SUMMER
IN
PHOENIX

<u>Other Titles Coming Soon from Lana Vargas :</u>

The Darkness that Follows Us

Three Words - A Novella

Summer
In
Phoenix

By Lana Vargas

First Paperback Edition Aug 2022

ISBN: 979-8-9863386-0-6(paperback)

Published by Birdcage Ink
www.Birdcageink.com

"I love you, and that's the beginning and end of everything"

- F. Scott Fitzgerald

PLAYLIST

Never Say Never - The Fray

Gives you Hell - All American Rejects

Enchanted - Taylor Swift

All I Ask - Adele

Jessie's Girl - Rick Springfield

Forget Me Too - MGK ft. Halsey

Dandelions - Ruth B.

See you later (10 years) - Jenna Raine

Two Ghosts - Harry Styles

Until I Found You - Stephen Sanchez

Saved - Khalid

 Scan the QR code to check out Elliot and Emory's Spotify playlist made by me + more songs !

I want to dedicate this book to my parents. The world didn't get to read my mom's book, but she's apart of mine. Wherever she is in the universe, I hope she's proud of it.

My dad, who has always put me on his shoulders to reach my dreams no matter how crazy they may seem, this one is for you.

You'll find a sneak peak of the prologue of my 2nd book at the end of this one, happy reading!

CHAPTER ONE

10 years ago

Age 9

"Emory get down here!" I hear mom yell from downstairs. She dressed me in a pink fluffy dress and curled my hair since I'm meeting the new neighbors from across the street today. Personally, I think I'm a little too old for these kinds of dresses, but it makes mom happy. She's gotten pretty close with Mrs. Cortes over the past few days, ever since her and her family moved into the blue house directly across from us. Even though I'm glad mom has a new friend now, I was pretty upset when I found out Mrs. Cortes only has two sons since there's not too many girls to hang out with in the neighborhood.

I hear unfamiliar voices in the living room, so I take one last look in the mirror before running downstairs. I leap down the last two steps which makes a loud *thud* noise that gets everyones attention to turn towards me. I freeze at the thought of being the center of attention.

"Mijita come meet everyone." Dad walks over to join me at the end of the stairs and puts my hand in his to pull me closer to the group of people. His hands are so much bigger than mine, and somehow they make me feel safe. His dark black hair is combed back with gel and his mustache is also combed, which is a new look for him. His caramel colored eyes are more noticeable with his hair out of his face.

Dad just recently started trying to teach me Spanish. His new nickname for me is 'Mijita' which just means daughter, I'll admit it sounds catchier in Spanish than it does in English. He always tells me he wishes my grandparents were here to teach me the language. They came to the United States from Mexico before dad was born to become small business owners of a restaurant, but they both died not too long before I was born. Dad says I have to embrace my Hispanic background, and be proud to be Mexican American. I just wish he would have taught me all this at a younger age.

As we get closer to the group of people who are staring I notice my dads' eyes never leave mom. He always looks at her like she's an angel. She's standing there in a long black dress, and her smile brightens up the whole room. Mom has those

11

features where you'd think she was a model when she was younger; her long honey colored hair that frames her heart shaped face, perfect brown skin, caramel colored eyes just like me and dad, and she somehow even makes the freckles on her face look beautiful. She passed freckles down to me, but I don't look half a pretty as she does with them. My parents met when they were in high school and they've been together ever since. They always tell me the story of how they met and it sounds like something straight out of a cheesy romance movie; girl drops her books on the floor at school, boy dips down to help her, and it was love at first sight. I hope to have a love like theirs one day, minus the cheesy meet cute.

"Emory this is Mr. and Mrs. Cortes." I finally look up from the floor to see a petite woman standing next to a tall figured man, both of them are smiling down at me. The woman is almost as pretty as mom; she has black hair cut to her shoulders, wide brown eyes, and the most radiant smile I've ever seen. The tall, dark haired man next to her looks the opposite of dad, this guy looks *buff*, and dad…well he isn't. The woman crouches down to be eye level with me while the man stays back and watches. I'm not as short as I used to be, but I'm only nine so adults still tower over me a little.

"Emory it's nice to meet you, your mom told me a lot about you. I'm Emily, that's my husband Miguel, and my two boys Elliot and Andrew." She jerks her head behind her, and I slowly slide my hand out of dad's to take hers and shake it. I look into her eyes and notice they're the prettiest shade of brown, almost like a milk chocolate candy bar. I look directly behind her to see her two sons. One of them looks a little older than me, maybe twelve? He's a little taller than me, and has the same dark brown hair as Mr. Cortes, but from here I can tell his eyes are the same color as his moms'.

"I'm Andrew." He says with a faint smile followed by a wave. I suddenly notice the other boy next to him, he looks about my age. He looks a lot more like Emily in my opinion, olive skin, short black hair, soft brown eyes, and a smile that makes my stomach feel like it's in knots. He walks up to me with a big grin on his face, and hugs me tightly without saying a word. I'm too stunned at the sudden contact to say anything.

"I'm Elliot." He says as he breaks away.

"I'm Emory."

"What's your full name Emory?"

"Emory Jewel Diaz." I say hesitantly. I've never told anyone my full name, but then again, no one has ever asked.

"What's yours?" I ask him.

"Elliot Jacob Cortes." The smile on his face hasn't left since he approached me. It makes me smile for the first time since I came running downstairs. "How old are you?" I ask. I want to know if I'm right about my guess on his age.

"I'm eight, I'll be nine this month on the twelfth." I just turned nine four months ago in August, so I'm not too much older than him.

"Hey I just realized we have the same initials, E and J." He points out. I didn't realize it until he said it, but it is a weird coincidence. I don't say anything back because I'm not really a sociable person, even though Elliot seems really nice. "I think I'll call you that now…Ej." He says. I didn't think it was possible for his smile to grow any larger, but it has. The only thing close to a nickname I have is the one dad gave me, and mom calls me Em sometimes. I kind of like Ej though.

"Okay." I wish I can say more, but my nerves are taking over in my stomach. A bright look covers Elliot's face, like something just clicked in his brain before he speaks up again. *He sure can talk.*

"I have an idea! You can call me Ej too, and it'll be like *our* thing." I think about it for a couple seconds before answering. Maybe it'd be cool that we had something that's just ours, plus it will be nice to have at least one friend. It's not that I don't want them, I just like being by myself. Dad says I'm like him in that way.

"Deal." A smile peeks through when the words leave my lips. I think this is the most I've smiled with someone other than my parents, it feels kinda…*nice*. Elliot hands me a small flower, and I take it in my hands to admire it. From the first look I think it's a daisy, but I'm not really familiar with flowers to know for sure. Its white petals are a little wilted around the edges, but it still has a really bright yellow center. It's beautiful. No one has ever given me a flower before, much less a boy.

13

"I picked it from our yard when my mom said her friend had a daughter, everyone says you should always bring a girl flowers." He's got his hands in his pockets with his head tilted down towards the ground. He seems *nervous*?

"Thank you. I wish I had something to give you." Mom always says to never show up somewhere empty handed, I just didn't think that would count for today in my own house.

"It's okay, we'll be across the street from each other, so if you really want to bring me something you can next time."

"Deal." I'll never forget this day, I made a friend, and I got my first flower from a boy. I have a strange feeling that meeting Elliot today changed everything.

CHAPTER TWO
8 years ago
Age 11

"Do you think you'll ever fall in love Ej?" Elliot asks catches me by surprise. I've never gave that much thought, I mean I'm only eleven so it's not exactly a priority. But those moments where my parents and I are having our regular movie nights, and I see the way they make each other happy just by being around each other, it gives me hope that maybe one day when I'm older I'll find a love like that. The kind of love where you know you're gonna be with them forever.

"When I'm older yea I guess...why?" I ask.

"I don't know, lately my parents have been fighting a lot, and I wonder if it's like that with everyone who falls in love." Elliot and I have been best friends for two years now, and we've spent everyday together on these steps of my house talking about anything you can think of, but today's conversation feels different, more deeper. As much as I want to ask if anything is wrong, I know what he'll say. He will never complain about anything, and somehow he always sees the positive in every situation. I honestly don't know how he does it, I could never be that positive all the time, but I guess we balance each other out.

"I think people fight no matter how in love they are in." I look straight ahead of me instead of at him to avoid him feeling uncomfortable. What I said is true, I think everyone fights. My parents fight, even if it's something as small as who's going to make dinner, or who forgot to wake me up for school in the morning. If they have big fights it's never around me or loud enough for me to hear, and it never lasts longer than a day because the next time I see them, they're dancing in the kitchen to 80's music like they always do.

"Do you think I'll ever fall in love?" He asks. He looks desperately at me with his big brown eyes, waiting for my reply. Elliot is the best person in the world, and I'm not just saying that because he's my best friend. I don't see why anyone wouldn't fall in love with him some day. So I say the only thing that feels right.

"Of course, I think it'll catch you off guard which is the best part...she'll be really pretty, and you'll get these butterflies in your stomach around her, you'll want to be around her every second of everyday, and you'll know you want to be with them forever." I know with every fiber in my body he'll find someone great, because it's what he deserves. He's the boy with the smile that can make anyone feel better, the one that runs from his house when he sees me on the swing in my front yard just so he can push me, the boy who's brought me a daisy everyday since we met, just because. Any girl would be lucky to have him. He stares back at me with a look on his face I've never seen. His eyes are dilated a little, and he almost looks stunned.

"Yea...I think I will find someone like that." He whispers so low I almost miss it. He smiles charmingly, making my insides tangle up in the way they do only when I'm around him.

"Emory time for dinner!" My mom shouts from inside.

"I'll see you tomorrow Ej." He says walking towards his blue house across the street. I turn to start walking inside my house, but stop when I hear his loud foot steps behind me. He's almost out of breath when he finally reaches me.

"I almost forgot." He's still panting when he pulls a white daisy out of his hand, and puts it in mine. It's the same kind he's given me everyday for two years. You'd think I'd be used to it, but it still makes my heart full knowing he thinks of me everyday before he comes over. I reach to pull a small leaf out of my pocket to give to him, the same kind I've given him for two years, since the day after we met. I didn't want to give him just a boring leaf, so I put my own little touch so he knows it's from me; with a little black heart drawn in the middle of it. It started off as a joke since a leaf was the only thing that was lying around the day after we met, but his face lit up when I gave it to him, and I knew I wanted to see it everyday. I place the leaf in his hand, and he gives me that perfect smile I've grown so used to. He turns back around to walk towards his house, and I stay there for a few extra seconds looking after him. As I see him approach his door, I notice the feeling I get only when I'm close to him start to disappear.

16

CHAPTER THREE

6 years ago
Age 13

You know those moments you just know will change your life forever? Today is one of those moments. I stare blankly in the mirror while flashbacks from the last year play like a movie in my head. The dark bags under my eyes from the lack of sleep almost match my black dress. *Things are going to be so different now.* I hear a faint knock on my bedroom door before I look up and see dad slowly make his way in.

"Hey, come downstairs there's some people I want you to say hi to." I've been avoiding going downstairs for a reason, but something in his eyes tells me everything I need to know; that he doesn't want to be alone down there. I've managed to stay up here in my room for the past hour, but I knew sooner or later someone would come and make me go down. It's already been the most exhausting day, and I just want to go to sleep and forget about all this, but I know dad needs me. So, I find the strength to pull back my tears that are fighting their way out, and walk downstairs with him hand in hand. My hands still feel so small in his, but this time I think it's me that's making him feel safe instead of the other way around. We haven't really spoken much to each other in the last week. I think we're both afraid to say *anything* to each other.

Everyone's eyes shoot up to us as soon as we make our way into the living room. My hands start to turn clammy with all the attention on me. Everyone is gathered in groups, talking amongst themselves with food surrounding them on the coffee tables. The air feels suffocating, but I manage to keep the tears at bay and plaster on the fake smile I've been giving all day. There's only so many times a person can say 'Thank you, I'm okay.' before they crack, and I have no idea how much longer I can take before I do just that.

"Emory dear, I'm so sorry. Are you ok?" A woman I recognize from mom's job extends a hand to place on my arm while she gives the same sympathetic look I've seen so many times in the last week. I give her the same lie as everyone else.

"Thank you, I'm okay." And just like everyone else, she buys the line. I mean how okay can you be after losing your mom? I don't know how to answer that truthfully. Mom was sick for awhile, I first noticed about a year ago on my twelfth birthday when she was too tired to get out of bed instead of making me my famous birthday breakfast: pancakes with strawberries for eyes, and banana slices for the smile. At the time I had just figured she worked a late shift the night before and wanted to sleep in, but she started to sleep in more often which wasn't like her. That was the first sign, then she started missing work, my school recitals, dad even started taking me to school every day instead of them switching off. She started to get pretty thin and that's when she went to the doctor. I'll never forget the day my parents sat me down on the couch and told me mom had cancer. That was the day I had my first panic attack. I don't think any of us realized we'd have so little time left. Of course mom would always tell me not to worry and that'd she'd beat it, but it was when I saw her chemo sessions were bringing her to the point of exhaustion that I knew I was going to lose her. There is no possible way to prepare for losing a parent, even when you know it's coming.

We had a good year though. After she was diagnosed we went out every weekend to the park, and made so many pancake breakfasts I *almost* got tired of them. I watched her and dad dance to their favorite 80's songs in the kitchen every morning, and she got in as much life lessons a girl may need. I'm thirteen now, and I'm realizing that there's still so much for me to learn that she won't be here to teach me. I feel tears prick my eyes but I wipe them away before they can stream down my face in front of anyone. The last thing I want to do is cry in front of a bunch of strangers. Everyone says their condolences as I do a walk through of the living room. I nod at them all and give them a convincing smile. After awhile I get exhausted saying the same thing over and over again, so I head outside to sit in the swing attached to a tree in my front yard that dad made for me a few years ago. I sway in silence looking in the distance. *How am I going to live the rest of my life without her? How is my dad going to go on without the love of his life?* Things are going to be so different without her, and I'm not ready for that. How do people even go on without their mom?

My staggering thoughts are interrupted when I feel Elliot approach me from behind. He pushes me back and forth on the swing very gently, just like he always does. The only sound I can hear is the wind whistling since we're both silently still. It's a gloomy day today, the skies are gray, and it looks like it might rain but it won't let up. It's my favorite kind of weather because these were the days mom would call in at work and spend the whole day with me watching movies and drinking hot cocoa.

"I'm not dumb enough to ask how you are, but you know I'm here for you Em." Elliot breaks the silence. Leave it to him to be the only person not to ask if I'm okay. I should have known if anyone could see through me, it'd be him.

"Do you think everything happens for a reason?" I ask. My attention stays towards the ground because if I look up into his eyes I'll break, and I don't want to break today. I hear him take a big breath in as if he's trying to be careful with what he says. I hate that everyone is treating me as if I'm so fragile lately.

"You know I always like to see the positive in a situation, but something like this..." He pauses. "It's bullshit." I've never heard Elliot curse, it almost makes me laugh.

"Bad things happen to good people Emory and it's bullshit, but we have to learn to accept it and move on, you can't let it stop you from going on and living. Your mom was the best person, and she brought my best friend into the world, so for that I'm grateful. One thing you can't say is cancer stopped her from living, she gave it hell for as long as she could, and I think you should remember her that way." I feel the heat of his stare on me, but I still can't bring myself to look up at him. My mom did give cancer hell. Her illness never stopped her from spending as much time as she could with me and dad, and she always had a smile on her face, at least in front of me. That's exactly how I'll remember her; happy and strong. I don't fight the tears that stream down my face anymore because I know I don't need to in front of Elliot. A sob that's been building in my chest finally plunges out. I've been holding the tears in all week, and if anyone is going to see me cry, I'm okay with it being Elliot. He's got his arms tightly wrapped around my body, as if he's trying to protect me from feeling any more pain. I let out more quiet sobs in his chest, staining his white

19

collared shirt with my mascara. After a few minutes, I finally look up at him into his eyes, and all the emptiness I was feeling before is gone for a split second. Looking in his warm brown eyes always makes me feel like nothing is wrong in the world, at least at that moment. "I love you Ej, but stop being so stubborn, and stop pretending you're okay, at least with me." He whispers while rubbing his thumb across my cheek wiping away all my dried up my tears. I feel my face flush at his warmth. Elliot and I have been friends for years, but we've never told each other we love each other. Of course we know we feel it, but hearing him say it for the first time makes my heart flutter. I try to get my heart rate back to normal, but he's so close and I know he can feel how fast it's beating.

"Love you too." I've never told anyone I love them except my parents, but telling him just feels right. He's my best friend, my safe space. Something about being in his arms makes the rest of today feel bearable, like as long as he's right here with me I can get through this, or anything for that matter.

"Here." He pulls me back by my shoulders and places something behind my ear. I already know what it is without looking at it, but I pull it out anyways just to see it. It's my white daisy with the yellow center. I pull out the leaf with the black heart drawn in the middle that I had in my dress pocket, and place it the front pocket of his shirt. Through all the craziness of today, I remembered to keep it on me for when I would see him.

"What do you do with all the leaves I give you anyway?" I ask curiously. We've been doing this whole exchange for about four years now, and I've never thought to ask. He looks at me nervously for a few moments before answering. "Some of them I keep, but a lot of them end up lost." He's looking down at the ground now. *Why is he so nervous*? I push the thought in the back of my mind, and entwine his hand in mine to pull him towards my front door to go back inside.

"What do you do with the flowers I give you?" He asks.

"Some of them I keep and some of them end up lost too." I lie. I keep every single one he gives me. It's the smile he gives me next that makes me take a big breath, and walk inside to finish the day strong. Elliot never left my side.

CHAPTER FOUR

5 years ago
Age 14

"I heard Olivia likes you." I tell Elliot. We're on the front steps of my house like always. He's sitting next me with his elbows rested on his knees, but his head snaps up as soon as he realizes what I said. Olivia is a girl who goes to school with us. She's a year older, but somehow Elliot got her attention. She told all her friends, and they made it a point to make sure I knew about it because they notice I spend so much time with him. If I wasn't so afraid of getting suspended I'd give her a piece of my mind. Olivia is the kind of girl who gets the attention of every boy in school. She's got long blonde hair, she always wears the fanciest clothes, and not to mention every one either wants to be her friend, or just be her. Then there's me, always in my band t-shirts and vans. Black is my favorite color so I try to incorporate it into what I wear every day. I like the way that I dress and I wouldn't change for anyone, but I can picture Elliot liking someone like Olivia, and I feel almost hurt by the thought.

In the last year I may have developed a *small* crush on him. He's grown into his features for only being fourteen. His jawline is starting to edge, and his skin cleared up from the preteen breakouts, so now he has perfect olive skin. He played football for awhile so he developed some biceps, and of course who wouldn't fall for his perfect smile; the one I've looked at everyday since we were nine, and somehow I still find myself excited to see it everyday. He's perfect, even with the dark bags under his eyes that he thinks I haven't noticed lately. I don't ask about it because I'm sure it's from his parents keeping him up with their arguing. It's gotten worse over the years, but I figured if he wanted to talk about it he would so I don't ever bring it up unless he does.

Elliot doesn't know about my crush of course. We're best friends and he could never see me as more than that. So to save me the embarrassment, I decided to bury it deep down. Sometimes when he does something Elliot-like I allow the butterflies to swarm in my stomach for a few minutes before caging them back up. I'm sure he would much rather be with someone like Olivia over someone like me anyways, so why say anything? Plus, if he knew about my crush I'm worried it would completely ruin our friendship.

"How do you know that?" He asks staring blankly at me.

"Her friends told me, I think she wanted me to know so I'd stay away from you or something, I may be a year younger than her but I'll still kick her ass." He lets out an amused laugh, which is my favorite sound in the world. His voice is getting deeper now, and I find myself purposely making lame jokes just so I can hear his deep laughter.

Olivia isn't the first girl to have a crush on Elliot that doesn't particularly like us hanging out all the time, but we promised each other a long time ago that no one will ever make us drift apart.

"Olivia is cool, but she's not someone I would go for." His confession surprises me. Here I thought Olivia would be a perfect girl for him, and somehow she's not his type? I thought she was everyone's type.

"What kind of girl would you go for?" I ask nosily. I wonder what kind of girl gets his attention if not Olivia. In the five years I've known him he's never even had a crush on anyone as far as I know, if he has he's never told me about it. He quickly looks away from me and inhales deeply before speaking again.

"The kind of girl who gives me butterflies every time I look at her, someone who could have the whole world on her shoulders but still smile as if nothing is wrong…" He pauses. His stare is back on me, except it's more intense, and he seems more firm with his words now. I feel my body stiffen under his gaze.

"Someone who has the most perfect round eyes, preferably caramel colored. Someone who's so beautiful it hurts to look at her." My mouth suddenly feels dry, and I can feel a huge lump forming in my throat that I can't swallow down. He could be talking about anyone, but deep down I know he's not. *There's no way he could like me back.* It doesn't make sense for a guy like him going for a girl like me. I clear my throat loudly before leaping up off the ground onto my feet. We're outside, but the cold air suddenly feels smothering.

"I should go inside to help my dad make dinner." I spit out. I can't manage to get out any other words at the moment.

I never want to jeopardize our friendship, so I don't saying anything more. He's my best friend and my favorite person, but if we crossed that line there is no turning back, and I never want to put myself in a position to lose him. My crush on him will just have to stay hidden for the rest of our lives.

Elliot smiles at me, but it feels different, almost as if he's forcing it. He rises and pulls a white daisy out of his pocket to place it in my hand. I pull out the leaf with the little black heart, place it in his hand, and pull him into a tight hug. He's always so warm, he's like his own sun. He smells like Axe body spray, I'm usually repulsed by that smell but on him I don't mind it at all. I pull back from our hug and start to walk towards my door when I feel a tight grasp on my hand, and before I can think I'm pulled into his hard chest. He's taller than me now so I have to look up to him. He leans into me and places his lips on mine. He tastes like mint, and his lips are so soft and gentle, ironically they're also warm, just like everything else about him. My heart is beating so fast I'm sure he notices, but he doesn't budge from kissing me. My body feels like it's floating off the ground, and the butterflies I keep caged up for him just broke out and are fluttering all around in my stomach. He pulls back after a few seconds, but it felt like much longer. He gives an Elliot-like smile, and I can't help but smile back. My cheeks hurt from how big I'm smiling.

"I just wanted you to be my first kiss." He doesn't say anything else before releasing me. He walks towards his blue house across the street without a second glance. I bring my fingers to my lips to touch them, noticing they have a tingling sensation that won't go away, and I can still smell the mint from him.

I just kissed Elliot.

I just had my first kiss.

It was perfect. Just like him.

CHAPTER FIVE

5 years ago

One month later, another moment I knew would change my life forever occurred. As I sit on the front steps of my house with my knees brought to my chest, I watch the moving truck in front of the blue house across from me slowly get filled up. Mr. and Mrs. Cortes are carrying a long tan couch into the back of the truck, each of them are on opposite sides, and I can hear Mrs. Cortes yelling instructions at her husband telling him to go left when he goes right. Andrew and Elliot follow behind with small boxes and somber looks on their faces. It's crazy how someone's whole life can fit inside a moving truck. I watch everyone's movements blankly, I should have went over to help earlier, but I can't get my body to get up to move, I feel frozen in place.

Elliot told me he was moving about two weeks ago. We were in our usual spot on the steps and he said him and his family were moving to Phoenix, Arizona, 373 miles away from here. He said it was because his mom wanted to be closer to her side of the family. I still remember my whole body going numb when I heard him say that he would miss me, and that he'll always keep in touch. My brain can't comprehend the thought of Elliot not being around anymore. No more daily talks on the steps, seeing his smile, getting to see his brown eyes light up when he gets excited, no more exchanging of daisies or leaves with the black heart drawn on.

The slamming of the moving truck door snaps me back into reality at the same time I see Elliot make his way over to me. I'll never get this sight of him again. He has his head down, and his hands are awkwardly in his pockets. I feel the tears wanting to come out but I push them back, I would prefer him not to remember me as a crying mess. I've already said my goodbyes to his parents and Andrew, I saved Elliot for last so I can keep my heart in tact for as long as I could.

"We're gonna head out now since it's a long drive." He says still not making eye contact with me. I think he's thinking the same thing as me; that if we look at each other we'll lose it.

"Okay." I choke out. I want to say more but the words won't come out. I want to tell him not to go, that I'll love him forever, and that he's my best friend in the whole world and it feels like he's taking a part of me with him, but none of that leaves my mouth.

He inches closer and is now directly in front of me. I lift my face to peer up at him to see his glossy red eyes. The dark circles under his eyes I pretended not to notice seem to be getting worse. His frown takes up his whole face, and suddenly all I want to do is make him smile just so I can see it one more time. He pulls me up to my feet and brings me into an almost suffocating hug. I take in a deep breathe and settle into him as I memorize his axe body spray scent, and how warm he always is. I hear his nose sniffle but I can't bring myself to pull back and look at him because I want to be strong until the end for him. So all I do is wrap my arms even tighter around him. I'd like to think me and Ej have our own language, and right now our hug is saying what our mouths can't.

"Never forget about me Ej." He whispers softly into my hair. I close my eyes tightly as the tears try to fight through.

"Never." I whisper. *Please don't forget about me either.*

"I love you."

"I love you too." *Always.* I won't say goodbye because I want to believe this isn't the last time I'll see him. I finally find the strength to pry myself out of his arms, if I don't let go now I'll stay in his arms forever. I take one final look into his creamy brown eyes that I'll miss so much. I'll miss the comfort they bring me on bad days. He looks at my face intensely before rubbing his thumb across my flushed cheek. With the way he's looking at me, it's like he's trying to memorize every crevice on my face or something. He gives me a small unconvincing smile, and turns away to walk towards the moving truck without another word. I feel like running after him to hug him one more time, but my feet are planted to the floor.

He gives one final look back at me and waves before climbing into the backseat of his mom's white BMW. I stare blankly as the car pulls away with the moving truck following closely behind. I push my feet off the cement and run until I reach the middle of the street to see the car drive away down the block. I feel something

25

brush against my ear and I bring my hand up to grab it. It's a white daisy with a yellow center, I didn't even feel him put it in my hair. I finally let the tears pool out of my eyes as I see the white car turn the corner and drive away, taking the other half of my heart with it.

5 years later

CHAPTER SIX

This is bullshit. I sit in the backseat of my dad's car, staring absently out the window, trying to figure out how the hell I got here in this situation; in a five hour car ride to see someone I haven't seen or heard from in five years. It isn't exactly how I wanted to start off the summer. Frankly I would have rather stayed back in LA, but since dad doesn't trust me on my own he said I have to go, and I guess I'm in no position to put up a fight with him.

It's been five years since Elliot Cortes promised he'd stay in touch after he moved, but I never heard from him or his family ever again. That is until recently when Mrs. Cortes reached out to my dad and arranged for us to stay with them for the summer. Mad was an understatement of how I felt after a couple years of silence, but after awhile I just chose to pretend like he never existed. It was working out pretty great until now. Dad says we're spending the summer in Phoenix because supposedly Elliot wants to see me, but I don't see why the sudden change. Me and Elliot under the same roof for three months? This will be *interesting*. I can already feel the bile building up in my throat at the thought of coming face to face with him again.

I'm sure he'll try and come up with some bullshit excuse as to why it's been five years since we've spoken, but nothing he says can make me forget all those nights I spent crying myself to sleep thinking of reasons why he decided to give up on our friendship. Did he meet a girl and she told him not to speak to me? Did he forget about me? Was I not important to him? All of which are questions that raced through my mind every day for the first two years of silence. Elliot moving away felt like the end of the world at the time five years ago, but I was about sixteen when I realized I needed to move on without him. I'm nineteen now, and quite frankly I don't want or need him in my life anymore. It's going to be a long summer to say the least.

I'm not necessarily upset with the rest of his family, but the fact that they never bothered to reach out either in five years stings a little, especially since after mom

28

died, Emily took on a small part of that role for me. I have a pull proof plan to ignore Elliot at all costs this summer, it should be easy enough.

I put my headphones in to avoid conversation with dad while he drives, not that he would start one anyway. We haven't really had anything to talk about lately, and by lately I mean since mom died six years ago. We hardly ever speak, and when we do it's usually him telling me how much I need to *be more responsible and get my shit together.* I can't really blame him though, I've been a pretty shitty daughter for the past few years. I come home past curfew every night, I got in too many fights to count in high school, I skipped so much school I only scraped by to graduate because I got in good graces with my teachers and did *a lot* of extra credit, and I'll admit that the friends I chose to keep around me weren't the best company. Sometimes I wonder if our dynamic would be different if mom were around, if she'd make us sit down and talk about what's bothering us. I also wonder if there would even be something bothering us in the first place if mom were still here.

I press the shuffle button on my music app and 'Never Say Never' by the Fray starts to play. The memory involuntarily comes flooding through my mind of me listening to this with Elliot when it came out, it became one of our favorite songs to listen to together. I hate him even more now for ruining a good song. I let my head fall back on to the seat and close my eyes trying to push the picture out of my head. The thought of being face to face with Elliot in a few hours has me on the edge of my seat, so I let the heaviness in my chest take over as I drift off to sleep.

"Emory we're here." I hear my dad's faint voice before I feel a soft nudge on my arm. I slowly pry my eyes open and I'm stunned by the bright sunlight burning my corneas. Why is it so bright in Arizona? I take in my surroundings as dad moves to the trunk to get our luggage. The house in front of me is so huge I'm at loss for words. It's two story all white house with black trimming around the edges, there are so many windows i'm wondering how many rooms this place has. The front yard has one of those fancy water fountains spewing, and I can smell the freshly cut grass. It also has one of those wrap around porches I've only seen in movies. It's the complete opposite of the house we have back in LA. There are two other cars in the drive way besides ours, I notice the white BMW right away, and the other is an older model truck that looks like it hasn't moved in months. I help my dad get the rest of our bags out of the trunk and we slowly walk towards the house. The trail up the drive way leading to the door is at an incline, and so long I'm out of breath when dad rings the doorbell. My heart is beating so fast I think it's going to burst out of my chest. I just hope Elliot doesn't answer the door, I haven't even thought of what I'm going to say to him. *Fuck you* seems like a pretty harsh thing to say to someone after five years, but that seems to be the only thing that comes to mind.

I hear the lock click so I swallow down the vomit that's wants to come out, and brace myself. The door swings open and to my relief it's Mrs. Cortes who answers with the brightest smile on her face. She still has her black hair, except now it's a little longer, and I notice some gray starting to come out at the roots, but she still looks stunning. She's wearing very light makeup but I can still tell she barely has any fine lines or wrinkles. If she didn't have the gray in her hair I'd swear she didn't age over the last five years. She lets us inside and we immediately drop our luggage that was weighing us down. *Holy shit they are rich.* The ceiling is so high it feels like I stepped into one those old cathedrals, their floors are a glossy petal white color, and to the right of us they have the most beautiful off-white staircase that wraps around and leads upstairs. The furniture looks like it rarely gets used from how brand new it looks. The sectional they have in front of the flat screen is black leather, which matches the coffee table in the middle of the room hosting a bunch of home decor magazines. Everything is so bright I feel like I'm in a museum. I can't help but look at some of the family photos that are scattered all around the room as my dad and Mrs. Cortes talk amongst themselves. Some are group family photos, some are just of Andrew, and when I catch a glimpse of a few of Elliot, I avert my gaze quickly.

"Emory, ay dios mío you're so beautiful and so big, come here." She pulls me into an immense hug, and sighs into my hair. I'm not much of a hugger, but she caught me off guard and I can't exactly push her off. She doesn't have to slouch down to be eye level with me anymore like when I was a kid, but the heels she has on do make her tower over me so I have to get on my tippy toes slightly to reach her height.

"We've missed you so much." She whispers into my hair. The mention of *we* makes me flinch. *You guys have a hell of a way of showing it.* I decide to keep the rude thought inside my head.

"It's nice to see you Mrs. Cortes." I manage to force a smile as we pull back from the hug.

"Emory just because it's been years doesn't mean you can't call me Emily." Loud footsteps coming down the stairs catch my attention, and my heart starts to speed up again, but it goes back to it's normal tempo when I see only Mr. Cortes approaching us. He looks the same too, *do these people even age?* He still has the same shade of dark brown hair with no sign of any grays. His eyes are the same hazel color I always seemed to be jealous of as a kid, and his facial hair is neatly trimmed with no signs of gray in it either. These two are a prime example that aging isn't always bad to you.

"I thought I heard voices, Emory look at you." He admires me before squeezing me in a tight hug that sort of hurts a little. This is the most hugging I've done with people in a long time, and I'm not sure I like it. He releases me, and approaches my dad to greet him with a firm handshake. I've never really spoke to Mr. Cortes so I don't know much about him, except that he seems to love his family.

"Miguel, good to see you." My dad says with a big smile spread across his face, it's been awhile since I see one of those on him.

"Andrew get in here!" Emily yells upstairs. Only seconds go by before I hear another set of footsteps coming down the stairs, these footsteps are more urgent and quick. His dark brown hair is cut short, and just as I remembered, he has the same brown eyes as his mom…and his brother. He's so tall now it's intimidating. His shoulders are broad, and his biceps are bulging out of his t-shirt, it seems like he

31

works out religiously. He also has dark facial hair now which is different, but it does emphasize his strong jawline. He's only three years older than me, but I swear he can pass for at least twenty five.

"Emory!" He shouts as he lifts me up off the ground. He squeezes me tighter than his dad did, almost stopping my breathing entirely. I really hope this hugging thing is a one time occurrence with them.

"How are you kid?" He asks.

"I'm good, you?" I reply dryly as he releases me. I try to catch my breath while he answers. "I'm good, same old shit." He says promptly.

"You're buff dude when did that happen?" He used to be a pretty scrawny kid, so the new look is a bit of a shock.

"Gotta stay fit for all ladies." He jokes. When we were growing up, all the girls in school wanted to date him, and that was before he looked like this. He's attractive, but he used to protect me like a big brother, so I saw him no other way. No other boys other than Elliot were allowed to even go around me when we were kids, otherwise they'd be answering to him. Even though he was super popular back then, and he seemed outgoing, I could always tell something was off about him, but I never asked. He definitely seems more confident now though.

"Look at you all tatted up now." He gestures towards my arms that are now covered in tattoos. He lifts each arm one by one to observe them. I got my first tattoo when I was seventeen when an old friend of mine learned how to do them, ever since then I get a new one every chance I can get. I have some quotes from books, my favorite songs, I have a dainty snake design going up my forearm that I got about a month after I turned eighteen, and the rest are pretty random: music notes, hearts, skulls, flowers, you name it I probably have it tattooed somewhere. Only one of them has deep sentiment, but no one knows about that one.

"You grew up a lot in five years kid." He says giving me a tight smile. *It wouldn't seem like such a shocker if anyone here kept in contact.* I decide to keep another rude comment to myself, and return a fake smile at him instead.

"Ok let Emory and Richard get unpacked." Emily announces as she helps me take my bags upstairs, while Mr. Cortes helps dad with his. I continue to observe my surroundings as we walk up the stairs in silence. More family pictures line across the wall leading up the staircase. Some are from when Andrew and Elliot were kids, some are from when they're older. I stop in my tracks when I see a picture of Elliot and I from when we were ten framed and hung up. It was halloween, and we decided to dress up as Cosmo and Wanda from the Fairly Odd Parents. We're back to back holding up our "wands" in the picture. I flinch when the memory tries to fight its way into my brain.

"You coming Emory?" Emily asks snapping me back from my thoughts. I follow her up the rest of the steps, and she stops at the first door on the right. We walk inside the room, and just like the rest of the house it's so bright and organized. I'm almost afraid to move anything.

"You'll like this room, it has a private bathroom. I figured you didn't want to share with the boys." The room is beautiful. There's a queen sized bed in the middle, with a pearl white comforter that compliments a cream colored bed frame. There's a nightstand next to the bed with the same cream colored shade, and the knobs are a clear crystal. The curtains are white which lets a lot of sunlight in, which I'll have to get used to. The room I have back home is completely opposite of this, but it'll do for the summer.

"We're so glad you guys are here Emory, we really missed you." I don't say anything back because I don't know what to say. It's not that I'm mad at them, but I am a little irritated that everyone thinks that I should just pretend the last five years didn't happen.

"You know I really hope this summer you and Elli—" She starts but gets cut off by a noise downstairs that sounds like a door closing. She looks away, and then back at me with a ghostly look. She doesn't have to tell me that Elliot is here, somehow I can feel it. My throat grows tight, and it feels like all the air just got sucked out of the room.

"I'll let you unpack mija, come downstairs when you're ready." She gives me one last hesitant look, and turns to walk away. The last thing I want to do is go down-stairs and face him, but I also know I can't hide in here forever. I used to imagine what I would say to him if I ever saw him again, but none of it was ever pleasant.

33

Maybe I could stay up here until everyone else goes to sleep, then I could tour the rest of the house. That sounds like a better plan.

A knock on the door makes me flinch out of my deep sleep. I look around the room to see my suitcase still on the floor unpacked, and it's pitch dark outside now. *When did I fall asleep?* There's another knock on the door, and this time I let out a loud grumble before getting up to answer it. My heart sinks down to my stomach when I see Elliot on the other side of the door with a plate of food in his hand. My breath hitches, and a feeling of nausea washes over me. He's looking very intensive at me, but all I can do is stare back with my mouth slightly gaped open. *He couldn't just leave me alone?* He seems to be good at that. I notice his hair is a buzz cut now, and I can tell by his stubble facial hair that he just shaved recently. He's definitely taller, but not as muscular as he was when we were kids. His eyes are just as richly brown as I remember which I *hate*. Also, *hello jawline*. This family definitely has some good, strong genetics. I obviously expected a change in his appearance compared to when we were fourteen, but I wasn't expecting this. He looks like a man. All the words in my head suddenly fall out of my brain.

"Hey Ej." He says tensely, breaking the deafening silence between us. His voice is so deep now, it catches me off guard. Hearing the nickname we used to call each other makes me instantly shiver, and I hope he didn't notice. I haven't heard it since we were kids, and honestly, it doesn't feel the same anymore. We called each other Ej because it was our thing, but I don't want us to have *anything* anymore. Just by standing in front of him my heart feels like someone has a grip on it, waiting to rip it out. "It's Emory." I say giving him a deadly stare. All the anger I have built up is gradually coming to the surface the longer I stand here with him. He averts his gaze down to his feet and swallows loudly as if I offended him. *I hope I did.*

34

"Emory...sorry. How you been?" He's still looking down kicking at his feet trying to avoid eye contact with me. My blood starts to boil. *How have I been? That's all he has to say? He falls off the face of the fucking planet for five years, and that's all I get?*

"I don't think you want me to answer that question Elliot. Frankly I'll be happy if I avoid all conversation with you while I'm here." I fold my arms across my chest defensively. He shouldn't have came up here, but I'll bet he probably thought that I would just run into his arms and pretend everything is okay, but that's not the case, and he'll learn it soon enough if he hasn't already. He breathes deeply and finally looks up at me. It's the first time in five years that I look into his eyes so close up. My mouth dries at the sudden sight. His eyes are different now though, they don't glisten like the used to, they almost seem lost. *I know the feeling.*

"Emory please, if you would just let me explain everything, I have so much to tell you and—"

"No." I say firmly, cutting him off mid sentence. Fifteen or even sixteen year old Emory would have killed for an explanation from him, but this Emory doesn't want anything to do with him. "I don't want to hear anything you have to say Elliot. You left and forgot I even fucking existed until now, and expect me to come running into your arms as if nothing happened!" I don't care if everyone can hear me downstairs. A frown takes up his whole face before he speaks again.

"I can explain everything Emory if you just listen. I care about you, and maybe after hearing what I have to say you'll understand why I did what I did." He's pleading now, it almost makes me relent, but I have to keep my guard up with him. I won't be hurt by anyone else ever again, especially him.

"No. I don't want to be here, I don't want to see you, I don't want to talk to you. It should be easy for you to pretend I don't exist since you were so good at it for five years." I slam the door in his face and turn back to plop down on my bed. I don't even feel a little bad for how I treated him. Maybe now he'll understand half of what I felt years ago. There is no way I can forgive Elliot, call it whatever you want, but I can't forget what happened. No one was there when I'd sit on my steps everyday staring at the blue house across the street, waiting for him to come out knowing he would never do it again. They weren't there when I would watch out for the mail man every single day for two years frantically checking for a letter from him. They don't know what it's like to get your heart ripped out of your chest, and even five years later still have pieces of it that haven't been mended back together. I was alone during that whole time, and he never even bothered to send a damn text telling me he's okay. Even if he didn't want to be my friend anymore I think I deserved at least some kind of explanation, but he never cared enough too give it to me.

I'm not going to let him get to me, I just have to get him out of my head. I start unpacking my suitcase, and hang up all my shirts and pants in the *huge* walk in closet the room has. It's not like I'll be needing a lot of space, my wardrobe mainly consists of t-shirts and jeans, but I appreciate the extra space. I move on to the small boxes I brought that include family photos, my favorite books, and a small black box that I don't even know why I brought with me in the first place. I haven't even opened it in two years. I brush my fingers along the top of it, and notice the black paint is starting to chip from how old it is, the gold lock on the front doesn't even lock anymore, but I keep it on because it compliments the black. I don't necessarily care to have it locked anyways, no one else even knows it exists, and I intend it keep it that way. I go into the walk in closet and place the box on the very top shelf out of sight. I never intend on opening that box ever again.

CHAPTER SEVEN

As I open my eyes, I take in the surroundings of my new room and I'm immediately reminded that yesterday was not just a bad dream. I actually saw Elliot yesterday, told him off, then stayed hidden in here all night just to avoid him. The encounter with him from yesterday keeps replaying in my head, the distraught look on his face when I didn't let him explain himself burns in my memory. I realize now that I may not be able to avoid seeing Elliot as much as I would like to since we are under the same roof, but I can at least avoid having any conversations with him. The last thing I need is for me to let my guard down and start being friends with him again. I've been down that road and it didn't end well.

Walking into the bathroom I mentally thank Emily for giving me the room with a private one, the thought of sharing a bathroom with two grown men doesn't sound appealing. I turn the shower on and wait for the water to turn hot to loosen my tight muscles. I already have a pounding headache from just thinking of when I'll see Elliot next. I won't be able to avoid him today because one: I'm hungry, and two I do want to see the rest of the house at some point. I let the hot water fall pour over me, loosening all the tense muscles in my body. I want to blame it on the road trip, but I have a feeling it has nothing to do with the trip, and everything to do with the fact that I have to share a house with someone I despise for the next three months. I thought I was miserable in LA, but it doesn't compare to this. Truth is, Elliot was the one person I thought would never hurt me, and the fact that he did it so easily cut a wound so deep I don't know if it'll ever heal. Seeing his face just reminds me of that empty feeling. It also makes me remember a time when I trusted people, and how it fucked me over in the end. I'm better off shutting everyone out, it's the only way to protect myself.

I have no idea what I'm going to do today. I'm in a new city, I have no friends, no car. I did want to try to find a summer job to make some extra cash, and it would also get me out of the house.

I get out of the shower and change into some jeans and an old band t-shirt. I brush out the knots in my long black hair that dangles down my back, and throw some

37

light makeup on my face to cover up the brown freckles on my cheeks. Dad always used to tell me to embrace them because they look exactly like moms', but as soon as I turned twelve I learned how to cover them up with a little foundation and face powder. I head downstairs and go into the kitchen to try and find something to eat because I can feel my stomach rumbling with hunger. I thought about taking the food Elliot brought up to me yesterday, but I also didn't want anything he offered me. My pettiness back fired on me, because now I'm starving.

Speaking of the devil, Elliot is sitting peacefully in a stool in front of the kitchen island when I walk in. My body goes frozen when we lock eyes, but I instantly recover and head towards the refrigerator while he goes back to reading the book in his hand. I notice out of the corner of my eye that he starts to fidget nervously in his seat, but I continue to look deep in the fridge for something quick to eat.

"There's pancakes on the stove." He speaks up. "No thanks, I don't eat them." I notice a blueberry muffin and grab that instead. I sit in the stool opposite of him, and quietly break little pieces off my muffin to shove into my mouth.

"Since when? You love pancakes." I can feel his fiery glare on me but I keep my head down. I used to love pancakes, specifically with strawberries for the eyes, and slices of bananas for the smile that mom used to make for me every birthday. After she died I didn't eat many pancakes anymore, it wasn't intentional, but next thing I knew it had been six years since I had one.

"Not anymore, a lot changes in five years." He flinches at my sudden harsh tone. I feel a heaviness in my chest that I can only explain as guilt. Why do I feel guilty for being rude to him when he deserves it? We have to come up with some sort of agreement so I can avoid situations like this.

"Look…whether we like it or not, we're going to see a lot of each other so let's make a deal. I'll leave you alone, you leave me alone and we'll both be happy." I finally look up at him and wait silently for his reply. *All we need is boundaries.* I didn't notice I was holding my breath until he responds. "I won't be happy."

"But I will." I let out with a rough tone. He nods absently, and looks at me with pleading eyes.

"I'll give you your space for now Emory, but let me just warn you that I'm not going to stop trying to prove to you how sorry I am. At the end of this if you never want to speak to me again that's your decision, but I won't go out without a fight." He gets up from the stool with force and walks out of the kitchen. Where was this "fight" years ago? Why does he suddenly want to show me that he wants to be in my life, when years ago he made it very clear he wanted no part of it? I thought when I told him we should ignore each other he'd be more than happy after how I talked to him yesterday, but if anything it made him come on stronger. *Fuck.* It doesn't matter what he says or does, because I can hold grudges, and he'll soon realize that he has no other choice but to give up.

The job search was a bust until I saw a now hiring sign on the door of a local bar named Sam's. Being a waitress at a bar wasn't my first choice, but beggars can't be choosers. The owner is an older man who of course is named Sam. He seems in his late fifties or so, his beard is a salt and pepper color that fits into this lumberjack persona he gives off, along with his plaid shirt and blue jeans. He didn't seem to mind I'm only nineteen as long as I could be there five days a week. I couldn't pass up the offer when he said I can start as early as a week from today. I need the money if I'm going to be able to afford my own place when I go off to college in the fall. My grades weren't the best in high school with how much classes I missed, but my high SAT scores definitely helped my case when I applied to the University of San Diego. I got my letter of acceptance a couple weeks ago. I prefer not to live on campus so I need to save up as much money as I can. I thought taking a year off after I graduated high school would help me save up some cash, but sadly that wasn't the case.

Sam gave me his information, and a date to come to do all my new hire paperwork. The bar is only about a twenty minute walk from the house which I can manage. This job will be good for me, I get to save up some cash, and avoid Elliot at the same time. Killing two birds with one stone.

When I walk into the house I immediately get hit with a strong aroma of food, reminding me I haven't eaten anything today except half a blueberry muffin during mine and Elliot's uncomfortable encounter this morning. I walk into the kitchen and I'm greeted by a very upbeat Emily at the stove.

"Hey Emory! I was wondering where you were." She has Cumbia music blaring on the bluetooth speaker as she dances in place in front of the stove.

"I went to look for a job, I actually ended up with a waitressing job at this bar named Sam's."

"You work at Sam's? The boys go there all the time, Sam is a good friend of ours." *Shit.* I just had to work at the one place Elliot would be when he's not here. *Nice going Emory.* I wonder if it'd look bad if I quit before I even start.

"Hey ma what's for dinner?" Andrew enters the kitchen with Elliot following closely behind him. He comes up to his mom's side and brings her into a side hug.

"Shrimp tacos. Can you guys set the table since you're here?"

"Fuck yes. You'll love moms' tacos Emory, they're the best." Andrew boasts enthusiastically while grabbing plates from the cupboard.

"Hey! Cuida lo qué dices!" Emily yells sternly to her son, pointing her wooden spoon in his direction.

"Sorry ma." Andrew says with a smug grin on his face before placing a peck on top of her head.

"Boys did you hear Emory got hired at Sam's." Emily announces. I was hoping it wouldn't have came up. Even though I knew they'd find out eventually, I didn't think eventually was right now. Emily was probably just trying to start up a conversation since me and Elliot are in the same room. I hope they don't keep trying to push us to talk while I'm here.

"Oh no shit? Nice Diaz. Me and E are always there." Andrew says. Emily silently walks over to him, and smacks his arm with the back of the wooden spoon.

40

"What did I just say about watching your mouth?"

"Ow! Sorry ma I keep forgetting." He says rubbing the spot where he was hit, while Emily walks back to the stove with a faint smile on her face. I'd be lying if I said I wasn't a little jealous watching them mess around with each other. It seems like a lifetime ago that was me and my parents, without the hitting with wooden spoons though.

"When do you start?" This time the question comes from Elliot. I spare a quick glance at him, contemplating if I should pretend I didn't hear him.

"Next week." I reply tensely. His entire face hardens, and I can't put my finger on why. I brush whatever that was away because I don't have to entertain whatever he's doing.

I'm quick to take the seat next to Andrew at the table so I don't get stuck next to Elliot. I decide to check my emails while we wait for Emily to bring everything to the table. My counselor from the university has been in constant contact with me since I mentioned that I wanted to change my major a few weeks ago. I originally said I wanted to major in Psychology, but the more I thought of it, it just didn't feel right. I've been avoiding her because I don't know what the hell I want to do with my life. I'm only nineteen how am I supposed to figure it all out right now? I'm jealous of those people who know exactly what their purpose in life is. The ones that know they're going to become a doctor, a nurse, or a teacher. I don't have a purpose, nothing seems important enough for me to pursue it. I have three months to figure out my whole life, no pressure or anything. I see another email from my counselor but I don't open it, instead I let out an exasperated sigh before exiting out of it.

"Everything okay?" Elliot asks from across the table. He probably thinks I won't be rude to him in front of Emily and Andrew, but he obviously doesn't know the new me very well.

"Yup." I answer sharply without looking up at him. Andrew clears his throat loudly before shifting in his seat uncomfortably.

"It doesn't seem like it."

"I'm fine." I snap back at him. Andrew bows his head down to look at his phone, but Elliot doesn't budge from holding intense eye contact with me. We don't have to

41

say anything because our eyes are doing all the talking. I just told him this morning to leave me alone, and here he is pushing the boundaries I asked for. I just have to get through dinner, then I can hide upstairs in my room for the rest of the night.

Of course it wasn't that easy, because dinner was awkward to say the least. I managed to avoid conversation the whole time thankfully, but I did involuntarily participate in a few staring contests with Elliot. I could feel the burning heat of his gaze a few times, and instead of being uncomfortable, I decided to play at his game and make *him* uncomfortable. Of course it didn't work since every time I won the stare down he'd wink and give me a little crooked smirk. *I hate him.* If he thinks he's going to win my friendship back with a few staring competitions and a smirk he's got another thing coming.

Instead of going up to my room to hide from him, after everything is cleaned up I decide to head out to the front porch for some air. Once I step outside, I see my dad rocking in one of the chairs. I look around for another seat since I don't want to take the one right next to him. We take in the view of kids riding their bikes down the long street, their laughter fills the neighborhood. The sound makes me smile to myself. I would do anything to be that innocent again.

"I got a job." I say hesitantly. In the past six years since mom has been gone, I can count on my hand how many decent conversations we've had. It's always the same routine; we ask each other how our days were, we talk about his job, and then the conversation dies off. It's gotten worse the last couple years though, he can't even look at me anymore.

"Where?" He asks while keeping his attention on the children playing.

"A bar, it's a waitress gig. It pays good and the tips will help a lot, I could use the extra money before heading out for school." His attention snaps to me now. His caramel colored eyes meet mine, but they're filled with anger. I remember when they used to feel comforting once upon a time.

"Really Emory? Is a bar the best environment you want to be in after what happened?" He's never going to let me forget it. It's been two years, and he doesn't know that I think about it almost every day. Tears threaten my eyes. This is what happens when I try and have a simple conversation with him, he always brings it back to that night. If it's not that night, it's another time I fucked up.

"It's a job. The owner is cool with Emily and Miguel, and Andrew and Elliot always go. It's fine, I wish you'd stop throwing that night in my face every time we have a conversation." I raise my voice a notch, but he doesn't react. I know I fucked up, but nothing I do now will ever make him see me differently. Who am I kidding though, even before that dad couldn't hold a conversation with me.

"I wish it never happened at all but it did Emory." He's got his disappointed face on again, but now when I see it, I just feel numb. "I thought coming here for a few months would help you get your shit straight, I didn't bring you here so you can work at a bar and mess around again." *Now I'm pissed.*

"Who says I'm messing around? I don't see you offering to pay for where I'm going to live when I move for college so I had to take matters into my own hands." My breath hitches, and my throat grows tight as the words get stuck, but I push through it. I have to get this out.

"If you weren't so busy throwing my mistakes in my face every time we talk maybe you'd actually see that I'm trying to move past what happened." I bolt out of my chair and storm back into the house without another glance at him. The room starts to spin, and my eyesight gets blurry as the tears slowly make their way down my face. *Why am I crying?* I should be used to feeling like shit after I talk to him. With everything spiraling in my mind from him, to being stuck here with Elliot, to having to pick a major in three months, everything is rushing over me all at once. I wouldn't be surprised if my dad didn't speak to me for the next three months after this. If he didn't, it wouldn't be much different than it is back home, after awhile I figured out a way to be okay with the silence. You kind of have to when you're a disappointment to everyone around you.

CHAPTER EIGHT

I've been tossing and turning for what feels like all night, thinking about how fucked my life is, and how I can't wait to leave it all behind in three months. I see a sliver of light shine through my window which peaks my interest. I look over at the alarm clock and it reads 5:18 am. *Fuck.* I haven't been up this early since…well since ever. I guess I could make the best of it instead of staying in bed all day trying to avoid my dad. Not only do I have to avoid Elliot, but now my own dad too. It'd be a miracle if I survived the summer.

I tug the blankets off and go into the bathroom to get ready for the day. I wash my face, and put a little makeup on to hide the bags from crying last night. The conversation with my dad replays back in my mind. I've known for awhile now that my dad was disappointed in me, but a little part of me wanted to him to be proud of me after telling him I got a job, but obviously that moment never came. We used to be close when I was younger, but after we lost mom I guess we just didn't have anything left to talk about. Next thing I know, it's been six years since we've had a meaningful conversation.

I'm not going to let what happen yesterday affect me today, so I slip on some comfy clothes and hope Emily and Miguel keep coffee stocked here. Downstairs is quiet as I suspected, it's Sunday so no one in the house works today, and I doubt they'd spend their day off waking up at five in the morning, hell I wish *I* wasn't up at this time either. I'm startled by Elliot who's on his laptop on the kitchen island when I walk in.

"You scared the shit out of me!" I whisper shout at him holding my hand over my chest, trying to regulate my heartbeat back to normal.

"Sorry, I'm an early riser. There's coffee." He says with a hint of a smile like he's proud he almost gave me a fucking heart attack. I don't want to accept his coffee, but that is the main reason I came down here. *Damn.*

"Thanks." I reach into the cupboard to get a mug, and pour some of the fresh coffee into it, then put two scoops of sugar, just how mom used to drink it. The silence in here is suffocating me so I exit the kitchen and head out the front door

44

before he can start up a conversation. The sun isn't fully out yet so it's the perfect time to catch the sunrise. I take a seat in one of the rocking chairs and stare at the beautiful sky. Its colors remind me of cotton candy: the pink's, blue's, and even yellow's are all blended together. Mom and I watched a lot of sunrises when she was ill, the treatments she was on would usually keep her up sick all night so she was always up before the sun. She once told me that her and dad's first date went on so long, they ended up watching the sunrise the next morning. I used to want a love like theirs, a love that consumes every part of you so much that you don't even take in the concept of time, but now I don't see it in the cards for me. Love like that can only end in heartbreak one way or another, I've witnessed it happen first hand.

"I see you still love sunrises." I hear Elliot close the front door behind him, but I stay silent looking out at the sky still deep in thought. *He just doesn't give up does he?* He doesn't say anything else before he walks off, and I hear the garage door open minutes later. Of course with my luck he would be an early riser, I can't escape him no matter how hard I try.

"Shit!" I hear a loud shriek and the sound of metal drop to the floor. I run in that direction before a single thought enters my mind. When I reach the garage seconds later I see him wrapping a towel around his hand. The once white towel is now stained red and I instantly go into alarm mode.

"Let me see it." I reach for his hand but he pulls back swiftly.

"I got it." He protests. *Now* he wants me to leave him alone?

"Elliot give me your hand or I'll reach over and grab it...your choice." He gives me a defeated look before placing his wounded hand in mine. I unwrap the towel to see a small gash on his palm. As soon as the pressure is off, it starts to ooze blood, so I cover it back up again.

"You guys have a first-aid kit?" He nudges his head in the direction of a cabinet to the right of him.

"Top shelf." I rush to the small cabinet and grab the kit from the shelf. I frantically dig through it and find gauze, ointment, and some strips to hold the wound together. I grab two chairs, put one behind Elliot to sit, and the other directly in front of him for me. "Sit." I tell him aggressively. Thankfully he doesn't try to rebel this time. I grab his hand to look at it again, but this time I feel warmth travel up my arms and settle into my stomach at the contact with his skin. I clear my throat trying to push away whatever that feeling was, and focus on cleaning his wound. I got it to stop bleeding for now by applying enough pressure, but I still need to clean it and put the strips so it doesn't re-open and start bleeding again. We don't say a word while I bandage him up, but I can feel him admiring me, which is just as uncomfortable. While I apply ointment to the wound our fingers graze for a short moment, and my heart instantly starts to speed up. It feels like my arm just got shocked and electric waves are traveling up my entire spine. I look up at him and notice he's breathing more rapidly than usual, not to mention his chest is heaving, eyes are dilated, and his hand is starting to get clammy. I'm sure it's because of the blood loss he just experienced. Our eyes lock in on each others', and suddenly I'm imagining I'm fourteen again looking into his gentle eyes, and everything is right in the world, *but I'm not fourteen anymore*. I snap back from my foolish thoughts and finish wrapping his hand with gauze.

"You're good at this." He says with a husky voice as he watches me attentively.

"It's nothing. When you get in a lot of fights you pick up on basic first aid." It's not something I'm proud of. Three years ago if someone even looked at me wrong I picked a fight with them. I would come home with busted lips, bloody knuckles, gashes, you name it, I had it at one point. Eventually my dad got fed up and just stopped helping me clean up, so I had to learn to bandage myself up.

"I can't imagine you fighting like that." He says with a small chuckle.

"I'm a different person than I was before you left." I reply stiffly while finishing wrapping the gauze tightly around his hand. I make sure it's secure and let go of his hand right away, ignoring that the warmth and static feeling I just had is gone now.

"I don't know about that." He says. I exhale loudly and eye him with challenge.

"Alright I'll bite…what's that supposed to mean?" I fold my arms across my chest and wait for his answer. "You told me you wanted nothing to do with me a couple days ago, but you ran in here to make sure I was okay when you heard me scream, sounds like the old Emory to me." He gives me a cocky side smirk, and I return it with an eye roll. Only he would see it that way. Anyone would have done the same thing if they heard him scream, I just happened to be close by. I decide to change the subject because I'd rather not get into this with him.

"What were you doing anyways?" *Not that I care.*

"I was working on my truck, one of the parts got away from me and sliced my hand."

"Sounds like you shouldn't be doing it." I say rising up out of the chair.

"Are you kidding, this is my baby. I want to get it up and running before the summer ends." I observe the truck in more detail. It's all black, but the front bumper and grill are silver. The paint is chipped in some places, but I'm sure he's planning on fixing that. The tires have cobwebs which tells me I was right when I guessed it hasn't been moved since it was first parked in this garage.

"What kind of truck is it?" I ask.

"1968 Chevy C10." He's got a proud smile on his face as he admires it. *Why the hell am I sitting here making small talk with him?* He doesn't seem to mind of course because he replies to everything I say without a tone of annoyance. I don't say anything else before I walk out of the garage. His rugged tone stops me in my tracks.

"I don't think you should work at Sam's." There is a lot of things I know he has to say to me, but I was definitely not expecting that.

"What?"

"Look Ej...Emory sorry. It's just, I see the way guys get handsy with the girls there, and I don't like the idea of you being on the other end of that." He gets up out of his chair to come stand closer to me, but I back away to keep distance between us.

"I don't need you to look out for me Elliot, I can handle myself. I've done it for years now." My tone comes out harsh, but I don't care. First my dad now Elliot, I'm exhausted having to prove to people I can do things on my own. After Elliot left, I was all on my own and had to take care of myself, especially with dad working a lot more to bring in extra money after mom died.

"I'm not telling you not to work there, I'm just telling you why you shouldn't. As your frien—"

"We're not friends!" I shout so loud my chest burns afterwards. He startles and goes completely still. I'm sure the neighbors heard me with how loud I just yelled.

47

"I don't know how many times I have to tell you that I don't forgive you Elliot. Everyone in my fucking life just throws me away as if I'm nothing, and you were the last person I thought would do that...but you did. We're never gonna be friends again, the sooner you realize that the better off we'll both be." I can only manage to get out jagged breaths, and I can feel heat radiating off my body from the anger. I turn around to walk back inside the house before he can say anything else, but not before I spot the mortified look on his face. I may have gotten distracted by him for a split second, but I have to remember that I can never trust him again. He makes it seem like I'm some fragile thing that needs to be protected, but it's too late for that. There's nothing left of me to break.

CHAPTER NINE

Good news is I didn't wake up before the sun today, bad news is that I woke up still under the same roof as *him*. Yesterday I let him and the stupid garage incident fog my judgement, but I won't let it happen again. Who does he think he is telling me I shouldn't work somewhere? He sure has a lot to say about my life when he clearly didn't want to be apart of it for all these years.

Today is a new day, and I'm not going to let him ruin it. I figure everyone is already gone to work since it's Monday morning, so I say it's safe to go downstairs to get some breakfast without running into anyone. It's not that I'm uncomfortable around Emily and Miguel, or even Andrew, but I'd be lying if I said I still didn't have a *smidge* of a grudge. Their betrayal hurt a lot less than Elliot's that's for sure.

When I walk out of my room into the hall, I trip over something and almost hit the ground before I stop myself by holding onto the wall. Annoyance settles into me when I peer down and see a small box of my once favorite chocolate bars with a note attached. Only one person in this house knows Kit-Kat's were my favorite candy as a kid. I scoff loudly before bending down to grab the note.

I remembered your favorite candy so that should earn me

some points.   - E

Does he really think getting me candy will fix everything? It would be a shame to waste a perfectly good box of candy bars, but I don't want to accept anything from him. I bend down to grab the box, and throw them into the trash bin near my bed. I'm honestly surprised he remembers anything about me at all much less my favorite candy from when I was ten. Thankfully when I go downstairs no one is in sight. Elliot must be off plotting on how to annoy me if he's not here like he usually is, and I have no idea where my dad went off too. I grab a banana muffin from the fridge and sit down at one of the stools. For the first time since I got here I actually do hope I run into Elliot so I can tell him to his face where he can put those candy bars.

"Morning Diaz." Andrew greets me as he enters the kitchen and goes straight to the refrigerator. I guess I forgot he'd still be here since he doesn't have a job.

"Morning." I say with my attention still on my muffin in front of me. He surprises me by taking a seat on the stool right next to me, and stares at me without a word.

"Can I help you?" I don't necessarily mean to come off rude to him, but the way he's looking at me while I eat is irritating me, plus I'm not exactly a morning person.

"It's just crazy seeing you all grown up now." He admits. I break off another piece of my muffin and pop it into my mouth. When he realizes I'm not going to say anything, he clears his throat awkwardly before speaking again.

"Elliot hates himself for what he did to you Emory." I nearly choke on my piece of muffin from the surprising mention of Elliot. I should have known Andrew would try and cover up for him since he's always done that.

"I find that very hard to believe." I spit out. As soon as I move to get up out of my seat Elliot enters the kitchen in a black hoodie and jeans, with car keys in his hand. He's like fucking Beetlejuice, as soon as you mention or even think his name, there he is.

"Good morning beautiful people." He announces cheerfully. Of course he's the kind of person who wakes up in the morning all cheery, I despise those kinds of people. It almost makes me want to vomit up my breakfast. He takes a seat across from me, and looks at me with a stupid smirk on his face. What's up with these brothers staring at me eat?

"Why are you smiling at me?" I ask with distaste, but his smirk doesn't budge.

"Did you get the candy I left you?" Andrew was just about to get up from his seat, but as soon as Elliot says the words, he settles back in his seat and listens in on our conversation. "I did, you'll see them at the bottom of my trash can next to my bed." I beam a smile at him, and finally his smirk is gone.

"Here I thought you'd hide upstairs to avoid me again." He smirks at me again, but this time with mockery.

"You underestimate my ability to pretend you don't exist." I spit back harshly. This is going against my rule of not speaking to him, but if he wants to play I can play too.

"You seem to be doing a great job so far." He says before getting up out of his chair. *Asshole.* He looks in Andrew's direction now as he speaks.

"I'm taking your car but I'll text you when I'm on the way back in case you have things to do."

"So he does know how to use the phone after he leaves." *Shit, did I say that out loud? Oh well.* Elliot's face goes pale, he almost looks hurt. Andrew just looks stunned with his mouth slightly gaped open. The kitchen is dead silent for what feels like a long time so I leave my muffin on the counter and storm out. Even though I didn't mean to say it out loud, I don't feel bad that I said it. He deserves worse than that. Like I said, if he wants to play so can I.

Later after dinner I decide to help clean up since I didn't have anything else to do, and because dad and I are living here rent free for three months so it wouldn't hurt to pick up some chores. I'm at the sink washing dishes when I feel his presence behind me.

"Let me help." Elliot says. I ignore him and keep at my task. I feel his heat before I see him directly at my side. He waits patiently for me to hand him a dish to rinse off. *Can't he take a hint?* I thought I made it clear I don't want to be around him, but it seems like the more I push, the more he pulls.

"When did you start getting tattoos?" He asks. I leave his question unanswered while I try to finish washing the dishes as quick as possible to get out of here.

"I guess you're right about your ability to pretend I don't exist." He says.

"I learned from the best." I grimace at him then turn back to the dishes. I shouldn't have said anything, but I guess I need to hurt his feelings for him to shut up.

"I see that black heart tattoo is very on brand for the new you." He dishes back. *Guess I was wrong about him shutting up.* He's referring to the black heart I have tattooed on my middle finger. He's not the first person to joke about me having a black heart.

"You should get a dick tattoo since that'll be very on brand for the new *you*." I give him a devilish smirk and his face blanches.

"I'll play along as long as you want Emory." *That's it*. I turn off the water faucet and turn to fully face him now, shaking with rage.

"See that's the thing Elliot, you think this is a game when it's not. I *hate* you Elliot, and it's not in the playful 'I really like you' way. I mean that I hate you with every fiber in my fucking body." I slam down the dish that's in my hands so aggressively I may have broken it, but I don't care with how pissed off I am right now. Hopefully that'll get him to shut up for the next three months. If he would have just left me alone after the first time I asked him too, then I wouldn't have to yell at him in the middle of the kitchen.

It's funny how someone who once brought out the best in you makes you become the worst version of yourself.

CHAPTER TEN

It's been one week since I blew up on Elliot in the kitchen, and we've only said about five words in total to each other since then. This is what I wanted, but why do I feel uneasy about it? Isn't that something, he can move away and act like I never existed for years, but I feel a little bad for yelling at him about how I feel towards him. Thankfully I haven't had too much time to dwell on it since I've been getting everything ready for my first day at Sam's today. I'd be lying if I said I wasn't a little nervous.

I slip on a white shirt that only covers the top half of my chest, leaving the whole lower half of my torso showing. Sam gives employees a choice of wearing either blue jeans or shorts, and I decided on jeans in a heartbeat, I already feel out of my comfort zone working at a bar I don't want to push it. I've only had one job before, but it was just babysitting the kids next door twice a week when I was sixteen. This is my first official job, and other than the small amount of jitters I feel pretty good about it, despite what Elliot had to say about it.

As if I wasn't uncomfortable enough, when I reach downstairs everyone is sitting in the living room watching a movie together. I see all their eyes immediately travel straight to my low cut top. Elliot averts his gaze quickly, and I hear my dad let a disappointed sigh. I don't have the energy nor the time to deal with either one of them today.

"Good luck on your first day Emory." Emily says with an encouraging smile.

"Thanks." I lock eyes with Elliot before heading out the door, and it's like we're having a mental conversation. He's probably saying something like *it's not too late to back out.* I give him a stern look and try and relay the message *don't even think about trying to tell me anything* with my eyes. As if he got the message, he gives me a bleak look and turns his attention back to the tv. I have about thirty minutes until my shift starts but I want to make a good impression by arriving a little early.

With the twenty minute walk there my mind has some time to wander; about what happened between me and my dad, the look Elliot gave me before I left, but I hate the fact that the one thing that's sticking in my brain are the occurrences between him and I last week in the garage, and then in the kitchen. I'm not going to apologize for what I said when everything I said was true. Everyone has always treated me as if I'm disposable to them, my old friends back home, even my dad at times, and maybe I am. It used to feel different with Elliot though, I felt like I was his everything just as much as he was mine. Then when I was proven otherwise it felt like my heart shattered into a million pieces, and I still haven't been able to mend them all back together. That's the reason I hate him so much. A hard pill I had to swallow after two years of no contact from him is that maybe he just didn't care about me as much as I cared about him. After that I learned my lesson and found a solution on how to not have that happen again, and that is by not caring about anything or anyone, and it's worked out for me so far.

I arrive at the bar with eleven minutes to spare until my shift starts. Sam greets me with a big smile and shows me to a locker put my stuff in. He also shows me the break room, the storage where all the liquor is kept, the bar and kitchen area. After the tour he introduces me to a girl named Katlyn. She's so breathtakingly beautiful I'm immediately intimidated. She looks around my age, maybe a little older, she's got long brunette hair that goes down her back, and long dark eyelashes that compliment her green eyes and fair colored skin. I notice she has freckles just like mine, she almost makes me want to embrace mine more instead of trying to cover them up.

"Call me Kat, none of that Katlyn bullshit." She says immediately after Sam leaves us.

"Okay, you can call me Em if you want I guess." I offer.

"Em…I like it, it's simple and cute. I'll come up with my own nickname for you eventually." I can already tell me she's got the kind of outgoing personality I'm not used to being around, this could either be really good or really bad.

"So Em, have you ever been a waitress before?" She asks while dragging me with her to clear a table off.

"Never." I take a damp towel to help her wipe the table and chairs off, and I see her give a slow approving nod out of the corner of my eye.

"I like you already, c'mon I'll show you where we put all this crap." She gestures to the pile of dishes she's balancing on her arm.

"We get pretty busy around six because everyone likes to stop by after work and drink themselves silly because they hate their lives." I thought *I* was blunt, but she takes the cake.

"The best thing to remember is to smile, that's what brings the tips in. Be nice and look pretty, with a face like yours it should be easy." She gently taps the end of my nose which pokes a nerve in me, but I bite my tongue.

"We get some families that come to dine in, but mostly it's men who hate their wives. Don't pay them too much attention when they flirt with you, it comes with the job, most of them keep their hands to themselves. Sam takes that shit pretty serious if they try to get handsy." I swallow the lump in my throat by her use of the words *most of them*. The last thing I want to do is prove Elliot right about the guys that come in here.

"You can watch me take orders and expedite for a bit, then when you feel comfortable I'll watch you." I nod silently as we approach a family and I watch in awe as she takes all their orders and answers all their questions as if she has it memorized, she makes it look so easy. Am I in over my head? *No, you're not Emory, you can do this.* I assure myself mentally. I'm not going to give up so easily like I always do. This job is the first thing I've done for myself, and when you get let down from other people so much, you just can't let yourself down.

The first half of my shift flies by, and just like Kat said, around six we got a rush of men in suits that come in right after work. Luckily most of them sit at the bar and not the dining area so I don't get too many encounters.

"So Sam said you're from LA." We're sitting in the break room now sharing a plate of fries. It wasn't even our break time but Kat says she always eats in between rushes.

55

"I'm only here for the summer. I'm visiting some of my dads' friends and then I'm heading to San Diego for college."

"Well shit, I've never even left Arizona." She has a regretful look on her face, but before I can ask anything she grabs the ketchup and douses her side of the fries.

"I've never left LA before coming here, it's not all it's made out to be." I admit.

"Anywhere is better than here, I'm twenty two and I've never been anywhere else."

"Why's that?" The question stuns her, and honestly me too. I wasn't exactly expecting to engage in a conversation, but I am curious.

"It's a long story, maybe one da— shit!" Her sudden panic startles me. "What?" I look in the direction her panic is aimed at, but I don't see anything in particular that would set her off.

"Oh my god he's here, he's so hot it hurts." Her breathing hitches, and she suddenly looks flushed.

"Who?" I look around frantically but I still don't see anything except middle aged men who are talking amongst their friends.

"You don't see that gorgeous human being at table one?" I'm still learning the table numbers, but number one is easy to remember since it's right by the entrance. I look in that direction and I freeze instantly. Andrew and Elliot sit in the booth across from one another deep in conversation. I'm almost afraid to ask her which one she finds *gorgeous*, not that I mind if she thinks it's Elliot.

"Which one?"

"The older looking one duh." I let out a breath I didn't know I was holding. *Why was I holding my breath?*

"That's Andrew and the other one is Elliot." I nudge my head in the direction of the boys, and her face hardens.

"Emory sweetheart, if we're gonna be friends you have to disclose these kinds of things. Especially when it contains information about you being friends with the most beautiful man I've ever seen." I wouldn't exactly say we're friends, but I don't correct her since it already looks like she's going to implode. "I can introduce you."

Something tells me if she even comes in close proximity with him she'll pass out, and I'm kind of intrigued to see what happens.

"Are you kidding? I can't meet him looking like this." She gestures to her grease stained shirt, but honestly she's still one of the prettiest girls here, even with the stains. Some girls are effortlessly perfect, I am definitely not one of those girls, but she is.

"Fine keep being a creep and eye fucking him from across the room then." I start to walk away but then I feel her grip my arm with just enough force to stop me.

"Okay okay fine can you introduce us?" She's pleading now. Andrew hasn't even said one word to this girl and he's already got his hooks in her. I grab her hand and drag her in the direction where the guys are still sitting. I can feel her hands start to shake in mine, they feel a little sweaty now which is gross, but I ignore it.

"Thanks by the way baby cakes, I owe you one." She whispers to me. I guess she found her nickname for me. I'll have to tell her not to call me that when she's not hyperventilating. As we approach the table Elliots' eyes snap up to meet mine almost instantly. I brush off the sudden warmth in my stomach and snap my attention to Andrew.

"Andrew this is Kat, Kat this is Andrew." I gesture between the two of them and the instant eye contact between them makes me a bit uncomfortable.

"Hi." Andrew speaks first, but he seems to be in a stunned state.

"Hi, I see you come in here all the time…not that I'm a creeper or anything who watches you. I mean I do watch you to see if you need refills or anything, but not in a weird creepy way I promise. Do you guys want something to drink?" She's talking so fast I can barely understand her, and from the look on Andrew's face he can't either, but I can't help but notice he also looks fascinated by her.

"I'll take a Corona thank you Kat, and my brother will have a coke." He replies with a chuckle. I hear her finally take a breath and write down their drinks on her note pad.

"I hope Emory isn't giving you a run for your money Kat." This time Elliot is the one to speak up.

"Are you kidding me? She's killing it. She took over a table and I didn't even have to ask, she'll do great. Not to mention the tips she's going to get from being a fresh pretty face around here." Kat says with a playful grin. I see the muscles in Elliot's jaw tighten but I don't comment on it.

"I'm glad." He says through gritted teeth.

"Are you guys eating?" I pull my pen out to write down their orders since Kat is still mesmerized by Andrew and I want to get away from this table as fast as I can.

"I'm good with a burger, well done with all the veggies on the side please." Elliot says closing his menu and handing it back to me.

"Dude we just ate." Andrew says looking at his brother with confusion written on his face. Elliot gives him a wide eyed look, which he then nods slightly before peering up to speak to me.

"I'll have a small order of fries, thanks Diaz." I take both of their menus before walking away, dragging Kat behind me. She backs away slowly but doesn't break eye contact with Andrew. Isn't she supposed to be the one pulling me around?

"Shit my heart just exploded. Thank you Emory I would have never had the guts to go up to him." She has her hand on her chest as if she's trying to catch her breath. I put the slip with their order on the counter for the cooks to see without even thinking about it, maybe I can do this job after all.

"The rest is up to you." I say firmly.

"By the way I have to comment how the younger one was looking at you, what's up with that?" She asks curiously. I don't want to discuss me and Elliot with anyone, much less a stranger.

"We've known each other since we were kids." I shrug my shoulders and walk away to clean off a table to avoid any other questions that I know she has.

"So you and him never…" She doesn't need to finish her sentence for me to know what she's asking.

"No." I reply tensely. I leave out all the details because then I would have to tell her the truth; about how when he left it felt like he took the other half of my heart, and I've never gotten it back. I push the thought out of my head because no one will ever know that side of the story.

58

"I could cut the tension between you two with a knife so excuse me if I find that hard to believe." She presses. This girl doesn't know when to quit.

"I'd rather not tell my whole life story to a complete stranger." That may have came out harsh, but I'm tired of people pushing me to talk about shit I clearly don't want to talk about. She doesn't seem fazed by my stand-off personality at all which I find a little annoying.

"Okay okay I'll drop it, but I'm just saying if a man ever looked at me the way he looks at you, I'd be running into his arms." She hands me a five dollar bill from a ten dollar tip that was left on a nearby table, and walks away with a grin on her face. If I'm not careful around Elliot, that's exactly what I'll be doing, and I can't let that happen.

I'm wrapping silverware at an empty table about an hour later, when I feel a presence behind me, only to look up and see a very nervous Elliot with both his hands in his jacket pockets.

"Me and Andrew are heading out now, we'll see you at home." A heavy feeling comes over my chest when I hear him say *home*. His house doesn't feel like home, but honestly neither has my house in LA for the past six years. I don't acknowledge him in the hopes he'll just leave.

"What time do you get off?" He asks.

"One." *Damn it why did I tell him that?*

"I could pick you up, no strings attached, I just don't like you walking by yourself at one o'clock in the morning." I quickly go through the pros and cons in my head of letting him take me home. On the one hand it would be nice not having to risk being ax murdered on the way home, but on the other hand being confided in a car alone with him doesn't sound appealing.

"No thanks, I like walking." Surprisingly he doesn't protest.

"See you later Emory." I expected more of a fight from him when I declined his offer, but maybe he's finally given up. I guess yelling at him in the kitchen did pay off. I walk up to the table that they were both sitting at to clear it off when I notice something under one one of the cups. I move it and find a $100 bill attached to a note.

59

If you try to give this back I'll just tell Sam to add it to your

paycheck - E

Unbelievable. Does he think I'm a charity case? I don't need his money. Who leaves a 100$ tip on a $20 tab anyway? Not to mention what nine-teen year old has money like this? I barely have enough to scrap up a 15% tip when I go out to eat. He always put me in these positions where I have to give him a piece of my mind when he does something I don't like, it's like he's doing these things on purpose to get me to talk to him or something. I wouldn't be surprised if he was.

It was a good shift. I took some orders on my own, the kitchen staff was pretty cool, and me and Kat had a few conversations; she can talk for days if you let her. I learned that she's an only child who lives with her grandma who can't work anymore, hence why she works two jobs. I've determined that she's an old soul trapped in a twenty two year old body. She collects things like pins, and healing crystals. She has a vinyl collection filled with music that was made way before we were even born. She says listening to anything made after the 80's is doing her ears a disservice. I said maybe ten words to her while I let her chew my ear off. She's not the kind of person I usually take too, but it felt kinda nice to talk to someone new.

"Do you need a ride home baby cakes?" I forgot to tell her not to call me that earlier, but now it's too late since it's stuck with her.

"I'm gonna walk but thanks."

"Sweetie you're not walking at one o'clock in the morning, I'd prefer that you don't get murdered, I kind of like you."

"I like walking." I assure her. She sighs in disapproval, but then a big smile appears across her face when she looks towards the entrance.

60

"On second thought I think you'll be just fine." I turn my attention to where she's looking, and see Elliot leaning against the wall outside the door. He's looking down at his phone so he hasn't noticed us staring yet. Out of my control, my face turns hot, and my heart starts to beat slightly faster at the sight of him. I grumble in annoyance not just at the sight of him, but also my reaction to the sight of him. *I'm going to kill him.* Kat and I get the last of our stuff, turn out the lights and walk out together. I look up to meet gazes with Elliot who's attention is fully on me now. I shift uncomfortably under his gaze, I'm not exactly used to people looking at me like how is now.

"Hey." He's chewing the inside of his cheek just like he would do when we were kids when he was nervous.

"What are you doing here?" I try to keep my tone calm so I don't make Kat uncomfortable.

"You said you like to walk, so I figured we could walk together." He says it so confidently my anger *almost* dissipates. I hear a low *hmm* sound from Kat, only to look over and see a smug smile on her face as she looks between the two of us.

"You two kids have fun, see you tomorrow baby cakes." She turns around to walk towards her car and I suddenly wish I took her up on her offer to drive me home. I nudge past Elliot, intentionally bumping his shoulder as I walk away. He follows behind me and we walk in silence for a few minutes.

"You just don't give up." I'm the one that breaks the silence this time.

"I told you I didn't like the idea of you out here by yourself, if you want to walk then I'm walking too."

"What the hell was the 100$ about by the way? I may not be rich like you guys but I don't need your charity." He looks surprised by my sudden angst.

"Is that what you think? Jeez Emory I don't think that you're charity I'm just trying to help you out."

"Well don't Elliot! I don't need your help." I snap back with anger laced in my tone.

"Why? What's so bad about me helping you huh?" His voice raises too which gets me to stop and face him. We're both stopped dead in the middle of the sidewalk staring each other down. "Because I don't need you! I've been fine without you. I don't need anyone!" Tears involuntarily fall down my face out of frustration.

"You're so pissed off at the world Emory, what happened to you?" His tone is softer now, and his eyes are filled with sympathy which only makes my anger rise more.

"Where has being a good person gotten me huh Elliot? I lost my mom, I lost you, I made shitty friends back home, my dad can't even stand to look at me…" I can only get out hollow breaths between each word, but I push through to continue.

"When you get fucked over by the world so many times, after awhile you just give up." I admit. I wasn't always like this, I do miss the old me sometimes; the version of me that loved life and everyone in it, who woke up everyday knowing she was loved which made her the happiest girl alive, but that Emory died and got buried a long time ago. After awhile I forgot that version of myself even existed. Elliot doesn't say another word. He looks like he's in pain while he searches my face. I don't have anything else to say so I turn to keep walking, and I hear him follow silently behind. A memory abruptly comes flooding into my mind, a memory I thought I forgot all about. I was sixteen, Elliot had already been gone for about two years.

My dad comes into my room with a pale look on his face likes he's seen a ghost. He hands me the envelope in his hands without one word, and he's looking at me like he's scared or something? I hesitantly take it from him and I notice the handwriting right away. My whole body turns ice cold, and it feels like I can't move. My fingers almost lose their grip with how numb my body is.

Emory Jewel Diaz
9312 Walsh Ave
Los Angeles, Ca 90066

I haven't seen his handwriting in so long, but I feel nothing but anger along with a little nausea looking at it now. Why reach out now after two years of silence? Did the girlfriend he stopped talking to me for dump his ass and now he can talk to me again? Or did he finally wake up one day and feel bad about leaving me high and dry? None of it matters though. I don't want to hear anything he has to say.

"Mail it back, I don't want it." I return the letter to my dad which earns me a look of utter disbelief.

"Emory you'll regret it if you don't hear what he has to say." I don't know why he is so adamant on me reading the letter when he's the one that seen how down I was after Elliot left and I finally realized he wasn't going to reach out. He should almost be as pissed off as me. I say almost because no one is more pissed off than me about the whole situation.

"I promise you that I won't." I put my headphones back in my ears and return my attention to the music I was playing before the past came back to haunt me.

That was the first and last letter I ever received from him. I'm sure the letter is long gone now, and I don't even know if I would read it if I was given the chance now. I didn't care then what he had to say in the letter, and I definitely don't care now.

"I'm not going to stop trying until you forgive me." He pulls me back to the present from the haunting memory. He just doesn't get a clue. I told him I don't want to speak to him, he doesn't let up. I even scream at him twice, and he still doesn't let up. I'm running out of ways to chase him away.

"Good luck with that." I snap while continuing to walk ahead of him.

"I'll wait." He assures me. I feel a very faint flutter in my stomach, but I push it away. I'm going to pretend that didn't happen.

"I hope you got a lot of time." I say. I notice that he goes still, and I don't miss the sudden distant look on his face.

"However long it takes." He whispers. It's not going to be as easy as I thought to get rid of this guy, no matter how many snide comments I make.

CHAPTER ELEVEN

"So what's up with you and Elliot?" Kat presses me as we sit at a booth folding napkins. It's a really slow day here in the dining area of the bar, and I'm actually relieved that she's here to help pass the time since she always has something to talk about. She and I have gotten acquainted in the two weeks I've worked here. She can be very pushy at times, and has gotten me to actually talk to her despite all my blunt remarks. We've had a lot of conversations, but I notice that she tenses up at the mention of childhood or family, so I steer clear of that. I learned that her dream is to move to Paris and meet a "hot french guy who can paint me like Jack painted Rose in Titanic." Her words not mine. Her favorite movie is Say Anything which honestly doesn't surprise me since she's obsessed with the 80's. She's strange, but in a Phoebe Buffay kind of way, in a sense that you learn to enjoy that about her. She's asked me this same question about Elliot before since she sees him wait outside for me after every shift now.

"Absolutely nothing." I continue folding and try to dodge from her gaze because I already know she's giving me the *you're full of shit* look. She doesn't believe me when I say I don't want anything to do with Elliot. I've let him walk me home the past couple weeks after work because he refuses to let me do it on my own, but all we do is walk in silence despite him trying to make conversation. I meant it when I told him I don't need him, if he wants to waste his time walking me home then that's his own decision.

"Emory I'm older than you which means I'm wiser, and I'm telling you that no guy who just wants to be your friend walks you home at one in the morning after every one of your shifts." She also doesn't give up on the idea that Elliot is into me. She also doesn't know anything about what happened between me and him. All I've told her is that we were friends as kids but we drifted apart. Technically I'm not lying, I'm just not filling in the important details. I intend to keep her in the dark about those details because I'd rather not dig up the past. I don't want to entertain her theory of Elliot being into me either. I thought maybe at one point when we were kids he could have possibly had a crush on me, but that theory quickly died after he moved and never spoke to me again. Let's just say I got the hint.

"You're in no position to give me advice when you haven't even said one word to Andrew since I introduced you other than asking what he wants to order." I point out bluntly.

"Hey smart ass, we're not talking about me we're talking about you. Did you ever see Elliot as more than a friend when you were kids?" I see trying to change the subject has backfired on me.

"I'm not talking about this." I start folding more aggressively to shove out the flashbacks that are fighting their way into my mind. I've been feeling very nostalgic lately and I don't like it.

"What was your first thought when you saw him again?" She's just like Elliot in the sense that they both don't know when to let things go.

"I wanted to puke, and then punch him in the face." I answer quickly, and of course she's unfazed by it.

"What happened that was so bad? I don't believe that you guys just drifted apart because every time you see him it looks like you want to set him on fire with your eyes." She's observant too. I'm going to have to remember that.

"Nothing happened." *Don't push it Kat.* I plea mentally to myself.

"Baby cakes I invented the word complicated...spill." She has a way of making you feel like you could talk to her about anything since she has a comforting vibe to her, but this is something I plan on keeping to myself. I've spent the last five years being closed off to everyone, it's an instinct not to open up.

I never thought I'd be relieved to see Andrew and Elliot enter, but seeing them sit down at their regular table means I can avoid her prying more. I nudge her arm and point with my eyes in their direction which catches her attention. I hear a little squeal before she gets up and skips over to their table. I decide to stay back because she doesn't need my help taking their orders, not to mention I prefer not to be there while she attempts and fails to talk to Andrew. It was funny to watch at first, now it's just painful. Andrew doesn't seem to mind it from what I've noticed though.

"I haven't seen you around here before." The voice behind me is unfamiliar and dark. I look up to see a man towering over me in height, he looks in his mid twenties, his tangled black hair sticks to his face from how sweaty he is, and his

65

body is slouching to the right as he tries to maintain his balance with one of his hands, while the other is occupied with a beer. His dark blue eyes are glossy and red, with one look I know that this guy is drunk off his ass. Under any other circumstance, I'd find him sort of attractive, but right now all I feel is disgust and uneasiness.

"I just started." I figure maybe if I entertain him for a little bit he'll go away, but that thought is proven wrong when I feel him creep closer to me. Goosebumps instantly rise on my arms out of alarm, and a cold chill creeps up my neck. I turn my attention to Kat and the guys, but from what I can see they're exchanging laughs at the table. I can't see much since the table I'm at is in the back area hidden away from their sight. Of course tonight would be the night this side of the place is dead, everyone is at the bar watching the baseball game that's on. *Fuck, breathe Emory it's fine.*

"You'd think with a pretty face like yours I would have noticed you by now." This time I ignore him and slowly rise up out of the chair to go join everyone else to get away from this creep. I only get a few steps in when he grips my arm so tight I can feel the bruises already starting to form. My back is to the front of his body before I know it and I can't get out of his hold.

"It's not polite to ignore someone who's talking to you." I feel one of his hands glide into my hair before he takes it between his fingers to smell it. *Don't cry, don't cry.*

"Don't touch me!" I continue trying to wiggle out of his grasp but he's too strong for me. He makes me want to go home and chop all my hair off from having his grimy hands all over it.

"What's the matter we're just having fun." His breath grazes against my ear and I almost vomit from the stench of whiskey mixed with beer. His grip on me gets stronger the more I try to get out of it. His slithering hands go to my waist and tears instantly start to well up in my eyes. *Fuck fuck fuck.* I look around for anyone that might be passing by, but there's no one in sight. With the game on the screen, along with the music blaring loud, it's too loud for anyone to hear me all the way over here. The next thing I scan around for is anything I could use against him, but my

66

pen is in my back pocket which he's blocking, and all the silverware is too far from my reach.

"Let go of me!" I shout as loud as my lungs will let me. Of course at that moment everyone starts to scream over the game masking my own. I don't even know if I'm loud enough since my body feels so fragile right now. He creeps next to my ear and takes another big whiff of my hair. Men like this absolutely disgust me. I shut my eyes and try to disconnect from my body, but I never stop trying to fight him off until his touch is abruptly gone and I hear a slamming noise behind me. I turn around to see Elliot on the ground, on top of the guy throwing hard punches directly at his face. I see blood everywhere through the wetness in my eyes. A snapping sound pounds in my ears that I can only imagine being the guy's nose breaking. Andrew rushes quickly behind and tries to grab his brother off the ground, but it's no use because Elliot doesn't let up on his punches in the slightest, even when the guy is clearly half conscious.

"Elliot stop you're gonna to kill him bro!" Andrew shouts aggressively still trying to pry him off. All I see is his arm flying up and down at the guy's face, followed by spats of blood. He's like a machine, never slowing down or letting up. Andrew tries everything to get him off; grabbing him by the shirt, pulling his arm back, even grabbing him into a bear hug to tear him off, but nothing works. He's like a pitbull with lock jaw. Elliot doesn't even look like Elliot right now. I feel a lump the size of a tennis ball settle in my throat, and my body doesn't want to move. Even with the brutal scene in front of me I feel disassociated from everything, but I find the strength to scream.

"Stop!" My lungs feel like they're on fire, and my tears feel hot as they stream down my face. Elliot stops mid punch and looks up at me with nothing but rage in his eyes. I gasp and take a small step back on instinct. "Come near her again and next time won't go as well as this time." Elliot points a finger at the stranger's bloody face. The guy is barely conscious, but he still manages to nod in agreement. He's almost unrecognizable with all the swelling and blood covering his face that I *almost* feel bad for him. I've been in fights before, but I've never wailed on anyone like that before. Suddenly Sam comes running up to us with a bat in his hands.

"What the fuck happened?" He asks the group. We all exchange wary looks at each other. My gaze goes from Elliot, to his bloody knuckles, then to the man on the ground who is now fully unconscious.

"This piece of shit had his hands all over Emory and you and your damn bat weren't around to help." Elliot shouts still full of rage, it fills the entire room making everyone else quiet. His whole body is shaking and I don't know if it's from the anger, the adrenaline, or fear. "I was counting inventory, I only heard shouting from Andrew I swear." Sam says defensively. He turns to give me an empathetic look. I hate people feeling sorry for me, I feel like I'm being suffocated with everyone looking at me with pity.

"Just get him out of here please." I announce to the every one. I can't help but hear how weak my voice sounds as I speak. I wipe the wetness from my cheeks and turn to walk to the bathroom to clean up. "Emory stop let me take you home." Elliot stops me by grabbing my elbow and pulling me back, but instead of seeing his face in that moment, I just see the strangers' dark blue eyes and evil smirk.

"Get the fuck off me!" I shout while twisting out of his grasp. I can still feel that assholes' hands all over me that my skin feels like it's crawling. I just need five minutes alone and I'll be fine. I storm into the ladies room and collapse against the wall as soon as I hear the door close behind me. I let a sob that's been lodged in my chest finally escape. I don't know if it's because that piece of shit assaulted me, or the fact that I just seen Elliot beat him to a bloody pulp, but I can't stop the sobbing from erupting out of me. No matter how loud the cries come out, my chest feels like it's collapsing in on itself, and I can't see a thing through the puddle of tears in my eyes.

How is it that my life came to this? I'm working at a bar where a fucking creep thinks it's okay to put his hands all over me, and I'm crying on a bathroom floor about how fucked my life is. I've had a lot of shitty moments in my life, but this one takes the fucking cake. I feel a burning sensation on my arm, only to look down to see the purple discolored finger marks. I lift my shirt up to see the same markings on my waist starting to form. I graze over the area with my fingers and I feel the vomit build up in my throat. I run to a stall and puke everything out: the disgust, anger, anxiety, fear. All of it. It still doesn't take away the fact that every time I close my eyes I see his blue eyes, or that I can still feel his touch on every inch of my body. I get myself to the sink and rinse my mouth out and gaze at my reflection in the mirror. My hair is still in tact, but I feel uneasy running my hands through it as I remember *his* hands being there just moments ago.

I hear the bathroom door creak open and I see Kat's brown hair in the reflection of the mirror. She approaches me very hesitantly as if she's scared to come up to me. She's got sympathy written all over her, and I can feel the vomit in my throat start to rise up again at the thought of her having pity for me.

"I'm so sorry Emory, if I wasn't busy talking to Andrew maybe one of them could have noticed earlier that you were in trouble, or maybe even I could have noticed." I hear her choke on her words, and she's got her face hidden behind her hair now. I know it's not her fault, but I can't help but compare her to everyone else who's never there for me when I need them.

"I just want to be alone Kat." I say while wiping the smeared mascara off my face with a paper towel.

"Emory please, if you don't want to talk to me then talk to someone else, what happened to you is going to start messing with your head, and it's hard to come back from that." Her voice is so sincere, almost as if she may know from experience.

"Please just leave." I give her a pleading look through the mirror reflection, hoping this time she'll just let this go. My whole body feels like it's being weighed down to the ground by thousand pound weights, and I just need to go lie down somewhere. She sighs in defeat and turns to walk away, but not before facing me again when she reaches the door.

"I get why you don't want to talk, but at least talk to Elliot. He's really worried about you. You shouldn't push everyone away Emory…at least not the ones that actually want to be there." The silence echoes when she leaves, and I'm left alone with the thoughts again. How is it that I'm surrounded by all these people, but I still feel so alone and empty inside? The old Emory would have assured Kat that it's not her fault for what happened and made sure she didn't feel an ounce of guilt, but the new Emory obviously wants to make everyone around her just as miserable as she is.

69

I hear the bathroom door creek open again and I roll my eyes without even looking towards the entrance.

"Kat I told you I'm fine." I clean the rest of the tears that snuck their way out and fix my clothes, which I decide I need to burn after this.

"Never thought I'd be in a woman's restroom but you leave me no choice." All the blood flow in my face flushes at the sound of his voice.

"Alright I guess I deserve it, let me hear the I told you so." I say turning to face him. My arms automatically go across my chest as I wait for the "*I told you the guys here were creeps but you didn't listen to me*" speech from him, but it doesn't look like he wants to argue, he just looks...sad.

"If I ever wanted to be wrong about anything it's this Emory." He inches closer to me, and this time I let him. I feel too exhausted to move or talk, I'm even too tired to fight him right now. The closer he gets to me the more the tears are on the verge of bursting out again. I catch a glimpse of the blood on his knuckles, and the spats of blood on his white shirt so I reach over to take a paper towel and run it under the sink with warm water.

"Come here." I demand while closing the gap between us. I softly graze his hands with the towel and clean off the red that stains them. Just touching his hands fizzles something inside me, but I focus on my task.

"You've been cleaning my cuts up since we were kids." He says with a low chuckle. I don't say anything because my brain is so mush right now I can't form any words.

"You want to talk about what happened?" He asks hesitantly. He's acting like I'm a bomb with a timer attached.

"I'm fine." I say shrugging my shoulders. I don't want to talk about what happened with anyone, I feel so embarrassed that it happened to me, and I can't stop replaying the detail of what happened in my head.

"You don't have to that."

"Do what?" I ask keeping my attention on cleaning off his hands. If I look up at him I'll break, and I can't break in front of anyone.

"You don't have to act like nothing bothers you." For some reason I snap at his words.

"What do you want me to say Elliot? That I have bruises from the pervert that groped me? That every time I blink my fucking eyes all I see is his grin, or how I can still smell the whiskey..." My voice breaks as another sob fights to come out. My body feels so weak that I feel like I'm gonna collapse at any moment.

"Why do bad things keep happening to me?" I whisper so low I don't think he hears me. I hope he didn't because I wasn't supposed to say that out loud. My legs bolt under pressure, but he catches me from falling to the ground and brings me into his chest. My sobs echo in the empty bathroom and I can't get them to stop. He's cradling the back of my neck with his firm hand while I bury my face into his warm chest. I can't help but notice a sense of safety washes over me. I still hate him, but after the night I just had this almost feels *nice.*

"I got you." He whispers in my ear. I don't know if it's just me being too tired to fight but I let him condole me, I mean he did have my back tonight I have to give hime some credit.

"How did you know what was happening? You heard me yell?" I ask still hidden in his chest. He clears his throat before speaking as if he can't get out any words either.

"I wish I heard you. I can't explain it but I just had a bad feeling, I'm sorry I didn't get to you sooner." Now his voice sounds like it's going to break.

"Thanks." I say in a raspy voice. I should say more but just saying *that* took a lot out of me.

"So does this mean I'm forgiven?"

"You wish." For the first time tonight, I smile.

CHAPTER TWELVE

My chest feels like someone is sitting on top of it knocking all the air out of me, and I can feel the tears start to gather up in my eyes. My room is pitch black, but I can see floating blue eyes, and dark hair standing in the corner of my room watching me. I remember his touch and how even after three showers that night I couldn't stop the feeling of my skin wanting to crawl off my body.

"Help!" I try to shout, but no one is coming. The pair of blue eyes inch closer to me, and I feel the room getting smaller and smaller. He beams an evil grin at me that makes me want to vomit. *This can't be real. How is he here? How did he find out where I live?* His icy hands come to rest on mine and pin them on top of my head despite my resist. I squirm to try and get out of his hold, but just like the first time my fight fails.

"STOP!" I beg. I scream at the top of my lungs until it feels like my chest is going to cave in but it feels like nothing is coming out. My body goes frozen as the scent of whiskey hits my nose.

"Nobody is here to save you this time Emory."

"Elliot!" I let out his name in an ear pinching scream hoping he'll hear me.

"Emory wake up!" I feel my whole body shake vigorously, and open my eyes to see a bright light and Elliot's lean body standing over me. I jump up so fast I almost fall over the edge of my bed, but he's able to catch me as he brings me into a tight hug.

"It was just a dream you're ok." I look around the room and see nothing but the same old room I've seen everyday for weeks, except there are no blue eyes, and no evil smirk.

"Elliot." I cry out as I curl my face into his neck. My nose immediately catches a scent of mahogany along with something sweet. I like his new scent, it beats the hell out of the Axe body spray he used to reek of when we were kids. I didn't mind it on him back then, but I much rather prefer this one.

"I'm here don't cry." I can't help but let all my tears fall onto the gray t-shirt he's wearing. *Wait did I scream for him in my dream?* I couldn't have.

"I'm sorry I woke you up." I can still feel the burning sensation in my lungs from screaming so hard. I'm sure I woke the whole house if he heard me since his room isn't even close to mine.

"You don't have to be sorry Emory." He grabs the back of my neck and pulls me close so our foreheads are touching. He's got his eyes closed as he rubs a thumb across my cheek so gently I barely feel his touch. I lean into his hand on impulse, but once I realize what I'm doing I pull back from him.

"I'm fine, thank you for checking on me." It's been almost a week since the incident, and I've had nightmares every night since. My dad woke me up the first night with a bat in his hands thinking someone was in the house, but every night after that Elliot has been the one right there when I open my eyes from the horrible dreams. He keeps asking me if I want to talk about it, but I don't want to talk to anyone about them.

"Emory —"

"Go back to sleep." I harshly cut him off. As much as I don't want to be alone right now I don't want to ask him for help, I'd like to save myself the embarrassment. It's pitch black again as I turn out my light, and my eyes start to wander to every corner of my room making sure no one is here, even though I know there's not. I don't know how to get rid of my nightmares, Emily suggested therapy but I won't be doing that again when all it did for me last time was make me more angry. The last thing I want is a complete stranger asking me questions about my life. I'm terrified at the thought that I might have to live with these nightmares for the rest of my life, and I hate giving that kind of power to the asshole that assaulted me. I hear my door slowly creak open making me click my light back on right away. Elliot is creeping in with a pillow and blanket in his hands.

"What the hell are you doing?" I ask propping myself up on my elbows to face him. He doesn't say anything as he lays his blanket on the floor next to my bed and drops his pillow down.

"What does it look like? I'm sleeping in your room tonight in case you have another nightmare." I stare at him in disbelief as he goes down to the ground and gets comfortable.

"No you're not." I give him a stern expression, but he isn't fazed by it.

"Either I sleep on the floor or in your bed, your choice." I scoff loudly at him.

"Fine suit yourself you're the one sleeping on the floor when you could be in your comfortable bed." I try to persuade him to go back to his room, but my attempt fails.

"Nice try Emory." *Damn.* At least I'm not scared anymore, the feeling is suddenly replaced with irritation. I will admit since *that* night I've learned how to be in the same room as him without wanting to tear my hair out. He did save me after all so I can't really continue to hate him with every fiber in my body, I just hate him a normal amount now.

"Emory can I ask you something?" He whispers.

"What?" I stare blankly up at the ceiling listening intently.

"If my mom never invited you and your dad to come this summer do you think you would have ever reached out to me?"

"No." I answer without hesitation. I could only imagine the disappointment on his face right now but I don't turn to look at him. I know I wouldn't have reached out to him, I wouldn't even be here in the first place if my dad didn't make me come. Five years can cause a lot of changes for someone, and not only was I afraid too see what it did to him, I was more afraid he'd see what it did to me. There are things from my past that I never want to bring up.

"I was planning on never talking to you again when I came here, but after *that* night I guess I don't hate you as much as I did before, but I still hate you." I turn on my side to stare down at him.

"I'll take whatever crumbs you decide to give me." He says it so genuinely I know he's not joking. My eyes catch a glimpse of the bruising on his knuckles from the punches he was throwing at *him.*

"I'd do it again in a heartbeat for you." He assures me. I gulp loudly at the sudden dryness in my mouth, and I'm suddenly at loss for words.

"I think I know how to help you with your nightmares." He says. I'm instantly filled with curiosity.

"How?"

"You'll see tomorrow, get some sleep Emory." I reach over to turn the light off, and a sense of worry comes over me thinking about what the hell he has planned for tomorrow.

"Hey Emory?"

"Yea?" I ask with my eyes closed as I try to drift off to sleep.

"I heard you scream for me when you were having your nightmare." *Shit, so I really did scream his name.*

"I guess I was hoping you'd save me again." I admit.

"Always." He whispers before I hear him drift off to sleep.

Something tells me now that I've given Elliot the time of day, there's no getting rid of him.

CHAPTER THIRTEEN

"Rise and shine sleeping beauty." I feel cold air hit me like a ton of bricks as my blanket gets yanked off me. I open my eyes to see Elliot creepily hunched over me.

"What the hell Elliot!" I spit out. I throw one of my pillows over my head to block the burning light from hitting my face. I'm not ready to leave my warm bed.

"Today is day one of self defense lessons from yours truly." His deep voice suddenly irks my soul more than usual.

"What are you even talking about?" I turn my head to look at the clock sitting on my dresser and it reads 6:32 am. *Yup, today is the day I fucking kill him.*

"It's six o'clock in the morning Elliot. If you value your life give me back my blanket and let me sleep." I turn my back towards him hoping he gets the hint and leaves me alone.

"Emory c'mon." He shakes my shoulder gently and then it registers in my mind what he said a minute ago.

"You said self defense lessons? What do you know about it?" I turn to face him now.

"I know enough. Andrew has trained in boxing since I can remember, and he showed me a few self defense moves growing up, some moves are better than no moves. I think getting your power back will help stop your nightmares." *Why do I have to get my power back so early in the morning*? I should murder him for getting me out of bed this early, but I have to appreciate the gesture. The only way to get me out of my funk is for him to help me help myself.

"I'll give you some time to fix yourself up because wow…not a pretty sight." He looks at me with scrutiny but then his laugh echoes when I flip him the middle finger. No one wakes up looking perfect in the morning, me especially, but apparently Elliot does since he looks like he just came from a damn shoot at GQ with his perfect skin and bright appearance. He hasn't shaved yet so his facial hair looks a little scruffy, but the look works for him. I'm realizing now that the buzz cut works for him too, not many guys can pull that off. *Oh my god am I checking him out*? I must be delirious from the lack of sleep. After a few minutes of self loathing I pry myself out of bed and pull into some workout clothes that I packed thankfully.

I hear voices when I get downstairs, and I slowly creep towards the kitchen where I hear Emily and Elliot having a conversation. I should give them some privacy but instead I hover back and listen intently anyways.

"I heard her screaming last night is she ok?" Emily asks.

"Yea she'll be ok. I'm going to show her some self defense moves, hopefully that'll make her feel better and help with the nightmares, I feel like I owe her that much." Elliot says with a hint of sadness in his tone.

"What you owe her is an explanation." She says sharply. *Explanation on what?*

"Could you keep it down please? She's gonna come down any minute." I quietly peek my head around the corner to see Elliot with his face in his hands while Emily is looking at him with worry all over her face. She starts speaking to him in Spanish and I mentally curse dad for not continuing to teach me when I was younger. I picked up on some, but not enough to hold a conversation, or in this case eavesdrop on one.

"Tienes que decirle á ella." *That I understand.* I've never heard her voice so stern.

"Yo sé, pero ahorita no ma." Elliot snaps back. I've never heard him speak Spanish before, I completely forgot he speaks it fluently since Emily made sure that it was both her sons' first language.

"Just be careful today mijo." She pleads. I want to hear more, but I think this is my cue to enter before I hear too much.

"Good morning." I try to play off being chipper so they don't suspect I was just listening in on their conversation.

"Morning mija, I haven't had a chance to make breakfast yet I'm usually not up this early." If she suspects I was eavesdropping she doesn't show it. "It's cool, I usually have a muffin or something, sorry if I woke you up last night by the way." She shakes her head immediately.

"You don't have to apologize, I'm just glad Elliot was there with you." She moves her eyes from Elliot to me, and tries to hide a smirk behind her coffee cup as she takes a sip. Elliot hisses through his teeth playfully at her before speaking to me.

"C'mon, let's go teach you how to kick some ass." He pulls me gently by the arm out of the kitchen and outside into the front yard. The sun is out but it's not beaming yet, and the air has the most perfect breeze. I guess I understand why he wanted to do this lesson early before the heat kicks in. It doesn't mean I like it, but I get it now.

"Lesson number one is to be aware at all times. I know it sounds like common sense but you'd be surprised on how many pervs take advantage when girls are distracted, anything can happen at any time." I nod my head in understanding, but my mind is wandering off to what his mom told him in the kitchen. *Should I bring it up?* No, then he'll know I was listening. *Do I even want to know what it is?* Actually the better question is why do I even care?

"Second lesson is pretty easy, just not for me." He brings me out of my thoughts and moves directly in front of me with a grim look on his face. I tilt my head at him in confusion.

"Knee me in the groin." He winces before I can even process his words.

"What?" I'm too stunned to say anything else. "It's a learning experience for you so I'm willing to be your guinea pig." He says regrettably.

"I think one day you're planning on having children and I don't need you throwing it in my face that I'm the reason you can't Elliot." I say.

"Don't be so dramatic I can handle it, just do it." He winces again. For a guy that says he can handle it, it sure doesn't seem that way with how much he's wincing *before* I've even done anything.

"No." I repeat rigidly.

"Emory Jewel Cortes would you just please knee me in the groin! Just think of how I didn't talk to you for five years and how piss—" I place my hands on his shoulders and bring my knee directly in contact with his groin before he even finishes his sentence. He immediately hunches to the ground in pain while he holds both his hands over the area of his pants, cursing under his breath.

"Great…job." He struggles with the words in between his shallow breaths. He stays on the ground writhing in pain. I've never done that to anyone before, but it did feel pretty good.

"Good news is I think I hate you less now." I dip down to be eye level with him.

"Glad to hear something good came out of it because this hurts like hell."

"You need some ice?" I don't know how much force I put into that so I guess I do feel *somewhat* bad.

"No I'm good. That was a good first lesson, but actually I think that's enough for today." His breathing returns to normal and his composure is calm now. He sits upright on the grass and I join him without a second thought.

"Don't get mad like last time, but I don't think you should go back to working at Sam's." He says. Sam gave me the week off after what happened, but he also said to take as much time as I need. I should be going back in a few days.

"That's not your decision to make." I reply with a cold tone.

"I don't like thinking that if I'm not there something could happen to you." He rubs his hand against his red discolored knuckles as if he's trying to retrieve the memory from that night.

"You don't have to protect me like I'm some damsel in distress, plus thanks to my new coach, I know how to knee someone in the groin and make them almost puke." I point out.

"I know you can take care of yourself, you're a badass." His deep laughter rattles through me.

"I am aren't I? " I joke. I won't admit it to him, but Elliot did something today that no one has ever done for me, he made me feel *strong*. It's a feeling I could get used to.

CHAPTER FOURTEEN

Today is my first day back at work since the incident, and it went as well as it could have. I swallowed my pride and apologized to Kat for how I made her feel the night it happened, and she cried telling me how sorry she was, which honestly made me a little uncomfortable. Sam kept checking on me every five minutes making sure I was okay, it got sort of annoying how everyone was walking on eggshells around me, but that seems to be the theme for anyone who's around me lately.

Elliot is in his usual spot after my shift ends. I hated the idea of him walking me home at first, but I am getting used to seeing him leaning against the same wall every time I get off work.

"I forgot to tell you this morning that I like your hair like that." He touches the ends of one of my braided pigtails with a warm smile.

"Thanks."

"I want to ask you something, and feel free not to answer if it's too personal." He says shifting nervously. *Shit.* I hate personal questions.

"Uhm, sure." I don't try to hide that I'm uncomfortable.

"I heard you and your dad arguing the other day on the porch…" *Shit shit shit.*

"What happened that has your dad so mad at you?" I knew it was coming, but I still feel like the wind got knocked out of me as the words escape him. That was the worst possible thing he could have asked me, I would rather he asked literally anything else.

"You were eavesdropping?" I ask defensively. I can't believe he was listening in on a private conversation, but then again I was eavesdropping on the private conversation between him and his mom in the kitchen the other day so I decide to ease up on him.

"You know what it's fine, and to answer your question, it's a long story." I don't want to talk about what happened that night two years ago. I was hoping if I pushed it deep down long enough it would stay in the past. I should have known it would come back to haunt me soon enough. My dad is already disappointed in me, I don't need anyone else giving me shit for what happened.

"We got time before we get home." He says. I can feel the sweat start to build up on my hands just thinking about confessing. On the other hand I'm sure if I don't answer now he'll just wait to bring it up another time. The question is do I want to confront my past or hide from it for a little while longer? *Fuck.*

"I made some shitty friends after you left Elliot..." My throat feels so tight it becomes hard to breathe, but I continue.

"They were always doing stupid shit like getting wasted before school, stealing whatever they could get their hands on, they even went as far as selling drugs at school, and I was stupid enough to be apart of it sometimes...not the selling drugs, but everything else, not that it's any better." He's staring back at me with no spec of judgment in his eyes, at least not yet. I'm going to throw up before I finish the story.

"One of the guys in the group had a crush on me but I turned him down, and I guess he wanted payback or something. One night about two years ago we were all walking home as a group like we always did, it was really late so no one was around. We were passing by this convenience store and I guess the owner always gave them shit so they decided to break in. I didn't want any part of it but I stayed and kept watch because they were my *friends*..." I choke on the last word because they were far from my friends.

"There was glass everywhere, the alarm was so loud, and I could hear them yelling at each other to grab stuff. I heard one of the girls yell for me, she said she cut herself on some glass so I ran inside to help her, next thing I knew I was waking up on the floor, all cut up from the glass, surrounded by cops shaking me awake to put me in cuffs." I can feel my whole body tremble with the anxiety of bringing up the old memory. I've tried so hard to push that night as far in the back of mind as possible, and right now it's literally fighting its way out.

"It didn't look good for me...broken front window, store was ransacked, and the fact that I was the only one there, so I got taken in. I spent the night in juvie since I was still seventeen at the time. Only reason why I didn't get put in real jail is because the cameras showed I wasn't the one who broke in initially." My chest feels so heavy, but I can't ignore that it also feels like a relief that I let it out. Elliot is probably going to think so little of me, just like my dad did when he found out.

81

Maybe *this* was the way for him to stop talking to me all along. I had never seen my dad more disappointed in me than when he had to sit me with me in front of a judge to convince them I was innocent. The look on his face that day still burns in my memory. From that day on I swear he's looked disgusted with me every time we're in the same room.

"What happened with the rest of those people?" He asks with distaste.

"The girl that pretended to cut herself on glass I guess felt bad afterwards and told me it was a setup the whole time. The guy I turned down was the one who knocked me unconscious when I ran into the store. I didn't snitch on them so nothing ever happened. They all stopped talking to me, but at that point everyone at school thought I was the one who did it, so to say it was hard to make new friends is an understatement." I don't know why I didn't tell the cops who really broke into the store. The cameras showed them break the window, but when they asked for names I stayed quiet as a mouse. My dad paid for the incident to not show up on my record which is the only reason it didn't get held against me when I applied for college.

"I'm sorry." I don't know if my mind is playing tricks on me or if he really just said that. "I'm sorry I wasn't there to protect you from shitty people like that." The look on his face is full of remorse. Leave it to him to find a way to blame himself for this instead of seeing how shitty of a person I am.

"I decided to be friends with them knowing what they did, and no one forced me to do some of the dumb shit with them. I could have walked away when they broke into that store that night, but I didn't." I point out. How can he think I'm innocent in any of this, much less any of this be his fault? "If I was there you wouldn't have made those friends in the first place." His voice grows louder as if he's angry, but I don't think it's with me.

"As stupid as they were, the decisions I made were mine, plus we both know even if you were there and I wanted to be friends with them you couldn't have stopped me." We both know how stubborn I've always been, so he knows what I said is true.

"Why is your dad so mad if you were innocent?" He lowers his tone and changes the subject.

"He's disappointed that I was even there in the first place. Plus I had to tell him all the shit that I *did* do with them, and that didn't go over so well. Him and I hadn't really seen eye to eye before that, and it only got worse after. At least before we were able to be in the same room, but he can't even look at me anymore 'til this day." I don't know why I admit all this but it came out so easily like word vomit.

"Well I'll never see you differently Emory. I know the real you. You're the girl that punched a kid in the face when we were nine because he called me four eyes when I got glasses, you were in the stands every time I tried out for football even when you knew I'd get pounded on, and after I made the team you're the one that cleaned up my gashes after every game. That's the real you. You may have covered her up in tattoos and put a block over her heart, but she's still in there somewhere." His words tug a particular cord in my heart that hasn't felt anything in a long time.

"I don't want you to be disappointed the more you get to know this version of me and realize the girl you knew is gone Elliot." I can't handle being a let down to anyone else.

"I'm counting my lucky stars you're even giving me the time of day, I'll get to know any version of you that you want to show me." For the first time since I've gotten here, a genuine smile of relief touches my face. Of all the reactions I thought he would have after I told him what I did, this was not it. We've still got a long road ahead of us, and I don't know if we'll ever get how we were before, but I guess we'll take it day by day. If I'm not careful he'll melt away every piece of ice around my heart that's protecting it, and that just can't happen when I put it there for a reason. I always thought I made myself tough enough to not have a weakness, but it just turns out mine was three hundred and seventy miles away from me and has chocolate brown eyes.

CHAPTER FIFTEEN

"I need your help spying on Andrew." Kat spills out like it's something so ordinary to say.

"What the hell Kat?" You'd think I'd be used to hearing crazy shit come out of her mouth, but she's definitely one to keep you on your toes.

"Not in like a creeper kind of way, I mean since you live with him tell me what he likes, what he doesn't like, what his type is, stuff like that." I roll my eyes and walk past her to the kitchen. I'm going to get a migraine if I have to talk about her and Andrew. It's been weeks since I've introduced them and every time him and Elliot come in now she doesn't make a move.

"Why don't you just ask him yourself? He seemed pretty into you." I'm clearing off a table when I feel her press gently into my side.

"You think so? Because I was too nervous to notice the few times I've talked to him. Do you think if I ask him on a date he'll say yes? Shit what if he says no? I'll have to get a new job because that's so embarrassing." She's rambling fast again which tells me she's either nervous, or partially insane. Probably both, it is Kat we're talking about.

"Kat calm down, just ask him out, and if he says no I know where he lives so we can egg his car." Her shoulders relax and she laughs contagiously. I am starting to open up to her, and to my surprise she's kind of growing on me.

"You always know what to say baby cakes." She slaps my butt softly with the towel in her hands. It used to get under my skin when she'd do things like that, but like I said, she's growing on me. *It surprised me too.*

"You know you have all this advice about guys but I haven't seen you hang out with any of them besides Elliot." She points out, and the realization hits me like a ton of bricks. I didn't come here to date anyone, hell I won't even be here in two months. Plus, the opportunity hasn't presented itself.

"I have better things to do than worry about dating." I admit.

"Mhmm." She drags on before walking away. She still thinks Elliot is into me as much as I assure her that he isn't. I bet if she knew the backstory she'd change her mind, but I still can't bring myself to tell her.

Andrew and Elliot enter the bar about an hour later right on schedule, they come almost everyday around the same time. I let Kat have their table even though they're technically in my section. I creep closer to them so I can eavesdrop on Kat talking to Andrew, hoping today will be the day she makes a move. Elliot's gaze meets mine as I pretend to clean a table off nearby.

"Can I get you guys a drink?" She asks as she approaches the table fiddling with the pen in her mouth.

"Corona for me and a coke for my brother, thanks Kat." They also get the same drinks and the same food orders every time they come, you'd think they get tired of it. I turn my head slightly to see Andrew peering up at Kat scanning her body. He's such a guy.

"Oh so he remembers my name." She tries to sound playful, but I can definitely sense how nervous she is by her shaky voice.

"Of course I do, you're kinda hard to forget." I make a fake gagging noise louder than I meant to, which gets everyones attention. All of their eyes turn to me but I quickly look away and go back to wiping the table that I've cleaned four times now.

"Listen umm…maybe I could get your number and we could go out sometime." She says twirling her hair with her index finger. It's like watching a scene in a bad teen movie that you can't look away from. Andrew looks like he contemplates it for a few seconds before answering. I don't miss the glance he spares at Elliot either.

"Yea for sure let me write it down." He grabs the pen directly from her mouth and I swear I think she's going to pass out right here from how red she got. He grabs her note pad and writes his number down and passes it back to her. They exchange an intense stare down that lasts a little longer than normal before Elliot clears his throat loudly, snapping the tension in half.

"I'll be right back with your drinks." She turns away and I can see the beaming smile that takes up her whole face as she walks to the kitchen. I follow quickly behind her, ignoring Elliot's feverish stare on me.

"Told you he'd say yes." I whisper as I help her pour a coke for Elliot while she pours the beer for Andrew.

"Fuck I thought I was going to throw up on him Em." She says wiping fake sweat off her forehead. I laugh because I know she's not kidding. I do have to give her credit though, she did ask him out.

"I guess his car will be safe from eggs for now." I'm only half joking, but I really would have egged his car if he rejected her.

"Thanks again baby cakes, you're a good friend." She grabs the two drinks and walks in the direction of their table. *Friend.* It's been a long time since I've had one of those that wasn't Elliot. I have to admit it does feel kind of good.

"This is for you." Kat hands me a fifty dollar bill with a smug grin spread across her face.

"What's this?"

"A damn pony. What does it look like Em?" She asks sarcastically before walking away. I see a $50 bill attached with a note and I already know who it's from.

You said not to leave you $100 tips, you never said anything about 50$. See you later   - E

He infuriates me, he always finds a way around everything I say. The new Elliot is definitely more stubborn and doesn't take no for an answer. Maybe we're more alike than I thought.

"Remember when we were ten and Jeremy from next door tried to take your bike so you ran over his foot the next day." Elliot reminisces while he's hunched over bursting out in laughter. Our walks after work now consist of him trying to bring up the past. Sometimes I bite the bait, other days I bite his head off for it.

"He shouldn't have tried to punk me for it, he ran home so quick and his mom came to talk to mine." I cringe at my mention of mom. I don't like talking about the past because something always tries to creep back into my mind, like an old feeling, or a flashback. I can't afford for that to happen when I've pushed it all so deep into the back of my mind for a reason.

"I miss her." Elliot whispers with sadness as if he reads my thoughts. *Me too.*

"So are you going to school in the fall?" I ask. My mom is a subject I don't want to touch on with Elliot, or anyone for that matter.

"No." His voice is dry as he looks ahead and avoids eye contact with me.

"Is it because you don't want to?"

"Yes." His tone is short, and I notice his shoulders tense up and his jaw muscles tighten. He's being really weird now. Why is college such a sensitive subject? I get that it's stressful, but I don't think I've ever seen anyone so tense when the subject comes up.

"Did you ever have a boyfriend growing up?" Apparently it's his turn to change the subject. I look over at him in utter sock because not only did that come out of nowhere, but this topic is uncharted territory between us.

"Uhh…no. I went on dates but never anything serious. What about you? I'm sure all the girls have been swooning over you like always." I say. Ever since we were kids Elliot was someone who the girls always noticed. He turns and gives me the smallest glint of a smile.

"Never any I was interested in." Elliot never had a girlfriend even while we were growing up, and trust me every girl would have jumped at the chance. It surprises me that even now he hasn't been with anyone, especially since he's insanely attractive. *Wait, what the hell? Did I just admit he's attractive?* It must have been a slip up in my brain.

"I wonder what it takes to catch the interest of *the* Elliot Jacob Cortes." I play it off as a joke, but I'm actually interested to know.

"Ha ha, I just always seem find something wrong with every girl that's interested in me." He admits.

"Ouch, what a dick." I say scrunching up my nose at his harshness. He rolls his eyes at me, out of annoyance I'm sure.

"Shut up, I won't ever judge a woman off her size or the color of her skin, nothing like that. Women are the superior sex, period…but I always find something off with every girl." I stop abruptly to step in front of him and reach my hand out to shake his. He eyes me with utter confusion.

"What are you doing ?" Despite his hesitation he still reaches out to shake my hand gently.

"Pretend we just met, find something wrong with me." I say. I'm actually really interested to hear this. He laughs nervously while shaking his head.

"It's impossible Emory." He subtly bites down on his bottom lip and scans my entire body. My body feels like it just rose a few degrees hotter with just that look.

"Come on you won't hurt my feelings, pretend you don't know me and we ran into each other at a grocery store in the frozen foods section or some shit since I can't cook." I can feel his heavy laughter in my chest. His laughter is like a blanket that wraps around you when you hear it.

"Emory you're perfect…from your long black hair, to the freckles that you try to hide with makeup but I can still see them peak through, but besides your looks it's the fact that even though it's rare you let people see it, your smile can make anyone smile, and I find it oddly cute that you break off little pieces of your muffin when you eat them instead of just biting into it, not to mention you're not afraid to call people out on their bullshit. I can't find one thing wrong with you." My heart skips a beat in that moment, I physically feel it do it.

"Uhm…" I scramble for words, but nothing comes out. Damn him, he's had a way of scrambling my thoughts around lately.

"C'mon let's get home, you're off tomorrow right?" I have whiplash with how fast he switches up. One minute he's telling me he can't find anything wrong with me, then he's asking about my work schedule. I nod my head silently since I'm still so lightheaded from his confession I can't even get a simple *yea* out.

"Good because we're going to the beach." He says.

"The beach...in Arizona?" *Isn't this place one big desert?*

"We do have beaches Emory." He responds dryly. We approach the front gate of the house and walk up the steep driveway. I never took advantage of being close to the ocean while living in LA but I should have. I make a mental note to myself to visit the ocean more often when I'm in San Diego. We walk into the house and I start up the staircase while Elliot makes his way to the kitchen. His voice stops me midway up the stairs.

"Get some rest Em we're getting up early, by the way Drew and your friend Kat are coming." I was not expecting *that*. Kat just got Andrew's number a few hours ago and we're already planning beach trips with them? I have to hand it to her, she works fast.

"What the hell?" I blurt out without thinking.

"Yea me and Drew were talking about the beach and how we wanted to go, and your names came up so we figured we could all go."

"Sounds fun I guess." Spending a whole day with Elliot, and not to mention having to deal with Kat and Andrew doing whatever the hell they do. This ought to be good.

CHAPTER SIXTEEN

I wake up to my loud and obnoxious alarm going off, and I instantly regret agreeing to spend the day at the beach. This is the first time I'll be spending the whole day with Elliot since I got here, so it'll be interesting to say the least. I don't even know if I'm at the point where I can tolerate being around him for an entire day honestly, but I guess today's the day I find out.

I brush out my tangled hair and put a little powder on my cheeks, even though the Arizona heat will probably have me sweating it off soon. I move to my top drawer where I have my one bathing suit I packed. I only brought it along because I thought they'd have a pool in this place, but now I'm glad I did because it saves me the time of having to go out and buy one before we leave. It's black of course and it shows a little too much cleavage for my taste so I find a wrap to go around me. I also throw on a pair of jean shorts to cover my bottom half. The last thing I need is for someone in the house to see me half naked. I wish I was one of those girls that could walk around confidently in a two-piece bikini and not think twice, but it's just not me. I've been this way since I can remember, even therapy couldn't help me feel confident. Don't get me wrong I don't think you have to be a certain size or look a certain way to be beautiful, but I've just never felt beautiful in my own skin.

I hear Elliot moving things around in the kitchen when I reach downstairs. I swear this guy wakes up at the crack of dawn, every time I think I wake up before him, he proves me wrong.

"Good morning." He greets me with a friendly smile before returning back to his task of shoving water bottles and sodas in a big ice chest. He's in a white button up shirt, but the top two buttons are left unbothered showing a little bit of his chest. I think I can see a sliver of a tattoo under the shirt, but I can't really tell from here. He didn't bother to shave today, but I've noticed that I like the unshaven look better on him. He looks sort of handsome today. *Damn it Emory snap out of it.* I clear my throat to shake off the unbecoming thoughts in my head.

"Need some help?" I approach the kitchen island and start gathering things trying to distract myself. The island is covered with what seems like every item from the refrigerator, it looks like he's trying to make sandwiches hence the bread on the counter top.

"Yea that'd be great actually. There's baggies on the counter if you wanna make some sandwiches. Me and Drew like ham and Swiss with everything but the mustard please." He makes a disgusted face when he says mustard. Still the same as when we were kids.

"I see you still don't have an acquired taste." I say playfully. He narrows his eyes at me with disdain.

"It sounds like you still have shitty taste." He reaches over me to grab something which makes me get a whiff of his manly scent. *Why does he have to smell so good?* It's distracting.

It does almost feels natural, us being here and having a casual conversation. I have noticed I've been laughing a lot more lately, it feels weird. I've also noticed I don't have the nightmares as much since he started teaching me the self defense lessons. Even though he's only showed me two moves, it's better than what I had before, which was nothing. I will admit that I'm not sure how I feel about getting more comfortable around him, letting my guard down is how I got hurt the last time, and I can't let it happen again.

"Earth to Emory." He waves his big hand in front of my face to grab my attention. I didn't even realize I dazed off.

"Sorry I just got distracted." I gather the ham and Swiss to assemble the sandwiches. Just how I remember: ham, Swiss cheese, lettuce, tomato and a *smidge* of mayo. I don't know how many sandwiches I made for him as kids when we would hang out at my house. I also don't know how or why I still remember exactly what this guy likes on his sandwich. *What is happening to me?* I assemble the rest of the sandwiches, place them in baggies, and put everyones names on them so we don't get them mixed up. If I get a sandwich with mayo on it all hell will break loose. I place them all in the ice chest and scan the room to see if Elliot needs help with anything else.

"What else do you need?" I ask.

"I think we're okay, we'll take the chest to the car when your friend gets here."

91

"How far is the beach anyway?" It can't be anywhere close by since I haven't seen a body of water since I got here.

"Me and Drew have been going to the same one since we moved here, it's about three hours away." I gasp loudly.

"You've lost your damn mind if you think I'm sitting in a car with you guys for three hours" I'm used to the beach being so close back home, but three hours? These people are crazy. Elliot's chest rattles as he laughs.

"Relax it'll be fun, we'll lay on the beach, probably play some volleyball. Drew always comes up with something to do, you'll like it." I'm still not on board about sitting in a car for three hours, not to mention the three hours coming back. The sound of a doorbell interrupts us and I slowly get up to get it since I already know who it is. I open the door to see a bright eyed Kat in a pink tie dye bathing suit looking stunning of course. This girl embodies the confidence I wish I had. I've never seen her outside her work uniform, so seeing her in this form is new to me. She's got daisy duke shorts to cover the bottom half of her body, while the top part of her bikini exposes her flat stomach. With the flip-flops she's wearing I can see that her toenails are painted sage green, which matches the rubber band she has on her wrist.

"Hey baby cakes." She greets as she welcomes herself inside, giving me a small peck on the cheek as she walks past. She doesn't know the word boundaries, but for some reason I let her slide on a lot of things I usually wouldn't with other people.

"I see you work fast, just yesterday you asked Andrew for his number and here you are spending the day with him at the beach." She smiles big at the realization.

"It was his idea not mine. I was actually kind of relieved when he said you guys were coming because I was so nervous about being alone with him." Her grin disappears as she brings her nails to her mouth and nervously chews on them.

"Just be yourself." I nudge her arm gently. She inhales and exhales deeply before putting her hands back down at her sides. You wouldn't think someone as confident as her would be nervous about anything.

"Maybe he just invited me because he didn't want to be a third wheel with you and Elliot and he couldn't find another date last minute." A frown immediately takes up her face. I'm the worst at reassuring people, but I can tell she really needs it right now.

"Okay first of all, Andrew can't third wheel with me and Elliot because we're not a couple, second of all I'm sure he asked you because he wants to go with you, and spend time with you, so stop being weird and just have a good time." The frown is completely gone now and is replaced with her genuine smile I'm used to. Maybe I'm better at reassuring people than I thought. Kat is naturally a happy person though so she's not that hard to reassure.

"You're right I need to stop being weird, thanks baby cakes." She squeezes my arm gently and bounces up and down in excitement. I hear Elliot scream as he enters the living room.

"Drew! Get your ass down here and help!" He drags the ice chest with one arm and stops by the front door.

"Hey Kat." He greets while pulling her into a quick hug. She winks at me from behind his broad shoulder. I flip her the middle finger jokingly and take a seat on the lid of the ice chest. I hear loud footsteps and see Andrew descend down the long staircase. He looks like a teen heartthrob straight out of a 90's movie with how his hair is ruffled. He has a button shirt with palm trees printed on it, except the shirt isn't buttoned exposing the six pack he has, he paired it with cargo shorts like his brother and flip flops. Kat's jaw is practically on the floor as she drools over him. Andrew notices her and his eyes go wide before approaching her. I see his eyes linger as they focus in on her face which fills me with curiosity of what he finds so amusing.

"Hey babe." He pulls her into a hug, a lot longer than the hug she exchanged with Elliot seconds ago. My eyes go wide as I look over at Elliot with suspicion. *Babe?* I mouth silently at him.

"He calls everyone that, he's kind of a man whore." He whispers low enough for them not to hear. I'm sure he's doing that for Kat's sake so she'll feel special, which makes me smile. If I would have known he was a "man whore" I wouldn't have told Kat to get involved with him, but then again Kat is more than capable of taking care of herself.

"Alright losers let's go we've got a long drive ahead of us." Andrew announces helping Elliot carry the ice chest outside. Me and Kat follow closely behind as we all walk to the white Mercedes parked in the driveway.

"I can't believe we have to drive three hours for the damn beach." I grumble.

"Sorry you LA folk get spoiled, but here we have to travel to see a nice body of water." Andrew says.

"You *LA folk*? Andrew you're literally from LA too." I scoff. He laughs uncontrollably as if he caught himself on his mistake but he finds it hilarious. As we all trickle into the car Andrew gets in the drivers seat, Kat goes beside him in the passenger seat, and Elliot and I are in the back seat together. Flashbacks of seeing this car drive away all those years ago come searing into my brain. Suddenly I'm fourteen again standing in the middle of the street watching the car get further and further away. Even after they were long gone I stayed there for what seemed like hours hoping that somehow I'd see the car come back, but it never did.

"You okay?" Elliot asks, probably noticing my little moment.

"Yup, just dreading this long ass drive."

"Don't worry Em I usually cut the time the GPS says in half." Andrew starts the car and types in the address into the built in navigation system.

"That makes me feel worse." I lay my head back on the seat behind me and glare out the window saying a silent prayer that Andrew gets us there in one piece.

"Rise and shine baby cakes." Kat's brown hair comes into my sight before the blaring sun does. I didn't even realize I fell asleep. I slowly get out of the car to look around at the rest of my surroundings and it's not what I expected at all, but it'll do. It's pretty small so I wouldn't go as far as calling it a beach, it's more like a lake, but to each their own. There are palm trees everywhere, grass areas with picnic tables, and children running around playing, their laughter blares over the loud music people are playing. The aroma of people grilling meat fills my nostrils and I suddenly remember I didn't eat breakfast. There are some people on the water in speed boats and jet ski's, and I notice there are even people in kayaks. I react with a squeal of excitement without even realizing it.

"What are you squealing about over here?" Elliot comes right beside me and glares in the direction of my attention.

"I've always wanted to do that." I point at the people paddling in the water who look like they're having so much fun.

"I've never done it either." He admits.

"It's on my bucket list." *Why did I say that out loud*?

"Hmm, I think I need to see this list." *Great.* I only have about 5 things on my bucket list, but I imagine as I get older the list will grow hopefully. I've never mentioned to anyone about it, but it just slipped out. That tends to happen a lot around him now, I need a filter for my thoughts.

The four of us walk to an area that has some benches right in front of the water and settle there. I walk to the edge to admire the place more while everyone else gets settled in. The water is so clean and clear you can see the little pebbles at the bottom. I look out to see that on the other side of the water there are big groups gathered having barbecues while our side is more secluded which I appreciate. Big groups of people tend to make me uncomfortable. I walk back to the bench where Kat has already placed a table cloth over top and assembled everything out for everyone.

"Wow you're very…organized." I say observing all the sandwiches lined up evenly, even the drinks are organized by brand, color, and in groups of three.

"Yea grams has severe OCD so growing up I involuntarily picked up a few things I guess." She didn't say anything funny or witty, it's so unlike her. She's only brought up her grandma once since we've met, but it was very brief before she changed the subject. I can tell she gets on edge at the mention of her family so I don't push it by asking questions.

"Why do you have that hideous wrap around you by the way?" She asks. *There's the Kat I know*. I immediately become self conscious and cross my arms over my chest protectively.

95

"I don't feel comfortable without it." I say. She makes a clicking noise with her tongue while her eyes scan me from my toes all the way to the top of my head, making me even more self conscious than I was before.

"Em you've got a great body, don't be afraid to show it off. Be confident in who you are. Yea you have curves but embrace them, more people wish they had them, I know I do."

"Yea right your body is perfect. I've just always been like this, I don't feel good in my body I can't help it." I shrug my shoulders insecurely. I wish I could be different trust me, I envy the type of people who wake up everyday and admire who they see in the mirror.

"Listen baby cakes, everyone's body is perfect in their own way which includes yours. It's easier said than done to be confident, but that's why you fake it 'til you make it, and it'll come with time." She says it so confidently I almost believe it. Elliot and Andrew are playfully shoving each other as they approach us at the table. I wonder how much they heard since they were so close. I hope they didn't hear me spill about me being an insecure mess.

"We grubbing first or what?" Andrew asks while grabbing the baggie with his name on it. He opens it and takes a huge bite before any of us can even respond. He looks up and notices us observing him.

"What? Usually by this time I've eaten like three times." He goes in for another big bite. I should have packed him a few more sandwiches with how he's inhaling this one.

"But it's barely eleven o'clock." I state with disgust watching him devour his food quickly.

"What's your point?" He asks. I roll my eyes at him while Kat looks at him from the side of her eye with amusement. *What does she see in him?* Maybe it's because I've never seen him in any other way than a big brother, but I think she can do better, but that's just my opinion.

"After this we'll do two on two for volleyball. Spoiler alert Em, you and Elliot get your ass kicked."

"Oh really? Care to make it interesting? Losers have to jump into the water." I challenge. It's becoming sort of natural to engage in conversation with him too, they all seem to be growing on me, and I'm not sure if I like it. I've stayed closed off to people for a reason and I don't want it to blow up in my face.

"That water is freezing." Andrew says staring out into the body of water with fear in his eyes.

"Why does it matter? I thought you were confident you'd win?" I hear Kat and Elliot try to hide their snickering, and all of Andrew's face muscles tighten. I remember how competitive he is.

"Deal." We shake on it and the rest of us dig into our sandwiches.

Me and Elliot won by two points. We're on the other end of a scowl from Andrew as he removes his shirt and shoes.

"Have fun in that cold ass water Drew." Elliot mocks. Kat pulls her hair into a pony tail and removes her shoes as well.

"Fuck you." He says while flipping Elliot off.

"You don't have to go in Kat, this was mainly for Andrew." I offer her an out, but she shrugs her shoulders nonchalantly.

"We were a team, if he goes I go." She runs towards the water and plows in letting out a small squeal when she hits the water. She's so free spirited, it's refreshing to see that there's still people out there like that. Andrew gazes after her with a look I can only explain as a mix of admiration, and uneasiness. Before I can question it, the look disappears before he follows Kat's lead into the water.

"Holy shit it's cold!" He belts out. They both stay in there for awhile talking amongst themselves while me and Elliot clean up the mess we all made from eating. When I look up, they're emerging from the water holding hands which catches me by surprise. I don't know where they'll stand after today, but all I do know is if Andrew hurts her, he'll have to answer to me.

"Fuck you guys." Andrew says as he wraps a towel around Kat before he wraps himself up in another. I'm not surprised that Elliot said Andrew is a *man whore*, but I am surprised that despite that, he seems different with Kat today, more gentle. He didn't even get mad at her when she missed the ball in our game, and he's the most competitive person I've ever met. I've caught him a few times looking at her in awe when he thought no one was looking, but I also notice fear behind his gaze too. I know the look all too well because it's the same look I give Elliot every time he says something that makes me think that I can fully let him in, knowing that I can't.

"C'mon I need some sun to dry off baby cakes." Kat drags me by the arm towards the large grass area and we sit beside each other letting the sun rays hit us. The guys follow after us bringing blankets along with them to lay on the grass for us. Andrew takes a seat on one and Elliot on the other. As soon as Kat notices she goes to join Andrew on the blanket, leaving me alone. I stay put but somehow I can feel Elliot's glare on me. I don't turn around to look at him until I hear him let out a low grunt before moving the blanket next to me and taking a seat. As soon as I feel his presence next to me my chest feels tight, like the air I'm breathing just got sucked up with a vacuum hose. Kat and Andrew engage in their own conversation too low for us to hear.

"So tell me about this bucket list." He lays on his back and puts his sunglasses around his eyes. I stay sitting up with my knees brought to my chest, looking ahead at the people enjoying themselves on the lake.

"No." I say pointedly.

"Why not?" He's staring directly up at the sky as he speaks to me.

"Do you have a bucket list?" I try to change the subject, but fail miserably.

"Quit trying to change the subject, but to answer your question yes I do actually. I already crossed everything off though." *Of course he did.*

"You're only nineteen and you crossed everything off your list? I haven't even crossed off one."

"Life is too short Emory, you could be here one day and gone the next so you have to live everyday as if tomorrow isn't going to come." His words hit me like a truck. I never really thought of it that way, I mean I'm not naive enough to think we have forever, but I think when you're young it's easy to forget your days are numbered just as much as anyone else's.

"Fine I have it on my phone." I hold a finger up to him for him to wait as I pull out my phone and scroll through my notes app. I find the one I'm looking for and tense up as I read it. I honestly haven't looked at this list in so long, and I feel anxious over knowing I'm about to share it with someone else. After telling him what happened two years ago, he didn't judge me when he easily could have, so maybe I can also trust him with this. *Here goes nothing.* I hand him my phone and let him read the items off in his head.

#1 : get a puppy

#2 : dance in the rain (with or without music)

#3 : kayak or paddle boat

#4 : fall in love

He's going to think it's childish and stupid, I mean it kind of is since I made this list when I was fifteen.

"I'm gonna help you with your list before you leave." He props himself to sit up with me now. He sure knows exactly how to catch me off guard.

"Elliot don't be ridiculous." I dismiss his idea immediately, he really has lost his mind.

"I'm serious." He looks over deadpanning me.

"Why?" I ask.

"Because I—" He stops mid sentence and stares at me with a pained expression as if he was going to say something but decided against it. "I just don't know when I'll see you after this summer so I want to help you. I owe you that much." Something tugs at my gut telling me that's not what he was originally going to say. I contemplate on asking what he meant to say before stopping himself, but I also don't

99

know if I *want* to know. If it was something important I want to believe he would tell me.

"Well…you don't have to do that, but thank you." Now is my turn to lay down on my back letting the warm rays of sun hit my body. I feel Elliot lay down beside me seconds later. My body suddenly starts to blaze, but I know it's not from the sun. How funny how his presence alone burns me more than any sun rays ever could. Elliot's hand softly grazes mine but instead of jolting it away, I let it stay there. He doesn't try to entangle our hands, his hand is just placed on top of mine for comfort, but I have a feeling it's not for me.

"By the way Emory, I think your body is perfect, whether you cover up or not people will notice you so I think you should embrace it." He doesn't move a muscle as he speaks. The butterflies I keep caged up in my stomach are out again, except this time I let them stay there.

I'm in deep shit.

CHAPTER SEVENTEEN

The room I have here is great, but I do wish I had a tv in here for days like this. Today is the last day I have off until I go back to work and I want to spend it stuffing my face and watching my favorite show. Elliots' parents are at work and the boys went to run some errands with my dad so I have the whole house to myself. I head into the kitchen to search the walk in cabinet for snacks, and thankfully Andrew has a sweet tooth so there is an endless supply of treats. I grab the bag of Oreos and head into the living room to sit on the huge couch that takes up most of the space in here. I flip through the apps and find the one that has my favorite show Friends on it. My mom used to be obsessed with this show so naturally I found a liking to it, I can recite every word from any episode. It became my comfort show after she died, so it brought me some laughs during a rough time. I scroll through each season to find the episode I want to watch and press play. It's the episode where Rachel tells Ross they'll never be together after finding the list of cons about her. I remember when I used to dream about having a love like Ross and Rachel's, but now that I'm older not so much. I think I'd prefer a love like Monica and Chandler, where you're so familiar with each other then one day it becomes more when you least expected it too.

I only get about ten minutes into the episode when the guys come storming through the door with bags in each of their hands. They seem out of breath from hauling the heavy bags up the long drive way but I don't move to get up and help. I keep my eyes glued to the tv, and laugh to myself when Joey gets Chandler an ugly gold bracelet he has to pretend to like.

"What's so funny?" Elliot asks setting the bags on the floor. I turn my head slightly just in time to see him wince while massaging his bicep.

"The show I'm watching." My eyes are back on the tv now because if I look over and I see him rub his bicep again I'll get lightheaded.

"What show is it?" He plops down on the couch right next to me.

"Friends."

"I just lost about fifty percent of the respect I had for you, I mean c'mon their friend group is so unrealistic."

"How are they unrealistic?" My tone comes out a little more harsh than I intended but I don't apologize.

"They're together *all* the time and never get tired of each other? Not to mention the shitty jokes."

"So you're telling me you've never had a friend you could be around all the time and never get tired of their company?" I spit out defensively. I won't tolerate any Friends slander.

"I mean yea you, but that's different." He shrugs his shoulders as if he didn't just make my heart flutter with his answer. *I hate that it did that.*

"What are you smiling at?" He asks. *Was I smiling*? Shit.

"Nothing." I shake my head to clear my thoughts and pay my attention back to the show.

"So what exactly is a lobster?" His question implies that he's actually interested in the show which makes me smile to myself.

"Didn't you hear Phoebe? A lobster only has one mate for life, so she says Ross and Rachel are each others' lobsters." I explain.

"Because Ross and Rachel are meant to be mates for life?" He's staring at the tv attentively now.

"Yes." I laugh under my breath and we continue to watch the episode in silence together. This is one of my favorite episodes because it's the one where Ross and Rachel finally get together after they watch the prom video.

"Let me guess they get together, break up sometime during the show, then get back together at the very end?" He asks. I roll my eyes at him because annoyingly enough he's right and he doesn't even know it.

"Guess you'll have to watch and find out." I shrug my shoulders nonchalantly which gets me a narrow eyed look from him.

"It's ten seasons Emory I'm not watching that shit." He folds his arms across his chest, but still doesn't take his eyes off the tv.

"Then I guess you'll never know." Now it's his turn to roll his eyes at me. I grab the remote to change the show since he obviously isn't interested in it, but before I can click out of it he grabs my hand to stop me.

"So are they going to end up together at the end of this episode? I feel like they're building up to that." *I knew it.* I gaze at him admiringly for a few moments but I don't answer him. I don't know if I like the comforting feeling I get now when he's around, and frankly I don't even know what it means. It might just be the fact that I'm getting used to being around him, but I also know I don't get this feeling around anyone else which freaks me out. This wasn't supposed to happen, I was supposed to hate his guts and never see him again after I leave for college.

"You okay?" Elliot asks startling me out of my wandering thoughts.

"Yea why?"

"It just looks like you went somewhere for a bit." He looks at me with scrutiny and I try my hardest to play it off that I wasn't just thinking about him.

"I was just trying to think if your body has been abducted by aliens since you're watching Friends with me."

"Yea it's not my finest hour, if you mention it to anyone I'll deny it." He smiles brightly. There he goes again making me feel all flustered with his stupid, nice smile.

"How about some self defense lessons later?" He doesn't look up from the show as he asks. It's at the good part where they're all watching the prom video and about to find out what Ross did for Rachel.

"Yea sure, but I can't promise I won't cause any bodily harm." Last time wasn't very pretty for him, he taught me a heel palm strike and I may have made his nose bleed. Maybe he deserved it a *little*, but I did feel a smidge of guilt.

"We're going to try something a little different today if you don't mind, I'd rather not end up in the hospital from a head injury." I eye him with uncertainty.

"What do you have planned?"

"It was Drew's idea, we went today to get some equipment, turns out he wants to help too so you'll have both of us as coaches."

"Oh great because that's all I need is another Cortes brother telling me how shitty my form is." I say sarcastically.

"Your form is pretty shitty Em." He says before bursting out into hearty laughter. I nudge his shoulder as hard as I can but of course he doesn't even budge.

"Fine, but I wanna see this new equipment."

"As you wish…after this episode though." I know he'll never admit to liking the show, but I can tell he does.

"Drew! Can you bring the stuff downstairs for Emory?" He shouts upstairs.

"Yea be right down!" Andrew shouts back. I don't know how they haven't lost their voices with how many times they shout at each other from different spots of the house. The episode finally shows Ross and Rachel kiss, and I hear a *tsk* sound come from Elliot.

"They get together just because of a video?" He doesn't try to hide his disappointment.

"They got together because the video showed that Ross actually cares about her, and he has all along." He turns to look at me with a twinkling in his eyes that makes my breath hitch. *He has to stop looking at me like that.*

"I know the feeling." *thump thump thump.* My heart bursts against my chest in a hectic rhythm, and I can hear it in my eardrums. I'm going to ignore that he said that because I don't know what he meant by it, and I don't want to know. We lock into each others' gazes so strongly that neither of us want to look away. We're so close that if I tilt my head just an inch, our lips would be touching. It's weird to explain, but it almost feels like my body is pulling towards him. He inches closer to me very slowly, making our noses touch, but before I can even think if I want to close the space, Andrew's voice echos.

"Alright Em I'm going to turn you into a weapon by the end of our sessions." His voice tears right through the static energy between me and Elliot, and the moment is over. Andrew looks like an actual coach in his tracksuit attire, he even has a whistle around his neck, he looks absolutely ridiculous.

"Can I at least have five minutes to get dressed?"

"You have two." He replies sternly looking at his watch.

"Now I'm taking ten." I flip him the middle finger before heading upstairs to change. I haven't spent a lot of time with the two brothers together except for the day at the beach, so this should be interesting.

"What the fuck is this?" I'm now standing with both hands on my hips staring blankly at a rubber version of a man's upper body half. This isn't what I had in mind for my training, but honestly I'm not surprised with these two.

"It's a dummy, duh." Andrew says while waving his hands in front of the equipment.

"I'm sorry are you talking about you, or the actual dummy?" I ask pointedly. Andrew scoffs loudly and rolls his eyes while Elliot stands off to the side watching our exchange with amusement.

"Are you going to be an asshole the whole time?" Andrew asks. I see his jaw tick, which makes me laugh at how easily he gets annoyed. I guess we're the same in that way.

"I don't know why you expect anything less from me." I respond dryly, but let him continue onto my lesson. "Okay seriously though, how is this going to help me? It can't fight back and teach me anything." He immediately snaps back into teacher mode.

"True, but I think my brother is tired of being a human punching bag, so that's where this guy will come in handy, Elliot and I will do the rest." I guess this could work, and it would help not having to practice my hits on Elliot. I feel like I can't get the full experience because I'm afraid I'll hurt him. "To put it short Em this is going to help you get all that anger out and not put any of us in the hospital." He exchanges a look with his brother and they both give a small nod of approval to each other before he continues.

"I want you to picture this dummy's head as the perv who touched you. I want you to remember how you felt when he had you and you couldn't move. I want you to remember that feeling when you thought no one was going to come save you." My chest starts to rise up and down in shallow breaths, and my blood begins to warm. I've tried so hard to repress the memory of that night, but at the mention of it, everything is coming up to the surface again. The memory of his hands, his blue eyes, evil mischievous grin. My nose burns at the memory of the stench of whiskey, and my hands curl up into balls at my side as I start to recall the feeling of helplessness I felt that night.

"That's it Em control your breathing…in through the nose, out your mouth. Use the anger for your favor. Now show me what you got Diaz." I let out a grunt and swing at the rubber man in front of me. Elliot has only taught me two moves so far so I just repeat the only three moves I've seen in movies, then let out another loud grunt when I knee the dummy where the groin would be if this was a real man. I try to catch my breath as I hunch over for a few minutes afterwards. My chest heaves and my arms feel like limp noodles, but I feel *relieved.* Andrew has a proud grin across his face as he glares at me, but Elliot is giving me a look that seems unsettled.

"Attagirl! See I knew you were pissed off, and it saved E some head trauma so everybody wins." He praises me. It instantly makes me feel stronger than I've ever felt before.

"Alright that was the first test, now I'm going to teach you how to get out of a bear hug." I feel Elliot yank me from behind so my back is to the front of his body. His arms are so tightly wrapped around the front of my chest that I can barely move. I try to squirm out of his hold but it's no use since he's got at least one hundred pounds on me and towers over me in height. My body starts to hyperventilate at the memory of me in the same position that night. My whole body starts to tremble, and I feel cold all the way to my bones, until I feel Elliots' fingertips rub against my arm, and my body starts to calm.

"Get him out of your head. He doesn't hold any power over you anymore Em, you got it." He whispers closely to my ear. His words rush over me like a tidal wave, and my nerves obliterate. I start to squirm fiercer to get out of his hold.

"Stop Squirming Diaz, that's how you burn yourself out before you even make your move." Andrew instructs while he observes me and Elliot attentively. "Grab a hold of his arms and drop your weight down, once you do that use your right foot to step on his, just don't break my brother's foot please." *No pressure or anything.*

"I trust you." He breath grazes my ear as he whispers. If I could see my arms I would see goosebumps forming. I want so bad to be able to turn around and look at him, but instead I exhale a big breath, and do exactly as Andrew says. I end up loosing my grip on his arms when I try to drop my weight, and I fail at my first attempt.

"It's okay try it again. If it helps don't think of it as E back there think of him as a random perv who grabs you as you're walking home from work." Andrew instructs, surprisingly patient.

"That'll never gonna happen bro I walk her home from work." Elliot says confidently.

"E shut up and let me train my student." Irritation floods his voice.

"Again Diaz, and this time pretend it's not E. I don't even care if you hurt him this time." Andrew watches us closely.

"Umm I do I care, very much." Elliot protests.

"Dude what part of shut the fuck up don't you get?"

"*What part of shut the fuck up don't you get?*" Elliot mocks his brother in his best imitation of his voice as possible. I can physically feel my brain cells dying the longer I stand here listening to them bicker.

"Go easy on me and I'll watch all ten seasons of Friends." If he keeps whispering things in my ear I'm gonna lose it.

"Let's be honest, you were going to anyways." Andrew looks like's going to have an aneurysm as he watches us laugh together.

"Are you two done?"

"Calm down Drew she's got it."

"Let me see then." I take another deep breath in and try the move again. This time I do the move perfectly and even add my own move at the end, while doing little harm to Elliot.

"Not bad, not bad at all Diaz. I like the palm to the face action you added at the end." He looks at me proudly.

"I learned from the best." I say looking over at Elliot. *Jesus, when did I get so soft?*

"Sweetheart he learned from me, so actually I'm the best." Andrew boasts.

"How you get that big head through the door every morning is beyond me." I joke. He rushes towards me before I can react, lifts me over his shoulder, and spins me in circles before tossing me to his brother. Elliot does the same thing while I'm thrown over his shoulder. We're all laughing uncontrollably, and it's the happiest sound I've heard in a long time. I can't remember the last time I laughed this much, I forgot how good and freeing it feels. After a few violent spins, Elliot places me very gently back on to the ground. He looks at me with his big brown eyes and reaches to tuck a hair that fell out of my ponytail behind my ear. It's some shit straight out of a romance movie. His thumb doesn't move from my cheek, and this time I don't move away like I usually do. My face turns hot, but it could be from the exercise. Andrew clears his throat very loudly, reminding me that we're not alone.

"I think we're good for today. Good job Diaz, see you in the house E." He makes prolonged eye contact with Elliot and winks before heading back into the house.

"What was that about?" I ask.

"Just Drew being Drew." He takes a seat down on the grass and brings his knees up to his chest, and I follow. It's almost like I *want* to be around him now.

"Do you have any tattoos?" I'm the one to start the conversation this time. I remember the day we went to the beach I thought I saw a sliver of one under his button up shirt, but I couldn't be sure. I tried to get a glimpse again when I saw him in a tank top, but it wasn't noticeable then either.

"Just one, but you can't see it if I have a shirt on so don't get your hopes up." He says the last part with a playful wink.

"What is it?" I can't imagine what kind of tattoo he would get, he doesn't seem like the type that would get one to begin with.

"I'm not telling you." He laughs nervously while picking off pieces of the grass.

"C'mon please, I wanna know." I pout and give him puppy dog eyes, hoping they still work even though I'm a little rusty. I haven't done them since we were kids.

"You don't have to do the puppy dog eyes Emory, anything you want and it's yours, but tell you what, I won't say yes but I won't say no, just not right now. It's kinda personal so no one has ever seen it." He's more gentle with his words, almost as if he's shy.

"Fine, but I'm gonna hold you to that." I relent.

"What's your most meaningful tattoo?" He asks eyeing my full sleeves of tattoos. I already know the answer as soon as he asks me, and it's not on my arm.

"How about this, when you show me your tattoo I'll show you my most meaning-ful one." He lets out a sigh of defeat. "Deal. I'll hold you to that." I easily could have just shown him my tattoo, but ironically enough just like his, no one has ever seen this one specifically, and I plan to keep it that way for a little while longer. Elliot's arm slightly grazes mine, and my whole body is ignited at his touch. My body instantly reacts to him now for some reason, but the only thing unsettling to me is the fact that I'm not even sure if I hate it anymore.

CHAPTER EIGHTEEN

Elliot decided to walk me to work today despite my protest, so here we are, walking in awkward silence. I'm slightly on edge from my realization yesterday that I *think* I'm attracted to him. How the fuck did this happen to me? It was so much easier when I hated him.

"Are you excited for San Diego?" He asks after walking in silence for awhile.

"Yea I am, all I need to do is save up as much as I can to live off campus."

"How much do you have saved up?" I don't know the exact amount I have since all my cash is in a piggy bank I've had since I was fourteen.

"Not enough." I admit sadly.

"I'm sure you'll have enough when the time comes." He says it with so much assurance I almost believe him.

"Yea and maybe you can come visit me in San Diego and we can go to a real beach." I say sarcastically. His whole body tenses up like I said something wrong, but I'm afraid to ask if I did.

"I can't wait." He says distantly. I have to get this guy out of my head, he's got me planning visits for the future. *This can't be happening to me.* When we finally arrive at the bar, we face each other before I go inside.

"Me and Drew will be by a little later." He says.

"Do you guys come just to spy on me and Kat or what?" I squint my eyes at him suspiciously.

"Sorry to break it to you, but the world doesn't revolve around you Emory Jewel Diaz." He says sarcastically followed by a low chuckle. I hate that I think his laugh is cute.

"Asshole. I'll see you later, thanks for walking me to work." I say before turning my back to walk inside. To my surprise, I'm pulled back by my elbow into his firm chest as he hugs me tightly. Something deep down tells me this hug is for him and not me. His warmth engulfs me and I inhale his woodsy scent. I still can't pick up on what the sweet scent that's mixed in is, but I'll figure it out. He holds on to me longer than I expect, but I don't try to push him away, even though hugs still make me uncomfortable. If I'm not mistaken, I swear that our heartbeats feel aligned in their rhythm, both beating rapidly, but always on beat together. He finally lets go and gives me a faint smile when we pull away.

"What was that for?" I ask warily.

"I guess I needed it. Have a good day at work Em." He doesn't say anything else as he turns to walk in the opposite direction. I catch myself looking after him, watching his back muscles contract with every step. I snap myself out of the trance before I look for too long like a creeper. When I walk into the break area, I see Kat putting her bag into her locker.

"Hey baby cakes." She greets cheerfully.

"Hey." I say while trying to tie my apron behind my waist. I fail the first time because I can't even concentrate enough to pull the strings together. She notices my struggle and comes behind me to help, tying the string into a tight knot.

"What's wrong?" She asks. Leave it to her to notice I'm a little on edge today.

"Nothing." I've got too much on mind to just pinpoint one thing that's wrong.

"You're a shitty liar you know that."

"Just drop it Kat." I demand before walking off to clock in leaving her in the locker room by herself. Eight hours of trying to get Elliot out of my head, all while Kat is breathing down my neck trying to get me to talk, I don't know how long I'm going to last.

"Wait so you like Elliot now?" Kat asks shockingly. It took me about two hours to cave and tell her what was on my mind about the whole Elliot thing. It wasn't entirely by choice since she kept pinching me until I gave in. "I don't know what to call it." I admit. My brain is in shambles from thinking too hard about this.

"Well how do you feel when you're around him?" She asks. I really don't want to talk about this, but I also don't want to keep getting pinched by her, so I go with the latter.

"I don't know I guess I feel...safe? When he gets near me my heart starts to beat a little faster, it's weird. All I know for sure is I don't want to feel this way." She stops wiping her table off and looks at me in wide eyed disbelief.

"This is the same guy who's guts you hated not long ago?" I nod. I'm just as shocked as she is at the sudden change of heart. It feels like overnight my mind changed about him.

"Well there's only one thing to do." She has a devilish grin on her face as she sits down in a chair nearby. I don't have a good feeling about what ever she's about to say.

"What is that?"

"It's simple, you have to go out with another guy to get Elliot out of your head." She shrugs her shoulders as if it's such a foolproof plan.

"That's kind of fucked up for the other guy don't you think?" Since when do I care about other peoples feelings? *Damn, I am going soft.* She exhales loudly before gesturing to the seat next to her.

"Sit and listen for a second baby cakes, I'm gonna spread some wisdom." I sit across from her with my arms crossed while I listen.

"It is a teeny bit fucked up, but think about it Em...you either go on a date with a hot guy, or you keep being confused over Elliot. The only way to get over one guy is to get under a new one, it's the oldest trick in the book." *Of course she'd say that.* I withhold the information about me still being a virgin from her because I'm sure she'd try and give me the sex talk. There's just some subjects I don't want to touch on with her. I hate to admit it, but what she says actually makes sense; not the part about getting under a new guy, but maybe I just need to go on a date with someone and that'll bump Elliot right out of my head, problem solved.

"I'm scared to admit that I think you're right." I say defeatedly. She beams a proud smile at me.

"I'm a genius I know, and lucky for you I'm such a great friend I'm even going to find you a hot date." She winks at me, and I suddenly feel terrified to the core.

"Considering you think Andrew is hot, I'm not sure if I trust your judgment." I joke.

"Shut up, but seriously please can I? I promise it'll be a respectable guy your age who is just as boring as Elliot." I laugh sarcastically and playfully throw a towel in her face.

"Fuck you." I say, this time with a genuine laugh. I have to give it to her, she can make anyone laugh when they need it the most.

"No thanks, you're hot and all baby cakes but I'm not into girls." She blows me a kiss and leaves the table, but I stay seated for a little while longer. Saying I'm nervous for her to pick a date for me is the understatement of the year, but maybe this will be good for me. Best case scenario, I go on a date with a great guy, we have a good time and I forget about Elliot, worst case scenario, I feel nothing on the date and I have to go another two months knowing I'm attracted to the guy I've spent the last five years hating. I really hope it's the first scenario. I like the way things are right now between Elliot and I, we've barely gotten to a point where I can have a decent conversation with him without wanting to ring his neck, I don't want to go backwards and mess it up.

A part of me does feel guilty for the guy I end up going on a date with, it's like I'm using him or something, but if all goes well there might even be a second date, and that one will be guilt free. Actually giving a shit about other people's feelings is exhausting.

"Hey Sam the usual please." I hear Andrew's deep voice echo as he and Elliot enter the bar. Sam nods his head at the guys as they sit in their usual spot of course. Kat looks at me with wide eyes, and I nod my head letting her take their table so she can talk to Andrew. I have no idea where they stand because I haven't had a chance to ask her since the beach, but from what I can see, they both like each other. I can tell Andrew tries to hide it more than Kat though. Out of the corner of my eye I see Elliot shift in his seat so he's faced towards me, and he waves faintly at me. *Stop being so nice to me.* I want to scream the thought out loud, but it stays in my head instead. It'd be easier to ignore my feelings for him if he was rude to me, but of course he had to be this sweet guy even when I gave him every reason not to be.

"Excuse me do you know where the bathroom is?" A deep voice rolls from behind me startling me a bit. I turn and look at a face that has my mouth gaping open slightly. His hazel eyes have little specs of green in them, and his slightly tanned skin is glowing so radiantly it's intimidating. His ruffled, curly hair almost resembles the color of butterscotch candy. It's like he was sculpted by gods or some shit with how perfect he looks.

"Sorry I thought you worked here, but if you don't know I can ask someone else." He says eyeing my name tag with a sliver of a smirk on his face. I didn't even realize I was staring at him in silence like a fucking weirdo.

"Sorry yea I do work here, the bathroom is straight ahead in the back." I point in the direction, and he follows it. He backs away but still holds eye contact with me, his charming smile never leaves his face. He's wearing a gray v-neck shirt that is definitely doing his biceps justice with how tight it is. This guy looks like he could be on the next cover of a magazine. He finally turns away, but not without sparing me a second glance.

"Who the hell was that?" Kat approaches my back making me jump at her sudden pop up.

"I don't know some guy, he just wanted to know where the bathroom was." I try to play it off that I wasn't just swooning over a complete stranger. "He's hot." She whispers while she fans herself with the menu in her hand.

"He's okay if that's your type." I shrug my shoulders and turn my attention to another task trying to act aloof .

"So breath taking hot isn't your type suddenly?" She places a hand on her hip and squints her eyes at me with suspicion.

"Would you stop? A guy like that has to have a girlfriend have some respect." I grab the menu out of her hand and gently hit her on top of her head with it.

"Remind me to teach you a little thing called body language. That man was eye fucking you Em, he doesn't have a girlfriend." I walk to the kitchen to get away from her interrogation.

"So I have a small confession." The guy from a few minutes ago startles me by popping up directly in front of my walking path. I stare at him with scrutiny, waiting for him to continue.

"I knew where the bathroom was I just wanted an excuse to talk to you." He laughs awkwardly before putting both his hands in his pockets while looking down at his feet. Am I making *him* nervous?

"And asking about the bathroom was the best you had?" He laughs again, but this time it's in delight. He's got one of those contagious laughs where you want to join in.

"You sure know how to boost a guy's ego." He scans my body slowly but seductively, and meets my eyes last.

"I'm sure you don't need the boost, my friend can't stop drooling over you since she noticed you." I look over at Kat and see her drop her head down right away when she notices us look in her direction.

"And you?" He asks bringing my attention back to him.

"Me what?"

"Well I'm kinda hoping I have that effect on you too considering I haven't stopped looking at you since you came in earlier." I gulp loudly. I open my mouth to speak, but suddenly it's too dry to say anything. How did *I* catch the attention of a guy like this?

"Either I really don't have a shot or you're just a woman of very few words." I didn't even realize I spaced out while staring at him again.

"Sorry…I'm Emory." I extend my hand out for him to shake. He scans me again from head to toe, and grabs my hand gently.

"Nicholas but everyone calls me Nick, nice to meet you Emory."

"Nice to meet you Nicholas." I think Nicholas sounds better than Nick so I decide to roll with that hoping he doesn't mind. From the radiant smile on his face he doesn't seem to.

"Well Emory how about I take you out sometime?" Usually I'm not into guys that are so forward, but this guy just radiates the kind of confidence that you have to appreciate.

"Uhhh…sure here's my number." I take my note pad out and write my number on a blank piece of paper and hand it to him. He smirks confidently before putting it in his pocket.

"Well I'll let you get back to work, I'll see you soon." I look after him as he strides away and approaches a table with three other guys. We make eye contact with each other as he sits down, and I'm embarrassed that he catches me still looking.

"Well damn that was fast, guess you don't need me after all." Kat says while carrying two plates in her hands. I already know they're the guys' orders since the burger has everything on the side just like Elliot likes it. He prefers to build the burger on his own for some reason, I'll never understand his mind. I completely ignore her comment and help her by grabbing one of the plates. I follow behind her to the table where Andrew and Elliot are talking amongst themselves.

"Here is your weird ass unassembled burger Elliot, and for you Andrew your grilled cheese, a little burnt." She places the plate in front of him, and puts the condiments in front of Elliot.

"Oh shit Em, twelve o'clock hot guy from earlier can't stop staring at you." Kat points out frantically.

"What the fuck is twelve o'clock?" I look in every direction with confusion.

"I don't know I just hear everyone say it, just look to my left." She nudges her head in the direction she's referring to.

"Then just say to the left." I demand before I catch eye contact with Nicholas again. He smiles broadly while he takes me in with his alluring eyes.

"Who's the guy?" Elliot asks looking where I am with a tight look on his face.

"Some guy that asked Emory out, isn't he gorgeous?" Kat says. My attention snaps to Andrew where he shifts uncomfortably in his seat, but he doesn't say anything.

"Did you say yes?" Elliot looks up at me wistfully.

"Yea I did actually, his name is Nicholas." He doesn't say another word as he looks down at his plate and starts to pick at some of the fries. Andrew is looking at him with a weird look on his face, but Elliot doesn't say anything to him.

"Do you think you should be dating when you're leaving soon?" He doesn't look up at me when he speaks this time.

"It's nothing serious, it's just one date." I assure him.

"What if it gets serious and then you have to leave in a couple months?" He pries. If I'm not mistaken there's anger traced in his tone.

"It won't, guys like that have a different date every night it's fine." I say dryly. I leave out that I actually don't mind if it's just a one night thing, since this could be my chance to get what I'm feeling for Elliot out of my head, or should I say what I *felt* for him before he started acting weird now.

"So you voluntarily go on a date with a guy who you suspect goes on dates with random girls all the time? Nice Emory." His jaw muscles tighten, and his tone is more aggressive now.

"Who are you to tell me who I can or can't go on dates with?" I return the harsh tone he's giving me. I can feel my blood boiling as my irritation starts to rise. Kat and Andrew exchange wary eye contact at our slightly raised voices.

"I'm the guy who's gonna watch you cry when that tool fucks you over." He forcefully pushes his plate across the table so hard it slams into Andrew's, and pushes himself out of the booth. He swiftly brushes past me nudging my shoulder as he walks in the direction of the bathroom.

"What the fuck was that about?" I ask after he's gone. Kat and Andrew are silent as they look down at the table awkwardly. Kat is now seated next to Andrew in the booth, I'm guessing so she can be included in what's going on right now.

"E is just trying to look out for you." Andrew finally says after a few moments of silence.

"No, he's being an asshole." I take Elliot's old seat to face them now.

"He just doesn't want you to get hurt." I appreciate Andrew trying to defend his brother, but Elliot is acting like an ass for no reason, there's no justifying that.

"She's not going to get hurt she's just using the guy." Kat speaks up now. I throw her a wide eyed look before reaching over to smack her on the arm.

"Ow! What was that for?" She asks rubbing the spot I hit.

"That conversation we had earlier was private." I say through gritted teeth. She gives me an apologetic look as if she didn't even realize she spilled the beans on my plan until now.

"What conversation?" Andrew asks looking between both of us with worry. *Shit.* I guess there's no use in hiding it now.

"I agreed to go on the date with Nicholas because I need to get your stupid brother out of my head, but after what he just pulled I think that did it." Andrew stares at me in utter disbelief with his mouth gaped open.

"Wait...you like E?" He finally spits out.

"I don't know!" I exclaim louder than I intended, getting the attention from people at nearby tables. I take a deep breath and continue in a softer tone.

"I don't know what I'm feeling, what I do know is I don't want to feel whatever I'm feeling for him, so I have to use someone else to get him out of my head. I don't know if I just find him attractive or if it's more, but I don't want to find out." The words spew out like word vomit, as if they were just waiting to come out.

"Why are you so desperate to hide your feelings? If you feel something just say it." He talks with his mouth full of his grilled cheese now. He really needs to read the room; i'm going through a crisis and he's stuffing his face.

"So I can get humiliated? No thanks." I smile coldly at him. Even if I did have the guts to say something, I know Elliot doesn't see me that way, I got that hint when he decided not to speak to me for five years.

"All I'm saying is I don't think going out with a stranger helps anything." He says defensively.

"Don't tell him about this or I'll murder you in your sleep." I point my finger at him trying to put on my most intimidating face. He makes a zipping motion over his lips and beams a goofy smile at me. I slide out of the booth at the same time Elliot comes back, and we collide into each other. He grabs my elbow to balance me, and we make eye contact, but something feels different now, he seems distant even though he's right here.

"Drew let's go home." Elliot spits out without giving me a second look. Andrew scarfs down the rest of his sandwich and takes a few swigs of his beer before sliding out of the booth.

"See you guys later." They both walk out silently, but not before Elliot throws me a spiteful look before exiting out the door. *What the hell just happened?*

"Don't worry baby cakes he'll get over it." Kat tries to console me, but I brush it off. It's not like he can hurt my feelings or anything, I'm just utterly confused as to why he's so upset.

"He's an ass, but now I know why I decided to never speak to him again when I got here." I clear off the table and notice Elliot left his burger untouched. I walk to the kitchen with the plates, but before I dump his food in the trash I grab one of our to-go boxes and place it in there so I can give to him later. Whether we're upset at each other or not, I still want him to eat. *Fuck, I am going soft.* I shouldn't give a shit about whether he eats or not especially after what he just pulled, but I figure we can talk about it later when he picks me up, and we'll clear the air. I'll find out what his problem is one way or another.

"What do you mean you're taking me home?" Kat is digging through her purse for her keys avoiding my question. I was about to leave to meet Elliot outside when she said he wouldn't be there and that she was driving me home.

"He called here and asked if I could drive you home because he's not feeling good." She looks like she doesn't believe that just as much as I don't.

"He's that pissed off? I didn't even do anything. If he wants to act like a child then fine, I can play this game too." I grab my stuff and stomp past her towards the door. I'll walk by myself if he wants to act like that.

"Em let me just drive you home, stop being so stubborn for once." I resist the urge to yell because it's not her fault what Elliot did. I'm trying to be a little better at controlling my temper, but situations like this test me. I let out a loud groan as we both walk out and approach a pastel green Volkswagen Beetle.

"Isn't she cute?" She asks rubbing the hood of her car.

"It's very…you." We get into the car, and of course everything is organized. It smells like alcohol wipes, and there is not one sight of trash anywhere. I guess her grandmas OCD did rub off on her in more ways than one. She's got a Bob Ross air freshener, and colorful crystals are wrapped and hung from a string on her rearview mirror. It feels comforting in here, like her in a way.

"I can't believe Elliot." I spit out as soon as she starts her car up.

"I'm sure he's really not feeling good. Mad or not I'd like to believe he'd walk you home if he could." I shake my head in disbelief. I thought this was something he would get over and realize he was over reacting, but from the sound of it, he's going to continue to be pissed off for no apparent reason. Not that I care anyways.

"To think I felt bad after he left and I almost cancelled the date with Nicholas. He's so...he's just...UGH!" I shriek out.

"Just talk to him and find out why he's so upset, there has to be another reason other than he doesn't want you to get hurt, I'm sure of it." So she believes that's not the only reason either, *so I'm not crazy.*

"Frankly I don't give a shit how he feels because now I'm pissed off too." I can feel my chest getting tighter as the anger settles in more and more. This would be a good moment to bring out the dummy so I can throw a few swings at it. We approach the house minutes later, and I undo my seatbelt quickly with the intention of barging into the house to give Elliot a piece of my mind. I can already feel my hands shaking from all the anger radiating off of me. Kat places her hand on mine before I climb out.

"Call me if you need anything, I'll turn right back around if need to crash at my place."

"Thanks." I don't say it out loud to her, but I am pretty lucky to have met someone like her; someone who's there for you unconditionally. I should express that to her more but I'm not so great at telling people how I feel. I open the gate and start up the long driveway trying to gather what I'm going to say to Elliot. I notice I'm still holding the to-go box with his food in my hands, and I almost chuck it into the trash can outside, but I'm too busy trying to control my emotions so I don't start screaming as soon as I walk though the door; it's going to take everything in me not to strangle him when I see him. I turn my key in the door knob and pry the door open. When I walk inside, Andrew is the only one in sight paying close attention to whatever is on the tv. If he heard me come in he doesn't acknowledge it.

"Where's your brother?" I ask trying to control my tone so he doesn't suspect that I'm fuming right now. "Upstairs, he says he's not feeling good so I wouldn't bother him if I were you." He finally unglues his eyes off the tv to look at me with a warning glare. I ignore his request and head upstairs to Elliot's room. I knock softly on his door and wait, but I don't hear a sound. Maybe he's asleep? Or maybe he knows it's me and he's ignoring me? I turn the knob and walk inside to see him laying on his twin bed throwing up a football with his headphones in his ears, staring up at the ceiling fan. *Looking just fine.*

His room is not how I imagined it, he's got books scattered all around his desk and on the floor. They all look like they've been read through at least ten times from how worn out the spines are. There are clothes thrown everywhere just like a typical guys room would be. I notice posters of Chevy trucks all over his pale white walls, and a basketball hoop on the back of his door. He looks so peaceful it pisses me off even more. I kick his mattress so hard the whole thing moves which startles him enough to yank his headphones out of his ears.

"What the hell Emory!" He shouts. He tries to settle back in bed to put his headphones back in, but I reach over and yank them away.

"No, you don't get to be pissed off Elliot, tell me why you're so mad and why I had to hear from Kat that she was the one that had to take me home because you *didn't feel good.*" I make quotation marks with my fingers as I say the last part because he definitely isn't sick from where I'm standing.

"I don't feel like talking Emory. I made sure you got home so what's the problem?" His tone comes out spiteful.

"What's the problem? You're acting like a child that's the problem. I know there's another reason you're upset so just say it."

"Why are you going on the date with that guy?" His voice is lower now, but his tone is still sharp.

"I don't know maybe because he asked? And because I can do whatever I want." I can't tell him the real reason why I said yes.

"So you're really gonna go on a date with someone who you already suspect is a player? I thought you were smarter than that Emory, but hey what do I know? You said so yourself you're not the same person anymore." I'm not going to lie, that one hit a nerve.

"Are you fucking kidding me Elliot? First of all, you have no right to be mad that I'm going on a date no matter who it's with. Secondly, instead of coming to walk me home so we can talk about it like adults, you decide to fake being sick to avoid me, real mature. I guess you haven't changed at all, you still know how to flake on people." He winces at my words. That was one a cheap shot, but he hurt me, so by instinct I wanted to hurt him to.

"He's a tool Emory he's just going to hurt you!" I almost shout that I'm just using Nicholas, but the words don't come out.

"This is my choice to make! You wanted to be my friend so bad, well friends don't make each other feel like shit for something they decide." I wave my hands around frantically because I'm so furious I don't know what to do with them other than wrap them around his neck. He exhales loudly making me realize the silence in the room now is very loud.

"Yea and when pretty boy breaks your heart who's going to be the one you're crying to? ME!" He gets up from his bed to face me directly now. I stand up a little straighter as I shout back at him.

"Jesus Elliot we're not getting fucking married!" I know my face is turning red because I can feel it burning up.

"You know what? Go on your damn date then, when he dumps you like trash don't come knocking on my door." I can't believe we got to this point. I've never seen him like this, and I've been mad before, but not this level mad. Maybe we both bring out the worst in each other.

"I knew deciding to be friends with you again would come back and fuck me over somehow, but hey I should be used to it right?"

"Oh and here I saved your burger from the restaurant...asshole." I throw the box onto his bed and turn around to storm out of his room.

"It wasn't supposed to be like this." He whispers behind my back. He says it so low I almost miss it, but I can't stay in this room another second to ask if I heard that right. I slam the door behind me so hard the picture frames on the wall shake. Tears prick my eyes but I refuse to let any of them come out. Emily comes running up the stairs at the same time I'm approaching my door.

"Emory I heard yelling are you okay?" The concern written on her face makes the tears well up even more but I push them back. I hate the idea of someone seeing me cry.

"I'm fine." My voice comes out strained while a sob is fighting to escape my throat. She squints her eyes at me and looks at me with sympathy. "Oh mija, you wanna talk about it?" She touches the side of my face to catch a tear I didn't know was streaming down my cheek.

"I'm fine." I turn my door knob, rush into my room, and lock the door behind me before she can say anything else. I sink down against my door and bring my knees to my chest, finally letting out the sob that wanted to come out. Elliot doesn't deserve my tears, but it's getting harder and harder to fight them. I may be an angry person, but i've ever talked to anyone like how I talked to him just now. He really had me fooled with walking me home, leaving me tips at work, self defense lessons, protecting me at the bar that night. All of it was just a way to get me to let my guard down and forgive him, and all it did was leave me hurt yet again. This is exactly what I was afraid would happen. You'd think I'd be used to being disappointed by everyone, but each time it happens, the ice I've put around my heart gets thicker and thicker, making it impossible to melt away. I think I'm better off that way.

CHAPTER NINETEEN

Elliot and I haven't spoken in five days, not that I'm keeping track. The times we did end up in the same room with each other, we avoided one another like the plague. I think the most he's said to me is *do you want dressing?* when he was passing me the salad yesterday at dinner. I have no interest in speaking to him and I'm sure he feels the same way about me. This is what I wanted anyway, the next couple months should be easy now that we're not speaking. Tonight I don't care about any of that because it's my date with Nicholas. We've been texting the last couple days, and he's actually a pretty nice guy once you get to know him. He's on vacation visiting with family for the summer, but he lives in LA full-time while he attends UCLA to become a teacher. He seems like the perfect guy, but somehow a certain brown eyed jerk is the one I can't get out of my damn head. When I first agreed to this date it was just to get Elliot out of my head, but now I'm going because I genuinely want to see if things go anywhere with Nicholas. Any feelings I *thought* I had for Elliot dissipated, and they're replaced with the urge to punch him in the face every time I look at him.

Nicholas won't tell me where we're going for our date, but he did say to wear something formal so I decided on a black silk dress. The straps are so thin I think they'll snap at some point during the night trying to keep my breasts contained. The dress is knee length, and I paired it with the red heels that were hiding in the back of my closet. I curled my hair and went with natural makeup since I don't want to over do it. I actually feel really pretty. I hear a doorbell ring downstairs and glimpse over at the clock to see it's eight o'clock sharp. *I see he's punctual too.*

"Emory!" I hear my dad yell from downstairs. My dad was insistent on meeting Nicholas even after I pleaded with him how lame it is on the first date. To my relief, Nicholas didn't seem to mind at all when I told him. I'm waiting to find something wrong with this guy, but nothing has come up so far. I descend down the stairs slowly, meeting eyes with Nicholas. His eyes rake my entire body from head to toe so intensely I almost get shy. He's in a black suit and tie that he looks very attractive in. His curly hair is combed through now, though I think I prefer the messy look he had at the bar. No one can deny he's good looking, anyone with eyes can see that, but as I approach him I notice that there are no butterflies in my stomach, no sparks, or heat rising up my spine.

"Shit, you look great." His compliment slips out but he immediately corrects himself. "Sorry sir." He directs at my dad who has his arms are folded across his chest, just like every dad does when they want to see intimidating to the guy taking their daughter out. Nicholas slowly lifts up one of my hands to place a small kiss on it, but even with that, there are still no jolts of electricity running up my arms, or butterflies trying to break out in my stomach, but it's also still early in the date.

"You look really beautiful Emory." I can't help but laugh nervously as he compliments me again.

"Thanks, you too. I mean not that you're beautiful I mean...uhm you look really nice." *Did I forget how to talk or what the hell?* I guess this is karma for making fun of Kat when she used to get tongue tied around Andrew. It also doesn't help my nerves that everyone is in the room watching us like hawks. The only sound is from the tv show that's playing in the background, everyone is silent and still as they watch. I hear heavy footsteps descending down the stairs and see Elliot slowly walking down with a scornful look directed at Nicholas. He eyes my date up and down with distain written all over his face, he doesn't even try to hide it either. Nicholas fidgets nervously when he notices.

"Hi, I'm Nicholas." He extends his hand out to Elliot, but all he does is hiss through his teeth and dismiss him. *Asshole*. Nicholas pulls back his hand and puts it in his pocket to save himself more humiliation. Elliot has been an ass lately, but I didn't think it was too the extent of being rude to a complete stranger. He's usually all sunshine and rainbows around people.

"So where you guys going?" My dad asks curiously.

"It's a surprise to Emory sir, but I'll be happy to tell you when she walks out." He gleams.

"Just try and have her home at a decent time." My dad tries to sound threatening.

"Of course, I wouldn't dream of having her home late."

"*Kiss ass.*" Elliot coughs under his breath loud enough for everyone in the room to hear.

"You have something you want to share with the class?" I ask harshly. He has a lot of nerve being rude to Nicholas when he hasn't even done anything to him.

"I think I'm just catching a cold." *He's a shit liar.* I roll my eyes and turn my attention back to my date because I'm not giving Elliot the time of day anymore.

"We should get going if we're going to make it to this surprise destination." I entangle our hands together and pull him towards the door.

"You're right, just one second." He pulls back to stay behind to talk to my dad as I'm walking out. I can't make out what he's saying, but I'm sure he's telling my dad where we're going to get extra points with him. I'll have to ask for some tips on how to get on my dad's good side since I can't seem to get a grasp on it. I try to resist, but end up taking a glance over at Elliot who has anger flooding in his eyes as he watches me walk out. There's something else behind his eyes paired with the anger, I just can't figure it out.

Me and Nicholas finally walk out together to his black Range Rover parked in the drive way. He opens the passenger door for me and waits for me to climb in. It's the twenty first century so I didn't think guys still opened doors for girls, but this guy is already full of surprises; like the fact that he's rich because this Range Rover looks brand new and fully loaded with the newest gadgets.

"Who was that guy in there? Your brother?" He asks as he climbs into the drivers seat.

"No, that's just Elliot." I don't have enough time in the world to explain to him the complications with me and Elliot.

"I just assumed because he was acting like an over protective brother or something."

"He's just a childhood friend, he can be protective at times." Childhood friend seems like the safe route as far as explaining our relationship.

"Have you guys ever had a thing?" He asks with scrutiny.

"No never, just friends who grew up across the street from each other."

"Sorry for all the questions I just don't want to get in the middle of anything if there's something between you two." He says politely.

"You're not trust me. I'm here because I wanna get to know you." A faint smile touches his face and he gently caresses my hand that's resting on the middle console. I try and be as polite as possible as I remove my hand from under his. For some reason it just didn't feel right, but it could be because I hardly know the guy. "I hope you have an appetite for where we're going." He successfully changes the subject at the mention of food because I'm starving.

As I look over, I see the blinds in the living room slightly parted, and a tall figure hovers over the window. I already know who it is, and I feel a ping of guilt start to creep in, but I push it down. Nicholas successfully pulls the car out of the long driveway and drives off. I take one last look out of my window at the house before it disappears behind me.

We arrive at a place called Bella Vista. I've never heard of it but it looks really fancy from the outside, and when we stop in front a valet parking booth I know it's already more fancy than I'm used to. Nicholas gets out first to pass the guy working at the booth some cash, then he comes over to open my door for me. I grab his hand that's extended out to me and climb out taking in my surroundings of beautiful twinkling lights wrapped around all the trees surrounding the entrance, along with an elegant pebbled walkway, and the kind of view that leaves you speechless, hence the name of the place.

"Mr. Graham this way." A man dressed in waiter attire leads the way to our table. We go all the way to the top floor, and all the words fall out of my brain when I see the view from where we're sitting. You can almost see the whole city from up here. I notice we're the only ones up here on this level for now which makes me wonder if that's on purpose or not. "This view is incredible." I say admiringly. Since I've gotten to Phoenix I've never taken the time to see it this way, it is a beautiful city, I should appreciate it more.

"Will it be the usual for the drinks Mr. Graham?"

"Yes please that'll be great David." The man nods his head and smiles at me before walking away.

"The usual huh? I take it you bring all your dates here." My tone comes out playful, but I'm actually curious to see if I was right about him being the type to have a different date every night. "Actually no, I'm friends with the owner so I come here a lot, you're actually the first date I've been on since I've visited the city." *I don't buy that line.*

"You don't believe me?" He asks as if he just read my thoughts.

"I don't believe someone as attractive as you hasn't been on a date for almost two months until now." I admit. I'm usually not this forward by telling someone they're attractive but what the hell, maybe a new approach will be good for me. Before he can respond, David comes back with a bottle of wine. I look up at Nicholas with a wide eyed look of uncertainty because I don't know if the waiter knows we're both underage, but he nods his head subtly telling me it's okay. I guess there are perks for knowing the owner.

"Enjoy. I'll be back in a few moments to take your orders." We both pick our glasses up and clink them together.

"To first dates." He says cheerfully before taking a sip from his glass. I bring the glass up to my lips to avoid saying anything. I'm still a little on edge so hopefully this wine will help. "It's true you know."

"What's true?" I ask.

"About not having been on a date until now. I wasn't planning on it especially when I know I'll be leaving after the summer, but when I saw you walk into the bar the other day I knew I had to know you. You're so beautiful, and you seem to have this edginess to you. It's refreshing to see someone who's unapologetically themselves, I like that about you." I give him a weak smile at his confession. Those are some of the sweetest words anyone has ever told me, but to my surprise my heart doesn't skip a beat, it doesn't even beat faster than usual.

"Thank you, and if you should know you're the first date I've been on since I got to the city too." I admit.

"I'll drink to that." He raises his glass close to mine again and we both take another sip. If I'm being honest it tastes a little bitter, I thought rich people were supposed to drink good tasting wine? David nervously approaches our table with two bottles of Corona in his hand.

"Excuse me, but these are from the gentleman over there, he says to have a great night." He nudges his head in the direction of whoever sent us the beer, and my heart falls to my stomach at my sight in front of me. A wave of nausea rushes over me when I see Elliot sitting at a table directly in my view all by himself, with a beer in his hands. He raises his drink up to me and Nicholas when he notices that we see him.

"You've got to be fucking kidding me." I whisper to myself.

"What is he doing here?" Nicholas asks coldly, still staring in Elliot's direction.

"Did you tell him where we were going?" I ask.

"No I just told your dad when you slipped out." He assures me. I glare at Elliot again trying to tell him with my eyes that I don't want him here, but by the way he's looking back at me tells he doesn't care. His eyes are narrowed in on only me and his lips are curved into a tempting smirk. Just the look alone makes my skin feel ignited.

"He must of been eavesdropping when you were talking to my dad, just ignore him." I chase down the rest of what's inside my wine glass, grab the bottle from the ice bucket to pour more into my glass, and chug that down to.

"You might want to slow down on the wine Emory this one is pretty strong." Nicholas warns me while trying to grab the bottle, but I keep a tight grip on it.

"It's fine." I assure him while taking more gulps. All I want to do is enjoy my time with this great guy and forget about the annoying asshole in front of me, but even as my eyes wander, they always go back to watching him attentively.

"Have you two had a chance to look over the menus yet?" The waiter asks as he approaches the table again.

"I'll have the scallops and an order of caviar, and you Emory?" I look over the whole exquisite menu, but decide on the roasted chicken because I'm not familiar with anything else, and I'm too embarrassed to ask for clarification.

"So you're rich huh?" I blurt out and immediately get embarrassed. Maybe this alcohol is pretty strong after all. Nicholas readjusts in his seat as soon as I ask the question. This date isn't looking so great anymore from where I'm sitting.

"Uhh no my parents are, my dad is a lawyer at a big firm in LA, and my mom runs a five star restaurant down there."

"Wow." He's probably used to this wine and dine lifestyle, where as I'm definitely not.

"Yea but I don't think of their money as mine. Everything I have now is because I worked for it. My dad wanted me to join the firm and go to law school but it's just not my dream you know, I want to be an impact on kids' lives." I nod my head as I listen intently to him, but out of the corner of my eye I see Elliot looking down at the menu with confusion all over him; I recognize the look because it's a similar one I had while going over the menu. A waiter approaches his table and I try my hardest to listen in.

"I think I'm good with the beer thank you, I don't really know what anything on the menu is except the chicken." I smile involuntarily, and try to hide it behind my hand, but I know it didn't work when Nicholas squints his eyes at me with confusion.

"Emory did you hear me?" I snap back to him and realize I have no idea what he just said. *I'm the worst date ever.*

"I'm so sorry what did you say? I think the wine is getting to me." I bring my hand to my forehead and rub it gently. I do feel a little tipsy, but that's not the reason I didn't hear what he said, and I think he knows it.

"I asked what your attending college for in the fall." He repeats. He's being so sweet to me, the least I can do is pay attention to him. I need to block Elliot out of my mind like I was planning to do.

"To be honest I haven't picked a major yet, I got accepted to the University of San Diego but I don't know what I'm gonna major in." I admit.

"I understand that, something will come to you when you least expect it. Whatever you decide to major in I'm sure you'll do great." He reassures me with a smile, and runs his hand along his tie nervously.

"Thank you." I say politely while awkwardly taking another swig of wine.

"Would you excuse me? I'm going to go find a restroom." He says slowly rising out of his chair.

"Of course, I'll be here." He gets up to leave the table without another word. I run my hand across my forehead to wipe away the droplets of sweat that are trickling down. If I don't get Elliot out of my head I could ruin a potentially good thing with Nicholas. I get up to walk to his table and his tender eyes find me right away.

"What the fuck are you doing here?" All he does is laugh mischievously at my anger, and takes another swig of his beer.

"You guys are the only ones that can enjoy this view and the great booze or what?"

"You and me both know you're not here for the booze when you can drink at Sam's for free if you wanted to, plus I've never even seen you drink since I got here. How the hell did they even serve you?" I ask furiously with my hands on my hips. He holds up an ID card in his fingertips for me to see.

"It's a fake." I try to snatch it out of his hand, but he's faster than me at putting it back into his pocket.

"You might want to go back to your table before your date realizes you're talking to me." The impish grin on his face grows wider. *I hate him*. He made it clear he wanted me to go on this date, and now that I'm on it, he wants to ruin it. If I weren't afraid of making a scene I'd smack that beer right out of his hands.

"Haven't you caused enough drama Elliot? What the hell was that at the house? Nicholas was trying to be nice to you and you blow him off, real nice." He shrugs his shoulders as if he doesn't have a care in the world. This is a new version of him I don't want to get to know. He's acting like...*me*.

"Not my fault you can't see how much of a tool he is, but I'm not here to start drama. I'm just here to enjoy the view and drink my beer, have a good night." He says dismissively. I grunt loudly and turn away to walk towards my table that is thankfully still empty. I would hate for Nicholas to come back and see I'm talking to Elliot, I think the date would be over right then and there.

"If a small part of you still cares about me at all please leave Elliot. Nicholas is nice and I'm trying to enjoy this date but I can't with you sitting in front of me." I plead.

"Why? Am I distracting you with my good looks?" He smolders at me before taking another swig of his drink.

"You wish." I spit back. I wish more than anything that he wasn't right. If only I had the power to set someone on fire with my eyes right about now.

"You look really nice tonight Emory." He admires my whole body and finally stops at my eyes. We lock into such intense eye contact that it feels like there's an energy field in between us. I struggle to break the stare down.

"Go to hell Elliot." I'm beyond pissed at him, but I have to let it go and give my full attention to my date. When I return to the empty table, Nicholas returns about five seconds after me.

"Sorry that took so long, I met up with my friend I was telling you about who owns the place and we were just catching up." He takes a sip of his wine, and if I'm not mistaken he seems on edge now. I notice his hands are slightly shaky, and he keeps fidgeting with his tie as if he's nervous about something. I'm not an expert on body language, but I know in my gut something is off.

"Nicholas I'm sorry if I've seemed a little distracted tonight, but I promise from here on out I'm all yours." I put aside the wine glass and give him my full attention despite my hesitation with his behavior. No more alcohol for me.

"I'm glad to hear it." He smiles pleasingly before David returns to the table with our food, which looks delicious.

"Will that be all for now?"

"Yes David thank you, and that favor we mentioned would be perfect about now." The waiter nods his head hesitantly, but not before he gives me an unsettling glance. *Was I just imagining the look he gave me?*

"Of course Mr. Graham." I tilt my head at Nicholas with suspicion.

"What's the favor you asked him?" Wariness is traced in my tone now.

"Nothing to worry your pretty little head about." What the fuck is that about? *"Your pretty little head."* The way he said it makes it sound like we're in the fifties when women were told not to meddle in men's business. Alarms are going off in my head, then my attention is pulled away when I hear commotion coming from another table. My face flushes when I snap my head and see the waiter from earlier grabbing Elliot by the arm and yanking him out of his seat.

"I'm dining here you can't kick me out." He shouts trying to wiggle out of the waiter's grip.

"The owner asked me to remove you sir, I'm sorry." I overhear. I rise up out of my seat to walk over to them, but Nicholas grabs me by the wrist to stop me in my tracks. "I wouldn't go over there if I were you, they were suspicious of him having alcohol since he looks pretty young, they think he's using a fake ID so they're just making him leave."

"If they were so suspicious why didn't they double check his ID before serving him alcohol?" I try to pry myself out of his grip, but the more I try the tighter it gets.

"Emory I'm trying to save you the embarrassment of going over there, he's gonna leave and that'll be that, let's just enjoy the rest of the night." He pleads.

"Okay asshole I'm going!" I hear Elliot shout before stalking off, fuming with anger. Suddenly it all clicks. Nicholas excused himself, and he said he was talking to the owner which is his friend, then I overhear the waiter say the owner is the one who wanted Elliot kicked out. *He didn't.*

"Did you tell the owner to kick him out?" The hand that still holds its iron tight grip on me gets clammy, and he hesitates before answering me which tells me everything I need to know.

"Of course not Emory I wouldn't do that." I know he's lying, my gut has never been wrong.

"Elliot might be a lot of things, but at least he's not a liar which is more than I can say about you." I twist my wrist in his hand so he can release me, but now his tight grip moves to my forearm, holding me in place.

"Stay here with me, I have a great night planned." With my free arm, I grab his hand that has a hold on mine to pry it off, but he doesn't budge.

133

"Nicholas let me go!" I exclaim. I remember that we're the only ones up here other than the waiters, but they're no help. I'm sure Nicholas told them not to bat an eye at what he does.

"If you leave with him we're done Emory." He says venomously.

"Fine with me, we were done the second you decided to get my friend kicked out." I don't even know the guy so I'm not sure what he means by *we're done*, but it won't be keeping me up at night that's for sure.

"Fine, just like my dad always used to say...trash deserves trash." He finally lets go of me and waves his hand dismissing me as if I'm an inconvenience to him.

"You might think you're hot shit because you have money, but at the end of the day it doesn't matter because you're still an asshole." I emphasize the last word by elongating it so he hears it very clearly. My eyes search the room for Elliot as I walk away but he's no where in sight. Suddenly I feel Nicholas come up from behind me and wrap his big arms around my entire lower half of my torso. I start to panic and try to pry out of his embrace, then Andrew's encouraging voice pops into my head.

"Stop Squirming Diaz that's how you burn yourself out before you even make your move ..."

"Control your breathing, in through the nose out your mouth, use your anger..."

"I need you grab a hold of his arms and drop your weight down, once you do that use your right foot to step on his..."

"I can already tell that you'll never be anything more than a classless bitch anyway, so it's no loss to me." Nicholas whispers in my ear. I feel like I want to vomit as I feel his breath graze my ear and get a whiff of the wine we were just drinking. I wave of déjà vu crashes over me, I've been in this same position one too many times. I take a deep breath and do the move exactly how I remember doing it that day with Andrew and Elliot, except now I put actual force into it because I actually want to to hurt this guy. I even add a head butt at the end like I've seen in fighting movies. His grip instantly loosens and he falls back onto the table gripping onto his nose.

"I think you broke my nose what the hell Emory!" Blood gushes onto the white table cloth as he tilts his head and pinches the sides of his nose together. Some

134

waiters approach him with napkins to hold to his nose, typical that *now* they come to help.

"I'll do it again if you ever come near me or Elliot again." I threaten. He stares at me in disbelief as he yanks the napkins out of the waiter's hand to wipe the blood off himself. I sprint out of the restaurant hoping Elliot didn't get too far. I feel so stupid, I should have listened to him, but I know my pride won't let me say that to him. I frantically look for his car, but then I remember that I don't know what car he came in. My chest feels so tight, it's getting harder and harder to breathe as the panic start to settle in. I don't know if Nicholas will come running after me, or worse if he'll call the cops. I feel firm hands grip onto my shoulders and I swing my arm back swiftly without even looking.

"Woah calm down Rocky, it's me." Elliot is holding his hands up in surrender, and for the first time tonight, I feel calm.

"You were right…Nicholas was a dick, and he's the reason you got kicked out, and he tried to grab me but I did what you and Andrew taught me and I made his nose bleed, I should have listened to you I'm sor—" Okay maybe my pride decided to take a backseat tonight, that was easy enough.

"Emory stop… breath." He interrupts me and grips both my shoulders to help me get control on my breathing. I inhale through my nose and exhale out of my mouth, staring into his calming brown eyes. I can already feel the nerves start to unravel and the anxiety subside.

"You don't have to apologize Em, but let's go before we get arrested for assault and underage drinking." He rests a hand on the lower part of my back as we walk towards his car that's in the non valet section of the parking lot.

"You didn't use valet?" I ask.

"Hell no, why would I pay someone twenty bucks when I can park my own car?" For the first time tonight I genuinely laugh. After how I treated him, I wouldn't blame him for leaving me here stranded, but the fact that he's here despite every-thing we said to each other tugs something at my heart. He said some hurtful things too, but I think he said it to protect me, while I was just trying to say anything to hurt him. We reach the white Mercedes and he opens up the passenger door for me.

135

"Who knew you were such a gentleman." I joke as I climb in.

"I'm full of surprises." *That's the understatement of the year.*

The car ride home is quiet for the most part, the only thing helping the silence is Elliot's music playing softly in the background. My head is resting on the window looking at the surroundings as they pass by. My mind is racing as it recalls the last hour of events. Maybe it was the adrenaline at the restaurant that had me amped up, but I'm starting to come down from it all now, and it's not sitting right with me how dumb I was to believe the front Nicholas put up. Here I was defending him against Elliot who was trying to be a good friend and warn me about him, and he ended up being a douchebag. I do have to admit that it felt really good to fight back though, to not feel helpless and have to wait for someone to save me. I saved myself this time.

"What's on your mind?" Elliot asks softly.

"I'm sorry he involved you back there." I've already apologized to him, but I want to get it across to him how horrible I feel about everything. I'm not one to apologize, so for me to say it twice to the same person hurts my ego a bit, but I can afford it in this case; I really fucked up this time. Even if we can't be friends after what we've said to each other, at least he knows that I'm sorry.

"I already told you that you don't have to apologize, but I'm sorry about the shitty things I told you. I need you to know that I didn't mean any of it." His voice cracks as he speaks.

"You were trying to protect me, and I came into your room and cursed you out." I don't look at him when I speak because a part of me is still ashamed, also because my body feels so drained now, just lifting my head up sounds exhausting.

"Still doesn't make what I said right, I indirectly called you dumb, and I said if he hurt you to not to come to me, which is the opposite of what I wanted." His grip on the steering wheel tightens until his knuckles turn white.

"Well doesn't matter now, I made sure he wouldn't come near me again. I just feel bad that he kicked you out."

"I'll be the first to admit that he was probably right to kick me out." Now I lift my head up to look at him with curiosity eating at me.

"Why were you at the restaurant in the first place? Tell me the truth this time. And why do you think Nicholas was right to kick you out?" We pull into the driveway of the house and he clicks the car off, but neither of us move a muscle.

"He was right to kick me out because I was trying to snag his date." There is no sign of comedy in his tone.

"What do you mean?" I undo my seatbelt to shift my entire body to face him. I notice his breathing get more shallow at our sudden closeness.

"I didn't want you to go out with him Emory." He says seeming embarrassed. I roll my eyes subtly because we already established this when we were screaming at each other in his room the other night.

"I already knew that, you made it clear the second I mentioned him." It isn't front page news that Elliot hated him before he even knew him.

"That's the thing, whether it was that asshole or someone else I would have felt the same way, I didn't like the idea of you on a date with someone else." He looks up at me with so much sadness in his eyes that my chest feels heavy at the sight of them. I try to open my mouth to speak but I come up blank. It's no shocker that Elliot is protective of me, so it would make sense that he doesn't want me going on dates with random guys, but then it hits me. The last word he said, someone *else*. I can't contain the small gasp that escapes my mouth at the realization.

"When you say someone *else*..." I can't even finish the sentence before he answers curtly. "I mean I don't want you going out on dates with guys Emory, call it selfish, me being an ass, I don't really care. The next guy that tries to take you out I will threaten him off, that much you can count on." His tone is no where near playful now. Either it just got really hot in here, or my body temperature just spiked.

"Why?" I ask with a shaky breath as I meet his burning gaze with my own. *Is he going to say what I think he's going to say?*

"Because I..." He stops mid sentence, and hesitates. "I just don't want to see you get hurt like you did tonight. You deserve someone who's going to worship the ground you walk on, not some prick that thinks he can treat people like shit because of his money." He gazes down at his finger nails as he picks at them nervously. A small wave of disappointment crashes through me hearing his answer. After tonight my worst fear got confirmed, my feelings for Elliot are way past just physical attraction. I don't know how or when it started, but I think I may have known *before* everything blew up in my face at dinner tonight, I just didn't want to admit it. Nicholas didn't give me butterflies in my stomach, he didn't make my heart flutter or make it beat faster when he looked at me, when he cracked a joke a genuine smile never reached the surface, and he definitely didn't feel warm or safe like Elliot. I felt absolutely nothing the second I stepped into that car with him. I kept waiting for that feeling to come, but it never did. As for Elliot, maybe it's the fact that when I got here I was adamant on never talking to him again and he just kept pushing until I let him back in my life, or maybe it was the night he protected me when no one else did, or because the day at the beach when I was feeling my most venerable and insecure, all he did was say a few words and I felt like the most beautiful girl on the planet. Whatever the reason behind my feelings may be, I have to accept them now, and learn how to cope with them. Of all those reasons I just mentioned why I have feelings for him, I can think of two big reasons why it's not a good idea to tell him. One, there's a part of me that thinks if he was so easy for him to leave me the first time, he could do it again, and I can't handle that. Two, I genuinely believe that if he had feelings for me he would have said something by now, so maybe he really just sees me as his friend whom he feels he has to protect. I try to ignore the *someone else* slip up from earlier because he clearly has. *How did this even happen?* A month ago I was the one who wanted nothing to do with him, and now I have a crush on him. *Fuck.*

"Well not to worry, I'm sure there won't be any more guys asking me out, I was surprised Nicholas even did." I admit. He laughs under his breath and shakes his head disappointedly. He moves so close to my face our lips are almost touching. All the air in my lungs gets sucked up at the close contact between us. It feels like there's a sudden electric charge in the air at our close proximity.

"It's a real shame that you don't see what other people see Emory." *Why does he keep saying sweet things to me?* I can't bury my feelings if he keeps saying things like that. His minty breath hits my lips, and my body feels like it's overheating being so close to him, so I snap out of my trance and back away to give myself some space.

"Are you sure you're okay? Do you have a concussion from heading butting the shit out of that guy?" He brings his hand to my forehead and my whole face drains. "You're hot Em." I break out into a coughing fit from the shock of his words.

"What?" I ask with a husky voice looking up at him.

"You feel warm, let's get you inside you've had a long night." He unbuckles his seatbelt before climbing out, and closes the door behind him. I sit in silence for a few moments so I can gather myself because I feel like I just got punched in the gut.

"Right." I mumble to myself before following his lead and climbing out of the car. I have had a long night. I just want to climb into bed and forget about how shitty this night was, and most of all I want to forget about my stupid feelings for Elliot. Something tells that's going to be easier said than done.

CHAPTER TWENTY

I specifically remember closing my blinds last night, but when I wake up they are pulled all the way back letting the sun burn bright into my eyes. I lift myself up out of bed and peer around the room to see if anything else is out of place, and my eyes catch sight of a note on the pillow next to me. I notice the hand writing right away.

Get dressed and meet me downstairs. I have a surprise for you.

- E

I stare at the note for a few seconds trying to dissect it. Elliot must of came in here and opened my blinds to wake me up so we can do whatever he has planned. Whatever the surprise is better be worth getting up this early for. It's not even eight yet. Why must he always wake me up so early? I've never been a morning person.

I decide to go with some black sweats and an oversized crewneck for my outfit of the day, and pair it with some white sneakers. I grab my bag and I throw in my sunglasses, sunblock, a scrunchy, and even some bug spray. I don't know if his plan will include outside activities so I decide I'd rather be over prepared, I never know with Elliot. I throw my hair into a messy bun and secure it with one of my hair clips. This is as good as it's going to get if he's dragging me out of bed at this time. I already hear him when I reach the end of the stairs.

I walk in the kitchen undetected and lean against the doorway to see him sitting in front of the kitchen island reading something on his phone with a cup of coffee in his hand, like always. He's like an old man trapped in a nineteen year old body, waking up at the crack of dawn drinking a cup of coffee. He looks so peaceful I almost don't want to interrupt him. I watch him perk up at whatever he's looking at on his phone, his smile looking so effortlessly *perfect*. I thought eight hours of sleep would help me forget about my feelings for him, but apparently I lose all my senses as soon as I walk into a room with him. Just thinking about the whole Elliot thing is going to give me a headache, so I decide to put it on the back burner for today and focus on whatever he has us doing.

"Morning sunshine." He greets me while still looking at his phone, as if he sensed me in the room.

"You better have a good reason for waking me up this early." I say in a threatening tone.

"Technically I didn't wake you up." He points out with a sly grin.

"You opened my curtains so the sun would come in, you know I like to keep it dark."

"Okay Dracula, but I think you'll be glad I woke you up so early once you see where we're going." I dismiss his lame joke and stare at him with interest now. He looks cheery despite everything that happened last night so I take it as a sign that we are never going to speak about it ever again thankfully.

"Can I have a hint?" I grab a muffin out of the fridge and walk back over to join him where he's sitting.

"Nope, and before you even try the puppy dog eyes aren't going to work." *Damn.*

"Fine, then can we go already?" I break off a small piece of my chocolate muffin and stuff it into my mouth, only to look up and notice him looking at me with praise.

"You want a piece?" I extend my muffin offering him some. He doesn't say a word as he mimics me by breaking off a big piece and shoving it into his mouth. I recall the night when we were walking home and he said he found it cute when I did this with my muffins, though I'm not sure why he thinks that.

"C'mon we don't want to keep them waiting." He says pulling me out of the kitchen. My hand increases in temperature at his touch, and I hope more than anything he doesn't notice.

"Who's waiting?" There is no use in asking him questions because he already has me half way across the living room and out the door before I know it.

"You'll see in about twenty minutes." He peers down at his watch and nods his head in approval. I let out an annoyed grumble and follow him to the all black jeep in the driveway.

"I can't have at least one hint?" I ask as we climb into the car, trying hard not to sound too annoyed.

"Can you just enjoy the ride and not be so grumpy?"

"I won't be grumpy if you let me sleep in past eight." I point out. He shakes his head at me with that stupid, cute smile on his face again. He starts the car and plugs his phone into the aux cord connected to the stereo. "My password is 120411, you can pick the music to pick your spirits up."

"I doubt it." I protest, but I still snatch his phone from him and punch in the password. I notice it's a date, and I wonder to myself what the significance is to him. I pull up his music app and look through his music choices since I don't know what kind he listens to now. There are a lot of good options here from Green Day, Gorillaz, Paramore, I even see Lynyrd Skynyrd in here which I have to appreciate since they were one of mom's favorite. As I'm scrolling, my fingers suddenly freeze when I find a playlist labeled 'Ej'. My hand goes so numb I almost lose my grip on the phone. My heart quickens as I open it up and find a long list of songs I used to like when I was a kid, some of them I still secretly enjoy. "You remembered."

"Remembered what?" He asks which makes me realize I said that out loud instead of in my head.

"All my favorite songs from when we were younger...you have them." I see him swallow hard before he speaks. I take it he wasn't expecting me to find this.

"Of course I remember, you know how many hours I had to endure listening to Taylor Swift? It's cemented into my brain Emory." I know he's trying to play off how nervous he was just a few seconds ago. I hold my smirk in while continuing to scroll down the playlist. He has it all from One Direction, Taylor Swift, Justin Bieber, The Fray, even the Jonas Brothers. Whatever you think a girl would listen to from 2009-2012, it's in here. I smile proudly before clicking one of the songs and hire up the volume of the stereo. I receive a deadly glare from him as it starts to play, and I laugh at his apparent irritation. "You're trying to kill me aren't you?" He spits out. I don't miss the very small sliver of a smirk he's trying to hide on his face.

"Oh c'mon I know you remember the words." I nudge him on the arm and start to mumble the words to Enchanted by Taylor Swift, one of the songs I listened to

142

repeatedly when we were growing up. No one else but him knows I love this song. I peek over at him to see him try to keep a tight face, but I can tell he wants to break. I know it's all just a front because he used to sing along to this song all the time with me when we were kids. I hear my favorite part of the song and a rush of pure joy comes over me as I belt out the lyrics at the top of my lungs, I don't even care if I'm not the best singer. I let my arms fly in all directions they want to go as I sing along, my head flies back into the seat so hard the clip falls out of my hair. I open up the window and let the strong wind hit my face. It's been a long time since I let myself go and live in the moment, to feel actual joy.

"Sing with me!" I shout over the loud music. He shakes his head aggressively still looking ahead at the road.

"I don't sing Emory, plus I don't remember the lyrics." *I know he's lying.*

"And I thought I was the grumpy one." I say rolling my eyes. I go back to mumbling the words waiting for the chorus to come back around so I can scream the lyrics again. The beat starts to pick up and I can feel the rumbling in my chest as I break out singing, but this time I'm joined in by a deeper voice who's just as loud as me, if not louder. I look over to see Elliot with his eyes on the road, but now he's screaming the chorus with so much enthusiasm, I'm suddenly speechless.

"C'mon Emory don't leave me hanging now." He screams over the music in my direction. I didn't even realize I stopped singing, the sound of him shouting the lyrics put me into shock apparently. We're both shouting the lyrics as loud as our lungs will let us as the song's intensity keep building. Both our windows are open, and even with the wind blowing hard and messing up my hair, I find myself wishing I could live in this moment forever. Just being able to let go with him like this makes my heart swell up. The song ends and we both try and catch our breaths not saying anything else for a few seconds.

"I knew you still remembered the words." I say playfully smacking his chest.

"I remember everything." His expression seems sincere now, so I quickly look away before I get sucked into his presence even more. I let the playlist skip to the next song and Never Say Never by the Fray starts to play. I remember this song playing the day me and dad we're driving to Phoenix, and how I was repulsed that it reminded me of Elliot. Who would have known that a month later I'd be in the car with him listening to it, not only that, but the fact that I would have feelings for him. Life is funny sometimes.

"I love this song." I smile to myself and hire the radio up.

"I know." He mutters softly. How am I supposed to get over him if he does things like scream Taylor Swift with me in the car, and keeps all my favorite songs on his phone? *I'm in deeper than I thought.*

We approach a building on the busy street and come to a stop. I can't make out the name on the sign yet so I rush to unbuckle my seatbelt before Elliot stops me by placing a hand on mine. "Close your eyes, trust me." *Do I trust him?*

"Elliot don't you think I've suffered enough?"

"I want it to be a surprise until the very last minute, please." He pleads. If I'm not mistaken he's doing the puppy dog eyes at me, or at least trying to but he's shit at it. I let out a defeated groan and close my eyes, and an excited squeal comes from him as I hear him get out of the car. Now that I can't see all my other senses seemed heightened. I can hear the sounds of traffic on the busy street clearly, and the smell of apples floods my nostrils. Maybe we're by a bakery? I feel his warm hand entwine with mine. *Hello butterflies.*

"I got you, just step onto the sidewalk and I'll take care of the rest." I nod my head and extend my leg until I feel a solid surface and press down on it. I bring my other leg over and follow the same steps.

"If you let me fall I'll use the moves you taught me to kick your ass." I threaten him, but my tone is the least threatening ever. "I don't doubt it." He very slowly tugs me forward while still gripping onto my hand. I want to peak so bad but I decide to keep my eyes tightly shut. I hear a door open and a loud bell rings overhead of me.

"Elliot!" An unfamiliar feminine voice rings in my ears and I'm overcome with confusion as to where the hell we are.

"Hey Stef good to see you." He says kindly. If he doesn't let me open my eyes in five seconds I'll open them on my own, consequences be damned.

"This must be Emory." The same female voice chirps in my direction.

"I'd shake your hand, but I was told to keep my eyes closed." If my eyes weren't closed right now I'd throw a scornful look in Elliot's direction.

"Is it here?" I hear him ask with excitement laced in his tone. *The anticipation is killing me.*

"Yup, in the back." I feel his big hands grip me again as he brings me forward taking very small steps. *Is that a scent of shampoo?* I grow more and more curious as we inch closer.

"Elliot you're killing me." I grit out. I feel like I'm in a suspense movie waiting for something to pop out.

"Alright I think you've waited long enough, open your eyes Em." I pop them open quickly and my mouth gapes open at the surprise.

"What's going on?" I'm shocked at the sight of a small white dog with brown spots looking up at me wagging its tiny tail. It has one brown eye and one black eye, and it has the cutest curly hair.

"Emory, meet Winston." I kneel down to the ground to bring Winston into my arms. He's so soft, and he smells like fruity shampoo, hence what I was just smelling. He starts to lick my face as soon as he's close enough to it and an excited giggle escapes out of me. I put him down on his back to rub his belly, and peer up at Elliot who has a look of adoration, I'm sure it's for the dog. "You like him?" He asks.

"I love him, he yours?"

"Nope. He's yours." My hand stops abruptly as my entire body freezes up.

"What?" I manage to stutter out. Stef and Elliot laugh under their breath as they notice how much shock I'm in.

"I messaged Stef a few days ago asking if they had any small dogs here and she said they just received Winston. We're friends so she put him on hold for me until you could come and look for yourself, but I knew you'd love him." My heart sinks into my stomach as I try and process what's happening. No one has ever did anything like this for me, and the realization hits me hard. A tear streams down my face, and Elliot's face hardens with guilt. He comes to kneel down next to me and puts a comforting hand on my shoulder.

145

"Hey what's wrong? I thought you'd like his different colored eyes, but if you don't like him it's okay Stef had another family lined up for him so you won't be hurting anyone's feel—"

"Elliot shut up." I say gently through the sea of tears falling down my cheeks. I bring Winston into my arms and he licks them off my face.

"Why?" I ask. It's the only thing I can manage to say right now.

"It was #1 on your bucket list." He whispers. I didn't know guys like him existed. He's so selfless and genuine in everything that he does without expecting anything in return. My feelings for him just grew ten times stronger. I don't deserve this, it's too much. I've been horrible to him and he still went out of his way to do this. "I love him, thank you."

"Then why are you crying?" He asks tucking a strand of hair behind my ear. The smallest gesture makes me feel like my insides are all twisted up.

"Because no one has ever done anything like this for me, and the fact that we were fighting when you messaged Stef, but you were still going to do this for me, I don't deserve it." I shake my head in disbelief that this is actually happening. He puts his hand on my chin, and lifts my head up so my eyes are looking straight into his. It's ironic how Winston has one brown eye that is almost the exact shade as his.

"Of course you deserve it, I was going to do this whether you were pissed at me or not, but you not being pissed makes it a whole lot easier." He smiles before his eyes move down to my lips, and I feel like I'm going to melt into a puddle. He *has* to stop looking at me like that. I hear someone faintly cough which breaks the tension in our stare down. I look up to see Stef staring at us with what I think is a scornful look, but I could be imagining it.

"We should finish the paperwork so you can take this little guy home." She says in my direction. I pick myself up off the floor and hand Winston to Elliot to follow her through a pair of doors toward the front. Now that I don't have to keep my eyes closed I can admire my surroundings. The business cards at the front desk read Tiny Paws Animal Shelter. Leave it to Elliot to want to adopt a pet instead of go through a breeder.

"Just have to print some paperwork to transfer ownership to you." She says in a perky tone typing away on her computer as I observe the place more.

"So you and Elliot have known each other for awhile?" She asks. I snap my head to look at her, completely caught off guard at the mention of him.

"Yea, I mean we met when we were nine and grew up together." I reply with a strained tone. *Why are we talking about Elliot?*

"He said you guys didn't talk for a few years is that true?" I definitely don't feel comfortable talking about this with her, hell I haven't even talked to Kat about it, much less a complete stranger. I'm more uncomfortable at the fact that Elliot confided in her about it.

"How do you know Elliot?" I change the subject because obviously she knows the answer to the question she asked me. She stops typing and looks up at me with her round blue eyes. Her long blonde hair flows so perfectly around her face, and her cheeks turn even more red than they were before.

"We used to hang out." She smiles awkwardly before her gaze goes back to her computer screen.

"So you guys had a thing?" I spit out. I don't know why I ask, but it was just sitting on my tongue ready to come out.

"No…Elliot doesn't date." Her tone is so edged she can cut glass with it. I remember one night when Elliot was walking me home he had mentioned he'd never had a girlfriend, but I genuinely thought he was lying. I mean how could someone as good looking as him be single for nineteen years?

"He seems different with you though." I don't miss the bitterness pouring out of her.

"What do you mean?" I shouldn't even be engaging in this conversation with her, but now she's got my attention.

"He seems happy now." I stare blankly at her without saying a word. I wonder if everyone notices this? I don't know how Elliot was before I arrived a month ago so I can't really say if what she's saying is true or not.

"How was he before?" I try to hide my frantic thoughts. I hated him after he left, but I at least imagined him happy and living his life, but hearing that he might not

147

have been makes me feel disturbed. Stef pulls the papers out of the printer and staples them together before she lets out a loud sigh of annoyance.

"It's not my place to say Emory, all I want to know is what makes you so different."

"Excuse me?" I blurt out.

"I don't know what makes you special enough to get his attention." She folds her arms in front of her and stares at me up and down with judgment written all over her face. *I wonder if Elliot knows she's a bitch.*

"I'm just gonna take a guess here and say that Elliot turned you down didn't he?" I stare back at her with a cocky smirk. She's got the wrong idea about me if she thinks I don't have a sharp tongue too.

"I don't get it, you're not even that pretty." A sarcastic laugh escapes me before I can stop it. I don't get into fights like I used to, I've tried hard to bury that version of myself, but maybe I'll let a *tiny* piece of old Emory peak through.

"Maybe, but Elliot actually chooses to hang out with me, while you he only calls for a favor, so if you wanna be mad fine I can't stop you, but if you're gonna be a bitch, I promise that I'm better at it than you." She snickers low enough I almost don't hear it. Before either of us can say anything else I hear the doors swing open and Elliot comes through with the dog in his hands. Winston is curled up into his big arms, and it is the cutest sight ever.

"Almost finished? I want to stop by the store and get some toys for him." He's completely oblivious to the intense stare down between Stef and I right now. "Just about." I answer beaming a fake smile in her direction, but as soon as she catches a glimpse of Elliot approaching us her whole demeanor changes.

"So Winston is about a year and a half and he's fully vaccinated, neutered, and chipped so everything is taken care of. Don't be afraid to reach out if you have any questions, Elliot has my number." She said that last part a little too cocky for my taste. If Elliot didn't just walk through those doors I'd be on the verge of reaching over this counter to pull that pretty blonde hair out of her head, but I was serious when I said I buried that version of myself, I never liked it to begin with. Girls like her are the reason I always got into fights in high school though.

"Anything else?" I ask rudely. I feel Elliot tense up next to me, I'm guessing he's sensing my impatient tone. I just want to get away from her and the flirty eyes she's making at him.

"Nope that's all, again you can reach out if you have any quest—"

"Yup got it Elliot has your number." I interrupt sharply.

"Thanks for your all your help Stef."

"Anytime Elliot." If he really doesn't notice she's flirting, he is the most oblivious person I've ever met. "I'll be in the car." I grab Winston out of his arms and storm towards the door.

"See you around." I hear him say to her from behind me. *Why is he still talking to her?* Also why am I so irked by it? He's not mine to worry about.

"I hope so!" Stef shouts. I know for a fact she wanted me to hear that. I swing the door open and step outside, the slight breeze that hits my face calms me down a bit. I hear Elliot trickle behind me as I walk back to the car. I pass by a small bakery which explains why I smelled apples earlier. Winstons' ears perk up as we pass by.

"Em wait up!" His heavy footsteps approach me as he jogs to catch up to me.

"What was that about?" He asks accusingly. "What?" I bite back.

"I've never seen Stef so off." His hands are in his pockets as he walks beside me, seeming uncomfortable. Now he knows how I felt back there between the two of them.

"She's a bitch." I don't care if that's rude because it's true. Laughter erupts from him surprisingly. "Of course you'd think that." He says trying to hold back more laughter. I thought for sure he'd try to defend Stef after I insulted her.

"She is, of course you didn't see it with all the flirty eyes she was making at you." I don't try to hide the bitterness in my voice.

"She's just a friend, she's known for a long time that I'm not interested in her that way." He admits. I can't help but let a victorious grin spread across my face, but I don't let him see it. "So you friend zoned her? Ouch." I put a hand over my heart to mimic like I'm in pain.

"If that's how you want to put it. She was interested in me, but I said we'd be better off as friends." This is exactly why I decided to bury whatever feelings I have for him, I definitely don't want to be on the other end of getting friend zoned by him, I'll save myself the stab in the heart.

"Are your parents going to be cool with having a dog at the house?" I ask. The realization hits me that there is no sign of a pet living at the Cortes house. What if they hate animals?

"I talked to them when I messaged Stef and they thought it was a great idea." A weight lifts off my chest. It'll be nice to have a dog, my parents never let me have one when I was younger.

"Well since he likes you so much we can share him. He'll sleep with me a couple nights, then with you." I offer as we approach the car. Elliot steps in front of me to open the door for me just like he did last night. I find it interesting that he never did that until after my date with Nicholas.

"You don't have to share him Em, I got him for you."

"I know I want to. He'll be ours for now, then when I go off to San Diego I'll take him with me, but you can still visit him anytime you want." I don't miss the doubt that covers his face now. "If that's really what you want."

"It's what I want, we'll make up a schedule." I look down at Winston who's fast asleep in my arms now.

As I'm here with Elliot with *our* new dog on our way to get toys, something I haven't felt since before mom died washes over me.

I feel genuine happiness.

CHAPTER TWENTY-ONE

My eyes open from my deep sleep with a very wide awake Winston looking at me with his different colored eyes. He starts licking my face and pawing at my hair so I'm forced to lift myself out of bed.

"Why are you up so early Win?" I ask half conscious while petting the top of his head. My dad is the one who came up with the nickname when we got home from the pet store yesterday. Everyone instantly fell in love with him just as much as I did, and the name Win just slipped out of my dad's mouth and it stuck. Me and Elliot made up a schedule of when he'll sleep with either of us, and who's responsible for taking him out for his walks on what days. Today is the first full day with Winston and he's already proving he's an early riser just like Elliot since it's only six in the morning. I groan loudly and sink my head back into my pillows. I'm joined by Winston who climbs on top of my head to rest his tiny paws on me.

"Elliot put you up this didn't he?" I ask, only to receive a head tilt from him and another slobbery lick to the face.

"Okay I'm up I'm up." I climb out of bed to head to the bathroom to clean up. I hear light pats on the floor behind me and I smile seeing Win follow closely behind me on my heels. I could get used to this little routine with him, but we're going to have to fix this sleeping schedule, I already have Elliot to wake me up before the sun I don't need Winston doing the same. If I'm going to function the rest of the day I definitely need some coffee so I throw on some sweat pants and an oversized shirt to head downstairs. To my surprise I don't even hear Elliot when I enter the living room. *Did I actually wake up before him?* My question is quickly answered when he enters through the front door from outside in a white v-neck covered in black grease.

"Morning Em." He says while kneeling down to greet Winston with head scratches and belly rubs. It's the purest thing seeing them interact with each other.

"It's six in the morning and you're already working on your truck?" I ask walking to the kitchen with him and Win following behind.

"I had a lot on my mind so I figured it could pass the time, I've been out there since five." He lifts his shirt up to wipe his forehead and a sliver of his abs peek out. *Fuck, is the heater on?* It feels like a sauna in here.

"Is it almost done?" I need to start a conversation before I pass out.

"Almost, I may even let you drive it when it's running." He winks and turns around to start a pot of coffee. I hear a vibrating sound coming from his pocket and it catches my full attention because who could possibly be calling this early in the morning? He grabs the phone out of his back pocket and stares at the screen like he's seen a ghost.

"Who is it?" I question. It must not be good if he's got that paled look on his face.

"Nobody, it's probably one of those spam numbers." He grabs a mug out of the cupboard, but I can see his hands start to subtly tremble out of the corner of my eye. *What's got him so on edge?* The ringing stops, but immediately starts to ring again, and he lets out a loud grunt of frustration.

"I'll be right back." He rushes out of the kitchen before I can question him more. I almost follow him to eavesdrop but I decide to stay put, if it's important he would tell me. I decide to use this time to feed Win, so I go into the walk in cabinet, pull out his bowl, and pour out some dry food. He starts to devour it like he hasn't eaten in days, then Elliot enters the kitchen shortly after with a look I can't seem to read.

"Was that Stef?" I joke. *Why did I just say that?* I almost vomit when I say her name. I know it wasn't her but I figured it would lighten the mood a little if I mess with him.

"What if it was?" *He's joking, he has to be.* "Was it?" I try to hide the panic in my voice, but by the grin he's trying to hide behind his mug I think he picks it up.

"What's your issue with her?" He asks.

"I just got a bad vibe from her." I shrug my shoulders and fiddle with my finger-nails to avoid eye contact with him. *Also because I know she likes you and she would date you in a heartbeat if you ever decided you liked her more than a friend. Plus she said I wasn't pretty...yea she's a bitch.*

"Are you jealous?" I want to smack the smug look on his face right off.

"No." I spit out quickly, staring back at him with threatening eyes. *Please drop it.*

"So if I called her up right now and asked her out you wouldn't have anything to say about it?" He's messing with me because he thinks i'll cave, but he must not know me as well as he thinks he does. So I do the only rational thing, I *lie*.

"It's your life Elliot date who you want, I mean personally I think you should date someone who's not a two-faced bitch, but if that's what you prefer then go for it." I feel Winston tug at my pants with his paws so I lean down and pick him up off the ground and bring him into my arms. When I come back up Elliot is typing something on his phone. I try to peek my head to read what he's typing, but it's no use with the angle he's got his phone at.

"Well me and her are going out tonight so it's good to know you don't have anything to say about it." I think he's bluffing, but knowing him he'd pull this whole thing off just for me to admit I'm a *little* jealous. He can be just as stubborn as me sometimes, he's just better at hiding it.

"Cool. Have fun." I know he caught my venomous tone. I walk out of the kitchen with Win in my arms and walk as fast as I can up the stairs and into my room. He just told me yesterday that he only saw Stef as a friend and then today he does a whole three sixty on his feelings? A part of me thinks he's only doing this so I can admit I'm jealous, but if admit to that I would have to admit that the reason I'm jealous is because I have feelings for him, and that is a road I don't want to go down. I hate the idea of him out with her; her perfect blonde hair, and naturally rosy cheeks. It's bad enough she's a bitch, but why does she have to be pretty too? *Ugh.* My only saving grace is I'm going to be working at the bar most of the night. Waiting on tables is way better than waiting around here for him to get back from his date with *her.* I need an intervention from Kat and fast to get him out of my system, my shift cannot come fast enough.

Elliot seems pretty tired today, so instead of us walking to work together I agreed to let him drive me. I was insistent on walking by myself, but of course he didn't accept that answer. "What time is your date?" I ask to break the awkward tension between us. We've barely exchanged any words since this morning.

"Eight." His answer is short and he doesn't spare me any eye contact. He didn't even bother to plug the aux cord in so there's not even any music to break the tension in here. "Where are you guys doing?" I pry.

"Don't know yet, maybe a movie and dinner." He shrugs his shoulders but keeps his gaze at the road as we pull up to the front of Sam's.

"Well have fun." I say grimly and move to unbuckle my seatbelt. Elliot places his hand on top of mine to stop me, which sends electric jolts straight up my arms. My whole body feels alive when I'm around him, I hate it.

"Emory if there is any reason you think I shouldn't go on this date, say it right now and I won't." His eyes plead at me as he searches my face. He's so close I can feel his body heat radiating off of him. His breathing sounds staggered as he waits for me to speak up. I swallow the lump in my throat and scramble through the thoughts in my head. *I can't tell him not to go because then I would have admit my feelings for him, and it would make it sound like I want him to myself. Do I want him for myself? That's the only explanation why I got so defensive when I found out him and Stef used to hang out.* If I were to pour my heart out to him, and he didn't return the same feelings, my heart would never recover from another heart break from him.

"Have a great time Elliot." I climb out of the car without a second glance at him. I walk inside as fast I possibly can, but not before I hear the tires of his car peel away, and I let out a breath I didn't know I was holding. My heart feels like someone ripped it out of chest and ran it over with a fucking truck. I can't stand the thought of him on a date with her, but I can't stand the thought of being rejected by him even more.

The place is pretty packed tonight, the bar is filled with people who are tuned into a baseball game on the flat screen, and the dining area is actually occupied for once. Sam waves at me as I walk past the bar. He's going a hundred miles an hour popping caps off of beers and sliding them down the counter towards the waiting customers. When I walk into the break room I approach my locker, but before I open it, I slam my palm to it out of frustration, I hit it so hard my whole arm starts to sting immediately afterward. "What'd the locker do to you?" I hear Kat's petite voice from behind me. Her hands are full as she approaches her locker to shove all her stuff in.

"Nothing." I say sharply.

"What happened?" She walks over to me with concern.

"Nothing. I have to go clock in." I slam my locker closed and walk out. I know she's not going to let this go, but I wish more than anything she would this one time.

"Fine have it your way, but I will get you to spill and you know it baby cakes." She shouts from behind me. A few hours ago I couldn't wait to tell Kat how I was feeling so she can talk some sense into me about how I'm way in over my head, but now I find myself not wanting to talk about any of it. I just want to get through this shift, and go home to crawl into bed. *It's going to be a long night.*

"Has Andrew asked about me lately?" Kat asks pulling my concentration away from the plates I'm trying to balance on my arm. I look sharply in her direction and then back at the plates trying not to drop them.

"No, why?" I ask. She lets out an annoyed groan and grabs some of the plates from me to my relief. We approach the table of six and assemble their plates in from of them. "Let me know if you guys need anything else." I smile politely at them and collide with Kat who's right on my heels.

"He hasn't texted in a few days and I'm just wondering if he's mentioned why. I like to know if someone isn't interested anymore so I don't waste my time." She places her hands on her hips while I grab a rag to wipe down the table that just left. I grab the loose change lying on the table and notice it's only a .50 tip. *Assholes.* At this rate it's going to take me forever to save up for a place in San Diego. I've been here a month and a half and I feel like I haven't even made a dent in my savings.

"I would tell you if he said anything, but why don't you just ask him yourself?"

155

"Because in order to do that he'd have to return my phone calls. He hasn't even came by here so I can't confront him either." Now that she mentions it Andrew has seemed a little off lately, then again so has Elliot, but then again so have I. I know my reasoning behind my off behavior, but I can't speak on their behalf. I hear a loud gasp from Kat, but I don't look up to see what's caught her attention because I'm sure it's just a hot guy that walked through the door or something.

"No fucking way." She grits out as she gapes at the entrance with a horrified look. I peer my head in the direction of her eyes and I feel like I'm going to vomit right here on this table. Elliot walks in confidently with his arm around Stef, and waves in Sam's direction before sitting in his usual booth. My hands start to shake as I wipe the table aggressively, trying to get the picture out of my head of Elliot gawking at Stef with her perfect wavy hair, and the way her petite slender body looks in the skin tight black dress she has on. *Slut.*

"Who is that with Elliot?" Kat asks with her eyes still glued on them. If looks could kill they would both drop dead from the way she's staring at them with fire in her eyes.

"Some girl named Stef, they've been friends for awhile. He didn't like her twenty fours ago, but *apparently* he does now." Resentment is laced in my tone, and Kat must of noticed from the look she's giving me now.

"So we hate her? Say no more." I can't help but laugh. This is why I appreciate her, she always has my back without me having to ask.

"She's a bitch but Elliot likes her, besides why should I care who he wants to date?" I gawk at her.

"Because you have feelings for him." My whole body tenses up, and I see a cocky smirk grow on her face before she continues.

"Baby cakes I may have only known you for like a month, but I can see right through you. I knew you felt more for him than you were telling me, whether you yourself knew it or not." Of course she knew, she knows everything.

"Why did you tell me to go on a date with another guy then?" I remind myself that I still have to catch her up on the shitty date I had since she still doesn't know what went down.

"I knew you wouldn't listen to me if I told you that you liked him, so I figured going on a date with another guy would nudge you to realize it on your own." I narrow my eyes in on her.

"So I had to endure a date with that asshole because you didn't want to tell me I had deeper feelings for Elliot?" I fold my arms across my chest and hold her gaze. I don't know if I still would have went on the date with Nicholas if I knew that on some level I liked Elliot more than I was letting on at that time.

"Didn't it work though? You realized you like him and I didn't even have to say anything." She shrugs her shoulders as if her work is done. I sink into the seat next to me feeling defeated.

"It doesn't matter what I feel because I'm not going to tell him. I'll save myself the embarrassment, besides he likes Stef." I play with a thread of the towel in front of me to avert from making eye contact with her.

"Please, I'm more attracted to Kelly at the bar than Elliot is to that skank, and I'm not even into girls." I try to suppress it, but I can't help but laugh half heartedly as she comes to join me at the table. Everyone should have a Kat in their life, she always knows what to say.

"Do you want me to take their order? They're sitting in your section." She nudges her head towards the two, who I notice aren't talking at all. Stef is typing away on her phone probably gaping to all her friends that she's on a date with Elliot, while he's staring blankly at the menu, though I don't know why he even bothers when he practically has it memorized.

"No I got it." I assure her. She throws me a sympathetic look before I get up from my chair, but I give her my best fake smile that I'll be plastering on for the rest of the night. I'm not gonna let them get to me.

"I'll be pretending to wipe off the table next to you if you need me." She heads in that direction with a devilish smirk. I don't know if I like that look on her. "Or you can actually clean the table next to me." I offer, half playful but also half serious since we really need to get these tables cleaned off.

"What do you think I am, a waitress?" She turns around heading in Stef and Elliot's direction while I stay back for a little while longer. I exhale loudly and count to five in my head before walking over and turning on the fake smile I've mastered.

"Hey guys what can I get you?" I take my notepad out of my apron and face the two of them. Just standing here irks my nerves.

"Emory I wasn't expecting to see you here." Stef says returning a fake smile of her own. "I could say the same about you two, Elliot didn't mention you guys would be stopping by." I throw a dark stare in his direction, but he doesn't meet my eyes as he fiddles with his silverware on the table.

"We just went to see a movie and we were both hungry, he mentioned this place so here we are." Her fake excitement is peeking through.

"Here you are." I say sarcastically through my teeth.

"If you ladies will excuse me I'm going to run to the restroom." Elliot pushes his way out of the booth and nudges my shoulder on his way in that direction. *What the hell is his problem*? I should be the one pissed off, and as a matter of fact I *am* pissed off.

"I'll let you look over the menu and come back." I tell her. I want to avoid being alone with her at all costs before I do or say something that'll cost me my job.

"I know what you're trying to do Emory." She says with an acidic tone.

"And what exactly is that?" I guess I'm in the mood to be amused so I stay and hear her out.

"You're upset that Elliot asked me out, and now you're trying to make it awkward between us, but it's not gonna work. I've waited almost four years for him to ask me out." She folds her hands in front of her and peers up at me with innocent eyes. "I'll have a side salad with Italian dressing please, and a diet coke for the drink." She tosses the menu at me and turns her attention back to her phone. Out of the corner of my eye I see Kat storm towards us with anger flashing in her eyes. I turn my head slightly to pierce her with my eyes and shake my head. She stops in her tracks and rolls her eyes furiously. If *I* want to drag this girl, I know she *definitely* does.

"Look I'm not trying to do anything between you and Elliot, I'm actually the one who told him to go out with you tonight."

"Good because I would hate to tell Elliot to not speak to you anymore, but I will if I have to."

"Do you really think he'd stop being my friend because you said so?" I ask with anger teased in my voice.

"I can be *very* persuasive when I want to be." There is no trace of innocence in her tone now. "*Slut!*" Kat coughs under her breath. She was probably trying to be discreet, but she was loud enough for the whole bar to hear. Stef looks from me to Kat with an intense scowl now.

"I'm gonna ignore the fact that you said that, just like I'm going to ignore the fact that if I tell Elliot to drop you off at home and never talk to you again he would do it in a heartbeat." I let an evil smirk slip out of me and her face turns as red as a tomato.

"I know you have feelings for him, but do you think you're the only girl that can be in his life Emory? Do you ever stop and think someone else could make him happy? He'll be better off when you leave." My smirk dies off as I digest her words. I have to give it to her, the girl brought her A game with the comebacks tonight, she knew exactly what to say to get under my skin. *What am I doing?* It's just like when we were kids and all the girls that were into Elliot were all so intimidated to date him because of how close he was with me. My chest aches at the thought that I'd be selfish to hold him back from being happy with someone, that's not what friends do. Does he have to pick *this* girl to be with though? Anyone else would have sufficed.

I rush away holding back the sob erupting in my chest. I hear Kat's concerned voice from somewhere in the room but I get away so fast she either doesn't try to catch up to me or she can't. As I pace quickly to the restroom I collide with a rock hard chest and I wipe away the tears gliding down my face.

"I'm sorry." I say tenderly not looking up from the floor. I'm already embarrassed enough I don't need a stranger seeing me cry tonight. A few months ago, what Stef said wouldn't have hurt me because I didn't care about anything or anyone, but now

I actually do care about Elliot, so facing the reality that he might be better off without me stings a little.

"What happened?" I recognize the voice instantly, but my eyes still don't look up at him.

"Em why are you crying? Did some guy do some—"

"No it's nothing there's something in my eye, I was actually on my way to the restroom to wash it out so excuse me." I try to brush past him but his hand grips my arm with enough force to jolt me to face him.

"Emory if you don't tell me what happened I swear to God…" I can hear his teeth grinding from how tight his jaw is getting.

"Why her?" I blurt out. I don't mean to say it, but I don't try to take it back either. His eyes search mine with confusion.

"What are you talking about?"

"Why Stef? You couldn't pick any other girl to go out with?"

"This is about Stef? Did she say something to you?" He looks towards the table where his date is with flames in his eyes.

"Does it matter? You brought her where I work Elliot, after I told you I don't like her. You knew I'd be here and you brought her here to parade her around, clearly you don't give a shit about how I feel." I twist myself out of his hold to leave him standing there with a blank expression. He knows I'm right and therefore that's why he has nothing else to say. I rush into the bathroom and turn the sink on to flush water on my face, rinsing away the salty tears running down my cheeks. It feels like someone shot an arrow right through my fucking heart. How I feel right now has nothing to do with Elliot bringing Stef here anymore, and more about what she said, and the fact that maybe she's right, but I can't tell Elliot that. If I wasn't convinced before that I shouldn't confess my feelings, I'm definitely convinced now. It wouldn't do any good for anyone. Elliot deserves to be with someone who's going to stay in Phoenix unlike me, someone who can actually make him happy, and I won't get in his way. I'm not even happy myself ninety percent of the time, how can I possibly make another person happy? I just have to find a way to push my feelings

160

for him deep down to never be acknowledged again. We're friends now, and that *has* to be good enough.

I dry my face and fix my appearance before heading back out. The weight on my chest is immense knowing I have to go back out there and face the two of them again. If I don't go back Stef will know she got to me, and I can't have that. I may be upset, but my ego is stronger than my emotions.

My eyes immediately find the booth they were sitting at and I find it empty. A sigh of relief escapes me, but then a sense of sadness follows right after. Elliot probably didn't want to deal with me and Stef throwing insults at each other the rest of the night so they went somewhere more private. She's probably trying to *persuade* him as we speak. *Slut.* Kat approaches me with a devious smirk on her face that puts me on edge.

"What did you do?" I ask. Kat has three looks: happy, sad, and evil. This is one of her evil looks, and I'm afraid to hear what she says next.

"I may have *accidentally* spilled beer on her as I was walking by trying to eaves-drop on the argument her and Elliot were having." She tries to hide her laugh behind her hand, but she can't contain it after a few seconds so she belts it out. I don't join her, instead I look at her with a vacant stare.

"Oh c'mon, I know you wanted to do the same thing, and frankly I don't know why you didn't."

"Because I'm trying this new thing called controlling my temper, also I'd like to keep my job." I point out.

"Em, Sam is the one that told me to do it after I told him who Elliot was with." I twist my head to face Sam who lifts a beer bottle over his head at us with a twinkling grin on his face. I laugh lightheartedly, then I realize what Kat said before.

"Wait what do you mean Elliot and Stef were arguing?"

"I think you should go home and talk to him about it. Sam said you could go since it's slow now, I'm going to finish these few tables and head out early too." I'm still supposed to work another two hours, and I don't like the fact that I'm losing out on more money than I already have, the clock is ticking for me to find a place. "Oh I almost forgot." She reaches into her apron and pulls out a white piece of paper with a fifty dollar bill wrapped in it. I hesitate before taking it out of her hands to read it because only one person leaves me tips like this.

I'm sorry for being an ass, see you at home -E

Does he think a note and a fifty dollar tip is going to fix everything? The fact that he does makes me more upset than I was before. I crumple up the note and shove the money into my apron so I can give it back to him when I see him later. The only thing worse then being mad at your friend, is *living* with the friend you're mad at. How the hell did I get in this position? A few weeks ago Elliot was just Elliot, now he's someone who I care about but I can never have. It's not like I ever imagined Elliot as my boyfriend or anything, I'm not even sure what I imagined him as. The whole thing has my brain in a cluster. All I know for sure now are two things: that I'm pissed at him after what he pulled tonight, and that I have to convince myself that I have no feelings for him what so ever.

I end up helping Kat clean up the few tables that were left and we leave the bar together so she can drive me home. I want to scream at Elliot, but also ask him what happened with him and Stef. Whether I'm mad at him or not I'll kick her ass if she hurt him. I'm just about to climb out of Kat's car when she stops me.

"I heard what Stef said to you Emory." *Uh oh,* she called me Emory. She only calls me that when she's serious.

"You know that's not true right? He's so much better off with you in his life. I didn't know him before you got here, but I don't have to because I know how he is with you now. The way he looks at you…it's the way everyone wants to be looked at Em. I think it'd be a mistake to not try and be something more with him." Here I thought she would be the one to talk me out of my feelings for Elliot.

"You don't get it Kat, what if someone *can* make him happier, and I'm just getting in the way because I suddenly developed feelings for him? Plus I don't even think he has feelings for me, I mean c'mon he was on a date with another girl tonight."

"If you really believe that, you haven't been paying attention." She snaps back.

"What if I pour my heart out and he decides he doesn't want me in that way? I can't handle that rejection." I finally admit my fear out loud. The silence in the car is deafening. I don't think I've ever seen Kat this quiet since I met her, actually that's a lie because the second I met her she talked my ear off. I don't think I've ever been this vulnerable with another person in my life, I'm not quite sure if I like the feeling or not.

"What if it turns out exactly how you want it to?" She implies. I haven't really given it much thought as to what would happen if he did feel the same way since I've convinced myself there is no way he could. The truth is I'm afraid to open up my heart to him because the last time I did I was ghosted for five years. I've been trying to forget about it and move on since Elliot has been trying so hard to prove he's sorry, but there is a subconscious part of me that's utterly fucking terrified of things going wrong again.

"Thanks for the ride Kat." I don't miss the disappointed sigh she lets out.

"Text me if you need anything." She offers. I don't know where Elliot will be when I walk inside, and I'm not sure if I'm ready to confront him. I know he's going to want to talk about what happened with Stef and what she said that made me so upset, not to mention he's going to want to talk about what I said to him. I haven't given much thought on the lie I'm going to come up with so I guess I'll just have to think of one on the spot.

"Any day now baby cakes." Kat exclaims from her driver's side. I didn't even realize I was frozen on the other side of the gate staring off in the distance. If I'm lucky, Elliot will have forgotten about the whole thing and went to bed, or he might even still be out with Stef. As much as I wish that wasn't true, it would mean I could avoid him for a little while longer.

My wish crashes and burns when I walk through the door and he's in the living room playing with Winston. We make prolonged eye contact with each other and my whole body burns under his gaze.

"We should talk." He says. *Shit.*

CHAPTER TWENTY-TWO

"We should go somewhere private." I offer. I don't necessarily want to be anywhere alone with him, but if we end up tearing each other throats out I'd rather it not be in the middle of the living room for everyone to see. He nods his head in agreement and slowly gets up from the couch. I notice he's still in his clothes he was in at the bar, his cuffs on his black button up shirt are folded back and a few of the top buttons are left unbothered, showing a sliver of the tattoo I thought I saw the day we went to the beach. My face turns hot, and the heat travels all the way down to my toes as he approaches me to walk upstairs. I'm supposed to be mad at him, but somehow my stomach clenches at the fact that he looks ridiculous hot right now. *So much for pushing my feelings deep down.* I mean I can still admire him, I have eyes after all. "Your room or mine?" He asks. *What?*

"What?" My mouth feels like sandpaper with how dry it just got.

"You said you wanted to talk somewhere private, your room or mine?" He repeats. I swallow down the lump the size of Texas that's in my throat, and start up the stairs nudging past him. "Mine." I hear his heavy footsteps behind me, but I can't find it in me to turn around to look at him, I have to keep my composure for a few more seconds. I close my door behind me, and Elliot props down on the bed with Winston prancing closely after him. Neither of us want to talk first that much is obvious, but the longer we sit in silence the longer it's going to take to get him out of my room.

"Where's Stef?" I guess I'll have to bite the bullet and start the conversation, but I'll make it known I'm not happy about it. I'm still standing by my door with my arms folded since I don't want to be close to him right now.

"After Kat spilled the beer on her I dropped her off at home." *Shit.* Is that why he seems so mad right now? Because a lousy drink got spilled on his perfect little date?

"I didn't tell her to do that by the way, but I'm still sorry you had to drop her off early." I don't even know why I'm the one apologizing, but I do *sort of* feel bad Kat did that to her. "The date was over before Kat did what she did, Stef had it coming I guess." He says with a smile peaking through. My shoulders ease a smidge at the sight of it. Okay, so he's not as pissed as I thought he was which is a good sign, but that doesn't change the fact that I still am.

"Why was the date was over before that?" I ask as I inch closer to him. I'm trying a new approach to this, starting off calm before I start screaming since last time didn't go so well. He hesitates for what seems like a long time I almost think he's not going to answer the question. "Kat told me what Stef said to you." He finally grits out with his tone far from gentle. Now it's my turn to hesitate to answer. I should have known Kat would tell him. I can't exactly deny it now, or can I? *No Emory, suck it up and face this head on.*

"She didn't say anything that wasn't true." The words feel like acid as they pour out. Elliot gently shakes his head in disapproval before he speaks up again. "So you really believe her then?" He questions tensely. What Stef said back at the bar just keeps repeating in my head. *He'll be better off when you leave.* One minute she was telling me he seems happier with me around, and the next she's saying someone else could make him happier, and that he'll be better off without me. I don't know what to believe.

"Yea I do…" I finally let out. His shoulders slump in disappointment at my admission. "You were fine without me for five years, so you'll be fine again when I leave, I'm just holding you back from being happy Elliot, just like when we were kids." He lets out a frustrated grunt and gets up from the bed to stalk over to me. Having him so close makes me stumble back until my back hits the door. He takes advantage of having me cornered and locks me in by placing both his arms on each sides of my body, with his palms on the door. His chocolate brown eyes pierce mine, and I can't bring myself to look away.

"Is that really what you think Emory? That I was fine without you? I thought of you everyday for five years, even though you weren't here you were still every-where; the music I listened to, every girl that talked to me I wished they were you, even down to the color of my damn truck is you. So if you *really* think that I was happier you're wrong because I was miserable!" *Thump thump thump.* My irregular heartbeats beat in my eardrums. I'm too dumbfounded to say another word, much less move. The only sound you can hear is both of our rapid breaths.

165

"It didn't seem that way, but whatever it felt like for you I promise it was ten times worse for me Elliot. You weren't there when I sat by the fucking mailbox everyday after school waiting for a letter, or when I'd stare at the phone waiting for it to be you on the other end. It was hell and you weren't there!" How did we end up arguing about this? This wasn't part of the plan, but here we are arguing *again*.

"I was trying to protect you!" He returns my harsh tone, and neither of us seem to be backing down. "From what?!" My chest is overcome with heaviness and my throat feels like it's closing in. How is it we always end up in a screaming match? His face turns into a frown and his tone is softer now.

"Being away from you was the hardest thing I ever had to do, but it was something I had to do at the time Em. The letter I sent you explained everything, but I knew you didn't read it when you didn't reach out." He completely ignores my question. *The letter.* The letter I took one look at and told my dad to send it back. Guilt immediately rushes over me, but then I realize that I don't have anything to feel guilty for. He should have known I wouldn't have opened it after two years of no contact, or he should have at least tried harder to get in contact with me when he realized I didn't read the letter.

"You think after two years I'd want to hear anything you had to say to me?" His face is so close to mine I can feel his breath across my face. It feels like there's a bubble surrounding us with how tight it feels to have him this close.

"I would never intentionally do anything to hurt you Emory." *Why do I want to believe him when he's given me so many reasons not to?*

"Then why bring Stef to the bar tonight when you knew I'd be there? You knew how I'd feel about it." A cocky grin forms on his angelic face, and I want to smack it right off.

"Why did it bother you so much? You said so yourself you don't care who I date."

"Yea well I lied, you can date whoever you want just not her." I don't feel an ounce of regret as the words leave my mouth. His eyes gaze down my entire body before answering.

"The thing is I don't want anyone else, not unless she's got long black hair and freckles, who loves the color black, and has a laugh that pierces my damn chest on the rare occasions I hear it. Who's too stubborn for her own good, and not to mention she's gotta have the guts to head butt the shit of someone in the middle of a restaurant because she's a total badass." My whole body goes limp, but I manage to stay upright. My breath hitches as I search his face for any sign that what he just said was a joke. *Was I imagining that? Have I gone completely insane?*

"What are you saying?" I ask between my jagged breaths. His chest starts to heave nervously as he inches even closer to my face so our noses are touching, and he gently rubs my cheek with his thumb. I'm sure my face is bright red now. *How did we end up here? We were just screaming at each other seconds ago.*

"I'm saying that I want *you* Emory, and I'm not gonna hide it anymore. Anything you want and it's yours just ask me. You want my heart? Done. You want me to grovel? Done. You wanna pretend you hate me for a little longer? Fine I'll wait. Every time you push me away I'm just going to to push back ten times harder because I know you feel something for me." His tone is threatening but seductive at the same time, and I'm overwhelmed with everything I'm feeling right now. I can't even remember why I was mad as I look deep into his eyes and digest the words that just came from him.

"What about Stef?" I whisper. My brain is so mush that's the first thing that came to mind.

"Stef is nothing to me. I just took her out to get you jealous because I knew you were just scared to admit you felt something for me. I know that's fucked up to Stef but it was the only way I could get you to see it. Besides after what she said to you I want nothing to do with her, that's why I told Sam to tell Kat to spill the beer on her." *He did what?*

"You did what?" My mouth drapes open from the shock of his confession.

"You really think I'd even want to look at her after Kat told me what she said to you? So I talked to Sam to put the idea in Kat's head, and thankfully your friend is easily persuaded and my plan fell through. I took her home and told her not to contact me again." He says confidently with the cheesiest grin. I cannot believe he did that just because Stef said something that upset me. *What is this guy doing to me?*

"You did that for me?"

"I would do anything for you, if you asked for the fucking moon I'd find a way to get it for you. Just please don't ask for the moon because it'll be very hard to get." I laugh at his cheesy joke, but it fades away when I see his feverish gaze scan my body again.

"I'm leaving after the summer Elliot."

"I already told you I'll take whatever crumbs you want to give me." *This guy is too good with his words.*

"Don't you think you'll be happier with someone who isn't leaving?" I want to make sure he knows exactly what he's getting himself into.

"What part of I don't want anyone else don't you get Emory?" He mutters. He exhales loudly, looking deep in thought.

"Fuck it." He whispers. Before I can say anything he brings his lips to brush against mine catching me off guard, but I don't try and pull away. His lips are so soft and gentle it sends me into a frenzy. I wrap my arms around his neck and bring him in closer to intensify the kiss. His warmth is radiating all through me, my brain is telling me to stop but my my arms just tighten around his neck instead. His hands glide down to my waist and he grips onto me hard enough to leave bruises, but I don't even care.

"Sorry if I'm a little rusty I haven't kissed anyone since I was fourteen." He smiles against my lips and awareness hits me. I stop and twist my face to look up at him.

"Hold on...you're telling me you haven't even kissed another girl?" *He has to be lying.*

"Why would I? I only ever wanted to kiss you." He's going to put me in the hospital for cardiac arrest if he keeps talking to me this way. He takes both sides of my face in his big hands and brings my lips back to his, but this time our kiss is more gentle. He glides his tongue into my mouth and I'm a goner. *Why weren't we doing this the whole time?* I spent weeks so pissed off at him when I could have been making out with him? *Way to go Emory*. Something about this kiss makes me feel whole again, like the more our lips graze against each other the more pieces it's mending back together inside me. I can't remember a time in the last six years when I felt like this. I feel something softly claw at my leg so I pry myself away from Elliot to look down and see Winston peering up at us. He paws at my leg again as if to tell me he wants attention now. "It's your night with him." I tell Elliot while picking Win off the ground to bring him into my arms. Elliot smiles at the both of us and takes him from me. He immediately settles in and closes his eyes in Elliot's embrace. I'll never get tired of seeing them both together.

"I'm going to go put him in my bed, I'll see you tomorrow Em." He grabs my hand and places it between his lips to leave a wet kiss on it.

"Goodnight." I whisper. I bring myself up on my tip toes to brush my lips against his one more time, but I quickly pull myself away before I get carried away.

"You're never getting rid of me now." He gives me one more peck on the lips before walking out the door, and my body instantly misses his heat when I hear the *click* sound of the door. I walk over to sit on my bed and a smile instantly covers my entire face as my mind recalls everything that just happened. One minute we're screaming at each other then the next he's got his tongue in my mouth, it all happened so fast I'm still trying to fathom that it actually happened. *Elliot likes me.* He doesn't care that I'm going away to college soon, he doesn't even see that as an obstacle. Of course I'm sure it will be when the time comes, but I figure we'll cross that bridge when we get there.

"Sorry if I'm a little rusty I haven't kissed anyone since I was fourteen." I recall his deep voice as it rolls through me and sends goosebumps down my arms. I find it hard to believe he's only kissed one girl, but when he said it I actually believed him. Truthfully I've only kissed one other guy other than Elliot, but trust me I wish I hadn't. I was sixteen and I went to a friend's party and got pulled into a game of seven minutes in heaven, how cliché. His name was Danny Reed and he was a horrible kisser. He used way to much tongue and his breath reeked of cheap booze. Elliot kissed me better when we were fourteen than Danny did at sixteen, so to say I regret it is an understatement.

169

My body feels like it's floating off the ground, and I don't want to come down. I hate that I'm going to have to tell Kat she was right, but I'm glad she was. My body immediately sinks into the mattress when I lie down, and I drift off in a deep sleep within seconds, thinking of a pair of beautiful brown eyes.

A gentle nudge on my shoulder wakes me up from my sleep, it feels like I just closed my eyes so it can't be morning already. I pry my eyes open to see Elliot shirtless, in plaid pajama pants, and with Winston in his arms. *Am I dreaming about Elliot?*

"Elliot?" My voice cracks as I speak out. I peek my gaze over to the clock and see it's only two in the morning. *This better be good.*

"Sorry to wake you but Winston was whining, I don't think he can sleep without you." My brain is not fully awake enough to process what he's saying.

"Can you put a shirt on please? It's already hard to concentrate on anything." He laughs deeply and places Win next to me in bed before leaving. I feel him nuzzle into my neck and is sound asleep in seconds. I'm trying to doze back to sleep when I hear Elliot creep back into my room. He's got a plain grey t shirt on now, if I thought the white shirts made him look hot, the grey ones take the cake.

"What are you doing?" I whisper. I'm wide awake now, and fully aware he's trying to get into my bed.

"I can't sleep without you either." He's doing his shitty attempt at puppy dog eyes again.

"Nice try."

"C'mon please? I like sleeping next to you, even when I slept on the floor that one night it was the best sleep I ever had." I grumble in annoyance and pat the spot next to me in my bed. He doesn't even try to hide his excitement as he crawls under my blankets. I settle us both in under the blankets and try to close my eyes, but I can feel his gaze before I even look over at him to see him staring at me in awe.

170

"You're so perfect." He mutters. Winston is snoring in the middle of us so we can't exactly move closer to each other, but he places his hand on my arm and drags it very slowly in an upward motion, and stops midway. Goosebumps start to rise everywhere on my body. It dawns on me that while Elliot poured his heart out to me, I didn't say how I felt about him.

"I went on the date with Nicholas because I was using him to get you out of my head, because I was in denial about my feelings, but before he even showed me how much of an asshole he was I knew I didn't feel the same way about him that I felt about you." I let out a sigh of relief as I finally get that off my chest.

"I was jealous when you told me you were going out with him that's why I got so pissed at you. It wasn't even at you really, I was pissed at myself that I couldn't just tell you how I felt." He glides his soft fingertips up and down my arm as he speaks softly. I can feel knots forming in my stomach from how nervous I am with our close proximity. I had a feeling there was a deeper meaning behind him being upset that night, but him being jealous never crossed my mind. My body is fighting my sleep because I want to stay up and talk to Elliot, but a yawn slips out. "Get some sleep, I've got something planned for tomorrow."

"Last time you said that we ended up with Winston."

"It's not another dog I can tell you that much Emory." He says closing his eyes peacefully.

"Ej." I whisper. His eyes shoot open, and even in the dark I can see the astonished look on his face.

"What?" He mumbles so low it's almost inaudible. I get lost in his angel-like features, and suddenly I feel like i'm a kid again looking at my best friend. I didn't think I'd ever want him to call me Ej again, but it just slipped out and I don't want to take it back. I feel like I can trust him again with this piece of me. *The piece that was only his to begin with.*

"You can call me Ej." I repeat. All he does is stare back at me with the happiest grin on his face and brings his index finger to my bottom lip to caress it. *Here come the butterflies.* He kisses my lips so tenderly I melt into my mattress. Winston moves in his sleep which breaks the kiss, but we don't stop admiring each other until my eyes finally close and I drift off to sleep.

At this moment I decide that I'm going to let him in completely, hoping it doesn't backfire on me.

CHAPTER TWENTY-THREE

I'm instantly enamored when I open my eyes at the sight of Winston curled up with Elliot, I could get used to this view. Seeing him in my bed next to me just reminds me that everything that happened last night wasn't a dream. It wasn't exactly how I planned the night to go, but I wouldn't change a thing if I had to do it over again. I grab my phone from the dresser beside me and see my phone has eight unread text messages all from Kat.

Did you and Elliot make up yet? 2:02 am

Please tell me you guys are making out or something right now 2:43 am

Emory Diaz if you don't call me right now we're no longer friends! 2:56 am

Just kidding about the not being friends part but please I'm dying over here!3:03am

EMORY!!! 3:23 am

If I find out you're not replying because you'd rather make out with Elliot I'll be so pissed 3:25 am

I'm going to bed but you better text me when you get up or I'll go over there and kick your ass 3:30 am

Love ya 3:33 am

I find it weird Elliot is still asleep when he's usually the first person in the house to be up and moving. I slowly creep out of bed trying not to wake the two bodies in my bed snoring away. While I'm tip toeing towards my door, I hear Elliot stir and mentally curse myself for waking him up, but to my relief all he does it settle more into the pillows and start to snore again. Once i'm in the hallway I dial Kat, she should be up by now. It only rings twice before I get an answer.

"You better have a really good story for me after not responding last night Emory Diaz."

"I didn't see the messages until now." I respond dryly.

"So that's all you got? Nothing juicy at all? What a bust." Disappointment fills her tone.

"Well…not exactly." I hear ruckus on the other end of the line, and a few moments of silence goes by. "Kat?" I look at my phone screen to make sure the line didn't go dead.

"I'm here! Sorry I was getting settled in to hear every detail of what happened." She sounds out of breath as if she was running.

"Well, he kissed me for starters." I know it actually happened, but saying it out loud makes it feel real. I can't stop a shy smile from cove-ring my entire face. "Tongue?" *Of course that's the first thing she wants to know.*

"A little."

"Ahh! Tell me everything." She shouts excitedly, and I go through the events of last night starting from after she dropped me off. Mine and Elliot's screaming match, him confessing his feelings for me, and then him kissing me. I left out the detail about him not kissing anyone else but me just because I feel like that should be something that stays between us. I also tell her that he ended up sleeping in my bed, she swears more happened but I assured her we only slept.

"So what does this all mean? Don't you leave for college soon?" She asks.

"Yeah I told him that but he doesn't seem to care, I don't know if he's just in denial or if this is just a summer fling." I hate the idea of us just being a temporary fling to him, but I push the thought out of my head for now. It hasn't even been twenty four hours since we confessed our feelings for each other, and I don't need that stress right now.

"I doubt it'll just be a fling to him Emory, you've got him wrapped around your little finger, I'm sure he'll be treading right behind you to San Diego."

"You really think he would do that?" I try to hide the panic in my voice.

"I'm sure if you asked he'd go with you anywhere, but my advice is just take it day by day, a lot can happen in a month and a half." *That's what I'm afraid of.* Kat has put it in my mind now that he would move to San Diego with me if we established that this is more than just a fling, and that is just too much to process

174

right now. The whole point of me picking a school far enough away was for me to learn how to be on my own.

"I gotta go, Elliot has something planned and I've got to get ready, I'll talk to you later." I rush out.

"Talk to you later baby cakes, and remember to use protection." She jokes. I groan loudly and press the end button, I should have known it was too early to talk to her. I stay out in the hall for a little while longer trying to imagine my life if I were to —and this is completely figuratively speaking—ask Elliot to come with me to San Diego. Would he even come? His family is here in Phoenix, and he's always been really close to them. It was easy for me to pick a school far enough away from LA because me and my dad haven't exactly been close for years. It'd be a lot to ask anyone, besides I don't even know where we we stand so it'd be really weird to even bring it up. *Why did she have to put that in my head?* I wasn't even thinking about it, and now it clouds my brain, but all I need to do today is focus on spending the day with Elliot.

I twist the knob to my door very gently and peak into my room, but my bed is empty. Winston is laying on my floor, and I hear gagging sounds in the bathroom. Awareness hits me and I rush to the door to try and open it but it's locked. "Elliot are you okay?" I shout. I knock aggressively on the door a few times before he answers.

"I'm fine Em don't worry." His reply is followed by more sounds of gagging and vomiting.

"Elliot you don't sound fine let me in!" I urge. My nerves grow into a ball in my stomach the longer I stand on this side of the door.

"I'll be out in a little just go downstairs and feed Winston." His voice sounds weak, and I want nothing more than to get in there.

"I'm not leaving until you let me in." I demand while shaking the doorknob again, but this time more aggressively.

"Dammit Emory please just go, I don't want you seeing me like this." He grits out with a slice of anger in his voice. I rest my forehead against the door in defeat. As much as I want to help him, I don't want to try and be there for him when he obviously doesn't want me to be.

175

"Come on Win." He perks his ears up and follows me out the door to go downstairs. I want to be mad at Elliot for not letting me in, but at the same time I feel guilty that I wasn't there when he woke up so I could help him. He clearly needs someone up there with him, but I also won't force myself to be.

"Morning Diaz." Andrew greets me when I walk into the kitchen, he's standing near the fridge shirtless, and stuffing his face with food.

"Do you and your brother believe in shirts?" I joke while reaching for the bag of Winston's dog food in the walk in pantry. I pour some out into his bowl and he devours it all as usual.

"You don't wear shirts when you have a body like mine." He beams a confident smile in my direction and winks at me. I roll my eyes annoyingly and head for the refrigerator.

"So I seen that Elliot wasn't in his bed this morning, any ideas on where he was?" His accusing tone tells me he already knows where he was, but he just wants me to say it out loud. His eyebrows are raised and he's peering at me with waiting eyes. I sometimes forget that him and his brother have the exact same brown colored eyes as Emily, it's so easy to get pulled into them.

"Are you implying something?" I ask trying not give anything away.

"Well all I know is I heard yelling from your room last night, then I heard Elliot go into his room. Funny enough when I went to get him this morning he was no where to be found." I know he knows that Elliot slept in my bed last night, but do I deny it? Do I just admit it? I'm saved by the bell when Emily walks in the kitchen in her lavender robe and slippers. Her black silky hair is pulled up into a messy top knot. I hope I look half as good as her when I'm her age.

"Buenos días, quieres desayuno? I can make some papas con chorizo." I haven't had that for breakfast since I was a kid when mom would to make it on the rare occasions dad asked for it.

"I'm good ma thanks though." Andrew takes another big bite of his bagel.

"You Emory? I feel like I've barely seen you lately where have you been hiding?" I give her a lazy smile before answering.

"No thank you Emily, and I've just been here and work. I get in late sometimes so that's probably why you haven't seen me." She pulls a mug out of the cup board and starts preparing her coffee pot.

"Makes sense, by the way your dad has been asking for you mija." My eyes widen in surprise. Why is he looking for me? I haven't done anything stupid since I got to Phoenix so what could he possibly want to lecture me about? I make a mental note to find him sometime today and talk to him.

"Where is my other beautiful son? He's usually already down here." She asks the room.

"He said he'll be right down, he was pretty sick this morning, he was puking in the bathroom." I admit. Andrew and his mom glance up at each other, and I don't overlook the silent look of panic they exchange. I don't think they know I noticed it.

"I'm sure everything is fine, he probably ate something bad last night." Emily says uneasily. It sounds like she's trying to comfort herself, but I can hear the alarm laced in her voice. She starts to move out of the kitchen, but stops when Elliot walks in without saying a word to anyone. His face looks drained of color, and the dark bags under his eyes are apparent even from where I'm sitting. His expression is tight as he reaches into the fridge and downs orange juice straight from the carton. We all watch him silently, staying very still.

"Qué te pasa mijo?" Emily approaches him and places the back of her palm on his forehead. I think that's what I miss the most, having someone around with the mom instinct to take care of you. I had to do that for myself after mom died, and on occasion I also had to do it for dad since he never dated anyone after mom passed away. When I got accepted into San Diego, guilt came over me for a split second because at that moment I knew my dad was going to be completely alone for the first time since mom has been gone, but I know she wouldn't want me to stick around. She would want me to go follow my dreams, whatever they may be.

"I'm fine ma I promise, I think I just ate something bad last night." He grabs his mom's hand from his forehead and places a peck on it before placing it back on her side. She stays in front of him for a few more seconds, but I can't see what she's doing since her back is to me. I see Elliot's whole body stiffen up before he shakes his head gently at her and she drops her head.

"I was just asking Emory if she knew where you went last night E, I went to get you this morning but you weren't in your bed." Andrew changes the subject, apparently trying to change the awkward vibe in the room, but of course he had to bring *that* up. I threaten him with my eyes but he just winks and beams a smug smile in my direction.

"So what's for breakfast ma?" Elliot asks while approaching the stool I'm sitting at. He gives me a warm smile before sitting next to me. I feel him grasp my elbow and rub his thumb gently across it. This must be his way of apologizing while everyone is around us. Emily lets out a soft chuckle which tells me she knows what Andrew was implying, but she either doesn't care that her son slept in my bed, or she really doesn't know because she doesn't say a word about it.

"I can make papas con chorizo." She moves to the stove and pulls out a pan from the lower cabinet.

"Actually on second thought I shouldn't eat so soon after puking, I'll just have coffee, but thanks ma." He says. Andrew stops mid bite of his bagel and makes a disgusted face.

"Really E? I'm eating I don't need to know about you puking your brains out." He throws the rest of the bagel on the counter aggressively.

"That's for being an ass trying to call me out in front of ma." Elliot whispers low enough for his mom not to overhear him.

"Well played." He nods his head with an approving look before he flips Elliot the middle finger.

"Hey none of that in front of me." Emily threatens piercing her eyes at her sons.

"Sorry ma." They say dryly in unison. They make me want a sibling, but also glad that I don't have one at the same time.

"Have you ate yet? You need the energy for what we're doing today." Elliot asks me while getting up to pour coffee into a mug.

"No I haven't, but are you sure we should be going out today? You sounded pretty bad this morning, and you don't look so hot." I peer at him with concern hoping he'll notice and call off the plans he has for today. He should be resting, we have the rest of the summer to do whatever he has planned.

"And every other day I *do* look hot?" He subtly winks at me, but from the snickers I overhear I know Emily and Andrew heard what he said. I can already feel my face turning red from the embarrassment.

"I'm just saying we could postpone whatever it is you have planned for another day when you're better." He scared the hell out of me this morning, and I never want to feel that way again. He hesitates for a minute before replying in a non convincing tone.

"I'm fine Em, I really want to do this today."

"I agree with Emory mijo, you don't look so good maybe you should take it easy and do it another da—"

"We're going today." He spits out before storming out of the kitchen leaving his mug on the counter. The three of us are silent after he leaves.

"Just watch him for me today mija." Emily says to me while trying to hold back tears. I hear her sniffle her nose softly before walking quickly out of the kitchen. I know I'm not imagining that, *she was crying right?* Everyone is acting weird, and I don't know why.

"You're good for my brother Em." Andrew says after everyone is gone. This is the most serious I've seen him since I got here other than the night at the bar when Elliot got into the fight.

"But?" I imply. He shakes his head immediately with his nose scrunched up.

"No buts, he's been through a lot and he finally seems happy again, and I think you have a lot to do with that." I recognize a fake smile when I see one, but I don't question it. I know Andrew loves his brother even though they never really show affection towards one another. Seeing him like this is new for me, but it does warm my heart knowing he always has his little brothers back.

"While we're on the subject of making people happy, I have to tell you that if Kat ends up hurt because of you I'll have no other choice but to kick your ass." I threaten. All he does is belt out in deep laughter while hunched over the kitchen island.

179

I'm glad to see he's in better spirits now from a minute ago even if it is at my expense.

"Yea I heard you've put those lessons from me and E to good use, and as for Kat I've just been busy so I haven't had the chance to call her." His tone suddenly turns cold at the mention of her name. *Did something happen between them?*

"Were you planning on calling her when you weren't busy anymore?" I pry.

"Look I know she's your friend but this is between me and her." He grits out with a hint of anger, but it doesn't make me back down in the slightest.

"It's real simple Andrew, if you're into her, just stop being an asshole and tell her that, if you're not into her, just stop being an asshole and tell her that. I thought you were at least decent enough to do that." I hear him sigh loudly and his face tightens highlighting his sharp jawline. Him and his brother almost have the same facial structure.

"It's complicated Diaz, you don't know half the shit I have going on, plus I'm sure Elliot has told you I don't do serious relationships." He fiddles with his fingers as he avoids eye contact with me.

"Then why get involved with her in the first place? You knew she liked you." I spit out.

"Because she was cute, and then I got to know her and she was nice, but I just can't get involved with anyone Em. It's complicated."

"Then tell her that, believe it or not I care about Kat, and I also care about you because I see you like a brother, so stop being a dick and call her." I demand.

"E was right, you're not afraid to call people out on their shit." He says seeming more relaxed now. "When have I ever been?" I joke.

"You should go get ready for whatever E has planned for you." He nudges his head towards the doorway of the kitchen. "Oh and Diaz, you should know that I see you like family too. You're like the little sister I never had, and even when you go off to your fancy school in San Diego I'll always be a call away if you need me." I offer him a bright smile and turn around to walk out of the kitchen. Who knew the other Cortes brother was a softie too.

Elliot and I are in the jeep again, and unfortunately wherever we're going we can't take Winston with us according to Elliot. I don't have the slightest idea what we could be doing, but he has a tendency to surprise me so I brace myself for the unthinkable. Elliot looks a little better than he did earlier, but he still looks off compared to how he is every other day. I packed some water bottles, aspirin, and some barf bags just in case he gets sick again, but I told him before we left that I'll only go if he promises to take it easy. The concerned looks of Emily and Andrew this morning are burned into my memory; something felt off but I can't put my finger on it.

"You're awfully quiet over there." He says accusingly. My gaze is on the colorful trees that are passing us by as we drive down the road.

"You scared the hell out of me this morning." I admit, still keeping my eyes away from him. "I told you I was fine." He tries to reach for my hand but I inch it away from his reach.

"Yea well you didn't sound fine, and the fact that you didn't let me in to help you hurt a little." *Since when do I talk about how I feel with other people?* This is all so different for me.

"I didn't want you to see me hurled over the toilet puking Emory." He doesn't hide his annoyance.

"Put yourself in my position, if it were me wouldn't you have wanted to help?"

"Of course." He replies with no hesitation.

"Then why can't you see it that way when it comes to you? I don't give a shit how you looked I would have been there for you." I bite out. It took me so long to finally let him in, and now he's the one closing me out.

"That's what I'm afraid of, I don't want you to stop your life to take care of me." He has the same defeated tone from earlier. I don't even know what he means by that since today was the first time he's been sick since I got here.

"One day of me taking care of you isn't going to interfere with my life Elliot." I point out harshly. He goes silent as he grips the steering wheel tightly.

"Please just let it go okay? I'm sorry. Next time I have food poisoning and I'm puking I'll be sure to ask for you." His tone is still off, but I decide to drop it. Arguing isn't the ideal way I want to spend the day after we confessed our feelings to each other. A few minutes later we come to a slow stop in front of an attendant at a booth. The older man hurtles out of his chair he was siting in to approach the car. He looks a little too old to be working in my opinion. His pale skin is covered in wrinkles, his gray hair is balding, and he has to use a cane to hold himself up to greet us.

"Hey Elliot long time no see." The man says happily.

"Hey Cal how are you?" Elliot greets back.

"Oh ya know still living the dream, you heading down to the lake?" He asks peeking into the car. Elliot nods his head and hands Cal a five dollar bill which he gives back right away.

"Yes sir, we have an item on a bucket list to cross off." I snap my head quickly when I hear what he said. *What the hell is he up to?*

"And who might this pretty lady be?" Cal asks looking at me with a friendly smile.

"This is Emory. Emory this is Cal, the best gate keeper in Phoenix." Elliot nudges his head towards me and I extend my hand to shake Cal's.

"Nice to meet you Emory."

"You too Cal." He gives a subtle head nod and presses a button that makes a loud buzzing sound before the big iron gate in front of us slowly starts to open.

"Good to see you again Elliot, have fun you two." They fist pump each other before we drive forward through the gate. I observe the beautiful surroundings as we drive through the pebbled trail that leads down to the lake. There are trees surrounding both sides of the trail, some have the most vibrant colors of orange, red, and even some pink in them, and there are huge fountains spewing out water scattered all around the open field area leading up to the lake. The grass here is so green it almost looks fake. I've never seen such a pretty view before, that is until I catch sight of the water, and I gasp at the beautiful sight. The clear water is sparkling in the reflection of the sun like diamonds. There are people on boats, kids swimming, and people paddling on kayaks. It's one of the prettiest things I've seen. I've obviously been to a lake before, but back home the water is never this clear, and the view is never this pretty, so I usually try to avoid it.

"You're telling me that this was close by, and instead we drove three hours to what you called a beach?" I blurt out.

"Hey don't insult my beach like that, plus I figured if I ever brought you here it'd be for something special."

"You used to come here a lot or something? Is that why Cal knows you?" I ask curiously.

"Yea, me, Drew and mom used to come almost every weekend when we first moved here just to get our minds off all the bullshit, dad would come sometimes too. I used to sit under those trees with Drew and we'd have competitions of who can skip a rock the farthest. Mom would pack a big lunch and we'd just stay out here all day until we were so tired we'd go straight to bed as soon as we would get home." A genuine smile reaches his face as he recalls the memories.

"That sounds really nice." I say. It reminds me of when me and my parents would come to the park every weekend when mom was sick. Even if it was just to sit under the sun and eat sandwiches, it was always a great day.

"Yea, but today me and you are doing that." He points to the people paddling in the kayaks in the water.

"You're joking right?" I question trying to hide my slight panic.

"It's on your bucket list." He insists. I should have known he had something crazy planned. I should have never told him about that damn list to begin with.

"It just sounded fun but I didn't think I'd actually ever do it." The panic settles in my stomach now.

"Well today you get to do it, and I'll be with you the whole time." He assures me, but it doesn't help the nerves in the slightest. Honestly being in a big body of water in a tiny kayak scares the living shit out of me. What if it tips over? What if I forget how to swim and drown?

"What are you so scared of?" I think he senses my internal panic. He parks the car close by the lake, and stares at me sincerely while I process my thoughts. I stare blankly at the two people in their kayak laughing at the fact that they keep going in circles because they don't know how to work the paddles.

"Emory talk to me." My body feels frozen and I can't even move my head to look at him. I never thought I'd be this petrified at this idea. I feel him gently grab my chin to tilt my head and look him directly.

"Em if you really don't want to do this just let me know, we'll turn around and go home to watch your stupid show." A small laugh breaks out of me.

"Friends isn't stupid." I whisper. He laughs deeply which rumbles my chest, somehow unsettling my nerves a tad bit.

"I don't like the fact that we're going to be in a big body of water in that small kayak." I admit.

"You really think I'd let anything to happen to you? I got you, but only if you really want to do this." I'm definitely going soft because I actually believe him when he says he wouldn't let anything happen to me.

"What if I fall in the water?" I mean it to come off playfully, but Elliot's tone comes out with no trace of humor.

"Then I'll go in after you. If you fall I fall." His words hover over me, and I know in my heart he's telling the truth, and my nerves dissipate all together.

"Ok." I guess I'm as ready as I'll ever be. He places a soft kiss on my forehead before opening his door to climb out. If his words didn't dissipate my nerves, that would have done it.

It takes about an hour for us to actually get onto the water since we had to wait for people to come back, and then get a ten minute lesson on what not to do when we're in the kayak. It's pretty self explanatory, you just use the paddle to move, and try not to don't tip over and drown. *Easy enough.* Elliot triple checks that my life vest is on properly before having me get inside the kayak. He pushes the boat off the edge of the water and climbs in himself. The way he pushes it so effortlessly is so attractive. *I need to get a grip.* Once we're off the edge I start using the paddle to push forward, and I'm quickly reminded I have no upper body strength, but of course Elliot is here to save the day because all it takes is a few long strokes of the paddle and we're already in the middle of the lake. I try to help, but every time I try to paddle we end up turning in a different direction so I decide to let him take the lead on this one. The way I'm positioned is very beneficial to me because from behind I can see his biceps flex every time he paddles us forward. His white shirt is a little wet from the water splashing up so I can see a little through it at his muscular back. I can't seem to be able to look away, he's so captivating. How can someone so perfect be into *me*? It just doesn't make sense. A better question is how was I able to deny it for so long that I was into him?

"Why are you attracted to me?" My thoughts clearly pour out of my mouth without consent. We stop abruptly so he can turn around to face me. His gaze is so fierce it makes me sweat from how nervous it makes me.

"You're kidding right?" He asks with no hint of amusement. I swallow loudly suddenly feeling like an idiot for even asking, but I'm in too deep now.

"I just don't get how you didn't find someone like Stef attractive, but you can like someone like me, she's perfect." My insecurities are slowly manifesting themselves and I can't find a way to stop them. It doesn't seem to phase Elliot in the slightest.

"Stef wasn't you Em. I don't give a shit how cheesy or cliché it sounds because it's true. She doesn't have your laugh, she never challenged me the way you do, I don't have history with her like I do with you, and you might not think so, but you're the most beautiful woman I've ever come across." He says sternly, but at the same time so gentle. If I wasn't already blushing I definitely am now. I can feel the heat spread across my face.

"It wasn't just Stef though, there had to be other girls that were interested in you while you were away, why not any of those girls?" I immediately regret saying anything. *Just stop talking Emory.*

"Did you not just hear me Em? Even though we hadn't spoken in five years I never got you out of my head as much as I tried to. I never went out on dates because every girl that would approach me I wanted them to be you." His confession inserts a little confidence in me I didn't have before. I've never been someone's first choice, and the fact that even when we were apart Elliot just wanted me, it means more to me than he'll ever know.

"Did you ever like me when we were kids?" I don't know why that comes out of my mouth, but I've always been curious, and now seems like an appropriate time to ask. He scoffs and starts to hover over and laugh, and I suddenly feel so embarrassed. *This just jumped up to the most embarrassing moment of my life. Maybe falling out of this kayak isn't a bad idea after all.*

"Like?" He utters in a the lowest voice I almost don't hear it.

"You could say something like that." He admits. I take that as a yes, but the laughing he did before he answered threw me off, despite that I don't ask for clarification.

"Well since you're confessing then I should too. I might have had a tiny crush on you as kids." This is the first time I admit out loud that I liked him when we were younger, even to myself. I was always in denial because I always believed he saw me like a sister like Andrew did. All the memories of us playing in my front yard, and hanging out on my front porch steps play through my mind. It was a simpler time and I wish more than anything to go back and cherish it more with everything I know now.

"Really? I always thought you saw me as your annoying best friend."

"Oh you were, but you were cute too." I joke. He brings his hand over his chest to mimic he's in pain before I catch sight of him dunking his other arm into the water. Before I can dodge him, he splashes a wave of water towards me soaking my clothes all the way down to my socks.

"Elliot!" I try to scoop up water to splash him back, but before I can he grabs on to my waist and pulls me into him. Hearing his laugh brings so much happiness to my heart. This is another one of those moments I wish I could relive forever. I try to squirm out of his hold, but he's gripped onto me tight enough to keep me pinned down.

"I'm going to kick your ass as soon as I get loose." I threaten him, but it's not taken seriously in the slightest since I can't keep a straight face. I keep trying to get out of his hold, but stop when I catch him gazing admiringly at me. He's serious now as he leans closer to me. My heart starts to beat faster just as it always does when I'm in close proximity to him, it's like my body knows exactly how to react to him.

He brings his lips to mine and I sink into the kiss, my face is soaked from the water, but he doesn't seem to mind at all. When our lips move together it sends a jolt down my spine. It feels like our lips are two puzzle pieces finally being put together. I feel complete. For only kissing one girl his whole life he's really good at this. I suddenly remember we're in a public place so before I get too carried away I firmly place my hands on his shoulders to push him away. I instantly miss his warmth when our lips part.

"There are kids around we can't make out in the middle of the lake."

"You're right, we should make out back in the car." I elbow him gently in his ribs trying to distance myself from him.

"You're crazy." I say shaking my head at him trying to stifle my laugh.

"Crazy about my girl." He boasts, and my body instantly goes still. *My girl.* I always found it cringey when guys called their girlfriends that in movies or books, but hearing it from his lips sounds perfect. *This man is going to be the death of me.*

"Who says I'm your girl?" His face turns bright red at my joke. I figure it's payback for soaking me with water. I burst out in laughter, and I see his whole body relax at the realization that I wasn't serious.

"You're gonna pay for that one!" He exclaims rushing towards me and starts to tickle my sides. I squeal loudly and try my hardest to squirm away from him. It's not fair since he's known since we were nine what spots are my most ticklish. I can't control my laughter, and he has the most joyous smile on his face that I decide here and now that I'll do whatever it takes to keep it on his face. All of a sudden he stops tickling me, and starts into a coughing fit that makes me go from playful to serious in seconds. He can't stop coughing as he's hunched over the kayak facing the water. I place a comforting hand on his back and rub in circular motions trying to calm him.

"I'm sorry Ej, I can't do strenuous activity for more than thirty minutes so we have to go back." His face is washed of color now, and I don't miss the hint of fear in his eyes.

"It's fine, are you sure you're okay though?" I have that bad feeling in my stomach again.

"Yea I'm fine, this happens sometimes when I do too much." His breathing starts to normalize, but he's still gagging while hunched over the kayak.

"Do you have asthma?" I pry.

"Something like that." Before I could question him further he comes back up, and grabs the paddle to settle back in his seat.

"C'mon I'll paddle us back." He says still seeming catching his breath. I place my hand on his to stop him.

"I'll do it." I say confidently settling back into my seat and grabbing my paddle.

"I'd like to get there before dinner tomorrow Emory so I think it'd be best if I do it." I roll my eyes at the insult, and begin to push my paddle forward in the water. It might take a little longer but I will get us there. "I can do it Ej." He insists while inching towards his paddle, but I smack his hand away with the paddle as he reaches for it.

"Elliot if you touch that paddle again I will revoke your privileges of calling me Ej until the end of time." I try to be as threatening as I can, but he laughs as if I was joking and puts his arms up in surrender.

"Fine, all yours baby." I push my paddle forward again, but this time we turn in the opposite direction I'm trying to go. I grunt loudly in frustration, and Elliot raises his eyebrows at me as if he's asking me if I give up yet. He must not know me that well if he thinks I'm going to give up so soon.

"You have to do one side at a time Em, push forward on your left then switch to your right." I let out a deep breath and do as he says which seems to work a lot better than my previous technique. As I'm paddling I'm finally taking in the gorgeous view, with the crystal clear water under us you can see all the different colored rocks, and some tiny fish swimming around. There's a nice breeze which is a change from the beaming heat.

"You knew you couldn't do a lot of strenuous activity, but you still brought me out here to do this?" I blurt out.

"I told you I was going to help with your bucket list." He replies sincerely. How can someone so handsome also be so compassionate? He went into a full coughing fit all because he wanted to help me do something on my list. A part of me feels guilty because that wouldn't have happened if it weren't for me.

"Don't you even feel guilty Em. I have coughing fits going up the damn stairs sometimes, it's no big deal." He shrugs his shoulders and looks around at the view.

"It sounded like a big deal, that's twice today you scared the shit out of me." I confess.

"You're cute when you're worried about me." He says beaming a cheesy smile at me. We finally reach the edge of the water, and one of the booth attendants that helps us bring the kayak onto the sand throws me a concerned look when they notice my soaked clothes. Elliot grabs my hand to help me up, but not before he laughs mockingly at me.

"Did you really have fun?" He asks as we walk back to the car with our hands entwined.

"Of course I did, but I could do without the wet clothes." We finally approach the car, and he opens up my door for me to climb in.

"This isn't the last of activities I have planned for us."

"You don't have to do anything else, we could spend the rest of the summer on the couch watching Friends and I'd be happy."

"I know I said I'd do anything for you, but you're pushing it with that one." I know he's bluffing when he says he doesn't like the show, but I'll get him to admit it eventually. He leans into me and places a quick peck on my cold lips before closing my door and walking to his side.

I don't know what the future holds for us, but I know as of right now I'm happier than I've ever been. Being with him just feels right. It's a new feeling, but it's one I can definitely get used to.

CHAPTER TWENTY-FOUR

"What the hell happened to you?" My dad exclaims when I walk through the door still in my wet clothes from the lake. His eyes go wide looking from me to Elliot, who's walking right beside me.

"I got a little water on me." I say through gritted teeth sparing a look towards Elliot. He's got his head down trying to stifle a laugh that's dying to escape.

"Uh huh." My dad says with suspicion. I don't want to tell anyone about Elliot and I until I know where it's going, but the way my dad is looking at us I can tell he doesn't need me to tell him anything.

"I'm going to to change if you boys will excuse me." I announce to the room before turning to walk up the stairs.

"Emory I need to talk to you about something whenever you have time." My dad shouts before I get far enough away. I nod in acknowledgment trying to hide my apprehensiveness. A million things swift through my mind of what he could have to talk to me about. Is it about college? Me and Elliot? Are we going back to LA early? Me and dad don't exactly have heart to heart conversations so whatever it is, it's not good.

Emily is walking down the stairs at the same time I'm walking up, and she gasps loudly at the sight of me. She's got the same wide eyed look my dad just had.

"Emory qué te pasó?"

"I got a little water on me, sorry I'm just headed up to change." I nudge past her to go into my room, and I'm instantly greeted by an excited Winston who franticly jumps on my legs. My room door was open the whole time so he could go in and out as he pleased, but from the looks of it he was laying on my bed the whole time we were gone. I pick him up into my arms and he greets me again with licks to my face. I already hate being away from him for so long.

"I missed you too Win." I hear a soft knock on my door, only to peek up and see Elliot standing in the doorway with his hands in his pockets. Winston tries to wiggle out of my arms so I put him down so he can run to Elliot. *Traitor*.

"I'm sorry for splashing you with the water by the way." He's giggling while he speaks which tells me he's not *that* sorry.

"It's water it'll dry." I say. I need to get into some dry clothes soon though because these wet ones are starting to get uncomfortable.

"I'll get you some dry clothes." He says walking towards my closet as if he just read my mind. I'm actually kinda curious on what type of clothes he would choose for me to wear so I leave him to it while I brush out all the tangles in my hair.

"What's in the box Em?" I hear him ask. *No no no.* I bolt to the closet, but before I can stop him he's standing there with his mouth agape with the black box wide open in his hands. I don't even know why I brought it here, but I seen it while I was packing and something just came over me when I shoved it into my suitcase. The last person I wanted to find it was Elliot.

"You kept them." He stands frozen in shock, but his eyes don't leave the black box in his slightly trembling hands. Inside is every single white daisy he gave me as kids. Everyday since we were nine until we were fourteen when he'd pick one out for me from his garden, i'd store it in this box. Of course they've become a little wilted over the years, but I couldn't bring myself to throw them out even after I was pissed at him, so I shoved the box in the back of my closet back home, and tried my best to forget about it. Sometimes a couple times a year curiosity would eat at me and I would pull out the box to reminisce, but then I'd curse him out and remember that I hate him.

"You weren't supposed to find them. I don't even know why I brought the box here when I haven't even opened it in yea—"

"Emory." He interrupts me, and I finally get a good look on his face. He looks like he might be crying. "I'm happy you kept them." I hear his voice crack before he walks up to me and hugs me so tightly I almost lose my breath.

"You don't think it's lame?" I ask only half joking, and he laughs deeply into my hair.

"Of course not, especially when it's not as lame as me." He lets out an exasperated sigh before pulling his shirt off, making me instantly turn red.

191

"Uhh Elliot we're not doing this right now." I say sternly. He looks me dead in the face before hunching over with uncontrollable laughter.

"Calm down Em we're not gonna fuck in a closet, I just want to show you something." He does that smirk I love, and grabs my hand gently to bring it to touch a place right over his heart. I don't look at the area right away because I don't want him to see just how red I am right now. My eyes instantly tear up when I see what's under my fingertips.

"I told you I only have one tattoo, of course it had to be about you." He whispers softly near my ear. *Can you have a heart attack at nineteen*? My heart feels like it's going to beat right out of my chest. There's a lump the size of a golf ball in my throat, and I can't get past it to form any words. My eyes well up at the sight of the small tattoo of a leaf with a black heart drawn in the middle, the same kind I gave him everyday since we were nine until we were fourteen. *He didn't forget.*

"You wanna know a secret?" I ask through the tears that are slowly rolling down my cheeks. He wipes some away with the thumb caressing my cheek while nodding his head. I guess he can't get any words out either. My hands are trembling from the anxiety of giving him a piece of me that no one knows about. I count to five in my head trying to gather up the courage to pull my shirt up halfway to expose my rib cage.

"No fucking way." He curses under his breath before he places his warm fingers on my skin to observe the dainty tattoo of a white daisy with a bright yellow center. When I got the tattoo I was seventeen, it was my first one, and it was also my own symbolic way of finally letting Elliot go. I told myself since I wasn't going to get closure from him I had get it on my own, and this was what I came up with. I didn't tell anyone I got it because with that comes questions I didn't want to answer, so I've kept it a secret until today. Showing him my tattoo, and him showing me his feels like even when we were apart we still shared something, and that we always had a part of each other whether the other knew about it or not. This whole time I was under the impression that he never reached out because he was happier without me meanwhile I couldn't even fathom my life without him, but turns out he was just as lost without me as I was without him.

"When did you get your tattoo?" I ask. His hand is still burning my skin, but I don't bother asking him to remove it.

"A couple days after I turned eighteen, Andrew said I should have at least one and this was the only thing that came to mind, what about yours?" He asks through shaky breaths.

"I was seventeen and my friend learned how to tattoo. Honestly it was my idea of finally letting you go." I admit. I suddenly remember we're still standing in the middle of my closet, and that he is still shirtless. I turn to sit on my bed and he follows quickly behind putting his shirt back on. He sits right next to me, and places his hand on my thigh before speaking.

"I wanted to call you so many times while I was gone just to check up on you, but before I knew it so much time went by, and I figured you were better off without me." His dreary expression yanks a cord at my heart. He'll never know how much I wanted to see a letter from him in the mail, or how much I yearned to hear his voice everyday until I was sixteen, and maybe even after that, whether I admitted it or not.

"Why did you leave?" The words struggle to come out. I can tell he's on edge now by the way he looks away from me, so I assure him by placing my hand over his that's still rested on my thigh. I wasn't ready to hear the reason he left before, but I am now. This is the last piece of him I need to know before we can move forward, and it doesn't matter what the reason is anymore because I know I'll be able to put it in the past. I never thought I'd get to this point where I could be open minded about anything, much less this.

"It's a long story." He says shortly.

"I've got time." I reply gently, trying my best not to scare him off by being too intense. It seems as if minutes go by before he entwines both my hands in his, and looks at me with remorse. "Elliot just tell me." I let out. Before he can open his mouth to speak there's a light knock on my door that interrupts us.

"Emory can I come in?" My dad asks from the other side of the door making my body jump and untwine my hand out of Elliot's grasp.

"Yea just a second!" I exclaim while examining my room to make sure nothing is out of place, it's bad enough Elliot is sitting on my bed.

"We're not done with this conversation." I point my index finger in his direction, and he gives me a distant nod. I can't exactly read the expression on his face, but I know it isn't his usual happy look. I go to open the door and see my dad standing in the doorway with his arms folded across his chest. He keeps a neutral look on his face even after he spots Elliot.

"Hey I was hoping we could talk if you've got a minute."

"Uhh sure me and Elliot were just talking, but we can finish later." I peer back at Elliot hoping he'll get the silent hint that me and my dad need some privacy. He winks at me before picking up Win and walking past my dad out of the room. I stare after him mentally reminding myself to find him later to finish our conversation because the way he was stalling to answer my question puts a pit in my stomach.

"Emory?" My dad snaps and I bring myself back to the present.

"Yea?"

"I asked if you want to talk here or go for a walk?" He already sounds annoyed, but it could be because he noticed I wasn't paying attention to him the first time.

"Here is fine." I'm reminded that I'm still in my wet clothes when I nervously put my hands in my pockets and feel the dampness. I never got my dry clothes from Elliot before he surprised me by opening that damn box.

I open my door wide enough for him to step in. I don't know if this is a private conversation or not but I decide to close the door just in case. His look is worrisome, I haven't seen this look on him since my parents sat me down to tell me that mom was sick, so to say I'm anxious is an understatement.

"Dad what's wrong?" I ask. Might as well rip off the bandaid, I know something is wrong, and we've never been the type to bullshit each other.

"I uhh…I wanted to talk to you about whatever is going on between you and Elliot." *I knew it.* He hasn't spoken more than ten words to me since we got here, and now all of a sudden he wants to play the concerned father? Where was that concern when mom died and I didn't come out of my room for weeks?

"What do you mean?" My defensive tone hardens his expression. I should have known we wouldn't last five minutes in the same room together, nothing has changed.

194

"I see that you guys have been spending time together lately, and I just want to talk to you about it and make sure you're okay."

"You don't have to worry, it's Elliot you've known him since he was nine years old."

"I also know how hurt you were when he left, I'm just trying to look out for you to make sure that doesn't happen again." He's staring up at me with a sad look in his eyes.

"I'll be fine dad, he said he wouldn't do anything to hurt me again." I point out. I find it weird we're having this conversation when he's never wanted to talk to me about boys growing up.

"You don't know everything about him Emory." He grits out. I feel my hands slowly curl up into fists out of anger.

"Dad I know him a lot better than you do, yes there's things I don't know yet, but I'll figure them out over time." I notice his body tense up as soon as the words leave my mouth. I know there's more to it than he's leading on, I can feel it in my gut.

"If there's something you know that I don't please feel free to share." I spit out with a venomous tone. He's acting weird just like everyone else has been lately, and I need to know why. He can't even look at me now, and it reminds me of the same situation I was in with Elliot minutes ago. It feels like everyone around me knows something I'm being kept in the dark from.

"It's not my place to say Emory." *So there is something.* I swallow the bile building in my throat before speaking again.

"Just tell me dad." I plead. Everything is playing back in my head; the conversation between Elliot and Emily the day I was eavesdropping, the weird looks between Andrew and Emily the morning Elliot woke up sick. I have to know what it all means or I'm going to scream.

"You need to talk to Elliot about it not me." My body feels like it's radiating with so much anger I might explode. My eyes start to collect tears out of frustration.

"Then why bring it up if you can't even tell me!" I scream. My dad's stunned face inserts guilt in my stomach. It's not just what he said that made me so angry, it's the fact that my gut feeling has been right this whole time and I ignored it.

195

"You might not see it this way, but all I'm trying to do is protect you. I don't want to see you crushed again when he...when *you* have to leave for college and he stays here." The break in his sentence tells me that wasn't what he was planning to say.

"Since when do you care about me getting hurt anyway? This is the longest we've been able to be in the same room since mom died. You can't even look at me, and when you do all I see is disappointment in your eyes. Good thing you only have to look at me for another month and I'll be out of your hair." I spit out angrily. He scoffs loudly, and turns to look at me with utter confusion.

"Is that what you think Emory? I'll admit I wasn't proud when I had to sit in front of a judge and prove that you were innocent that night two years ago, and yea I've given you a hard time, but that's only because I want you to learn from your mistakes." He looks down at his feet now, and I swear I can hear him sniffle his nose, but I just stare at him silently waiting for him to continue. "I'm sorry I made you feel like I was disappointed in you, you've made mistakes just like we all have."

"Even before that night you never talked to me the way you did before...mom died." I choke on the last words. I can feel both of our anxiety building up at the mention of mom, it's a subject we both have never touched on since the funeral six years ago. You could cut glass with the tension in the room now.

"You look just like her you know? So beautiful. The more you grow up the more I notice it. Your smile, the freckles on your face that you try to hide just like she did when she was a teenager, even your damn laugh sounds like her. After she died every time I looked at you I saw her, and I would just want to break down. I know that makes me a shitty father, and you didn't deserve that but it's true Em. She was so good at being your mom, being my wife, doing it all and making it look easy, and I couldn't even be a good dad to you after she was gone. I was ashamed, but not in you, in myself." I see a single tear fall down his face which makes me also start to tear up. I didn't even see him cry the day of mom's funeral. I've never seen him be this vulnerable much less with me, and I suddenly understand him on a deeper level. After mom died we both had our own ways of grieving, and in the end I guess we both shut down, and ultimately shut each other out. At least I had Elliot for a year after she died, but my dad didn't have anyone, and I didn't even notice what he was going through.

"You worked extra hours to keep a roof over my head and I made it harder on you. I completely ignored how alone you might have been feeling after you lost the love of your life." How did we let this happen? Six years of avoiding each other when we could have been helping each other heal from her death.

"You're the best thing that has ever happened to me Em, you're my whole life. I'm sorry if I ever made you feel less than that mijita."

Mijita, his old nick name for me when I was growing up. The loud cry that's been stuck in my throat finally escapes, and he stands up to walk over to me to hug me tightly. I let myself take a huge breath of relief at the contact, the kind I've wanted so badly since I was thirteen. I feel like we understand each other a little bit more now, but now I feel even more guilty I'm going away for college.

"Now I feel like shit I'm going to San Diego and leaving you alone." I pull away from his hug and wipe the wetness from my eyes. He snorts a laugh and looks at me with endearing eyes, it's a look I haven't gotten from him in so long.

"It's only two hours Em, plus I won't be alone." He says fidgeting in his stance. "What do you mean you won't be alone?" *Did I miss something?* He looks at me hesitantly before speaking again.

"I've been seeing someone for about six months." He brings his fingers to his mouth to bite at his fingernails as he looks at me with weary eyes, and I can't help but let out a surprised gasp. Either I haven't been paying very much attention, or my dad has been really good at hiding this relationship because I had no idea. I don't know how to feel about it, but I am relieved he won't be all alone when I leave him.

"What's her name?"

"Lorena, but everyone calls her Lori." He's speaking as if he's on edge waiting for my reaction. He probably thinks I'm going to flip out, and honestly the old Emory would have, but this new version of me is happy for him. I would never expect him to be alone for the rest of his life, plus I know mom would want him to be happy. She would want *both* of us to be happy.

"Is she pretty?" I joke to ease the mood which earns me another deep laugh from him, I missed hearing his laugh. My thoughts take me back to hearing his laugh when him and mom would prance around the kitchen at breakfast, or when we'd break out into pillow fights on movie nights.

"Yes she is very pretty, and she's really nice too. I know you'd love her, she already loves you after I told her about you." He gloats.

"So I take it you didn't tell her I'm an asshole then?"

"No I figured she'd realize that one on her own after she met you." He nudges my shoulder gently with his fist. It feels good to have a moment like this with him.

"Ouch." I gasp while holding my heart mimicking that I'm hurt. We banter back and forth a few more times before he dismisses himself out of my room, and I'm left with a content feeling in my chest. The only way I can describe it is when you're a kid getting up on Christmas morning and you're excited to get your parents up to open all the gifts under the tree. That's what this feeling is, a sense of excitement for what's coming for me and dad from here on out. A part of me wants to march over to Elliot's room and demand he tell me what's going on, but I feel so happy right now and I want to enjoy it for a little while. I've always got tomorrow.

Opening my eyes to see Elliot huddled over me in a black hoodie wasn't my ideal way to be woken up, but here we are. The sun isn't out so that tells me it's not morning yet. The time on the clock says 12:04 am and I let out a low growl. He has a habit of doing this, and I'm so close to killing him for it.

"No, hell no…not again Elliot, let me sleep!" I whisper loudly before turning my back to him.

"Trust me baby you want to get up for this." His use of *baby* makes any anger subside.

"What are you talking about?" I push myself up now full of curiosity.

"Meet me downstairs in five minutes, you might want to change into something warm." He kisses me on the forehead before walking out of my room leaving me more confused than ever. What could we possibly have to do at this time? The better question is what is he doing up at this time? He's a grandpa who's usually asleep by nine o'clock every night. I don't know what we're doing, but I decide to go with putting on my white running shoes just in case, and my favorite black hoodie. I grab my phone and very quietly tip toe down the stairs trying to avoid the squeaking of the steps to not wake everyone up. Elliot is pacing back and forth at the end of the stairs when I reach him.

"Alright what's so important you have to interrupt my beauty sleep?" I whisper placing my hands on my hips.

"First of all baby you don't need beauty sleep because you're hot, and second of all look out the window." He nudges his head towards the living room window that faces the front yard. I eye him suspiciously, but walk over and peer out to see that it's pouring rain outside. I didn't even know it rained in the summer time here.

"Have you never seen rain before?" I ask sarcastically. All he does is roll his eyes at me.

"Yes smart ass I have, but if you don't feel like scratching something else off your bucket list then fine we'll just go back to sleep." He starts to walk up the stairs but I stop him by grabbing onto his forearm.

"Hold it...what are you talking about?" I pull him back to face me which reveals the biggest smirk I've ever seen on his face.

"You said you wanted to dance in the rain." *He can't be serious.*

"You can't be serious."

"When do I joke about your bucket list?" He insists. *He's officially lost his mind.*

"I put that on my list when I was younger after I saw Troy and Gabriella do it on the rooftop in high school musical." I scoff. The idea sounded really cute when I saw it in movies growing up, but now that the opportunity is in front of me, getting soaked from the rain at midnight doesn't sound like the greatest idea.

"When are you going to stop making excuses and start doing things out of your comfort zone Ej? I'll go out there by myself if I have to, but I'd have a lot more fun if you were there." I think he's full of shit when he says he'll go out there by himself, but a small part of me knows he'll do anything to prove a point.

"Okay fine." I agree to his crazy plan. His smile gets even brighter than before. He leaves a wet kiss on my cheek and entwines our hands to walk us to the front door. *How could I ever say no to that smile?* I stop us abruptly as a thought enters my mind.

"Wait…you were already sick this morning I don't think it's the smartest idea to go out in the rain." I would feel like the worst person if he got pneumonia or something just because he wanted to help me cross something off my bucket list. He grabs my chin softly to tilt my head up to look at him, his touch sends shivers down my body and I'm not even in the cold yet.

"Don't worry about me I'll be fine, I wanna do this for you baby." There he goes with the *baby* again. I swear if this man came to me one day and asked 'Would you please help me rob this bank *baby?*' I wouldn't even hesitate.

I nod my head in approval before he pulls me towards the door. As soon as it opens I hear the droplets of rain hit the ground, the sound is so therapeutic to my ears. It's coming down pretty hard, but of course Elliot doesn't show any sign of hesitation. I let out an exasperated sigh and pull my hood up before he drags me outside. The water hits me and my body instantly feels frozen, but somehow Elliot still feels warm to the touch. I decide to take the hood off my head to let the water fall onto my hair and my face, I might as well enjoy it while it lasts. I look up towards the sky with my eyes closed, and stick my tongue out to let the rain catch on it. A cheerful laugh comes out of me which catches me by surprise because I didn't even know I could laugh like that. I feel like I'm a kid again playing in the rain without a care in the world.

Elliot is right, I need to learn how to get out of my comfort zone and live a little more. I would have never in a million years even thought of doing this, but I'm so glad he made me do it. He has a way of bringing out the best in me, even when I thought there wasn't any left. I glance over to admire him, but he's already looking at me with an enamored look on his face.

"May I have this dance?" He extends his hand for me to take it.

"Really?"

"Isn't that what Troy asks Gabriella? Or is it only romantic when he does it?" He jokes keeping his hand extended towards me. I finally grab it and he pulls me gently into his firm body. I'll never understand how we could be out in the cold rain, but he still feels like a sauna.

"Troy was hot so it was okay." I burst into laughter as I wrap my arms around the back of his neck for support. A playful scoff comes from him, and he tightens his grip on me before whispering close to my ear.

"You're lucky I'm in love with you because you're a pain in the ass." My laughter dies and my body freezes, but I know it's not from the cold. I feel all the muscles in my body stiffen, and I can't bring myself to look at him.

"You don't have to say it back, but I'm in love with you Emory Jewel Diaz. I love your snide comments, your laugh, your forgiving heart, your bravery, your beauty, I love every damn thing about you, and I'm not afraid to say it to you everyday until you're ready to say it back." I feel the hot tears slide down my cheeks. I don't know if I'm ready to say it back, and I don't want to unless I'm one hundred percent sure. I feel him grip harder onto my waist and we start to sway back and forth slowly. The rain is letting down harder by the second, but we seem unfazed. My heart is so happy and full at the moment, I never want to leave. I never knew it was possible to feel this happy with someone else. These past weeks with Elliot have been a rollercoaster of emotions to say the least. I came here this summer hating his guts and ready to ignore him for three months, but I ended up falling for him. I have no idea how that happened, but I'm so glad it did.

"Oh and one more thing." I feel him reach into his pocket and I hear his phone click as it unlocks. I finally pull back to see what he's up to.

"What are you doing?" He's typing something in his phone but the rain droplets are making it blurry to see his screen, and then I hear it.

"It wouldn't be right if we didn't dance to this song." *This man is fucking perfect.*

He pulls me back into his embrace and we sway slowly to the song that's playing from his phone, the same one we sang in his car the day we got Winston, and the song that'll now be my favorite forever. Enchanted by Taylor swift plays softly in the background, and I'm overcome with disbelief that he did all this for me. I don't just mean specifically this; since the moment I got here he was determined to make me realize he's changed, and even after I forgave him he never stopped proving it to me. He made sure I got to do everything I wanted to do before I left him, the only thing is now I *never* want to leave him. I don't know if that means I'm in love with him because I've never been in love before, but I imagine it feels something like this. I feel him dip me down and he brings me back up to sway slowly again.

"I have to say, not bad." I say smiling from behind his back.

"I looked online for a five minute dancing lesson before I woke you up." He admits laughing softly in my ear. *Of course he did.* Elliot has made me feel more alive in the nearly two months I've been here, than I have in nineteen years. He makes me want to be fearless and chase life head on. He calls me brave, but he's the one that made me strong enough to be brave. He calls me beautiful, but he's the one that made me feel confident enough in my body to feel beautiful. He calls me fearless, but he's the one that made me feel powerful, it's him. I can't necessarily give him *all* the credit, I'd like to think I had something to do with it, but I can honestly say the Emory that showed up at his door two months ago, and the Emory dancing with him the rain now are two completely different people.

Is that what love is? To be utterly consumed in another person? To want to better yourself because of the influence someone has on your life. To randomly have the guts to dance in the freezing rain with them at midnight, and have them be your very first thought in the morning, and the last thought before you go to sleep. If it is, then I'm absolutely without a doubt in love with Elliot Cortes. I think a part of me always has been, I just buried her deep down where I couldn't find her. I pry myself away and look up at him with admiration. His chiseled jaw line and messy facial hair makes him look so effortlessly handsome. I never thought I'd be in love with a man who has a buzz cut since it's never been my thing, but like I said, it's funny how life works sometimes. When I admire t him I can't help but let a smile spread across my entire face. My jaw is starting to hurt with how much I've been smiling lately.

"Why are you so smiley suddenly?" He asks leaning his forehead against mine, peering his chocolate brown eyes back into mine.

"You." I answer honestly. He grasps the back of my neck so gently, and brings his cold soft lips to touch my own. The way his lips just fit perfectly into mine as we intensify the kiss just feels like we complete each other in every way possible. Like our lips were made just for one another. I remember when he told me when he kissed me at fourteen he knew he didn't want to kiss anyone else, and now I know exactly what he means because I never want to kiss anyone but him ever again. I want to tell him I love him, this feels like a good moment with the rain and the kissing, but I hesitated after he said it so he'll probably feel I'm just saying it because he did, and I want him to know just how much I love him.

I love him so much it hurts.

CHAPTER TWENTY-FIVE

Did I set an alarm, what is that noise? I immediately realize the obnoxious sound coming from my phone is my ringtone so I quickly prop myself up from my pillows to answer it without looking at the caller ID.

"Hello?" I grumble lowly. *This better be good.*

"Hey Emory it's Sam, sorry to bother you, but I wanted to see if you're able to come in today? One of the girls called off so it'll just be Kat by herself and she requested you to come in to help out if you can." It takes me a few minutes to fully process that it's my boss on the line right now. I wasn't scheduled to come in today, but I guess working the early shift won't be so bad, at least I'll get off early enough to still be able to spend time with Elliot.

"Yea of course, give me thirty minutes?" I ask slipping out from under my covers. I walk to my closet to lay out my work clothes which are a little wrinkly, but I'm sure they won't mind. Frankly they're lucky I'm going in at all.

"Thanks Emory you're a life saver." Sam says in a cheery voice before hanging up. If it wasn't for Kat asking for me I probably would have said no since I didn't get to bed until about two in the morning. Elliot and I stayed outside a little longer than we should have. The rain let up after awhile but we stayed out to keep dancing, and talked until we both couldn't keep our eyes open anymore. We talked about everything except the fact that I'm in love with him, and the so called thing he's been keeping from me according to dad. It was on the tip of my tongue to ask him about it, but I couldn't bring myself to ruin the good moment we were having, and especially not after his confession of being in love with me. I'll ask him about it tonight, and after he tells me whatever it is, we'll move past it and I'll admit that I'm in love with him. I mean, how bad can this thing everyone has been so weird about be?

I can't think too much about it right now because I'll just psych myself out, so I concentrate on getting ready for work. I brush the tangles out of my hair and throw on some light makeup to hide the dark circles under my eyes. I decide to try something new and let my freckles show today. It feels different, but a good different I guess.

Before I get dressed I figure I should go ask Elliot if he can drop me off since there is no doubt that he's wide awake right now reading something on the kitchen island and drinking coffee. I leave my room and jolt downstairs to see no one in the kitchen, so I pace to the living room window to peer out, but I don't see him working on his truck in the drive way either. He can't possibly be sleeping at nine in the morning? He's usually been up for hours by this time. I walk back upstairs, go to Elliot's door, and lean my ear against it not hearing a sound. I take it upon myself to slowly turn the doorknob and creak the door open, only to see him snuggled up in his blankets sound asleep with Winston in his arms. I wish so much that I was cuddled up with the two of them. It is unusual he's still asleep right now, but he's probably beat from staying up so late so I decide to let him sleep. Since I'm walking to work I'm technically already late so I rush back to my room to throw my clothes on, and I'm out the door in minutes. Emily is putting on her jacket by the front door when I reach the bottom of the stairs, and her face brightens up when she sees me.

"Good morning mija where you off to this early?"

"I got called in to work, I'm actually running late since I have to walk. I was going to ask Elliot but he's sound asleep." I turn towards the door to leave, but her worried voice stops me.

"Elliot is still asleep? Is he okay?" There's a certain edge to her tone that puts that bad feeling in the pit of my stomach.

"He's fine, he didn't get much sleep last night so I'm guessing he's just catching up." I assure her. *Why is it such a big concern that Elliot is still asleep?* "Did you need a ride? I was just going out for groceries and the bar is on the way." She says as she reaches for her purse.

"Uh yea that'd actually be great, thank you." I offer her a slanted smile and we both walk out the door towards her white Mercedes in the driveway. I've been here almost two months, and this will probably be the longest I've been alone with Emily since I've been so caught up with Elliot; I wonder if she has her suspicions about us. We crawl into the car and she plugs in her phone to the aux cord right away. It's only when I peer at her from the corner of my eye that I notice her hands are trembling. It's a little chilly, but not cold enough to have someone shivering. I should ask if she's okay, but the music blaring from the radio interrupts my thoughts. I hear Free Bird by Lynyrd Skynyrd start to play and an involuntary smile creeps onto my face.

"Mom loved this song." Memories of her singing along to this when she'd drive me to school run through my mind, I wish more than anything I didn't take those moments for granted.

"I remember. She's the one that made me love this song so much." She puts the car into reverse and backs out of the long driveway, her hands are still shaking slightly on the steering wheel. "You're turning out to be just like her you know, so strong willed, and not to mention beautiful." She taps a finger on my cheek which makes me aware that her hands are toasty warm, so she can't be shaking because she's cold.

"That means a lot coming from you since you two were so close." I admit. Emily was over at our house just as much as Elliot was. Her and mom were always having lunch or going shopping together, they even started a book club at one point, but it only lasted three meetings before they got bored of it.

"She made me promise to take care of you when she knew she was sick, I'm so sorry I didn't follow through with that promise when we left." I hear her voice hitch so I place a reassuring hand on her shoulder. *Since when do I console people?* This new Emory is getting exhausting to keep up with.

"You had to do whatever you had to do, I'll admit I wasn't accepting of it at first, but I get it now that you had to leave to be closer to your family, and I know mom gets it too." Her eyes go wide subtly enough that if I wasn't looking directly at her, I wouldn't have noticed. She doesn't say anything more until we pull up in front of the bar with three minutes to spare.

"I hope you know that you're the best thing to ever happen to my son Emory." She says before I open the passenger door to leave. My hand stays frozen on the handle. I should have known she knew something was up between us, moms know everything. I'm able to crane my neck to make eye contact with her warm brown eyes, the same exact ones she passed down to her son. They give me a sense of comfort while I'm looking at her because it's like looking into Elliots'.

"But?" I ask warily. I'm getting déjà vu again since I had almost the same conversation with Andrew. She lets out a loud breath and brings her soft hand to my cheek. It's weird how comforting this is, but Emily has always had the mom instinct down to a science so she's naturally very comforting.

"No but mija, at the end of the day I know you're the reason he's here, and I couldn't be more grateful for that." *What does that even mean*? I want to ask for clarification, but I'm one minute from being late and I still need to go put my stuff away and clock in. All I do is offer her a soft smile that probably just came off as awkward before climbing out of the car. "*You're the reason he's here.*" Her voice keeps repeating over and over again in my head as I try make sense of it while walking back to the locker room to put my stuff away. It wasn't just what she said, but the way she said it. She was so off, like her mind was a thousand miles away.

"You're my hero for coming in baby cakes, I love you." Kat peers from around the corner in her usual peppy voice. As if she senses my confusion, her peppiness is replaced with concern. "What wrong? Trouble with your boy toy already?" Her comment strikes a nerve with me, but I brush past it.

"No it was actually his mom, she said something and now I can't get it out of my head." I pull my apron on and tie it in a knot behind my back before going to clock in, with Kat following behind me on my heels.

"What'd she say?" I don't know if I should be telling her something Emily said to me, but if I don't tell someone about it I'm going to go crazy.

"She said that I'm the reason why Elliot is here, but how can I possibly be the reason why he's here? She's his mom isn't she the reason he's here?" I try to play it off as a joke, but Kat's whole face drains as she stares back at me. If I wasn't already on edge I would definitely be now.

"Why do you have that look on your face?" I demand.

"What look? I'm just tired Emory." *She called me Emory.* A big red flag for Kat when something is up is when she doesn't call me baby cakes or Em.

"Katlyn Harrison if there's something going on, as my friend you have to tell me." I say in my most stern tone. This is my first time since I've met her that I've used her whole name, but if there was ever a time to use it, it's now. I already have to deal with everyone else acting weird, I can't deal with her too.

"Em I don't know anything, if I did I would have told you. I think you're just reading too much into what she said." It doesn't take me off edge one bit, but I decide to drop it for now. Maybe she's right and I'm just overthinking this because of everything else going on in my head. The dining area of the bar is empty as I suspected it would be at ten in the morning, but there are a few regulars being served at the bar area.

"I talked to Andrew yesterday." She seems annoyed at the mention of his name which shocks me because not too long ago she was really into him.

"Next subject…I want to hear everything between you and Elliot, it's the reason I had Sam call you in because I wanted to hear it in person."

"That's the reason I had to drag my ass out of bed this early?" I put a hand on my hip and look her at with narrow eyes trying my best to be intimidating. "Duh, now fill me in on all the juicy details." She takes a seat at one of the nearby tables, and crosses her legs peering up at me with awaiting eyes. I tell her what Elliot did for me last night and also my bucket list that he's been helping me with. I also tell her that he admitted he was in love with me and why I didn't say it back right away, but I'm planning on saying it today. She listens intently as she always does, not interrupting me once even when I know she was dying to.

"So you're in love with him?" She asks after I finish.

"Yea…I am." I don't hesitate this time. It feels wrong that I'm admit-ting it to her before I even tell Elliot, but I figured it could be good practice saying it out loud before seeing him later.

"Who knew Elliot was such a romantic." She looks off into the distance as if she's deep in thought, then Sam approaches the table we're sitting at with a case of beer in his hands that he seems to be struggling with.

"Sorry to interrupt your therapy session girls but could you help an old man out and carry these cases to the storage room?"

"I guess I could spare some time." Kat says sarcastically.

"We'll talk more later." She whispers to me as we follow closely behind Sam. I've never had a girl friend to vent with, it's different than when I talk with Elliot. I don't know what I did to deserve a friend like Kat.

I never realized how many cases of beer we go through until now. It takes us almost two hours to bring all the cases back and unload them into the storage. Kat and I pulled most of the weight since Sam gave up about half way through, blaming it on his old age and bad back. I'm bending down to grab the last box when I hear my phone ring in my back pocket and see a number I don't recognize across my screen. I hesitate because it could be one of those spam callers, but I notice it's an Arizona area code so I pick it up.

"Hello?" I say with uneasiness.

"Emory it's Andrew." I don't know how he got my number or why he's calling, but my grip immediately loosens on my phone as I hear how shaky his breath is on the other end. *Something is wrong.*

"It's Elliot, he's in the hospital. I'm texting you the address now, me and my parents are here." I don't hear much else after that, all I hear is a shatter followed by a high pitched ringing in my ears. The room feels like it's spinning, and I can't seem to remember where I am right now. My vision gets blurry, and a wave of nausea wraps around me like a blanket.

"Emory! What's wrong?" Kat's frantic voice is what snaps me out of my episode. My phone is on the ground, and so is the box of alcohol that was just in my hand which explains the shattering sound I just heard. I can't seem to find my voice as I try to speak. *"It's Elliot, he's in the hospital."* Andrew's voice blares in my mind repeatedly, getting louder each time I recall it.

"Emory you're scaring me who was that?" Kat shouts at me. I don't respond right away, instead I quickly start to retrieve all my stuff. *I have to get to him.*

"It was Andrew, Elliot is in the hospital. I have to get over there." I shout as I kneel down to grab my phone. I notice the screen is completely cracked, but I shove it in my pocket anyways since it's the last of my worries right now.

"Emory wait I'll drive you there!" Kat is by my side in seconds, and Sam doesn't pay us any mind as we both storm out. Either he already knows what's going on, or

209

he sees the look on my face and decides not to bother. Either way I don't care even if I get fired over this. We climb into Kat's car and she starts it up without even bothering to put on her seatbelt. I give her the address from Andrew's text and she makes a sharp u-turn before speeding off, swerving through all the cars that are in the way. With the way she drives we'll be at the hospital in no time which is fine with me.

"What did Andrew say? What's wrong with Elliot?" She asks frantically while honking at the cars that are moving too slow.

"He didn't say anything except that Elliot is in the hosp—"

"Move out of the way asshole!" She screams out her front window at the car in front of us. They seem to be going the speed limit, but that just won't do for her, or me at the moment. I'm still trying to process everything so I haven't let the panic settle in yet, instead guilt starts to creep in first. What if he's sick from being out in the rain last night? Or what if his asthma is affecting him because the kayaking we did? I don't know what I would do if something happened to him because he was trying to do something nice for me. I can't think about anything else right now other than getting to Elliot as quickly as I can. Thankfully Kat pulls into the hospital parking lot minutes later, and I jump out before she can even put the car in park. I sprint through the two double doors and approach a front desk clerk.

"I'm here to see Elliot Cortes." I haven't been able to step foot in a hospital since mom was sick. The horrid smell of strong cleaning supplies, the sick patients walking around, the somber looks in the waiting room, the stressed looks of doctors pacing the hallway, it all brings back memories I pushed into the back of my mind years ago. The panic is starting to trickle in now.

"Are you family?" She questions peering at me through her thick glasses. Her red hair is pulled back into a bun held with pencils, and she's obnoxiously chewing on gum.

"We're his sisters." I gesture to me and Kat who's stuck to my side like glue now that she's caught up to me. It feels disturbing to call myself his sister when I've made out with him, but I know they won't let me back there if I would have said I'm just his girlfriend. Am I even his girlfriend? *Focus Emory you've got bigger problems.*

She looks between me and Kat full of doubt. Her and I look nothing alike much less like Elliot, but she doesn't have to know that. She lets out a loud sigh and starts to write something on a sticker. It seems like she doesn't believe me, but she also doesn't want to deal with us which works for me. She hands us our visitor stickers with sass.

"He's in room 306." She grits out before returning to her typing on her computer. I grab Kat by the arm to drag her towards the elevators as soon as the words leave her mouth. "Nice going with the sister thing." She compliments. The elevator doors finally open after waiting for what feels like forever, and we make our way in. We stand in dead silence as I feel the elevator creep up floor by floor. I push back the vomit that wants to come out because my only concern right now is Elliot, I don't care about anything else.

"He's fine Em." Kat tries to assure me. *I just need to get to him.* The elevator doors swing open and I step through as soon as there is a big enough opening not even waiting for them to open all the way. I look left and right trying to read the small numbers on the doors in front of me, but as the panic starts to settle in more my vision starts to blur, and my ears have the high pitched ringing sound again. I feel a tight grip on my arm pull me towards the right.

"This way." Kat directs me in the right direction, and we pace quickly towards room 306 while passing nurses and doctors who don't pay us any mind. The dimly lit hallway gives me the creeps, it's like something you see in a horror movie. Thankfully I catch a glimpse of Elliots' parents, Andrew, and my dad sitting in chairs lined up against the wall in the hallway.

"Emory!" Emily shouts jolting out of her. She brings me into a tight embrace right as she approaches me.

"Thank you for coming." She whispers into my hair still holding on to me. Her voice sound so fragile and defeated.

"I'm so sorry this is all my fault." I say with regret. She lets go from our embrace to look at me with a puzzled expression. "What do you mean mija?" She asks.

"Elliot wanted to help me cross things off my bucket list this summer so we went kayaking, and we were in the rain last night, and now he's sick because of me." I whisper trying my hardest to hold back the tears that want to burst out.

"Oh Emory, it's not your fault, not one bit." She grabs my face and rubs her thumb up and down very slowly along my jawline. Her fingers are so cold that if I didn't already have chills from the nerves her touch would do it.

"Then what's wrong?" I didn't intend for my tone to come out so harsh. She looks back at everyone behind her, but they're all quietly looking down at the floor and not up at us. I notice the tears welling up in her eyes when she snaps her attention back to me.

"Emily what's going on?" I'm going to go fucking crazy if someone doesn't tell me what's going on right now.

"He's been asking for you." She jerks her head toward the door and walks away to join her husband who's still seated in his chair. Kat is sitting by Andrew now with her arm wrapped around his shoulders supportively. From her reaction to his name earlier I don't think they're on speaking terms, but knowing her even if they weren't she'd be there to support him no matter what, she's a softie for people who need consoling. I make prolonged eye contact with my dad, but all he does is give me a slight head nod towards the door in front of him, room 306. I was so anxious to get here and be with him, but now that I'm here, I'm almost scared to go in.

I take a deep breath, count to five in my head, and walk inside to see Elliot gazing up at the small tv in the corner of the room. He's got a shit ton of tubes in his arms, his skin is pale which makes the dark circles under his eyes more apparent, and the low beeping sounds of the monitor beside him make me want to vomit. I remember hearing the same beeping sound day in and day out with mom, until one day there were no more beeps. Even after she was gone I heard them in my sleep for months. I come back from my memories just in time to see his face brighten up at the sight of me.

"Ej!" He exclaims with excitement while trying to push himself up with shaky arms. He winces before I can rush to his side.

"Hey I'm here don't try to get up." I help him untangle the tubes that knotted from him trying to get up. I notice a saddened look is directed towards me as I focus on the task.

"Elliot what's wrong? Why are you in here? " He averts his gaze and fiddles with the tubes connected to his hand.

"Emory there's something I need to tell you." I sink into the uncomfortable chair next to his bed without saying another word, staring up at him with uneasiness. After a few moments of him not saying anything I entwine his hand with mine. It's not warm anymore…it's ice cold which makes me wince, but I don't let it go because I need the comfort right now, and something tells me that he does too.

"I should have told you a long time ago…I just didn't know how." *Thump thump thump.* I ignore my irregular heartbeat and only pay attention to him. "This isn't how I wanted you to find out." He grits out.

"Spit it out Elliot." I demand. My tone comes out rude, but the anticipation for his response is slowly killing me.

"I'm sick Em, I've been sick for awhile." His eyes are glistening from the tears that are gathered in his eyes.

"What do you mean sick?" A single tear trickles down his cheek and he looks like he's in so much pain. I notice I'm holding my breath as I wait for his answer.

"Lung cancer." *No no no no no.* Cancer has already taking too fucking much from my life, not Elliot. *Please, not Elliot too.* I swallow down the big lump in my throat. I'm on the verge of tears but I don't cry.

"How long is awhile?" I whisper.

"What?"

"You said you've been sick for awhile, how long is awhile?" I let go of his hand because I can feel the sweat building up on mine.

"Since before you got here." *Crack.* This time the cracking sound isn't from my phone falling to the floor, or a case of beer, it's the sound of my heart breaking into a million fucking pieces. There is no way Elliot wouldn't tell me something *this* big even if I was pissed at him when I got here. There's no way, I must of heard him wrong.

213

"Did I hear that right? You knew you were sick with cancer *before* I got here?" I try to mask the anger building up inside getting me ready to erupt. He doesn't say a word, he just nods his head silently and more tears trickle down his cheeks.

"I want to know everything right now, no more bullshit." I spit out with authority. My leg starts to bounce as I anxiously wait for him to speak up.

"Promise me you'll keep an open mind Emory, I don't want to lose you." He pleads. His face is red from all the tears he's wiping off, but I'm too pissed off to comfort him.

"If you don't tell me right now you're going to lose me anyway." He tries to grab my hand, but I move it away the second he reaches for it. I can feel my blood boiling with rage, but I need to sit this through and hear everything he has to say for my own sake.

"About six months ago I went for a check up because I wasn't feeling right. I thought it was allergies or asthma, but they did a scan and it showed that I had a tumor in my lungs." *Don't cry Emory, don't cry.*

"They said by the time they caught it, the cancer was spreading too fast, it had already started to move to the rest of my body. So that's when I asked my parents to get a hold of your dad so you guys could come here for the summer." *Oh my God.*

"So that's why I'm here? You knew you were dying and you felt guilty that I was pissed at you so you dragged me here for the summer?" I grit out. I've never been this livid in my entire life.

"It's not like that Emory, I wanted to see you before—"

"Before what Elliot? Say it. You wanted to see me before you died!" I scream at him so loud he flinches, but he stays silent.

"How long?" My voice is so low I'm surprised he caught it. The hitch in his voice tells me he knows exactly what I'm asking.

"They gave me six to eight months...six months ago." The rage travels to every crevice of my body before I jump out of my chair to walk to the other side of the room. I don't know what I'll do out of anger if he says the wrong thing from this point forward.

"Let me make sure I have this correctly…you could have died any fucking day while I was here and you didn't think to tell me Elliot?!" I scream loud enough that the people next door could probably hear me. "Elliot do you know how unfair this is to me? You've known you were dying for six months, yet I find out because you're in the hospital? What if you didn't end up here today? Would I have found out at your fucking funeral or what?" My chest is on fire as I shout at him, and I don't feel an ounce of guilt this time.

"There were so many times I was going to tell you but I—"

"But you didn't! How are you going to tell me you're in love with me, and the next day I find out that you're fucking dying!" I can barely get in full breaths, and I feel like I'm going to collapse at any second.

"I'm sorry Ej, there's more if you just listen."

"I wish I never came here this summer." I whisper. A look of pure devastation washes over Elliot's face. Honestly right now I feel like the old Emory…*numb*. His saddened look doesn't even phase me.

"Emory please you have to understand where I was coming fr—"

"I don't want to hear anything more you have to say Elliot. You told me you'd never hurt me again, but I guess just like everything else that was a lie right?" I spit out angrily before storming out the door. I hear it slam shut behind me, and finally let the tears pour out. Suddenly I remember that everyone is still outside the door so I pull back the tears, and wipe the evidence of emotion off my face. Everyone probably heard me screaming hence why all their expressions are paled. Then something dawns on me.

"All of you knew." The silence is deafening between everyone as they look to each other, waiting to see who's going to answer.

"Elliot said he wanted to tell you himself Em." Andrew stands up with his hands nervously at his sides. Kat is hiding behind him peering at me with tears streaming down her face.

"So you guys knew he was dying but still kept me in the dark." I say pointedly.

"Put yourself in our position Emory, we promised him not to say anything. We told him so many times to tell you but he just kept saying it wasn't the right time."

215

Emily speaks up this time. She can't even look at me anymore, that seems to be the theme for everyone today.

"I'll be at your house packing, I'm catching a flight back to LA." I announce while storming away. I feel a hand tighten on my arm only to look back and see Kat.

"Em please stay, you'll regret it if you leave and something happens to him." She pleads. Something else dawns on me, like a puzzle piece finally clicked in.

"How long have you known?" I ask. Her face drops before she answers. Everyone had me fooled, but with her for some reason the betrayal stings a little bit more.

"I just found out yesterday I swear." I let out a loud scoff out of anger. Everyone has been lying to me, and I was the only one kept in the dark. Kat barely met Elliot a couple months ago, and somehow she finds out he has cancer before I do? None of it makes any sense. I finally opened up to people, and once again I'm proven why I don't in the first place.

"So you lied to me today? You knew something was up with what Emily said to me and you still didn't say anything? You said you'd tell me if you knew anything, but you're just a liar like everyone else." I turn my back, but she yanks me back to face her again.

"Emory please you have to understand the position I was in, I promised Andrew I wouldn't tell you." She's sobbing through her words now. I've never even seen her sad, much less cry.

"That's all that matters to you huh? Is that the reason you became my friend? To get close to Andrew? Congratulations you got what you wanted." She winces at my words, but I don't feel any emotion what so ever as I witness it.

"Of course not please let's talk about th—"

"No!" I yell interrupting her. A few nurses peer up at us but then quickly go back to what they were doing.

"Just leave me the fuck alone, you guys at least owe me that much." I speak to everyone now, and she finally lets me walk away this time. I remember that she was my ride here so I guess I'll be walking home. It's about a thirty minute walk, but I figure it'll give me time to think about how much my life has went to shit in less than 24 hours. Everything is starting to add up now, like yesterday when we went kayaking.

"I can't do strenuous activity for more than thirty minutes."

"You have asthma?"

"Something like that." I replay our conversation and feel so stupid for missing the signs when I know them all too well from seeing mom go through it. More memories swarm into my head: him sleeping a lot more, waking up puking, the dark circles under his eyes, it's all coming together now. I blame myself for being so oblivious to it all and believing him when he said he was fine. I just started to trust him again and he proves to me why I didn't want to in the first place. There were so many times I could have figured out what was going on, but something happens to my brain when Elliot is around, suddenly I get so consumed in him I forget to use my common sense.

I'm pissed off, hurt, confused, and lost, all at once. My chest is tightening by the second from the immobilizing anxiety that's building inside. I haven' t had a panic attack since the day I found out about mom, and I'm suddenly faced with the same crippling emotions. My mind travels back to yesterday again, when dad tried to tell me Elliot had something to tell me, and of course the second he took me out in the rain I didn't care to ask about it anymore.

Elliot is sick.

No, he's dying.

How does a person wrap their head around the fact that the person they're in love with is dying, and you didn't even notice? I thought it was just the beginning for us, but it's the opposite. I feel like someone plunged a rusted knife into my chest and left it in. I grow more angry at the fact that he used up all his time to fall in love with me, and to make me fall in love with him when he knew he wasn't going to be around for much longer. How is this all fair to me? I receive weird looks from the people walking past me as they witness my mental breakdown on the side walk, but I don't pay them any mind. I hear brakes screech beside me but I keep looking forward. If it's Kat I have nothing to say to her, and if it's some random creep I just won't pay him any mind and he'll just drive away.

217

"Emory!" I hear my dad's deep voice exclaim from the car.

"If you're here to change my mind about going back to LA save it dad, I can't be here anymore." I don't stop walking, but he stays beside me in the car moving very slowly.

"Just get in the car, there's something you should see before you book that flight, and if you still want to go afterwards I'll buy the ticket myself." I stop abruptly to turn and face him, making him press aggressively on the brakes. I wipe off the dry tears with the back of my hand and walks towards him.

"Get your credit card ready." There is nothing he can say or do that'll convince me to stay, but I'll let him try.

CHAPTER TWENTY-SIX

I must of told my dad fifty times that this is a waste of time, but here I am waiting downstairs for this so called thing that's going to change my mind about going back to LA. He did say he'll pay for the flight if I still want to go after, so I guess it'll save me the money. I'm sitting on the couch looking up flights when dad comes down the stairs with a folded piece of paper in his hand. I didn't notice yesterday, but his hair that's usually jet black is showing streaks of grey in it now, I'm not sure whet-her it's from stress or old age. Now that we can stand to be around each other there are small things I've noticed about him, like how his mustache has little specs of a salt and pepper color now, or how now that he's older his eye color is lighter.

He sticks out the piece of paper out to me but I don't take it at first. I just stare at it with uncertainty, contemplating if this is even worth my time.

"You said you'd hear me out before you booked the flight." He says. I groan and snatch it from his waiting hands. A cold chill inches up my spine when I unfold it. *What the fuck? How am I holding this in my hands right now?*

"The day you told me to send it back I kept it instead. I figured one day you'd regret not being able to read it." His voice interrupts my racing thoughts. My fingers grip onto the piece of paper so hard I'm afraid it'll rip. I can't seem to control my breathing as my chest moves up and down in shallow breaths. *It's Elliot's letter.* The letter I bitterly told dad to send back when I received it in the mail three years ago. I look at it in my hands as if I'm looking at a ghost; in a way I guess I am. This letter is sixteen year old Elliot writing to sixteen year old Emory, both of those people are long gone. I never thought I'd see this again, but now I don't know if I want to read it or not. As if dad reads my hesitation he speaks gently to me.

"You know when I found out mom was sick I felt a lot of what you're probably feeling right now." I can't help but hiss through my teeth.

"Oh yea? She knew she was dying for months and didn't tell you?" I ask sharply. He's not the one I'm angry with, but he's the closest one here.

"No…but when we did find out she was sick I remember feeling so stupid because I felt like I should have seen the signs, maybe they would have caught it sooner if I did. I imagine that thought has entered your mind once or twice." He takes my silence as an agreement. "There was no way for you to know what was going on. I should have told you before we got here, or at least made you read the letter, but Elliot begged me to let him tell you when he was ready. I'm so sorry." He actually sounds like he's genuinely sorry.

"I keep replaying all the red flags in my head and how I should have caught them, especially after knowing what mom went through. Most of all I feel so stupid that I was the only one that didn't know. Maybe if I did I wouldn't have wasted so much time being pissed at him."

"I'm sure no matter what he's grateful for whatever time he has with you. I know I was grateful for the years I got with your mom." His face drops to an almost pained look.

"What was it like?" I instantly feel guilty for asking and making him relive all the painful memories.

"It was the hardest thing I ever had to do to see her go through that, and it hurt even more knowing I couldn't help her." I don't miss the hitch in his voice along with his inability to keep eye contact with me now.

"How did you do it? How were you able to watch someone you're in love with slip away and still have the strength to be there for them?" I'm trying so hard not to break as I say the words.

"There were days I just wanted to stay in bed and give up but I couldn't, because if she was going to keep fighting then so was I. Instead of seeing everyday as a day she was getting closer to…*dying*, I saw it as another day I got to spend with her." He looks off into the distance and a bright smile covers his face, I'm sure he's thinking of all the precious memories he has with her. Someday all the moments Elliot and I have will be just that, memories that I look back on when I'm missing him. He's not even gone yet and I feel like a piece of my soul is missing.

"Do you love him?" He asks. I nod my head without thinking twice about it. I'm so pissed off at him, but yet I still can't deny I'm madly in love with him. *What has my life came to*?

220

"Then my advice is to stay here with him, make everyday you have with him count." He reaches out and touches my hand for comfort. I missed having the comfort from a parent, I didn't even realize how much I needed it. I let a loud distressed cry flee from my throat.

"I can't! I can't watch him die! I'm not as strong as you dad. I can't stay here with him knowing one day he won't wake up, and I'll be left here trying to pick up the pieces of what's left of my heart. How is that fair?" My vision is becoming more and more blurry with all tears collecting in my eyes.

"You're right, you're not as strong as me Em, you're stronger. You know why? Because your mom was the strongest woman I knew, and a part of her is inside you." I close my eyes tightly trying to recollect my thoughts. *I can't do it.* Everyone gives me too much credit, I'm not strong.

"It's a gift you know, to find that kind of love so young, don't waste it Emory." Was this his plan? To guilt trip me into staying?

"I can't lose him again." Losing Elliot a second time would crush me completely, not even therapy could help this time. I went to a couple sessions a few months after he left when dad started getting worried about me acting out. The only thing I kept doing after the sessions was to count to five in my head and control my breathing when I feel like I'm getting overwhelmed, everything else went through one ear and out the other.

"The sad truth mijita, is either way you're going to lose him. Wouldn't you rather know you made the best of your time, or would you rather run away?"

"I can't." I whisper weakly shaking my head aggressively.

"Do you know why we named you Emory?" He asks.

"Uhm…because you thought it was pretty?" *Why are we talking about this now*?

"Well that was part of it. Emory comes from the British origin meaning strength." This is the first time I've heard this. I mean who looks up the meaning of their name anyway?

"What's the whole point of the this dad?" I ask tensely. He shakes his head tenderly as if he's contemplating whether to say something or not.

221

"Your mom had a miscarriage before you Em, she was so crushed I couldn't get her out of bed for weeks, but then we found out we were having you, and from that point on you made her stronger, and we knew you we're gonna be a fighter. Hence how we came up with Emory." This is new information as well, I never even knew mom was pregnant before me. It makes me sad that they had to go through that pain of losing a child.

"I'm sorry you guys went through that, and with all due respect, I still don't get how my name is significant to the situation." I say. I'm still not sold on staying, but he can't say I didn't try to hear him out.

"My point is that Elliot needs you more than ever right now, be strong for him, and don't sit here and tell me that you can't because you're strong enough for it I know you are, your mom and I named you Emory for a reason."

How can I be strong for someone else when I can't even be strong for myself? Also how does he expect me to be strong through all of this when I already feel like I'm going to crack at any given moment?

"I thought you weren't on board with me and Elliot? Isn't that the whole reason you came to talk to me yesterday?" I ask.

"That was before, when I knew he was keeping this from you, and before I realized how much he loves you. When Emily was taking him to the hospital this morning, he didn't even care about himself, he asked for you. He was worried if you were okay since you weren't here." *Fuck, why did he have to tell me that?* It's making it even harder to just walk away from Elliot.

"Read the letter Emory…" He pleads before getting up from the couch to walk upstairs. I feel like I'm sixteen again staring at the letter for the first time. My hands are aggressively trembling as I hold it still. A part of me wants to rip it up, go upstairs to pack, and pretend I never saw it, because if anyone has the ability to change my mind about leaving it's Elliot, and that's exactly what I'm afraid of. I can't stay here and pretend like everything is fine when I know every night when I go to sleep it could be the last time I see him. I knew mom was getting close when she was too weak to even get out of bed, she wouldn't eat, and when she did she couldn't keep anything down, it was brutal to watch. I can't go through that again. I want to remember Elliot how he is now, the energetic, happy, caring man that I still love more than anything. Why do I feel a tinge of guilt if I don't read the letter? Like I owe it to him or something? *Here goes nothing.*

Dear Emory,

I know I'm the last person you figured you'd hear from, but there's a lot to catch you up on and I have a feeling if I tried to call you'd just hang up on me so a letter it is.

It's been about two years since I've seen you, but I'd be lying if I said I haven't thought about you every single day since. Leaving you was the hardest thing I ever had to do, but it was something me and my family needed to do at that time, maybe now that we're older you'll understand that. The truth is we left because they found a cancerous tumor in my lungs when I was 13, and we had to move closer to a treatment facility. We tried treatments in LA for about a year, but they weren't working so mom found a facility here in Phoenix. The treatments actually worked since I'm in remission now.

I want you to know that you're the best thing to ever happen to me Emory, you're the reason I wanted to seek outside treatment and fight. When I was sitting through my chemo sessions all I thought about was you. Your smile, your hair that always smelled like strawberries, your freckles that you hate but I love, the kiss we had when we were fourteen. Even through all the pain, the thought of seeing you again someday made me push through it. In a way, you might have saved my life. I hope I get to thank you in person one day.

Since I'm confessing things I should probably tell you I still haven't kissed anyone else since I kissed you. Do you remember that day? How I told you I wanted you to be my first kiss? Well, in all honesty that was before we found the facility in Phoenix, and we noticed the treatments weren't working so I didn't know how much longer I had. I didn't want to leave this world without kissing you so I did, and if you were my first kiss, and my last then I'd be happy. You have to understand that when I didn't call or write after I left it had nothing to do with you Emory. You don't know how many times I wish I could have called you just to hear your voice, but I stayed away for you. I figured if you were pissed at me for not calling, it'd be easier than you being crushed if something happened to me. I seen how you were after your mom died and I couldn't be the one to put you through that again. I don't want you to think it's because I didn't care about you because God do I. I love you Emory. I've wanted to tell you that for so long. No matter what happens after this I'm so glad my parents chose to live in the blue house on Walsh Ave across from yours, because it brought me you. Whether you choose to forgive me or not I want you to know that you kept me alive, and for that I owe you everything. There were times I wanted to give up so bad and let the cancer take me, but the thought of never seeing you again hurt more than any treatments I had to endure. I understand if you need some time before reaching out after you read this, it's a lot to take in, but however long you need i'll be waiting. Whether it's 10 months or 10 years I'll pick up when you call.

   Til I see you again.   - Ej

The letter is now drenched in my tears, and the black ink is smeared, but I still manage to re read it about two or three more times. Everything hits me like a hundred pound weight on my chest. Elliot was sick when we were kids. *Oh my God.*

   He left LA to seek treatment and he didn't tell me to protect me, because he *loved* me even back then. I think back to fourteen year old Elliot, and how scared he must of been hearing he had lung cancer. You're supposed to be a kid with no worries in the world at that age, and he was worried about dying. *Fuck.* Picturing younger him going through all those chemo sessions, and taking all the medication makes my stomach churn with nausea. I was holding a grudge against him while he was fighting for his life, and I didn't even let him explain himself. I knew I was a shitty person, but this is a new level of shitty.

The day of my first kiss with him lingers in my mind, I remember it like it was yesterday. Now it turns out he kissed me because he thought he was going to *die* and he wanted to kiss me in case he did. It's all gluing together like a jigsaw puzzle in my head. He wrote this when he was sixteen when he was in remission, and I never opened it. I could have had three years with him instead of three fucking months. Not only that, but I wasted the first few weeks when I got here being pissed at him, when I could have been making the best of the time I had left with him. The reality of my mistakes pound a hole into my chest, and my legs buckle sending me sinking to the ground on my knees. I hear the loud impact of me hitting the floor in my ear drums. I let all my built up emotions out: the anger, the sadness, the regret. All of it comes out in one loud blood churning cry that has my dad running down the stairs in seconds.

"Hey it's okay, let it out mijita." He brings me into his chest and cradles me, and I let him for once. I let out another cry because I can't get the tightness out of my chest. I can't leave Elliot, not now. I already abandoned him when he needed me once. Seeing him get worse every day is going to crush my soul, but leaving him now would crush it a million times more. I'm going to spend every waking moment with him and create beautiful memories that I'll get to look back on for the rest of my life. I'm going to see every day I wake up to him as a gift just like I seen everyday with my mom as one.

I don't care if my heart is shattered into a million pieces when Elliot leaves this world, I have no use for it without him anyways.

CHAPTER TWENTY-SEVEN

When I finally build up enough courage to walk up to his hospital room everyone is still waiting outside in the hallway. The grim looks on their faces tell me more than their words ever could; that they're worried and scared, but I don't think any of them would admit it out loud. I know because among other things I'm feeling the exact same way. Emily notices me first and hesitates before approaching me, almost as if she's scared of what I'll do or say. I don't blame her from how I acted when I left. She places her cold hands on each of my shoulders and gives me a troubled stare, so I decide to talk first.

"What you said today, about how I'm the reason why he's here. What did you mean by that?" Her eyes are red and her mascara is smeared from crying so much. She looks so vanquished, but can you blame her?

"When Elliot found out the cancer was back he refused the treatment, he said that he didn't want to put himself through that again…" She chokes on her words but manages to continue.

"I begged him to do it but he said he was done fighting…then he found out you were coming." She tries to give me her best fake smile, but I can see right through it. I'm too familiar with them.

"He started the treatments again because he said he wanted to stay around long enough to see you again." *Of course he did.*

"I told him when I got here I didn't want to know why he left, I could have known then and I wouldn't have wasted so much time." My voice cracks, and I let out a muffled sob. I haven't cried this much since the night of mom's funeral, I forgot how exhausting it is to actually feel pain. Emily wraps her arms around me tightly and buries her face in my hair. She smells like mom, they always wore the same perfume which is Chanel number five. Being wrapped up in her scent feels like I'm being hugged by mom right now, it feels so consoling. We stand in silence together for a few moments until I hear her faintly whisper into my ear.

"I'm so grateful for you Emory, because of you I get to have my boy a little while longer." For her son being in the hospital she's not as distressed as you'd think she'd be, but I can tell she's just trying to be strong for her husband and Andrew.

"Emily, Miguel." I turn my head in the direction the voice came from to see a man in dark blue scrubs with a clipboard in his hands approaching us. His ginger hair is combed neatly into a side part, and his facial hair is neatly groomed. He looks fairly young, not too much older than me and he's already a doctor. Meanwhile I start college in a little over a month and I haven't even picked a major yet.

"Dr. Conrad what's the news?" Elliot's dad is now at Emily's side grasping tightly onto her hands as they wait for the doctor to speak. I haven't had any conversations with Miguel this summer, all I know is Elliot and Andrew don't seem close to him. Now that I think of it Elliot rarely ever talks about his dad.

"The scans we did show that the cancer has spread from his lungs throughout his internal organs. Soon it will go to his heart, I'm so sorry to say but he's in the end stage now. I believe he's only got weeks left, maybe a month." I don't hear much after that. *Is the room moving?*

He's only got weeks left.

He's only got weeks left

He's only got weeks left

The words echo in my head over and over again. I guess I'm in the right place if I have a heart attack. I thought I had more than a few weeks with him, I mean mom was sick for awhile before she passed away, but I guess Elliot *has* been sick for awhile, I'm the just the only one that didn't know it. I want to roll into a ball on the floor and cry, but I can't. I told myself I would be here with him until the end so that's what I'm going to do, the end is just a lot sooner than I was expecting.

"So what do we do from here?" Miguel speaks up since Emily is staring vacantly at her hands folded in front of her.

"Since he's nineteen he has the choice to either stay here under continuous care, or he can stay at home for the remainder of the time." The doctor speaks with a sympathetic tone, but his face is emotionless. He probably has at least a dozen of these conversations a day so he's become numb to it all. It must be tough to be the bearer of bad news over and over again, and to see all the distraught families after they hear such devastating news. I knew that doctors were heroes, but this definitely puts a new perspective on them for me.

"I'll give you some time to discuss it with him, of course we don't expect an answer right away. Again I'm deeply sorry. Elliot is a strong kid and I wish I could have done more for him." He sounds genuine as he speaks. I wonder if this is the doctor that's been handling his case since he was younger.

"You've done more than enough for him over the years, thank you Dr. Conrad." There's my answer from my previous question. He shakes hands with Elliots' parents before stepping away and peeking out a sliver of a smile in my direction.

"Can I see him?" I plead.

"Of course mija, if he'll listen to anyone right now it'll be you." Emily finally speaks up in a brittle voice. I walk past them silently to make my way to the room Elliot is in. *You can do this.* It took me so long to get the courage to do this, but now that I'm in front of his door I start to shake from all the nerves.

He's sound asleep when I go inside the room. I don't want to wake him so I just sit in the chair beside his bed and stare at him admiringly. It's already been the longest day and it's not even over yet. I went from having a normal day at work, to my whole world flipping upside down. I woke up this morning thinking I had so much time with Elliot, to finding out I only have weeks. I break down into a puddle of tears stifling my cries to not to wake him up.

I don't want to know a life without Elliot Jacob Cortes in it. He's a bright light for every single person he meets, only someone special could do that, and saying he's special is an understatement. My only regret is that I didn't realize everything sooner, I let years go by without talking to him when I could have let him explain himself on why he didn't reach out after he left. I wouldn't blame him if he woke up pissed at me for how I acted towards him earlier. I should have been more understanding of where he's coming from. That's the thing with Elliot, he was suffering and he still thought about me, he didn't want me to relive the pain I went through when I lost mom so he shielded me from feeling the same with him. He's so selfless, the world needs people like him. It's unfair how someone who has always put other people's feelings first was the one that was hurting the most. I can't imagine the things I'm going to have to do without him. He won't be there when I graduate college, get my first apartment, or when I get my first adult job. When Elliot told me he loved me a thought came into my head that he could be the one I spend my life with. The one I could walk down the aisle with one day, maybe even start a family with someday, but now the thought is gone. Everything is gone; the hope, the opportunities, the future I thought we could have, it's all leaving with Elliot, and so is the other half of my heart.

I hear him stir in the bed softly, and I look up at him already staring at me with sadness in his brown eyes. I don't have time to wipe the tears off my face before he does it for me. I don't even try to hide the somber look on my face.

"How bad is it?" He asks with his finger resting on my chin. His hand that's connected to the IV is so cold, it's not the same warm Elliot I've grown so familiar with, and that's hard to stomach, but this is what I signed up for and I'm not going to leave his side.

"Weeks, maybe a month." I tell him dryly. Guilt eats at me telling me I should have said it in another way, but I know he wouldn't want me to bullshit him. He's emotionless as the words leave my mouth so I try to change the subject.

"I read your letter." His eyes lighten up right away. A small smirk pokes out through the sadness, and it's the most beautiful sight.

"How? You said you sent it back."

"Turns out my dad never mailed it back when I told him to." He chuckles deeply leaving him breathless.

"Remind me to thank him for that." He says when he finally catches his breath. I hold his cold hand in mine, now it's my turn to let him feel my warmth. I usually don't run warm, but compared to his freezing hands I'm the damn sun right now.

"I want you to know that I get it Elliot…all of it. I get why you left, I get why you didn't tell me you were sick, I even get why you stopped taking your treatments. I just want to know why you thought I couldn't handle the truth?" I can see his eyes start to water already which triggers my tears, but I manage to keep them at bay for now.

"It wasn't that Em I swear, I just thought that *maybe* by some miracle I would beat it again just like the last time. I didn't want to believe that after I finally got you back I was going to end up losing you again, I couldn't believe that." He starts to cry uncontrollably as he chokes out the last words. I've never seen him cry like this, and it shatters my heart.

"Hey…you're not gonna lose me Elliot. I'm not going anywhere I promise." I assure him wholeheartedly. I already knew I was staying, but now it feels real as I say it out loud to him.

"Emory you can't. I already told you that I don't want you to stop your life to take care of me, it's not your job." He sounds so defeated, I don't know how to help him other than squeezing his hand tightly.

"I'm not stopping my life, I don't start school for a month and a half. I want to do this Ej, please let me do this." I beg. He still doesn't look sold on the idea yet. This is the first time I've called him Ej in five years, but it feels almost natural. "I don't want you to see me when I start to get worse Em."

"I don't care, I know you would do it for me." I know without a doubt what I say is true.

"Yea because I'm in love with you." He doesn't hesitate when he says the words. I cursed at him and said awful things to him an hour ago, but yet he still admits he loves me with no hesitation. I'd be lying if I said I didn't feel butterflies in my stomach right now.

"Yea, and I'm in love with you." It's not exactly how I wanted to tell him that for the very first time, but it felt like the right opportunity. He needs to understand how I feel about him, and that I'm not going to leave him when he needs me the most. He stares back at me with astonishment, and we're both so silent you can hear the ruckus going on outside in the hallway now.

"What did you just say?" His glare is so intense I could catch on fire from it. I can feel the sweat start to build up on my neck from how anxious I am. I've never said this to anyone before and I don't want to fuck it up.

"I am in love with you Elliot Jacob Cortes. I think I have been for awhile I was just trying to hide that part of me. That's why I'm going to be here for you until the very end. When you're too weak to walk on your own I'll be right there, when you don't want to get out of bed I'll stay in bed with you, and when you wake up feeling sick I'll be right there. I'm still going to love you as much as I do right now, maybe even more if it's even possible." I wipe his wet cheeks and leave multiple soft kisses on his hands as he sits in silence staring at me in utter shock. He starts to rub circles on one of my fingers while staring at it with longing. He speaks so low now, it's almost a whisper.

"I've dreamed about putting a ring on this finger some day Em. I wanted to beat this damn sickness and move to San Diego with you. I wanted to marry you when you were done with school, and when we were ready I wanted to have a family. I always pictured there'd be a little girl running around the house with her black hair, and freckles she got from her mom." I don't stop the waterfall of tears that run down my cheeks. Of all the things I was prepared to hear that was not one of them, but they're the most beautiful words I've ever heard.

"Don't forget a little boy with beautiful brown eyes he'd get from his dad." I don't know what comes over me to say that, but it feels so right coming from my lips. "I've been in love with you since I was eleven years old Em, it was the day I asked you if you thought I'd ever fall in love. Do you remember what you told me?" I shake my head because I can't physically say any words right now.

"You told me that I'll fall in love without even realizing it, that I'll get butterflies in my stomach every time I'm around them, and I'd want to be around them every single day. Truth is I fell in love with you before I even knew what love was, you don't even realize the impact you've made on my life. You're it for me baby, and I don't care if I've only got weeks left because if I get to spend them with you that's already more than I could ever ask for." We're both crying so hard we don't speak for several minutes. Just when I thought I couldn't love him more than I already do he says things like this. Honestly I never imagined myself falling in love. I never thought it was in the cards for me because maybe I was being punished for all the bad things I've done in my past, but being loved by Elliot is proof that there's some-one out there looking out for me, and if this is the only thing they'll give me in this lifetime I'll gladly take it.

In another life maybe Elliot and I have the fairytale ending where the guy finally gets the girl and they live happily ever after together, but although this isn't exactly one of those stories I'm going to make sure we still get to live a small version of *our* fairytale ending.

"I wanna go home Em." He says trying to compose himself.

"Ok. I'll have your parents talk to the doctor about you going home tomorrow, but for tonight you should get some rest, it's been a long day." I get up from the chair to walk out of the room, but I'm stopped when he softly grasps me by my wrist.

"Can you stay here with me?" I wasn't going to leave his side anyway, but he would have been hard to say no to if I was. I prop myself back in the chair, but I see him scoot to the edge of his bed and softly pat his hand on the empty side, staring at me with raised eyebrows.

"You're joking right?" *He's definitely lost his mind.*

"C'mon I like sleeping next to you, please?" He pouts his bottom lip out and attempts puppy dog eyes, I don't have the heart to tell him he sucks at it. "The nurses are going to be in and out of here we could get in trouble." *Now I'm worried about getting in trouble for something?* What has he done to me?

"I get a pass since I'm dying." He tries to joke, but I narrow in on him with anger flashing in my eyes. "Too soon?"

"You think?" I grit out. I finally give in and climb into his small hospital bed with him trying not to lay on the tubes he's connected too. He tucks us both under his thin blanket and I bury my face into his firm chest. I can hear his shallow breaths, but he comforts me by stringing his fingers slowly through my hair.

"I wish I didn't spend the first few weeks I got here so pissed at you. I wasted so much time with you when I could of bee—"

"Emory don't do that." He interrupts with a strict tone. "I didn't tell you I was sick when you were mad because I wanted you to forgive me because you wanted to, not because you felt like you had too. You also had every reason to be mad, so don't even think about feeling guilty."

"What if I never forgave you?" I ask with wonder.

232

"That was never going to happen because you of all people know I am nothing but persistent." He says, and I finally let out my first laugh of the day.

"How am I gonna live without you?" I mean to ask the question in my head, but I accidentally end up saying it out loud. I bring my fingers up to touch his face and begin gently brushing his cheeks while staring at him admiringly. I want to remember him this way; defined cheek bones, buzzed cut hair, dark facial hair that I thought I hated on guys but I love on him, his light brown eyes, warm smile. This is *my* Elliot. The Elliot who's been in love with me apparently since we were eleven years old, the man who sings Taylor Swift with me in the car, and kept a playlist of all my favorite songs even after all these years, the one who got a black truck because he knew it was my favorite color, and got a tattoo as a reminder of me after years apart. He says I made an impact on his life, but he has no idea how much of one he's made on mine. He made me open up my heart again, to trust people again, he helped me feel confident, and ultimately worthy of someone like him loving me.

"Are you kidding me? You're going to go off to college and do so many great things, I know it. You're going to meet someone who treats you exactly how you should be treated. I know this because after I'm gone I'll personally pick him out and send him your way, you'll know it's me who sent him because he'll have a strong unique name like...Easton or some shit." He says confidently.

"Easton huh?" I ask trying to enlighten him. I have no plans of being with anyone else after Elliot, but I know if I tell him that he'll give me a big lecture on how he wouldn't want that for me, but it's true; Elliot has had my heart since we were kids whether I realized it or not, and I don't plan on giving it to anyone else.

"Yup, and one day you're going to get married and have kids who will have the same spunky attitude as their mom, and you'll have the life you've always wanted. That's what I want for you baby. I don't want you to stop your life after I'm gone. Even on the days where it feels like you can't I need you to get up and live your life. Promise me." I nod my head silently, holding back the sea of tears that want to burst out again. I've done enough crying for the day.

"I promise." I whisper softly.

CHAPTER TWENTY-EIGHT

Elliot was persistent on not spending another minute in a hospital bed so his doctor discharged him this morning. I made sure he was okay and settled in before coming down to the bar. They assigned him a nurse who will be taking care of his treatments, and she'll be at the house later so I figured now was as good as a time as ever to do this.

"Hey Emory I wasn't expecting you. I heard about Elliot, I'm so sorry." Sam says when he sees me approach the bar. He continues to dry the cups used for cocktails while he looks at me with sympathy.

"Thanks Sam, I actually came here to talk to you. I wanna thank you for the opportunity you gave me, but I really need to focus on Elliot right now, so I can't work here anymore. I'm sorry about the last minute notice." I thought all last night about whether I should quit this job or not. I feel terrible for quitting on the spot when Sam has been a good boss, but if Elliot only has weeks left I don't intend on spending eight hours a day away from him.

"I completely understand Emory, and I respect that you came and told me. If you ever find yourself back in town and need a job the door is always open for you." He offers me a sincere smile, and I beam one back at him in return.

"Thanks, that means a lot." I will miss this place and the people I work with, and I'll definitely miss the money. If I have to live on campus for the first year in order for me to do this for Elliot, then so be it.

Out of the corner of my eye I see brunette hair I've become too familiar with pass by on the way to the kitchen. I haven't talked to Kat since I told her off yesterday at the hospital, despite all the messages and voice-mails she's bombarded my phone with.

"Hey." I say slowly approaching her.

"Hey." She looks down to avoid eye contact with me. I don't blame her for being short with me, I shouldn't have said all those things to her yesterday when she's been a good friend to me since I've met her.

"I'm sorry for what I said Kat, you didn't deserve it." I choke on the words as they come out. I'm not used to apologizing, but I fucked up and I need to fix this. I never thought I'd have a friendship I wanted to fight for other than Elliot, but Kat snuck her way into my heart and became someone really important to me, whether I say it out loud to her or not.

"Yea I did, it was fucked up not telling you, and trust me I wanted to when Andrew told me, but I knew something that big you should hear it from Elliot. I'm sorry baby cakes." She starts to whimper, and I move closer to hug her tightly. I sink into her embrace because honestly the hug was more for me than for her. I've cried more in the last twenty four hours than I have in my entire life and I'm exhausted.

"How is he?" She asks into my hair still not letting me go.

"He's okay considering, he's at home now. I just came to tell Sam I'm not coming back, I need to spend as much time with him as I can." She nods her head and pulls back from our embrace with a sympathetic look on her face. Having sympathy for me seems to be the theme for everyone lately, I hate it. "He's lucky to have you Em." I wasn't planning on making any friends while I was here, and the fact that I'm leaving with a friend like her makes my heart full.

"Thanks. I should go before the nurse gets to the house, she's showing us how to give him his meds."

"Call me?"

"I will." I go in for another quick hug, but she holds onto me a little longer than I wanted. *I still hate hugs.*

"I love you Em." She whispers. "Love you too." I actually mean it when I say it. Some people go their whole lives looking for a friend like Kat, and I was lucky enough to stumble across her when I least expected it. Along with Elliot, she's helped me learn to open up to people, and most of all she showed me there's are good people still in the world. I'm going to miss the hell out of her when I leave.

Elliot's nurse goes into grave detail with everyone in the house about his around the clock treatments, the side effects the medication will cause, her schedule of when she'll be here, and everything in between. She's really sweet and very patient with us when we ask her questions on everything we're unsure about. She looks about twenty five, her black wavy hair kinda resembles mine in a way, and she has the most beautiful blue eyes I've ever seen. She's leaning over Elliot to set up his IV bag when it hits me that I would love to do this; helping people and their families during their difficult time. Of course it'd be tough to see patients really sick, but I can picture myself doing this and being really good at it. Me having been through this situation twice in my life now, it'll be my way of turning my bad situation into something good. Seeing the way his nurse instantly knows what to do, and how to explain it to us is so admirable. *Holy shit did I just pick my major?* It took me almost the whole summer, and the love of my life dying to figure it out, but I guess I did. I know Elliot will be proud of me when I tell him.

The thought evades my mind that he won't be here to see me help people. It's taking some time to finally accept the fact that the time I have with him is limited. Of course I know it's going to happen, but sometimes I like to pretend that he's not sick, and that this is just a thing we have to get through for him to get better in the end. It might be a bad idea to think like that, but I'm still learning ways to cope with all of this all while putting on a strong face for Elliot.

"Any more questions before I head out? You have my work number just in case, but I'll be back tomorrow to check on him." The nurse says finishing positioning Elliot comfortably. I shake my head at her, while I stare expressionless at him in his bed. He has his head down, fully concentrated on the tubes stuck in his hands. The nurse told us he'd be pretty out of it most of today from all the different meds he's on. She must have noticed the longing on my face because she sits next to me on one of the nearby chairs.

"He's okay all things considering you know, if he gets nauseous it's completely normal considering how many meds he's on, and I'm a phone call away if you need me." She places a reassuring hand on my shoulder trying to comfort me, but it doesn't seem to help in the slightest.

"Is he your boyfriend?" She asks.

"He's a little more than that." We're far enough away from him that if we speak in low voices he won't hear us. I feel like calling Elliot my boyfriend is such a mediocre title for the way I feel about him.

"I've been in your position you know, my husband passed away last year from cancer, it was…rough to say the least, but I was there for him every single day until he passed away." I would have never guessed that she's been through the same experience, but that just shows you never know what's really going on in someone else's life.

"How did you comfort him through everything? All of a sudden I don't know how to be around him, or what to say." I confess. It's a thought that's been stuck only in my head since he came home from the hospital, but I never thought I'd say it out loud to anyone.

"Hun the best thing to do is treat everyday as if it's his last, and tell him you love him every chance you get."

"Is that why you became a nurse? Because of what happened to your husband?" It may have came out more straight forward than I wanted, but she doesn't seemed fazed by it.

"No, but it's the reason I transferred from being in the emergency room to being an at home nurse. With this I was able to take all my experience I had with taking care of my husband, and use it to help other families who are dealing with the same thing."

"That's really admirable." I admit. I see a proud smile cross her face.

"What's admirable is you doing this for him. Being there for him, comforting him, I promise it means the world to him." I stare back at Elliot to see him fast asleep now.

"Whats your name?" She asks sweetly.

"Emory."

"I'm Hope, nice to meet you Emory." I beam a genuine smile at her this time. I don't think she even realizes that she helped in more ways than one today. Her name is perfect for her because that's exactly what she's given me, *hope.*

I'm going to need as much as I can get to get through the next few weeks.

CHAPTER TWENTY-NINE

A loud sound of metal dropping and maybe even glass breaking startles me awake. The noise sounds like it's coming from downstairs. I reach over to check the spot next to me to find it empty and cold. Elliot insisted I sleep next to him since he says he can't sleep when I'm not next to him now. Fear springs into me at the realization making me jump up to sprint downstairs. He's not supposed to be out of bed by himself. My eyes widen with shock at the sight in front of me when I reach the kitchen. There is broken glass scattered everywhere across the floor, and the kitchen island is full of ripped up papers. I catch the sight of Elliot leaning over the kitchen table breathing heavily. I try my hardest to avoid the glass to get to him but there are tiny shreds everywhere, I picked the wrong time to run down here barefoot.

"Elliot what the hell is going on?" Seeing him like this startles me. As I search his body for any cuts from the glass I notice that he's trying to hide a bottle of whiskey behind his back. I recognize the bottle from his dad's stash that he keeps in the china cabinet in the living room. The bottle is almost completely empty, and I know for a fact it was full when it was behind the glass. I can't deal with a drunk Elliot right now.

"I was trying to get something to drink, but I couldn't grasp the cup." He whispers taking another swig from the bottle. I try to go for it but he moves it away from my reach too quick. I know he's going through a lot, but did he really have to turn to alcohol?

"You shouldn't even be drinking with all the meds you're on." I try to grab the bottle from him again but he brings it to his lips for a big gulp. I feel rage building up, but I try to repress it because I know this isn't him.

"Does it matter? I'm dying anyways." He's got a big smile across his face now, but it's not his usual warm sunny one, this one feels dark and ugly. He starts to break out into uncontrollable laughter that sends goosebumps down my arms, along with a feeling of uneasiness. All this mess because he couldn't get a cup out of the cupboard, he must be spiraling.

"What's with the papers ripped up huh?" I question with acid in my tone.

239

"I was tired of looking at all my medical bills my parents have to pay so I took care of the problem." His laugh turns sinister, and I'm trying my hardest not to slap the smirk off his face. *This isn't him Emory.* I have to keep mentally reminding myself of this because I'm starting to lose my patience and I can't do that with Elliot, not when he's falling off the deep end like this.

"Let's just go to sleep Ej, please." This isn't exactly what I signed up for when I said I'd be here for him no matter what, but I guess this is the ugly part of love that you hear about; the part that you have to accept when you really love someone. I try to lift him up from the table, but he's way too heavy for me. I grunt out of frustration trying to figure out how the hell I'm going to get him up the stairs in one piece. *Andrew.*

I leave Elliot sitting down at the table while I run back upstairs in a full sprint to Andrew's room. I'm surprised everyone else in the house isn't up with all the ruckus, but they must be deep sleepers or something, me on the other hand wakes up if I hear the wind howl outside. I don't even bother knocking on his door before I storm in and shake him awake. Before he opens his eyes I catch the sight of what looks like an almost empty pill bottle beside him on his dresser. It's too dark to read the label so I decide to let it go for now instead of jumping to conclusions. I can only deal with one Cortes brother at a time.

"Em? Whats wrong?" He asks looking up at me with squinted eyes.

"Come downstairs please, it's Elliot." I'm doing pretty good at holding back my tears because this isn't the time for that. He leaps out of bed as soon as I say Elliot's name and sprints out of his room leaving me in the dust. Sounds of things clashing plunges a queasy feeling into me just thinking of what Elliot is doing downstairs. When we reach him he's standing up now, and he still has the bottle in one of his hands, the other is pulling all the dishes out of the cupboard sending them straight to the ground in hundreds of tiny pieces. He's got the most wicked smile on his face I'm almost afraid to approach him, and by the way Andrew is stuck to my side he is too.

"E what the fuck is going on?" He shouts at his brother, but Elliot doesn't even notice. Andrew looks down at the ground at all the broken glass and lets out a grumble of annoyance before walking over to Elliot. He doesn't even try to avoid the glass since now it covers every inch of the floor.

"Elliot stop!" Andrew never calls him by his full name, he always just calls him E, so he must be scared. "You can't drink when you're on your meds what the fuck are you thinking?" He shouts.

"Why? Maybe I'll go quicker if I drink myself to death huh Drew? It'd be better for everyone don't you think?" Elliot says humorously. I feel the burn from the bile that's now sitting in my throat. *How could he even say that?* Does he really think the rest of us will be better off after he's gone? Does he have no idea how he affects all of our lives? He might want this to be over, but he's not thinking about how everyone else is going to feel after he dies. Emily and Miguel have to go on without their son, Andrew has to go on without his only sibling, and I have to go on without the other half of my heart.

"Elliot you're acting like dad give me the fucking bottle!" He goes for the bottle and pries it from his brother's hand with anger. I stand still as a statue at the mention of their dad. I never even knew Miguel drank a lot, that must be the reason why they both don't seem close to him. If their dad does have a drinking problem he has a good way of hiding it because I had no idea. I think Andrew forgot I was here otherwise I don't think he would have just said that. His weak eyes meet mine, but I don't say anything or move another muscle. He turns his attention back to his brother, and wraps his arms around his shoulders to walk him out of the kitchen. Elliot's eyes are bloodshot red and swollen as if he's been crying. I want to know what's going through his head to help him, but he can't even form a coherent sentence right now, much less tell me how he's feeling.

"I just want it be over Drew, I'm so tired of being a burden...especially to Emory." *Crack.* There goes my heart breaking again. He thinks he's a burden to me? Did I make him feel like that? Oh my god what if I did unintentionally? How can someone who is always there for everyone else be so against people being there for him? It hurts my heart that he thinks he could ever be a burden to me, or anyone else. He doesn't realize how loved he is.

"Emory loves you E, let's just go to sleep." The three of us walk up the stairs very slowly to try to avoid Elliot tripping over his own feet.

"That's the problem, loving me doesn't benefit anyone in the end." *This is just drunk Elliot talking, he doesn't mean any of it.* I assure myself mentally. Andrew throws me an apologetic look before walking into Elliot's room to prop him on his bed, and he's fast asleep as soon as he hits the mattress. I'll have to call the nurse to come earlier tomorrow to put his IV back in, honestly I don't even know how he pulled it out without me hearing. Andrew stares at him for what seems like several minutes in silence, he looks so *lost.* I know he loves his brother, he's always been so protective of him, but unfortunately this is one thing he can't protect him from. I imagine that however I'm feeling, Andrew feels ten times worse, he's just not showing it. I should know, I became pretty good at masking my emotions.

"Get some sleep Diaz." He says as he storms out the door. After he's gone and the house is silent again, I quietly crawl into the bed to curl next to Elliot who's snoring loudly now.

"I love you." I whisper quietly enough not to wake him before I finally let the tears spill out and fall onto the blanket, then everything turns black as I drift into a heavy sleep dreaming of the broken man next to me that I want more than anything to fix.

CHAPTER THIRTY

The kitchen is a wreck and I have to clean all this mess up before Emily wakes up and sees it. The last thing I want is for her to know Elliot did this, frankly I wish I could forget that he did this. It's only five in the morning, but after I cried myself to sleep last night I only slept for about twenty minutes, the rest of the time I spent thinking of ways to show Elliot how much he means to me. Nothing came to mind, but right now my only priority is to clean up every shard of glass from the floor before anyone else notices. I also notice that the bottle of whiskey is still sitting on the counter with only a few drops of alcohol left in it. I still can't believe he drank a whole bottle by himself, the most I've ever seen him drink was the one beer on my date with Nicholas. The ripped up papers scattered around the island catch my attention. From my understanding of Elliot's gibberish last night, they're his parents medical bills for his treatment. I grab the pieces and try to piece them together as best as I can to look at what Elliot is so upset about. He's already got so much going on he shouldn't have to feel guilty about his medical bills, but that just shows how selfless he is. He's terminally ill, but somehow he's still worried about how his parents are going to manage.

I piece one of the papers together somehow and peer at the itemized receipt with a total bill of $608.87 just for his medication. *Holy shit.* I had no idea his treatments were this much. Him saying he feels like a burden makes more sense now after seeing this, but it's far from the truth. His family loves him so much they'll do anything for him, I just wish he'd see that. How do I make him realize everyone around him is here to support him no matter what? There's no way to get through to him with how he's thinking right now.

"That's the problem, loving me doesn't benefit anyone in the end." His painful words keep playing in my mind on replay. Back at the hospital I thought we were on the same page about me staying and taking care of him, he never once mentioned him feeling this way about it. This must be what people mean when they say sometimes you have to put in more effort when the other person in the relationship can't. I have to be strong enough for the both of us right now.

I hear light footsteps come down the stairs so I hurry and toss all the shreds of paper into the trash can and go back to sweeping up the little glass that's left. I got distracted, shit. I hope that's not Emily because she'll flip out if she sees this. Maybe I can play it off like I broke a couple plates or something? *Yea, that's the plan.* I look up only to see Elliot staring at me with anger behind his vacant eyes. They're still bloodshot red, and now the circles under his eyes are almost black. We both glare at each other in complete silence. I can hear his wheezy breaths from here, along with my own jagged ones.

"You don't have to clean this up Emory it's not your mess." He doesn't move from where he's at, but I see his eyes scan the room at the damage he did just hours ago. His expression is full of remorse, and all I want to do is run up to him and hug him, but I can tell he probably doesn't want that right now. I feel my body pulling towards him like a magnet that's close to it's other half.

"I have to clean it before your parents wake up, I don't want them to see it." I don't want to say anything that I think will set him off since I know he's still in a vulnerable place.

"You're not gonna clean up my mess Em I got it." He finally approaches me and tries to grab the broom out of my hands but I snatch it away too quick. I get a sense of déjà vu since just hours ago we were doing the same thing with the bottle of whiskey. He exhales a big breath and I see his jaw muscles tighten out of frustration as he tries to grab the broom again, but I keep it away from his reach.

"Elliot go back to sleep you shouldn't be out of bed." I say sternly while bending down to pick up the big pieces of glass left on the floor.

"I don't want to be in bed I want to help you clean up." He persists. His tone is getting impatient but I ignore it, he must have forgot that I don't stand down easily either.

"You'll cut yourself on the glass, you don't even have shoes on." I point out.

"Fuck Emory just give me the damn broom I don't want you to do this for me!" He yells so loud I feel the vibration in my chest. The nurse said he'd get mood swings with the strong meds he's on so I'm trying not to take it personal, but it's hard not to when the person you're in love with screams at you when you're trying to help them. I'm usually one to scream back, but one of us has to stay calm, and Elliot is way past that. His face turns into a frown instantly.

"Baby…I'm so sorry I didn't mean to scream at you I just don——"

"It's fine Elliot." I interrupt him as I grab the broom from out of his hand, I didn't even realize he took it from me. I go back to sweeping as if he isn't just standing there looking at me with grief. I know I can't really be mad at him, but I also can't ignore what he did. Before I can say any-thing else to him he walks out of the room without another word.

What am I doing? I don't even know how to be around him anymore. Before he ended up in the hospital I felt like we were closer than ever, now it's like we both don't know what to say to each other anymore. I don't want to say the wrong thing and make him upset, and I'm sure he feels the same way about me. I need to figure out a way to get us back to *us* again.

I hope everything goes according to plan because this is my best idea yet. Elliot has been avoiding me since he stormed out of the kitchen this morning so I had to ask Andrew for his help to lure him out here. I don't know if he's angry, or if he feels guilty over what happened between us, but I'm hoping what I planned will help us feel connected again. I want so bad for us to get back to how we were before. I meant it when I said I wanted to treat each day I get with him as a gift, and hopefully after this he'll let me.

I have the whole bed of his truck lined with blankets, and luckily Emily was able to find a couple lanterns in the garage because it's starting to get dark out here. I also have a basket full of snacks, some sandwiches for the both of us, and water bottles. I figured a picnic paired with the beautiful stars in the sky should be romantic enough, I hope. I'm new at this relationship stuff so I'm not really familiar with how to do nice things for another person. I hear the front door close and I squeal quietly with excitement. I peer around the truck to see Elliot walking down the driveway with

Andrew right beside him guiding him so he won't fall down. It's dark enough out here that they can't see me yet.

"Drew what the hell are we doing out here? I'm tired." He complains loudly.

"Just trust me E." As soon as they get close enough Elliot's eyes widen at the sight of me, and his steps get slower and slower as he hesitates to approach me. Thankfully Andrew pulls him forward and gives me a salute before turning around to walk back towards the house. I feel disturbed as I watching him approach me with his hands in his pockets. I thought we were past the point of being nervous around each other, but he obviously is right now. Now it's my turn to fight for him and show him how much he means to me. He did it for me for weeks when I first got here.

"Emory what are doing?" There's no trace of anger or annoyance in his tone anymore so that's a good sign.

"Come here." I tangle our hands together to walk us over to the bed of his truck. As soon as he sees my setup that smile I know and love comes over his face.

"What is this?" He asks. I switch on the lanterns so he can get a better look at what I planned for us.

"You did this for me?" He asks in disbelief. I nod before helping him up to sit down on the blankets. I feel his hands trembling in mine so I hold onto them a little tighter than usual to support him.

"I've never done anything like this for anyone so if it's lame cut me some slack alright." I admit reaching into the basket to pull out the waters I packed.

"Are you kidding? It's perfect." He beams. I missed seeing his smile so much. I want to cry at the sight of it, and it's only been a day without it.

"What's this about Emory? I treated you like shit this morning you shouldn't have done this for me." *Since when is he the negative one? That's supposed to be me.* His smile is gone now and all I want to do is bring it back.

"I wanted to do something nice for you." I admit. I lean into him for a kiss, but he turns his head slightly so I end up pecking his cheek instead.

"What's wrong? I planned this picnic for us to spend time together and now you can't even kiss me?" I bite out angrily. He looks down at our hands that are still tangled together and lets out an exhausted breath before speaking.

"Drew told me you almost left to go back to LA after you found out about me. I think you should have went." An involuntary gasp escapes me, and I let go of his hand immediately.

"What do you mean?"

"You shouldn't have seen me like that last night, you shouldn't have to clean up my mess, and you definitely shouldn't have to deal with me screaming at you for trying to help me. It's only going to get worse from here Emory. I can't be selfish and let you stick around and watch me *die*." His voice croaks at the last word. I'm not going to let him give up on us, or himself. I know he's scared so he's trying to push me away; I know the pattern all to well because up until a few weeks ago I did the same thing.

"You should know by now that no one makes me do anything I don't want to do, if I wanted to be back in LA that's where I would be, but I'm not." It's not front page news that I don't let anyone control my actions. I'm here because I want to be here, point blank period.

"You don't get it Em."

"No you don't get it. I know what I signed up for when I stay—"

"I can't be a burden to you too Emory!" He shouts making me flinch. *There it is*. I was planning on easing our way into that portion of the conversation, but here we go.

"Is that what you really think? You think you're a burden to the people that love you?" I wonder how long he's been feeling this way.

"I know I am…My parents have argued about money problems from my medical bills since I can remember, Andrew never got to have a normal childhood because he had to take care of me while my dad was drunk and mom was out working her ass off to pay the bills. I can't take you down too." This man, the one who's always positive about every-thing you throw at him has always been just as broken as I am. Here I thought they were this perfect family who never had problems, but they're just as fucked up as the rest of us. Hearing that Elliot has always felt like a burden to everyone breaks my heart. How can someone who's made *me* feel so loved not know how much *he* is loved? To think he was always suffering in silence is a punch to the gut.

"Loving you isn't a burden Elliot, not to your family, and especially not to me. Loving you is the reason I believe there's a higher power somewhere out there looking out for me, because there's no other explanation as to how someone like me gets to love someone like you. You can push me away all you want, but I'm just going to push back ten times harder." I assure him with everything in me. Ironically enough he told me something similar the night he confessed his feelings for me. I can tell his eyes are welling up, and he almost looks *relieved*. He brings me close into a rigid hug, and I swear I can feel all of his emotions. I feel all his sorrow, hurt, regret, hope, and disappointment in this one hug, and I want nothing more than to take it all from him and put it in myself, consequences be damned.

"I love you Em."

"I love you too." God I love this man. If anyone deserves more time it's Elliot Cortes. If I could trade places with him I would in a heartbeat, because a world without Elliot in it is a disservice.

We spend the rest of the night stuffing our face with chocolate bars and staring up at the stars. It was a perfect night with the perfect man.

We're gonna be okay.

CHAPTER THIRTY-ONE

"Shit!" I hear someone scream from downstairs, followed by possibly something metal falling? I jump up from the bed in seconds to check if Elliot is in the bathroom again. Last night was a pretty hard night for him, he woke up six times to throw up, but at least this time he let me come in and help him. The bathroom in the hallway has no sight of Elliot when I push the door open which makes me instantly aware that he's probably the one making all the noise down in the kitchen. *Not again.* I push myself down the stairs taking two steps at a time and enter the kitchen nearly out of breath to see him placing two plates on the table peacefully. He walks over to the cupboard to grab two cups, and I notice his hands start to shake as he tries to grip tightly onto them so I decide to step in. I don't want a repeat of last week when he got mad he couldn't grip onto a cup and decided to break every dish in the cupboard. He ended up telling his mom what happened, she was mad for about five seconds before saying she needed new dishes anyways.

When he notices my presence he smiles warmly at me. I pretend not to notice that the circles under his eyes are even darker than before, and his usual olive toned skin is washed out, but he's still perfect to me.

"Morning baby." He beams before placing a wet kiss on my forehead. His voice has gotten more fragile over the past week, the nurse said it's normal but I can't help but miss the deep comforting voice I've grown so used to.

"Good morning." I take the orange juice out of the fridge and pour some into both the glasses.

"I'm sorry I kept you up last night." He sounds embarrassed so I immediately reassure him. "You say that every morning and I always say the same thing, you don't have to be sorry." I face him and place a quick peck on his cold cheek. I knew he only had weeks left when he came home, but I didn't exactly prepare myself to see him decline so fast. He's no longer warm to the touch, his skin tone is now pale white most of the time, and his cheekbones are no longer defined, more sucked in than anything else. Despite that he still has his beautiful smile, his chocolate brown eyes still make me melt as soon as I look into them, and being around him still makes my heart flutter more than ever. He's still my Elliot, that much hasn't changed in the slightest. *He turned me so soft.* He went straight through the blocks around my heart as if they weren't even there, and I haven't been the same since.

"Well I still feel horrible so I made you breakfast." He nudges his head towards the table where the two plates are full of food. A proud smile crosses over his face while I walk over and take a seat, and my heart leaps out of my chest when I notice what's on the plate. As if he senses my sudden change in emotion he speaks up. "Whats wrong?"

"How did you...uhm, how did you know?" I whisper. Sitting on my plate is a pancake with a smiley face, with strawberries for the eyes and cut up bananas for the smile, just like mom used to make me every birthday. I haven't even had regular pancakes since the day she died much less this. I know Elliot is trying to do a nice gesture, but something about seeing this in front of me makes me feel sad.

"I asked your dad what your mom used to make you for your birthday." He slowly moves to take a seat next to me to interlock our fingers.

"My birthday isn't for weeks." I say warily. My birthday isn't until August 24th, he should know this. I'll never forgive him if he forgot my birthday.

"I don't know if I'll be here by then Em, and I wanted to do something special for you while I can." *Fuck.* His words hit me like a ton of bricks fell on top of my head. It's all too much right now, with being surprised with mom's famous birthday break-fast, to Elliot making me realize he's probably not going to be here for my twentieth birthday. I stare back at the food laid out in front of me and my eyes start to well up with tears without me even realizing it.

"Oh god I'm sorry baby I should of asked first I'm so stu—"

"No it was really nice what you did, I just wasn't expecting it. It just reminds me of when I would wake up every birthday and the house would smell like her cooking, and her and my dad would be dancing around in the kitchen..." I stop myself before I break down in a puddle of tears as the memories play back in my mind. Elliot brings his hand to cup my cheek and presses his forehead to mine.

"You don't have to say anything else, I'm so sorry."

"It's fine." I whisper wiping the few tears off my face with my shirt. I hear him let out a prolonged breath before he speaks up.

"I don't have many lectures left in me so I need you to listen to me." He chokes on his words but pushes past it. *Shit, hold it together Emory.*

"You can't run away from your past forever, all those memories of your mom aren't things you should avoid Em. I know it hurts to think about them, but if you think about it, the pain from her being gone is a reminder that she was so special to you. Grief is the only reminder that you loved her so much."

"Yea she was pretty great..." I say softly. I've always tried to avoid any conversations that involve my mom, not because I didn't want to talk about her, but because it hurt too damn much to remember that she isn't here anymore. I've steered clear of everything that reminded me of her to avoid the pain the memories came with. I boxed up all her clothes, and all the photos the day after her funeral, and I haven't spoke about her since; until dad brought her up last week. Maybe Elliot is right about running away from my feelings, I can't do it anymore, it hasn't gotten me far anyway. Opening up to him seemed to work out well for me so maybe I can do the same for mom. So I do the only thing that feels right and pour syrup on my pancake and take a bite of it with the strawberry and banana. The sweetness coats my tongue, and I feel like I'm six years old again eating this with mom next to me as she steals strawberries off my plate, they were her favorite.

"Thank you." I tell him. *What am I going to do without him?*

"So since this is my early birthday breakfast do I get a gift too?" I gloat trying to lighten the mood.

"Soon." His smile fades and a frown takes over before I can question him more.

"Whats wrong?" I take another bite of food as he hesitates to answer. How did I go this long without pancakes? They're so good. *Okay focus on Elliot, food later.*

"I don't want you to avoid everything that reminds you of me when I'm gone like you did with your mom. I know that sounds selfish, but I want you to want to remember me Ej, not push me in the back of your mind to avoid the pain." His breath hitches and I put my fork down to reach my arm across the table to grab his hand. I gently rub my thumb across his and I feel my chest tighten at the thought that he thinks I wouldn't want to remember him.

251

"Elliot Jacob Cortes…you are the love of my life. I'm going to remember you everyday until the day that I die. You take up every thought I have, every good memory of mine has you in it, everything around me is you. I promise I'll never forget you, even on the days it hurts to remember." We're both sobbing now while gazing into each other eyes. I've never been so sentimental with anyone, but I knew if I didn't tell him that now I would have regretted not saying it all. He wipes his face with the back of his hand and starts to get up out of his chair. His arms start to shake vigorously as he tries to pull himself up, and I move to help him but he slowly shakes his head.

"I got it, but you can do me a favor by having this dance with me?"

"What?" I ask in confusion. He bows in front of me with his hand out like princes do to the princesses in movies. I'm still so confused until I hear music playing. I look around hesitantly, but I grab his hand anyway and he pulls me up against his hard chest.

"Elliot what are we doing?" We start to sway slowly, and then I finally recognize the song that's playing. Jessie's Girl by Rick Springfield starts to play from his phone, and a bright smile creeps onto my face. I used to love this song when we were kids, but I never admitted to my parents that I actually liked some of the cheesy 80s' music they'd dance too. He takes my arms and puts them over my head edging me to dance while he sways his body to the beat of the song. My stiff dance moves loosen when I see him having fun and hear his laugh echo through the kitchen, it's the most beautiful sound I've ever heard. We're dancing around the whole kitchen while the song plays, exchanging small kisses when we pass by each-other. Even Winston finally wakes up and trickles in the kitchen spinning in circles around us and wagging his fluffy little tail. Suddenly it hits me that I found a love exactly like I wanted as a kid, the kind of love I witnessed growing up. The kind where you wake up everyday grateful you get to experience it, the kind that caught me off guard and consumed me in the best way. Even if I only get to experience it for a short while, it's more than what most people get. I admire Elliot dancing around with Winston with the biggest grin across his face, and I know this is definitely another memory I'll remember forever.

CHAPTER THIRTY-TWO

"Emory!" It's pitch black in Elliot's room but the door is open which is letting the light in the hallway come through from the bathroom. My heart starts to pound so hard I can feel it throughout my entire body as I race to Elliot. I can already hear the sounds of him hacking so I go into full panic mode and swing open the door without knocking. He's laid out in front of the toilet covered in sweat, white as a ghost. I try to put on my bravest face as I rush over to the sink and cup my hand under the water to collect and splash onto his face.

"Hey it's okay." I whisper to him as I run back and forth from the sink to the toilet where he lays there almost lifeless.

"No it's not okay Ej, none of this is okay, I just want it to be over." His voice sounds so frail it hurts my heart to hear him this way when he's the one that's been keeping me sane lately. Every night this week we've been in this same position, and he always says the same thing 'I'm fine, let's go back to sleep.' Today is not the case though. He's giving up, I can feel it, but I know he wouldn't give up on me, so I can't give up on him.

"Hey look at me." I say softly grabbing his chin to face me. This angle lets me get a good look into his eyes, they're still the brown color I love, but now they're glossy and bloodshot red.

"You don't get to give up Elliot Cortes you hear me? I'm not done annoying you yet. Please keep fighting, I know it's selfish for me to ask you that but please...I need you." He wipes one of my tears falling down my cheek with his thumb.

"I'm sorry I said that. I'm just tired, and I'm *scared* Em." He says sobbing uncontrollably into my chest. I wrap my arms around him as tight as I can, wishing I could protect him from all the pain, the fear, and most of all, from the inevitable.

"I know, me too." I whisper into his ear truthfully.

"I want you to promise me something." By his tone I know what he's about to say is going to shatter me, but I listen anyways.

"Promise me that you won't close yourself off to someone else. I need you to move on after I'm gone."

"Elliot stop I —" I try to interrupt him but he cuts me off sharply to continue. "No Em I need to say this." He says slightly out of breath. As hard as it is I nod silently and listen as he continues.

"I want you to fall in love and be happy, and to actually *live* Emory, don't shut down and push everyone away again, promise me." I hesitate before answering. We had a similar conversation the day he was in the hospital, and I knew then I never wanted to fall in love after Elliot, because how could anyone ever compare to him? He's given me enough love to last a lifetime in the small amount of time we've had together this summer. So as much as it hurts, I decide to lie to him.

"I promise." If he knows I'm lying he doesn't show it. He looks at me with admiration and my heart starts to flutter the way it only does around him.

"You know I used too be so mad at the universe, or whatever is out there, for only giving me nineteen years when worse people have gotten more, but then I think it can't be so bad since out of billions of people it gave me you, and I'll spend everyday until I'm gone thanking it for that." *Me too.*

"I wish we had more time." I admit. I've never said it out loud to him before.

"Me too baby, me too, but the way I see it, if the universe brought us together once it'll do it again, and that time I'm never letting you go, and we'll have all the time in the world. I promise I'll find you in the next lifetime, and every one after that." I'm done trying to hold back my tears, I'm full on sobbing on the bathroom floor now. We don't say anything after that because we don't need to. Frankly I'm not ready to say goodbye to him, so I won't do it now.

CHAPTER THIRTY-THREE

Elliot and I have been spending as much time as we can with each other over these past few weeks. We finished all ten seasons of Friends at Elliot's request, but the agreement was that if anyone asks, it was mine. He swears he didn't like it but I caught him laughing at all the jokes. Him and Andrew finished teaching me a few lessons of self defense. Elliot was too weak on some days so Andrew did most of the instructing while Elliot was there just to watch and give moral support. He even helped me write the email to my counselor on deciding my major, now I have my schedule all set up for my classes that start in a couple weeks. We also had a lot more pancake breakfasts, danced in the kitchen just like my parents did, took Winston out for walks almost every morning when he was feeling up to it, and we talked about everything you could possibly think of. He even taught me a few things about work-ing on his truck, he finally got it running again. It was a little version of our forever.

Elliot is next to me sleeping still, last night was another pretty bad night. We spent half the night passed out in the bathroom next to the toilet, and the other half of the night was spent with him crying in my arms. Not being able to help the person you're in love with when they're in pain is something I wouldn't wish on anyone.

I decide to use this time while Elliot is still fast asleep to go downstairs to feed Winston, and see if my dad is awake to catch up with him. I haven't really spent too much time with him since we came home from the hospital, but this time it's not because I want to avoid him it's just because I've been so occupied with Elliot. Now that we're on better terms a part of me does feel bad since I won't be seeing my dad as much once I go off to college, but it is a relief that he has someone now and he won't be all alone. When I get into the kitchen no one is in sight unfortunately. I pour some food into Winston's bowl and place it on the ground for him to eat. I've done a lot of thinking about the situation with Winston when I leave. Since I don't have much money saved up I'll have to live on campus at least for the first year of classes until I can get my own place, which means Winston will have to stay with my dad for the time being. It breaks my heart because I've grown so attached to him, and he's some-thing that reminds me of Elliot so I'm going to need him more than ever.

My phone in my hand starts to ring and Kat's name pops up on the screen. She's called a few times this last week to check up, I'll admit that on some days I'm too exhausted to tell her everything that's going on so I don't pick up. She's been trying to get me to leave the house, but I'm always too afraid something will happen while I'm gone so I've declined all her offers. I've been such a bad friend lately, but I'll have to make it up to her before I leave, who knows when I'll see her again.

"Hey." I greet.

"Hey baby cakes, just wanted to call and check up on you." Her voice is less energetic than usual which today, I appreciate. "I'm fine." I lie. *I'm a mess.*

"Don't bullshit me Emory Diaz you've never been good at it." I can fake it with everyone else but her and Elliot.

"I'm not fine." I hear my voice crack but I push back the tears that want to fight their way out. I don't think I have much tears left in me.

"I'm coming over." She says.

"No it's fine, I'm just waiting for Elliot to get up and I'll be with him most of the day, I'd end up accidentally ignoring you." I already feel like a horrible friend again.

"Great so I have until he wakes up to hang out with you, I'll be over in five." The line goes dead before I can protest. If anyone can't take no for an answer it's her so I can't really be surprised. Just as I start to head out of the kitchen to get dressed Andrew is in the doorway looking just as restless as me.

"Hey." He whispers before passing me to get to the fridge. His eyes are swollen and red as if he's been crying but I pretend not to notice, guys get a little weird sometimes when they talk about crying.

"Hey." I reply back. I start to walk out but the sound of things clattering against each other followed by Andrew's scream sends chills up my spine and stops me in my tracks.

"There's no fucking orange juice!" I don't think I've heard him scream this loud before.

"Your mom hasn't had a chance to go shopping." I say gently, trying not to anger him more. Truth is everyone in the house is too scared to leave because we're afraid something will happen with Elliot while we're gone.

"Fuck!" He yells again, but this time he slams his hand flat on the countertop which sends a cup flying to the floor shattering into a bunch of tiny pieces. I flinch and step back to avoid the glass on the floor. If these brothers are going to get in the habit of breaking dishes I'm going to have to start wearing shoes when I come downstairs. Andrew doesn't move an inch, he has his head buried in his chest while his arms are stretched out in front of him bracing the counter. I hear a low gut wrenching sob come from him, but I don't approach him yet.

"I take it this isn't about orange juice." My lame joke gets a small laugh out of him, but it's followed by his hysterical crying.

"It's not fair Emory. My brother is the best of us, he can't die..." Sounding defeated seems to be the theme around here lately, but some-thing about seeing Andrew like this tugs something at my heart. I've never seen him cry, and honestly I don't really know how to react. I hesitantly approach him and wrap my arms around his limp body, and he begins to sob into my shoulder. He's got at least one hundred pounds on me so keeping him upright is an obstacle but I manage. "I don't know what I'm going to do with him Em." I can barely comprehend him through his words blending together, but that I got. *Me either.* Elliot affects everyone he meets in the most beautiful way that we all can't seem to see a life without him, and knowing Elliot that's exactly how he wanted to live. My mind goes back to when I planned the picnic for me and Elliot and he told me Andrew had to take care of him when his dad was too drunk and his mom was working. This guy has always taken care of his little brother as if he was his own child, and now he's going to lose him. Me being an only child I'll never understand the pain of losing a sibling, but seeing how close Andrew and Elliot are gives me an idea of just how much it's going to affect Andrew when he's gone.

Elliot hasn't gotten out of bed all day, it's unsettling seeing him this way when he was always up and moving before the sun was up. After I spent some time with Kat earlier, I used up some of my day making food for Elliot, then I helped while he threw it all up. We rewatched a few episodes of Friends, even Hope came over to change his IV bag and made sure he took his meds. Her and I talked for a little bit and I told her that she helped me realize I wanted to do this for a living after college. She was nice enough to give me her personal cell number to have if I ever needed anything.

I settle Elliot in bed before I climb in and let my exhausted body sink into the mattress. I feel him tilt my head towards him before he kisses me deeply. His body is freezing cold, but the warm feeling I get in my stomach when I kiss him is still there. When he pulls away a feeling of emptiness overcomes me.

"What was that for?" I ask curiously. It's not like he needs a reason to kiss me but it caught me off guard.

"Just like I wanted it…you were my first kiss, and my last." *No.*

"I love you so much Emory." He whispers when I don't say anything. I suddenly feel my chest collapse in so I can't form any words.

"Don't say goodbye yet." I plead. No tears are coming out because my sudden panic is the only thing I can feel right now.

"Remember what you promised me." He whispers. *No no no. Please don't say goodbye yet, I'm not ready.*

"I love you Elliot." I can't say goodbye so I won't. Tears are streaming down my face like a waterfall. I thought I had no more tears in me to shed, but I guess they were waiting for this moment right here to come out.

"Andrew! Emily!" I scream as loud as I can and hope they can hear me because my body is too frozen to go get them. I hear rushed footsteps coming towards us and everyone comes parading into the room, but I can't take my eyes off Elliot. Everyone's devastated expressions tell me they already know what's going on which thankfully saves me from explaining it. Andrew rushes to his side first and Elliot tries his hardest to smile.

"We had a hell of a time bro." Elliot says as cheerfully as he can to his brother. I catch a glimpse of a single tear rushing down Andrew's face as he looks back at him. I can tell he wants to let more tears spew out but he doesn't want everyone to see. *Poor Andrew.*

"Yea we did. I love you little brother." He replies through gritted teeth trying to put on a strong face.

"I love you too. Remember what I asked you to do." Elliot whispers bringing his forehead to touch Andrew's. They exchange prolonged eye contact before they break away with swollen eyes. "I got you."

"Just like always." Elliot whispers to him. He steps away to let his mom approach him while I move to let his dad come on the other side of him. I definitely see their dad in a different way now after hearing what he's done, so I try to avoid him more than I already have. Whatever they both say to their son I don't hear because all I hear now is the loud ringing in my ears again. The room seems to be getting smaller and smaller, and my chest is getting so tight it feels like it's going to tear open. My dad notices my full blown panic attack and places his hands on my shoulders telling me to take deep breaths and count in my head. All I hear is his voice echoing, it sounds like it's a million miles away as the room starts to spin. The breathing technique might work in other situations, but not for this kind of heartbreak. It feels like someone plunged a jagged knife into my chest and keeps twisting it deeper and deeper. I can only get out short breaths, and I faintly hear Emily sob into her husband's chest as they walk away from Elliot. I rush to go to his side again and thankfully he's still conscious, but barely. His breaths are getting more labored by the second. The tears haven't stopped streaming down, and my body is tired of fighting them off so I don't.

"I'll see you soon." He says weakly while beaming his smile at me, the one that's made me melt since we were kids.

"I'll find you in the next life time." I whisper back. The same words he told me that night we sat on the bathroom floor.

"Not if I find you first." I see his chocolate brown eyes one last time before they close. His smile still remains until that too slowly fades away.

259

"Elliot." No reply. *Fuck.* "Elliot!" I shout louder and shake him a little harder this time. *Fuck.*

"Emory…he's gone." I feel Andrew come up behind me and grip onto my arm to pull me back. *Please don't leave me.*

"Baby!" I try one more time, but when I don't get a reply my body goes limp. *I love you.* I don't collapse onto the floor because Andrew catches me before I fall. He pulls me into his chest and I can't stop the loud sobs that are escaping my throat. I'm crying so much I can't seem to catch my breath in between whimpers. The sounds I'm letting out are something between a sob and a blood churning scream. The only pain I can compare this too is if someone digs into your chest with their bare hand and pulls your heart out, but this hurts a hundred times worse than that.

Goodbye Elliot.

CHAPTER THIRTY-FOUR

I almost didn't go to the service today. I got dressed, put make up on to cover the puffiness in my face from all the crying, and I stood in front of the mirror for twenty minutes convincing myself not to go. I kept getting flashbacks of my mom's funeral and all the hugs from strangers. All the times I heard 'I'm sorry for your loss' and I didn't want to go through it again, but I felt like I owed it to him.

In the end I'm glad I went, it was a beautiful service. I didn't say a eulogy. How is someone supposed to sum up how amazing Elliot was in a small speech? You just can't. Plus I'd like to think that however we felt about each other is only between us. Just as I suspected, a lot of people attended; Sam showed up, it was the first time since he opened the bar that he closed it for the day, some friends Elliot made in high school, Cal the gatekeeper from the lake, Hope, I even thought I saw Stef wiping tears away from the corner of my eye. Kat thinks I should have told her to leave, but today I have no interest in talking to anyone I don't have to. I didn't cry as much as I thought I would, but not because I wasn't sad, because I know he would have wanted me to be strong today. As the day goes on it gets easier and easier to ignore the pain, nod my head and smile at everyone who comes up to me. The real pain will start everyday after this when I have to go on without him.

Everyone came back to the house after the service for the reception, but I skipped out on it to start packing. I leave for San Diego in a few days and I have nothing ready since I've been so preoccupied with helping plan the funeral. As I'm on my tip toes trying to get stuff off the shelves of my closet a black box comes flying down and opens at the impact from the floor. A numbing pain runs through my entire body as I see the white daisies all over the floor, the flowers I kept from when we were kids. At the very sight of them my heart shatters into a million pieces. It wasn't long ago Elliot found them and I told him about my tattoo and he told me about his. How am I supposed to do this? How am I supposed to go on without him? *I can't do it.* I go to pick them up from the floor, and I notice all of them are brown and wilted now, they look so *sad*. I feel the exact same way; wilted from not having Elliot around to bring me back to life anymore. He was the light in all my darkness, he took all the light with him, and now I'm left back in that same darkness he tried so hard to pull me out of.

I hear a light knock on my door and I quickly wipe my face out of habit even though there are no tears on my face this time. Andrew is standing on the other side of the door in black dress pants and a white button up shirt with his tie loosened. He has a box in one hand and the other hand in his pants pocket.

"Hey." I say with my arms folded across my chest staying in the doorway.

"Can I come in?" He asks looking down at the box avoiding eye contact with me. We barely exchanged words at the funeral. I think we both know there's nothing the other can say that will make the pain go away. I nudge my head in the direction of my bed and he moves past me to take a seat. "How are you?" He starts to pick at his nail beds nervously, still not looking at me.

"Fine." *It's a lie.*

"Same here." *That's a lie.* "So what's up?" I ask tightly. I don't want to be rude, but I don't really feel like conversing with people today. He exhales loudly and slowly opens the box before pulling out an envelope and placing it in my hand. I look down at it to see it has 'Ej' written on the front, and my heart sinks all the way down to the floor at the sight.

"What is this?" Only one person called me Ej. No one else even knew about that nick name, it was only *our* thing.

"A few weeks before he died, Elliot put some stuff together and asked me to give it to you after his funeral, he wanted you to read the letter first and then open the box."

"I can't." I shake my head and try to give the letter back but he doesn't move a muscle.

"I'm not going to make you open anything if you don't want to, but my brother loved you so much Em, and this was his last way of showing you just how much he did, so I think you want to open it." He leaves to walk towards the door without saying anything more. Before he grabs the handle to walk out I grab his attention.

"How does someone move on from someone like him?" I didn't plan on asking anyone the question that's been hanging around in my head, it just sort of came out.

Andrew has always seemed like a big brother to me so it seems only right he's the one I feel the most comfortable with asking the question to.

"My brother was the best person I've ever known Emory, those kinds of people become part of you and stay with you forever, so to answer your question...you *don't* move on, you just learn to live with the pain that comes with losing them."

"He loved you too you know." I want him to know how much Elliot admired and loved him. "I know." He gives me a tight smile before reaching for the door handle again.

"Hey Andrew." I call out to get his attention again. He exhales deeply and turns around to face me again.

"Take care of Kat while I'm gone ok? She may hate your guts right now but give her time, she's worth it." Kat informed me that she wasn't on speaking terms with Andrew at the moment, despite him trying to get on her good side again. I didn't ask why they stopped talking in the first place because it didn't seem like she wanted to talk about it. Their moment at the hospital was just her comforting someone who needed it, but she assured me it meant nothing to her. I know she was lying. Apart of me feels like there's something else going on with her that she's not talking about that might be holding her back.

"Don't worry Diaz, something tells me it's just the beginning for me and Kat." He lets a smidge of a smile peak through before finally walking out of my room.

The brown box with the lock on it sits on my bed tempting me, along with the envelope in my hands that feels like it's weighing my whole body down. On one hand I want to see what he left behind for me, but on the other hand I don't know if it'll make moving on easier or harder for me. I exhale deeply and gather up the courage to rip open the letter. I owe it to him to hear what he has to say. I don't get through the first sentence without shattering into a thousand pieces.

Dear Emory,

I don't even know how to start this letter but here it goes. If you're reading this it means Andrew gave you this after my funeral, he always did follow

263

through for me. I want you to know that these past few months with you have been everything I could have asked for. Even when you were pissed at me, knowing that everyday I got to look at you was the greatest gift. Thank you for giving me a chance to love you, and thank you for giving me the kind of love people only dream about. You gave me the kind of love in 2 months that people go their whole lives looking for, and for that I could never thank you enough. Some people go their whole lives looking for their soulmate, and I was lucky enough to have found mine when I was nine years old. I love you so much Ej, there wasn't enough time in the world to show you how much I do, but hopefully this letter and what's in the box will show you a glimpse of it. I want you to open the box now and pull out the envelope with the #1 on it and then come back to this letter.

I can't see anything through all the tears in my eyes, but I manage to move my shaky hands toward the box and pull out the other envelope. When I open it up I see a screenshot of an email between him and someone else. I grow more confused as I look at it so I go back to the letter like Elliot said to do.

You're probably confused as to why it's a picture of an email, but let me explain. I overheard you talking to your dad about you needing the extra money when you leave for college that day on the porch, so when you started working at Sam's I gave you big tip amounts to help you save up money because I knew you wouldn't take it otherwise. When you quit I couldn't do that anymore so I did the next best thing I could think of. One of my friends from high school moved to San Diego to run his dad's apartment complex, and it just so happened to be close to your campus. So I emailed him and put a down payment on a one bedroom apartment (and yes they allow pets so

Winston can stay there with you) all you have to do is call him so he can email you the paperwork to sign. This was the best thing I could think of to get you as an early birthday gift, I hope you love it.

Now, there's a phone in the box I want you to grab it, it's my phone. The passcode is 120411 if you don't remember it. The same passcode it's been since I was fifteen. One of the best days of my life, the day we met. December 4th, 2011. I need you to go to my notes.

I told you I had a bucket list baby.

I'm still trying to process what I just read before I reach for the phone.

He got me an apartment. He left me those big tips to help me save up for an apartment, and that was when I was still mad at him. I drop the letter on the bed and rest my head in my hands trying to process all the thoughts that are going through my mind. I wish he was here so I could thank him. Hell I wish he was here so I could hold on to him and never let him go. I already knew Elliot loved me, he didn't need to do any of this, but the fact that he did is one of the reasons I fell in love with him. His heart was so good and pure, too pure for this world.

I gather up the strength to open the box and grab the phone. I'm not at all surprised he remembered the day we met, I feel kind of shitty that I didn't, but that's Elliot, he always remembered the little things. I punch in the code and go to the notes app, and just like he said there is only one note titled 'Bucket List' I click on it and there is six items listed.

1. ~~Get Emory to forgive me~~

UPDATED BUCKET LIST

2. ~~Take Emory kayaking~~
3. ~~Get Emory a dog~~

4. ~~Take Emory to dance in the rain~~
5. ~~Get Emory to fall in love with me~~

There is no way this man was real. How could someone this selfless have existed? I don't see this as making it easier to live without him, if anything it's making it harder. I stare at the list for a few more minutes before I go back to the letter. It's getting harder to continue, but I've already gone this far.

Now that you've seen my bucket list you know that all I ever wanted to do is make sure you got everything you ever wanted, and my only wish is that you continue to get everything you want baby. I just want you to be happy. I want you to go off and meet a great guy who reminds you everyday how amazing and beautiful you are. I hope you go and start a family one day and you have the greatest kids because it's what you deserve, and I'll be watching you and cheering you on. I'll be sure to send you the best guy I can find.

I've got one more thing in the box I want you to have, so when you're ready reach in there and grab the black box with my name on it. It has a lock on it but the key is taped to the bottom. Come back to the letter one more time after you open it.

This is all too much to take in. He already gave me everything by just existing, he didn't need to do this. I feel my chest sink at the idea that I'll never get to tell him I love him one more time, or hold him one more time. I take another deep breath trying to control my tears and reach into the box to pull out the last item. Just like he said there's a key taped to the bottom of the box and it takes everything in me to finally put the key in the lock to open it up.

My body goes into shock when I see what's inside. My hands almost lose the grip they have on the box but I manage to keep a tight grip somehow. My chest heaves as

I try to catch my breath from the tightness around my heart. In the box is all the leaves with black hearts drawn in the middle, the ones I gave him when we were kids. *He kept all of them.* He told me when we were younger that he threw most of them out, but then again I told him I did the same thing with my flowers when I didn't. The leaves are mostly all dried up by now, but I can't believe I'm looking at them again. My eyesight is blurry from the pool of tears, and I'm sure my makeup is all smeared off, but I go back to the letter one more time bracing myself for whatever is coming next.

When I found out you kept all the flowers from when we were kids it made me feel less stupid for keeping all my leaves you gave me. Now you know that I've always loved you. I kept these because it made me feel like I always had a part of you with me, and I figured you should have them back to always have a piece of me. I hope all of these things shows you just a small piece of how I feel about you, but even this doesn't scratch the surface. I always thought our kind of love was only in movies, that one person couldn't possibly take over so much of your heart, but you did exactly that to mine baby, and that's why I'll live on even when I'm gone, because I left my heart with you. It was always yours anyway. You're my lobster, or whatever Phoebe said. I love you so much. I know right now you're probably wondering how you're going to go on without me, I know because if the roles were reversed I couldn't live in a world without you in it, but you have to keep going Emory, live the best life you can...make me proud.

I'm not going to say goodbye, so I'll just say see you later. Until we meet again in the next lifetime baby, I'll be waiting.

- EJ

You have to keep going, live the best life you can...make me proud.

I lift my head up towards the ceiling talking wherever I know Elliot is listening.

"I promise."

EPILOGUE

1 year later

"Everything is all set don't worry about it. The caters are reserved, the dresses are ordered, everyone sent in their RSVP, the venue is booked, flights are booked, it'll be perfect."

"Thanks mijita it means the world to me and Lori that you're apart of this." My dad hasn't sounded this happy in a long time, it makes my heart swell up. Him and Lori are getting married in a few weeks, and they asked me to be the maid of honor. I was on the fence about it when they first asked, but I actually like Lori so I agreed to it. Anything to make dad happy, and this woman makes him really happy. It almost gives me hope that I could find someone to make me happy after Elliot, but I don't think I'm at that point yet.

It's been a year without him and I still wake up most days expecting him to be sleeping next to me, but planning the wedding, along with my summer classes has been keeping me busy enough to not think about the pain of missing him as much.

The wedding is happening in Phoenix since my dad and Lori moved there about three months ago from LA. Turns out my dad loved Phoenix more than he did LA, and Lori was happy to go with him. This will be the first time I've been back to Phoenix since I left last year after Elliot passed away. I just wasn't ready to face anyone again, and honestly I still don't think I'm ready, but I can't miss my dad's wedding.

I've been in contact with Kat almost everyday since I left, she's actually been helping me plan the wedding, her organization skills have came in handy. I've also stayed in close contact with Andrew and Emily. Elliot left Andrew his truck, and he actually offered it to me before I left, but I wanted him to have something left of his brother so he ended up keeping it. He always sends me updates on the upgrades he puts on it which makes me happy that I made the right choice. He's doing much more with it than I ever would have. Emily always calls to check up on me which makes me still feel connected to Elliot in a way.

"I gotta go dad I'm walking to one of my classes." Today is the first day of my sophomore year, and my classes for this term are ten times harder than the last. I'm taking the BSN program, and to say it's a challenge would be an understatement, but in three years I'll be on the road to helping people, and making Elliot proud.

"I'll talk to you later Emory, say hi to Winston for me."

"I will, love you dad."

"Love you mijita." The line goes dead and I continue my walk to my class in silence. I've made a few friends since being here in San Diego. None of them are as outspoken and bubbly as Kat, but honestly who is? They're pretty great in their own ways though. It was a big change being in a different city all by myself, but I'm adapting. Having my own apartment off campus helps me keep my sanity, and having Winston with me helps out a lot especially on the days I miss Elliot more than usual. I still have days where something reminds me of him and I want to cry myself into a puddle of tears, honestly I don't think that feeling will ever go away, but on the really hard days I read over the letter he wrote for me before he died and I'm reminded how lucky I was to be loved by him. I'd like to say that so far I've followed through with my promise. I'm moving on without him just like he wanted me to, but there's also not a day that goes by where I don't wish he was here with me.

I walk into the classroom and most of the seats are empty since I always try to be about ten minutes early. I take a seat in the middle row and pull out my laptop along with my books I need for this particular class. As I'm getting settled in I accidentally knock one of my notebooks over to the ground.

"Damn it." I say while reaching down to grab it, but I'm beat to it when someone else reaches down to grab it for me and holds it out. I look up to meet with a pair of amber colored eyes that take me by surprise. The guy that's in front of my view has headphones stuck in his ears, but is staring at me with his full attention. He has tattoos plastered all over his his pale skin, and his chiseled face structure compliments the honey color of his short hair. He's dressed in a black t-shirt that emphasizes his biceps, along with ripped jeans and loafers. He's got that kind of rich, bad boy vibe to him, but I don't like to judge people off their first impression, *anymore*.

"I think you might need this." He says with his eyes still searing into mine.

"Thanks." I reach over to grab the notebook out of his hand, and he settles into the seat right next to me, of course.

I look over at him out of the corner of my eye to see him on his phone now. He side eyes me while he's hunched over his desk and catches me looking at him like a creeper. *Shit.* I quickly look away, but not before I see him smirk to himself.

"Nice tats." His deep husky voice vibrates in my ears.

"Thanks, you too." He smiles brightly as he admires his own tattoos. His smile tugs something at my heart, which alarms me because I haven't had someone's smile do that to me since Elliot.

"Whats your favorite one?" He tries to subtly examine my entire body with his eyes, but I notice and shift uncomfortably in my seat under the blazing heat of his gaze. I know the answer to his question as soon as he asks, but I look over all my tattoos anyway. I smile to myself before answering. "This one." I point to the one on the inside of my left wrist; the leaf with the black heart drawn in the middle of it. I got this one as soon as I got to San Diego last year, it made me feel like Elliot was right here with me for the new journey I was taking. The unnamed guy admires my tattoo and nods his head in approval without saying anything.

"What's your favorite one?" I ask. I don't want to be rude so I decide to continue the conversation.

"I don't have one, every one I get has its own story behind it."

"Damn, that's deep. I just get mine because they make me look kinda cool." He chuckles lowly to himself, and the sound sends a warm feeling into my stomach that I try to ignore. *Stop it Emory, it's just because he's cute.* I can't deny that this guy is attractive, but I almost feel guilty for finding someone attractive so soon after Elliot.

"What's your name?" The stranger asks. Guilt eats at me, but I decide to tell him just in case we sit next to each other again this semester.

"Emory." I hold out my hand and he grabs onto it for a handshake. A jolt of electricity goes down my entire arm at the contact. *What the hell was that?*

"I'm Easton, nice to meet you Emory." I can't tell if my mind is playing tricks on me, or if I heard that correctly.

A memory flashes through my mind of when Elliot was in the hospital and he told me that after he's gone he'd send me the best guy he could find. *"He'll have a strong, rare name like Easton or some shit."* I recall the memory from that day, ignoring the stinging feeling in my heart that it brings along with it. I took it as a joke at the time, but this can't be just a coincidence right? I've never met someone with that name before, and now I meet this attractive guy one year after Elliot told me he'd send me someone with the *exact* same name as him.

"Nice to meet you Easton." I beam my best polite smile at him and we don't let go of each others' hands for several more seconds.

"We should probably exchange numbers, just in case we need help with homework or something." He offers. I have to give him props on being forward.

"Yea sure, for homework or something." We both exchange shy smiles before I hear more students start to trickle in and the professor starts the class shortly after.

I can't say I'm surprised Elliot is keeping his promise even after he's gone. I take another glance at Easton before staring up towards the ceiling looking up at Elliot, wherever he is.

Since he kept his promise, now I just have to make sure I keep mine.

BONUS CHAPTER
Elliot

Emory gets here today, and I'm a bundle of nerves just thinking about seeing her again. I mean I've been in love with this girl since I was a kid, what do I even say to her? 'Hey I'm sorry I didn't talk to you for five years, I was busy trying not to die, but I'm in love with you so please forgive me?' Jesus I'm such an idiot. I can't believe it's been five years since I've seen her face, heard her voice, smelled her strawberry scented hair, or felt the warmth she brings when I hug her. I wrote to her when I was in remission a few years ago hoping she'd hear me out, but I can't really blame her that she didn't want anything to do with me. I couldn't even be mad if she decided to punch me in the face as soon as she sees me.

I found out I only had six to eight months to live a few months ago, and as soon as I got the news Emory's face is the only thing that crossed my mind. At first I denied the treatment the doctor offered me, the first time was horrible to endure, but then recently my mom said Richard and Emory agreed to come visit for the summer, or should I say Richard said yes and he's forcing Emory to come along. So, I got back on my medication the same day she told me, because I couldn't imagine leaving the world without seeing her again, even if she does hate my guts. I need to tell her everything; the real reason I left when we were younger, why I cut off contact with her, the fact that I only have months left and all I want to do is spend them with her, but most of all I need to tell her that I haven't been able to get her out of my head since the day I left her in LA five years ago.

It was the hardest decision I ever had to make to cut off contact with her, it was a long conversation I had with my mom at the time. Mom being mom she said she supports whatever decision I made, but she also made it known she didn't like the idea of us not having Emory in our lives anymore. After a lot of considering, I decided it was better for her if she didn't hear from me in case something happened, I couldn't do that to her. I seen how hurt she was when she lost her mom, and I'd be selfish to risk her going through that again just because I couldn't live without her.

The plan today is to go right up to her and get her to listen to what I have to say and start fresh. I don't want to waste any more precious time with her. Mom did warn me that Richard made her aware that the Emory we knew five years ago, isn't the same Emory that's going to show up on our doorstep; which makes me a little hesitant on my plan, but I've never been one to stand down from a challenge if I need to. If she doesn't want to listen to what I have to say the first time, then I'll just keep trying everyday until she does. I'll use whatever time I have left trying to get her to understand how I feel about her.

Andrew just texted me to warn me she'll be arriving in about twenty minutes so we'll probably get to my house around the same time. I'm out picking up my meds at the pharmacy since I didn't want to make her uncomfortable when she arrives by being there. I'm going to give her some time to get settled and then I'll try and speak to her. The last thing I need is for her to start screaming at me in the middle of the living room.

"Elliot." My name being called by the pharmacy staff pulls my attention away. I walk over to the counter to see Mariana behind the register with my medications in her hand. I was hoping she wasn't working today, it was awkward the last time I was in here when she asked me out and I respectfully declined. Don't get me wrong she's a beautiful girl, but only one girl has had a hold on me since I can remember, and now I compare every girl to her every single time. I haven't exactly had time for girls anyway, with the cancer treatments, remission, sulking over Emory, and now cancer treatments again.

"You know the drill with the meds or do you need Peter to go over them?" She asks tensely. Being rejected isn't a good look on her, she used to be so polite every time I came in here.

"I'm good thanks though Mariana." I say politely. Unfortunately I've grown familiar with these meds. They'll help me stay alive a little longer, but the side effects are a bitch: nausea, vomiting, loss of appetite, disorientation, fatigue, pain, the list goes on and on. I reach over to grab the bag from Mariana, but her cold fingers linger on mine long enough to make me uncomfortable. She's making flirty eyes at me, and I clear my throat loudly hoping she realizes just how uncomfortable I am under the gaze of her dark green eyes.

"Can I ask you something? What made you reject me?" *Does she really want to get into this now?* I don't like hurting people's feelings, but I can tell she's the type that doesn't hear the word no a lot.

"I'm in love with someone else." I say blankly. *That* should get my point across. Her wide eyed look tells me she got the message so I don't need to clarify. I walk away and send a friendly smirk in Peter's direction in the back. He's been filling my meds since I moved here so we've grown pretty familiar. He's the kind of guy you just know by looking at him that he has so much wisdom, we've had a few conversations, but nothing too serious.

When I first got to Phoenix I was fourteen, and the very next day after we arrived, I was at the oncologist. They had a great facility here with top of the line doctors and treatments that my parents couldn't pass up the opportunity for me, no matter how hard it was to leave LA at the time. They put me on chemo sessions twice a week, I was taking more pills than I can count on one hand—which is why I know Peter so well—and don't even get me started with the child psychologist my mom insisted I see.

I'm the first one to always see the positive in a situation, but the only thing worse than going through cancer treatment at fourteen years old, is having to talk to a stranger about going through cancer treatment at fourteen years old. In the end it all worked out, I eventually beat cancer and was in remission for awhile, until recently that is.

Three words. Three words is all it took to shake up my entire world.

Cancer is back.

I still remember the sharp numbing pain that traveled throughout my entire body when my doctor told me those words. I'd be lying if I said I still didn't have nightmares of that day. I wasn't even worried about myself at the time, I was mainly worried about mom, Andrew, and of course Emory. I guess I was worried about dad too, but a part of me still hates him for what happened that night, even if it's been years. Drew was never the same after that, he thinks I don't notice, but I do.

275

Now I'm back on the medications, but good news is I'm only doing chemo sessions once a week instead of two. Every time I think of giving up and letting the cancer win I think of Emory. Her face, her smile, and the fact that I want to see both of those things everyday this summer for as long as I can.

As I sit in my driveway staring up at my house, my stomach feels like it's tangled in knots. Drew texted me a few minutes ago saying they just arrived and she's in her room with mom. I have no idea what mom could be telling her, but I hope she's talking me up before I make my move. *Why am I so scared?* It's Emory, the girl I've known since I was nine years old; the one who would sneak me in through her window every time my parents' fighting kept me up at night, which was often. The one who purposely tripped a kid in front of the entire school after he pushed me in the cafeteria in 7th grade. Even if she isn't exactly the same person she used to be, she's still my Emory somewhere deep down, I just have to dig her out.

I somehow gather up the courage to go inside, but no one is in sight when I walk into the living room. I look around and see Drew walking in from the backyard.

"She's still upstairs." He says not waiting for me to ask anything. As soon as I start to head up the stairs, mom is coming down with a disappointed look on her face. *I don't like that look.*

"Give her some space mijo, I told her to come down when she's ready." *Damn it.* I was ready to go up there, but I'll respect her space.

Later came sooner than I expected since Emory still hasn't came down and her dinner is getting cold. Mom went up there earlier to bring her down, but she didn't even come to the door when she knocked. Now is as good a time as ever to go up there I guess, I'll bring her some food and try and get her to hear me out. Killing two birds with one stone. A wave of unsettling nerves crash over me walking up the stairs, my hands can barely grasp on to the plate with how much they're shaking. *Get a grip Elliot.* As long as she doesn't slam the door in my face at the sight of me, I'll take that as a good sign, I can work with that.

I lightly tap her door and wait for it to open. My heart is beating so fast, and I'm so lightheaded I think I'm going to pass out right here. What do I say? *I didn't even rehearse.* There's no answer so I tap on the door again and wait.

I'll just say what comes to mind it'll be fine. *I think.* She opens the door swiftly and we both freeze as we stare back at each other. It's so quiet you can hear our synchronized breathing. She's different, but still the same if that makes sense. She's covered in tattoos now which is definitely different, but she's still got her long black hair that I love. I can still see her freckles peeking through even though she tries to cover them up with makeup, and her eyes are still the beautiful caramel color that's made me melt at the sight them from day one. Her expression hardens the longer she stares at me which tells me she's not going to initiate a conversation.

"Hey Ej" I say shyly. *Shit I shouldn't have called her that.* I don't even know if she still wants me to call her that.

"It's Emory." She says throwing me a deadly stare. *Well, there's my answer.* I need to tread lightly here because anything I say can tip her off the deep end.

"Emory...sorry. How you been?" *How has she been? That's all that came out of my mouth?* I look down at the ground and kick at my feet to avoid eye contact with her. I deserve to be chewed out by her, but my heart can't take that while I'm looking at her.

"I don't think you want me to answer that question Elliot. Frankly I'll be happy if I avoid all conversations with you while I'm here." She folds her arms across her chest defensively. Alright so this is going to be *a lot* harder than I thought. *You got this Elliot.*

"Emory please if you would just let me explain everything, I have so much to tell you an—"

277

"No." She firmly cuts me off. *Okay I deserve that.*

"I don't want to hear anything you have to say Elliot. You left me and forgot I even fucking existed until now and expect me to come running into your arms as if nothing happened!" She screams so loud I feel the rumble in my chest. *I never forgot about you.* I almost say my thoughts out loud, but I'm sure she wouldn't want to hear it anyways, and I don't blame her one bit. If she wants me to beg I will.

"I can explain everything though Emory if you just listen. I care about you and maybe after hearing what I have to say you'll understand why I did what I did." I plead. I stare into her eyes trying to reach any part of the old Emory I can find, I know she's still in there somewhere. This isn't her. This is the version of herself she had to become after being disappointed. I created this, so it's my job to fix it.

"No. I don't want to be here, I don't want to see you, I don't want to talk to you. It should be easy for you to pretend I don't exist since you were so good at it for five years." She says harshly before slamming the door in my face, leaving the plate in my hands. *Ouch.*

I knew it probably wasn't going to be easy to win her back, but I also didn't think it'd be this hard. I'm going to do whatever I can to get her back. I'll do anything she asks me to do to hear her laugh again, and to see her angelic smile. If she wants me to grovel I will, if she wants me to get on my hands and knees and beg I will. I've got the summer to spend as much time as I can with her. I'm definitely not going to tell her I'm sick because I want her to forgive me because she wants to, not because she feels like she has to. I feel like shit that she's going to be the only one that doesn't know, but I have to give her some time. *I'll tell her soon.*

My only priority right now is to get my girl back, even if it's the last thing I do.

AUTHOR NOTE

I was five years old when my mom passed away of cancer. I don't remember much about her except that she was beautiful and kind, and had a smile that could light up every room, much like Emory's mom in this story. It didn't hit me until I got older how much a girl needs her mom. Cancer took so much from me, but writing this book was a way for me to get some of that back, and in some ways heal some of the old wounds I still had from losing my mom so young.

If readers take anything from this book I hope it's that they realize it's more than just your typical love story. Yes it is a love story, but it's more about learning to love *yourself.* Also that you don't always have to be so strong and independent. There's always people waiting to help you if you just ask for it, they just might end up surprising you.

I wanted this story to be in Emory's point of view so the readers can see her gradually go from this insecure young girl with so much anger she's yet to heal, and see her turn into this beautiful young woman who not only openly loves other people, but most importantly herself. It was a way to let her be someone that can be related to, and give people hope that one day they'll be okay too. While it makes me sad to think people can relate to what some of these characters feel and go through, I hope you can find peace in knowing that it'll get better for you too.

This is a story about *finding* yourself after you've experience loss. My wish is that Emory gives at least one person hope that you can do exactly that.

Enjoy a preview of Kat and Andrew's Dual POV spin off 'The Darkness that Follow Us' in the following pages. See you guys soon!

Trigger Warning :

Contains a heavy mention of drug use, addiction, and domestic violence.
Please only read if you are comfortable.

PROLOGUE

Kat

7 years ago

Waking up to loud noises in the pitch black darkness is a reoccurrence in my house. Whether it's mom and dad fighting, or one of their creepy friends trying to get into my room, it's all become normal to me. I've become well acquainted with not only the darkness, but the sounds of my parents screaming at each other mindlessly until they're too tired to yell anymore. Hell, I'm not even sure I'd call them parents since they haven't given me the time of day since I can remember.

Every night I imagine what my life would be like if I was born into a family where my parents care about me and not where they're going to get their next fix from, but hey, you have to play the hand you're dealt. Don't get me wrong I know there are kids who have much harder lives than me which is why I don't pity myself, but it's hard to see the good in a situation like finding both your parents passed out, and needles scattered across the living room at the age of seven. I learned how to administer Narcan that day because I thought my parents had overdosed. I'm fifteen now, but I'd be lying if I said that image still doesn't haunt me today. Not to mention I'm scared shitless of coming home from school and finding them like that again. Some things you can't get over no matter how hard you try, and believe me I've tried.

Most kids know more or less who they want to be by the time they're fifteen, or they at least have dreams of who they want to be. For me I know exactly who I *don't* want to be thanks to my parents. I promised myself at a young age I'd never touch a drug in my life, and one day when I'm ready to be a mom I'll never make them feel how I've felt my entire life. *Alone.*

"I'm done Chris!" I hear mom shout from the living room. We live in a small trailer home so the walls are pretty thin, I can hear everything. At night when all the yelling stops it's so quiet I count how many times the water drips from the kitchen faucet, and it helps me sleep sometimes. The silence has become comforting to me. It's better than the alternative of arguments and loud parties my parents throw with

282

their friends. I usually do my homework on the bus rides home because it's imposs-ible to get anything done with all the noise.

"You say that every time and you always come back." I don't miss the slurring of my dads' words as he shouts back at mom. He's either high or drunk, but my money is on both.

I slowly creep out of bed to put my ear up against my door to listen in on them. I try and be very quiet because if they find out I'm eavesdropping I'm dead meat. I don't want to be on the other end of dad's wrath when he's high.

"Not this time, you'll never put your hands on me ever again!" My mom shouts loud enough I'm sure the neighbors heard. I'd be lying if I said I wasn't used to hearing mom get slapped around and thrown into walls by my dad, but every night that happens the next morning she acts as if nothing happened. I narrowed it down to two options on why that is: she was either too high at the time to care what happen-ed, or she's too scared to leave him. My guess is the latter.

I've only seen my dad hit my mom once, and let's just say when I tried to inter-vene I got the message to never do that again; I learned how to cover bruises up with makeup at a young age. I wish I could say my dad was this good person who turned bad because of drugs, but honestly he's always been like this. I want to love him because he's my dad, but every time I look at him all I feel is disgust and disappointment.

"Fine, then take your worthless daughter with you on your way out." He shouts with disgust in his tone. It's no surprise my dad doesn't give a shit about me, but it still stings when I hear him say it out loud. I've tried to be the best daughter I can be; I cook, clean, I even put him into bed after he's passed out, but another thing I realized at a young age is that nothing I do will ever be good enough, he'll never love me the way a dad is supposed to love his daughter.

My parents got pregnant with me at sixteen, it's not the ideal age for most I'm sure, but he's made it known time and time again that I was never wanted from the moment they found out mom was pregnant. Sometimes I wish they never went through with having me, but those are dark thoughts I shove deep down inside.

No one knows my home life is like this, only my grams. She's tried to take me away once when I was eight, but mom wouldn't let her. At the time I thought it was because deep down my mom actually loves me and wants me around, but when I got older I figured out it's because grams gives her money every month for me, which I've never seen a dime of it might I add. Bottom line was; no Kat, no money, and of course mom needs her drug money so she decided to keep me around.

Footsteps approaching my door catch my attention, and I dart to my bed and hide under the covers without a second thought hoping they don't suspect I've been listening this whole time. My doorknob rattles and I hear mom's voice on the other end of the door as she tries to push it open. I always keep a chair propped up under the knob ever since some of my parents' friends tried to sneak into my room one too many times to be called an accident. It's happened more often now that I'm older.

Mom's voice sounds weak on the other side of the door which is the only reason I get up to open it. It wouldn't be the first time she's cried wolf for me to open the door, and let's just say the few times I fell for it dad ended up chasing her inside leaving my room a mess from them throwing shit at each other while I tucked away in my closet.

"What's wrong mom?" I ask trying to pull off my best groggy sounding voice to make it seem like I just woke up. I stand in the doorway with my arms folded across my chest defensively before I let her inside. Her eyes are bloodshot, and her makeup is smeared across her face from crying. Don't get me wrong, I want to love my mom more than anything but I can't help but resent her when I look at her. I resent her for choosing drugs over raising me, for staying with my dad all this time and dragging us both down in the process, but most of all I resent her for not wanting to ever get clean for me, or herself for that matter. I know my mom used to be beautiful because grams showed me pictures from when she was younger, but over time using hard drugs really got to her I guess. Her thin, dry blonde hair looks like it hasn't been brushed in weeks, her face is sunken in and covered in red patches. The only thing that's still hers are her emerald green eyes that she passed down to me, but right now the dark bags under those green eyes are so dark they almost hide the black ring forming on her left eye. It looks fresh so dad must have just given that to her, which would explain the breakdown she's having right now.

"I'm leaving Kat." She says barging past me. *Wait what?* Usually when this happens she locks herself in the room while dad passes out on the couch, then everything is back to normal the next morning. She's never been like this which sends a nauseating feeling to my gut. She paces back and forth of my room picking at her finger nails frantically before she sits down on my bed. Wait, she said *I'm leaving.*

"Wait what?"

"I can't be here anymore Kat, I have to leave." There she goes again with the *I* and not we. *Please don't leave me here with him.* I look at her with pleading eyes hoping she can magically read my thoughts. Who am I kidding though, mom wouldn't even know what I was thinking even if I wrote it down for her. *I can't stay here with my dad, I just can't.*

"I can go with you, I have some cash lying around so we can stay at a motel until we find somewhere permanent." I'm only fifteen so I can't exactly have a real job yet, but I do some baby sitting gigs for the neighbors and they pay under the table. I've saved every dollar I've gotten since I was thirteen hoping that by the time I was eighteen it was enough money to get the hell out of here.

"No I have to go by myself, but once I'm settled somewhere I'll come and get you." I feel the vomit wanting to come out but I push it down. *Please take me with you.* I don't necessarily want to go with her, but she is the lesser of the two evils.

"Please let me go with you." My eyes glisten with tears as I plead to her.

"Three days tops hun and you'll be with me." She places a cold boney hand on my cheek and rubs her thumb in circles. It doesn't comfort me in the way that a moms touch is supposed to comfort you, maybe because this is probably the longest she's been in the same room as me since the day I was born. Like I said, if I had a choice I wouldn't go with her either, but anywhere is better than being stuck here with dad.

She gets up from the bed and walks out of my room quickly with nothing but a blank stare in my direction, looking emotionless. I guess I can survive three days with dad. I'll just lock myself in my room until I have to go to school or when I have to eat. *Three days and it'll be over.* I'm not saying going with mom will magically make my life better, but maybe now she'll have a chance at getting clean.

I hear her going through her dressers and the bathroom cabinets collecting her things. I don't even have to look to know she's probably just collecting some clothes and the drugs she has laying around the house. Dad stays seated in the rocking chair while a baseball game is blaring in the background, he's got the deadliest stare right at mom. It send chills directly up my spine when I catch a glimpse of it. She takes one last longing look at me before walking towards the door.

Something comes over me when I run after her totally forgetting to put shoes on. She's already loading her stuff into the trunk of a car when I get outside. The cold air hits me like a ton of bricks in my chest, but I stay put on the front steps staring blankly at her put her stuff into the car at lightning speed. I don't recognize the man in the driver's seat, but the devilish smirk he's throwing in my direction makes me want to vomit right here.

"Three days Kat, I'll be back for you." She yells before crawling into the passenger seat of the strangers car. Why do I have this weird feeling this is the last time I'm going to see her?

Dust flies everywhere when the car peels away taking my mom with it.

"Please come back." I whisper into the darkness.

To Be Continued in 'The Darkness that Follows Us' ...

ACKNOWLEDGMENTS

To think that I started this story when I was 13, and now I'm sharing it with other people is so surreal, I couldn't be more grateful. There were many times I almost gave up, but I'm so glad I didn't because I'm so happy with this story.

There's so many people to thank, but I want to start off with my little sister Kayla, for putting up with me coming into your room a hundred times day to ask you what you thought of a chapter. Also without you I wouldn't have written Emory the way she is now. She started off as a "sunshine" character but I changed her last minute to be inspired by you, and now I wouldn't want it any other way. I love you sis.

Dad, you've made so many sacrifices for me to reach my dream without thinking twice about it, and for that I'll never be able to repay you. Watching you go through so much and still be so strong while I was growing up was so inspiring, and in so many ways it helped me write this story. You are one of the greatest gifts the universe gave me, I couldn't ask for a better dad. I love you.

Grandma, thank you for being there whenever I need you and never making me feel crazy for chasing my dream. Thank you for helping raise me to be the woman I am today. If I ever get to be half as strong as you are I'd be so lucky. Thank you for inspiring me to write the character Hope, named after you. I love you.

Geniece Trevino, where do I even start? I'm so thankful we crossed paths again right when we were supposed to. You gave me the confidence to pursue publishing this story and I'm so thankful for it. Without you I'm pretty sure this book would have stayed on the top of my closet being forgotten about. Your patience, knowledge, and kindness will never go unappreciated. Thank you so much.

Yos, the kind of friend you are inspired me to write Emory and Kat's friendship, and it turned out to be one of my favorite things in the book. Thank you for always being there when I need you. I love you.

Thank you to all my friends and family who supported me when I told them I was writing a book, having all your support pushed me to finish this when I thought about giving up. You guys know who you are and I'm so grateful for every single one of you.

Thank you so much to Abraham Pineda who brought the vision in my head to life for all the artwork that went into this book. Your talent is unmatched!

Also big thank you to Heather and everyone at Bird Cage Ink who helped me in the process of finishing this book. You guys are so amazing at what you do, and you make it look easy, but your hard work doesn't go unnoticed.

I also want to especially thank everyone who took their time to read Summer in Phoenix. I hope you guys loved reading it as much as I loved writing it. I have lots more coming for you guys that I can't wait for to read. I already love every single one of you!! Feel free to DM me on any of my socials I'd love to hear what you guy have to say about the book and chat <3

With so much love, Lana.

Follow me on Social Media! (:

How well did you read Summer in Phoenix?

Let's test your knowledge! Scan the code to take a short quiz

CPSIA information can be obtained
at www.ICGtesting.com
Printed in the USA
BVHW070014090223
658191BV00023B/664

9 798986 338606